LOLA MILES

Daffodils in Winter

Cover Design by DeborahAnne Neri

Editing by Steph White (Kat's Literary Services)

Proofreading by Vanessa Esquibel (Kat's Literary Services)

First edition

*This book was professionally typeset on Reedsy.
Find out more at reedsy.com*

As always, to my husband and children.
And to you, the reader. Thanks for liking fucked up stories as
much as I do.

Contents

Acknowledgement

Someone, anyone, pinch me. When I first set out on my writing journey, I truly never anticipated self-publishing one book, let alone two. It's been a surreal, out-of-body experience and I could never have done it without the support of my readers.

I'm still surprised that I have readers, but that's a tangent for a different day.

Daffodils in Winter is emotional, angsty, heartbreaking, and hopeful. I'd be remiss to say that I wasn't deeply impacted while writing this book; the memories of my own loss played on repeat as CeCe and Dante's story came to light. I'm breaking the fourth wall to implore you, as the reader, to put the book down if miscarriage, pregnancy loss, or anything else associated with those two things will trigger you.

Thank you to my husband, for once again picking up the pieces of our house when I'm too engrossed in the writing/editing process. These stories would not be possible without you, especially this one.

Thank you to Kat's Literary Services, a literal godsend of a company. Thank you Steph White and Vanessa Esquibel for the support, guidance, and help you've both given to me. The frequent changes, questions, and email ramblings can't be easy, but you both have helped me so much and I am indebted to you.

Thank you to Deb Neri for my gorgeous book cover. You are

so incredibly talented and I can't thank you enough for your patience with my madness.

To my BETA readers, Kristi and Lizet, your insight, feedback, and critiques helped to fine-tune this story and center the narrative. I can't wait to ask (demand) that you both participate in future readings because your comments were so incredibly helpful.

Thank you to the Author Agency for organizing my release tour, ARC distribution, and reveals. Both Shauna and Becca have helped to promote this book and I would not have the audience or reach without them.

Thank you to my parents, my family, and my friends for supporting my writing and encouraging me to pursue it.

And finally, thank you to my children for giving me the courage to be vulnerable with the world. Everything I do, I do to show you that you can be anything and everything, all at once. But still, you are never allowed to read Mommy's books.

Warnings

For those of you who do not wish to go into this book without the complete trigger and content warning list, please read below. Please note that this book is a work of fiction.

Trigger Warnings: This book contains references to pregnancy, pregnancy loss, graphic violence, and explicit sexual scenes. This book also contains references to parental loss and the death of a loved one. Please, take care of yourself and your well-being when reading.

Some things to know about *Daffodils in Winter*:
   Told in dual POVs
   Obsessive and OTT (over the top) MMC
   Dramatic and strong FMC
   Surprise pregnancy and pregnancy loss

Playlist

"I Will Wait" - Mumford & Sons
"Behold the Hurricane" - The Horrible Crowes
"Babel" - Mumford & Sons
"Charmer" - Kings of Leon
"Crazy Bitch" – Buckcherry
"Hard to Love" – Lee Brice
"Hey Now Girl" – Phantom Planet
"Son Of A Sinner" – Jelly Roll
"Body" – Loud Luxury
"I Fall Apart" – Post Malone
"Slow It Down" – The Lumineers
"Something in the Orange" – Zach Bryan
"Irish Eyes" – Rose Betts
"Roses and Violets" – Alexander Jean
"Save Me" – Jelly Roll
"Rudie Can't Fail" – The Clash
"Ride" – SoMo
"Ride" – Chase Rice
"Eyes on You" - Chase Rice
"Him & I" - Halsey & G-Eazy
"God's Plan" - Drake
"Red" - Taylor Swift
"exile" - Taylor Swift (ft. Bon Iver)
"this is me trying" - Taylor Swift

"Let Her Cry" – Hootie & The Blowfish
"Only Wanna Be With You" – Hootie & The Blowfish
"The Promise" – Tracy Chapman
"I Miss You" – Blink-182
"Addicted" – Simple Plan
"I'm A Mess" – Bebe Rexha
"Can't Take My Eyes Off of You" – Ms. Lauryn Hill

Prologue

CeCe

When my best friend, Ava, told me about the barbecue at Greyson's house, I knew that Dante would be there. It didn't take a genius like Serena to deduce that he would be present at the house he shared with Greyson and Lincoln, but the sight of him shocked me all the same. The night we met, Dante's colorful tattoos were on display; illustrations in the old school or American traditional style decorate from his wrists to his neck.

I'd never tell him, but his body art is what drew me to him in the first place. Growing up surrounded by fifteen male cousins, tattoos and piercings were standard. One of my older cousins, Wolf, even became a tattoo artist and appointed himself the family tattooist. I have no ink, but that doesn't mean I can't appreciate his.

When we arrived at the backyard party, Ava had a damn-near panic attack thanks to the mountain of cannoli she made, as though it was a bad thing she was a kick-ass chef and could whip up Italian desserts flawlessly. Serena and I had to talk her out of throwing the tray in the bushes.

Wasting that sugary confection would have been grounds for best friend dismissal or a review of our relationship, at the very least. Ava claims I'm dramatic, but tossing out hours of work because some frat boy you barely know may be turned off by baked goods is absurd. Thankfully, she got over her shit and handed the tray to Lincoln, who instructed us to make our way outside when we were ready.

I look up as we walk through the patio doors, noting the people scattered about the yard; the crowd isn't large, but it's still intimidating. The house, which is entirely too beautiful and homey for three college guys, has a large backyard that allows for patio space, an outdoor kitchen, and plenty of grass. Honestly, it's nicer than my parents' house.

Unwittingly, my eyes catch on Dante as soon as we walk outside. Standing in the center of a group of guys playing flip cup, he's dressed casually in black board shorts and a fitted white T-shirt. His backward white baseball cap hides his dark hair and calls attention to the scruff decorating his chiseled jaw.

Holy fuck. It should be illegal for a guy to be that good-looking—it's unfair. In his shorts—that are definitely European cut because I think I can see the outline of his dick—and his tight shirt, his skin is a canvas, showcasing the art I saw briefly on Thursday night. His legs, which weren't visible on Thursday, are packed with tattoos. From this far away, I can't make out any of the images clearly, but the pops of red, blue, and yellow that I see are woven with bold black lines. It's too bad he has the personality of a golden retriever on cocaine because he is freaking beautiful.

My thoughts must be broadcast on my face because Dante looks up, meeting my eyes instantly. The smile that breaks out on his face is goofy and endearing, and absolutely fucking adorable. I hate him for it. He runs over, literally sprints across the yard, and stops inches from me. I brace for impact; he's so fast that I'm sure he won't stop his legs in time. I'm used to collisions. Ava is my best friend, after all, and has the coordination of a baby giraffe, but something tells me that Ava's small, soft frame hurts a fuck-ton less than Dante's muscular body if he were to ram into me. I almost yell at him to slow the fuck down but bite my tongue.

I was a bitch to him on Thursday, and that seemed to ignite some warped fantasy for him. If I had it in me, I'd be sweet to him, but there's no way in hell that's happening, so silence will have to suffice.

"Red, you're here. Fuck, you look good," Dante pants. He sounds like he just ran the New York City Marathon.

"Stop calling me Red." I huff but offer a quiet, "Thanks," for his compliment. I'm a bitch, but not a rude bitch, and my mother would kill me if I didn't acknowledge his words.

"Anytime, beautiful. You're an English major, right? There are a few people I want you to meet. Come with me?" Dante requests, holding out his hand for me to take. I contemplate him, weighing my options. On the one hand, I can refuse him and pretend I'm too busy for his impromptu meet-and-greet. But I'm also curious as to whom he wants to introduce me to. Giving him a small nod, I'm caught off guard when he tugs on my arm and plasters me to his side, leading me toward a group of people sitting on the patio, drinks in hand.

Looking over my shoulder, I call to Ava and Serena, "If I'm not back in thirty minutes, tell my parents I've been kidnapped by a psycho from New Jersey."

Serena releases a laugh, but Ava rolls her eyes in response. "I'm sure you'll be fine," she shouts back. Dante gently pulls me before sliding his hand down and capturing my fingers with his own. His move is possessive, a display of whom I belong to, or so he thinks.

I pull on my hand, growling, "Would you stop being a caveman? I'll follow you, but let go of my hand."

His groan is low and deep, shooting lust straight to my core. "Fuck, Red, I love it when you get mouthy with me." His hand tightens around mine, holding me in a vice-like grip.

"Freak," I mumble under my breath. If Dante hears me, he doesn't respond.

—

The only thing worse than being attracted to Dante is being surprised by him. The people he introduced me to are the editors and writers of the Marymount Review, the literary magazine on campus. Maybe I shouldn't be shocked that he remembers my love of literature and major based on our conversation Thursday night, but I am. In my experience, guys would nod politely anytime I spoke about books, literature, or anything remotely academic. Dante seems to remember every facet of the information I shared with him.

I don't like feeling indebted to anyone; whenever I feel the scales are imbalanced in someone else's favor, my skin itches, and I feel the immediate need to level the score. With Dante and this introduction, I sense the imbalance intimately. I also feel a little turned on by his consideration, but that's beside the point.

Within the group of people he introduces me to, there's one guy who seems especially interested in me and what I have to say—the copy editor, James.

"So, are you planning on joining the staff of the review?" he asks.

I shrug my shoulders, relaying my indecision. "I'm not sure. I'm more of a writer than an editor. Although, it would be amazing to meet and collaborate with other like-minded students." The thought of working alongside others invested in prose, poetry, and literature makes me giddy, even if editing is not my favorite.

"Oh, you write?" he questions, looking me over closely as though seeing me for the first time. "A beautiful woman that writes. You should join our writing workshop next weekend. Give me your number, and I can pick you up, maybe get some dinner afterward." Before I can respond, Dante releases a low growl and pulls my body against his. I try to step out of his embrace, but he locks his arm, keeping me in place.

"The last thing Red wants to do is jump on your pencil dick, Jimmy," Dante scoffs. "You either invite her because you take her shit seriously or get the fuck out of my house." Startled by his threat, I look up into Dante's face, set in a severe expression. He looks ready to beat the shit out of James.

"My name is James—" he starts, but Dante cuts him off.

"I don't give a shit what your name is. Don't disrespect my girl and her talent again, you fucking weasel." Dante's vibrating against my back, his anger rising like palpable energy. Clearing my throat, I grab the hand at my waist and squeeze as hard as I can. To him, it probably feels like butterflies flapping against his skin, but it succeeds in turning his attention to me.

"I need to use the restroom; can you show me where it is?" I ask, doing what I can to pacify the situation. I *should* correct Dante and tell him that I'm not his girl. I *should* be insulted that he thinks he knows me intimately after speaking with me for two hours three days ago. And I *should* skin Dante alive for inserting himself where he doesn't belong, but if he's right and James was playing literary scholar to get his dick wet, then fuck him.

Leveling one last look at James, Dante's eyes meet mine, and he nods. Not bothering to release me from his hold, he turns us toward the house and rushes me inside.

—

Dante:

Fuck that guy, fucking cocksucker. When I told Red that I had people I wanted her to meet, I didn't expect her to get hit on right in front of my fucking face. It took every ounce of willpower I had not to deck that prick.

I'm normally a pretty calm guy, but Red brings out every protective and possessive instinct I have. It doesn't help that she looks like a fucking siren in her tiny jean shorts, with her long hair hanging loose down her back. As soon as I saw her across the yard, my dick went hard as a fucking post and started weeping to get inside her.

I won't tell her that, though, because I'm not a fucking creep like Jimmy. Seriously, fuck that guy.

I know that her request for the bathroom was a bullshit excuse to defuse the situation, but I won't call her out on it. She's given me the perfect excuse to get her alone. I look down at her tucked against my side and bite back my smile. Her stunning face is set in a scowl as she matches my stride to get inside.

"You want me to slow down, Red? You've got some short legs," I tease because, damn, she's tiny; she can't be more than five feet of tight curves. She's got the personality of a warrior princess and the balls of a linebacker, though.

"Fuck off, I have long legs," she huffs.

"Red, your legs are the size of a toothpick. I'm pretty sure my six-year-old cousin is taller than you."

"Tell me, does your little cousin like his big cousin Dante?

Will he cry at your funeral? I know twenty-six ways to kill a man without leaving any evidence," she says in a low voice. Something must be fucking wrong with me because my dick gets harder with her threat. My mom used to watch *Alias* with Jennifer Garner, and fuck, I've always liked a strong female that could beat the shit out of me if she wanted to.

I stop her before we reach the patio door and turn toward her. I widen my stance and reach down to adjust my dick, trying to hide my hard-on from the people that are no doubt staring at us.

"What are you...? Oh God," she pauses, lowering her voice before continuing, "did you just get hard because I threatened to kill you? What kind of fucked-up foreplay is this?"

"Fuck, your voice sounds so good when it gets all deep and raspy," I moan, leading her through the doors. "Come on, I'll take you to my room to use my ensuite." I walk her through the kitchen and toward the stairs in the front of the house. She must actually need the bathroom now because the little viper doesn't stop me when we stride up the stairs and into my bedroom.

Turning on the light, I watch Celeste take in the space. My room's not the primary—Grey got that because he owns the damn house—but it's a generous size and fits a king-sized bed, dresser, nightstands, and desk. Each bedroom in the house has an attached bathroom, which is an ideal setup. Growing up, I had housekeepers and suites, so living in a traditional college dorm room my freshman year was akin to *Naked and Afraid*; I was always naked because I knew jackshit about laundry, and my roommate was fucking terrified of me.

"Nice collection," Red comments from my desk. Above my desk, I have a shelf filled with vinyl records, the classics on display: The Clash, The Doors, The Eagles, The Beatles, and Led Zeppelin. I don't give a shit what anyone says, there's nothing like good rock music from an era where men wore pants tight enough to squeeze their dicks off.

"See something you like?" I ask. She runs a hand along one of the vinyls, tracing the edges with her dainty finger.

"This is my dad's favorite band," she says in a soft voice. "I think I know every record on this album." She laughs, pulling The Clash's *London Calling* album out. Looking over her shoulder, she asks, "Do you mind?"

I shake my head because is she serious with this shit? Why would I mind that the girl that gets me harder than a fucking light post wants to play one of my favorite albums? Like an old professional, Red drops the vinyl on the record player and ques it to play "Rudie Can't Fail." I raise a brow, surprised by her pick. She bobs her head to the music, mouthing the lyrics off-key like a bad karaoke singer.

"Fuck," I groan, rubbing a hand down my face. She looks at me sharply, her movements halting. "You're fucking perfect, Red," I sigh. It's not a lie; she's everything I want, everything I crave, bundled into a petite package.

She rolls her eyes. "And everyone says that I'm dramatic. Your music collection would be better if you had some country artists and bands mixed in." She goes back to singing, turning her back on me and ignoring my presence. Fuck that.

Stalking over to her, I cage her in from behind, being careful to leave just enough space that if she says no or tries to get away, she can. She doesn't do either of those things, though. No, the little cock tease presses into me and continues singing and dancing like an extra in a music video. Her hips work against me while she sings about being reckless. I coast my

xv

hand along her thigh, raising it until I reach her hip and pull her back, letting her feel how fucking turned on I am by her and everything she is. She sinks deeper into me, grinding her ass against my cock before bending over and giving me a view that has me nearly fucking weeping.

Her ass in the air, she continues her slow dance, moving her ass side to side and up and down like a goddamn stripper during a lap dance. I still her hips and reach my arm around her waist to tug her up, bracing her against my body. Bending down, I bring my mouth against her ear.

"Red, if you keep doing that, I'm either coming in my pants like a fucking teenager, or I'm getting on my knees and worshipping that pussy. Either this stops now, or you give me those pretty lips," I growl, nipping her ear before trailing kisses down her jawline. She becomes languid and fluid in my arms, dropping her head back to give me better access to her smooth skin.

"Fucking hell, Red," I pant between kisses, "you taste fucking delicious. Tell me, does your pussy taste as sweet as the rest of you?"

She releases a low moan, spurring me on. My hands travel over her body in gentle passes, from her breasts, which are the perfect handful, to her narrow waist and the delicate flare of her hips. I can't fucking get enough. "Is your pussy weeping for me? Are your panties a fucking mess for me?"

"Why don't you find out, Dante." She lets out a breathy sigh. I still, wanting to make sure I heard her correctly.

"I need to hear you say that one more time, Red." I spin her around and pin her to my desk. "Be real detailed and tell me exactly what you want."

Her eyes narrow, and her lips twist up in a smirk. "Get on

your fucking knees and eat my pussy." She emphasizes her point by grabbing my shoulders and pushing me down. With her small stature and my behemoth body, she doesn't get very far, but I follow her direction and sink to my knees. Looking up at her, my hands go to the waistband of her shorts. I pause, waiting for her next direction. "Take them off," she orders in a husky tone.

Fuck, I knew she'd be like this, demanding and hot as fuck beneath my hands. I make quick work of her shorts and panties and stare at the prettiest fucking sight I've ever seen. "Fuck," I groan, "look at this pretty little cunt." I lean in, breathing in her scent and burying my nose in the strip of red curls. Lifting my head, I ask, "Baby, can I taste you?"

"Please," she moans, shifting her hips forward. As soon as the words are out, I seal my mouth to her cunt, lapping up the wetness and sucking her clit into my mouth. She bucks against me, grinding her pussy into my face and spreading her wetness. I reach up and grab her hips, pulling my head from between her thighs to lift her onto the desk and spread her legs wide.

"Hold your legs, Red, let me fucking eat," I command. Despite her earlier bravado and dominance, Celeste submits and spreads her legs, holding them at an impossible angle while I feast. I work one of my hands over her thigh and to her tight opening. With my mouth sucking on her clit, I run the tip of my blunt finger against her, spreading her hole before diving in.

Fuck, she's tight. Pushing in and out, I feel her pussy muscles clench, drawing my finger in deeper with every pass. "Fuck baby, you taste fucking delicious," I say. "Fucking come for me; let me feel that cunt squirt all over my face." Like my

xvii

words are a detonator, her pussy flutters around me, and I feel her explode against my fingers and tongue.

"Dante, holy shit," she screams, grabbing my head and holding me tight against her center. I lick her through her spasms, cleaning her orgasm off her skin and swallowing her essence down, making it a part of me. I feel her hands tug my hair, and I look up into her lust-drunk eyes. "Fucking kiss me, douchebag," she says.

I stand up and dive in, not giving a shit if I get her cum all over her face; I'll lick it off her fucking skin. Her lips are firm and soft against me, demanding a control that I won't let her have. I pull back, cradling her jaw between my palms. "Open up, baby," I order. As soon as she opens, I spit into her mouth, giving her a taste of her cunt before I claim her lips again in a blistering kiss. Our tongues battle, twisting and dancing until her hips start to gyrate against me.

Breaking the kiss, I trail my lips down her neck, pausing at her shirt's neckline and sucking the skin just above her breast. "Can we take this off, Red?" I mumble, grabbing the hem of the offending fabric.

"If my shirt comes off, you need to be naked too," she responds, pulling at my T-shirt. Say no-fucking-more. I rip my shirt off and tear my shorts down. I didn't bother wearing briefs today, so my hard cock is out and demanding Red's attention.

"Jesus," she murmurs, looking at my dick. I glance at her before looking down at my cock. My eyes shoot back up immediately. Jesus Christ, she's naked and on full display.

"Goddamn, Red, you're going to fucking kill me." I grab her around the waist and toss her over my shoulder. The first time I fuck this girl isn't going to be on a goddamn desk.

xviii

I'll save that for the fourth or fifth time. Maybe the fourth *and* fifth.

Setting her down on the bed, I watch as she lays back, a fucking goddess spread for sacrifice. She bends her knees before opening, giving me a prime view of the heaven cradled between her thighs. "God fucking damn," I growl. "You going to let me fuck that cunt, baby?" I ask, my eyes still on her wet pussy. I run a hand over my cock, squeezing out a drop of precum before working it back down.

"Fuck me, Dante," she whispers, running a hand up her sides and cupping her breasts, inviting me in. I fucking pounce on her, tearing her hands away and replacing them with my mouth. Pulling one pert nipple into my mouth, I suck, working the areola into a peak before transferring my attention to the other breast.

I reach over to my nightstand and grab a condom, tear the wrapper, and make quick work of rolling it over my cock. Lining myself up with Celeste's opening, I surge forward into her warm, wet, tight-as-fuck heat. I feel her body still and see a wince cross her face. Her cunt is holding my cock in a death grip, squeezing the shit out of it, and fuck, if I die here, I'll know I reached heaven. She's almost too tight. Fucking shit. "Red, Celeste, are you a virgin? Fuck," I grind out, stilling myself inside her.

"Well, I was a virgin, but I'm not anymore. Clearly," she answers with her sass. If I weren't so worried about hurting her more, I'd take her over my knee and spank her ass for that comment and failing to tell me that she'd never had sex before. I'm sitting here, my dick harder than it's ever been, about to explode from one fucking thrust while I just impaled her with my cock.

I start to pull out, but she wraps her legs around me, preventing me from moving. "Don't you fucking dare, Dante," she whimpers, angling her hips and thrusting upward. I grit my teeth, stealing myself against the need to pound her. "God, fucking move," she pleas. With my size and girth, Red's going to be sore for fucking days, but I can't say that I'm disappointed that I'm the first cock she's ever had.

If it were up to me, it would be the only cock she'd ever fucking have.

I shift, throwing my body on the bed and bringing her with me until she's on top of me, straddling my hips and controlling how deep she takes it. "I'm not fucking happy you didn't tell me that you had a virgin pussy, Celeste," I reprimand, using her full name. "You're going to ride this cock and fucking take what you can. Next time I fuck you, I'm going to tie your ass up and leave you on the edge for fucking hours. You'll be so desperate for me that I'll have you in fucking tears, begging to come." I give a light smack to her ass, urging her forward. "Now, fucking ride that cock, cowgirl, and let me feel that virgin pussy take all nine inches of me."

Like my words ignited a fire, she sinks down, taking me to the fucking hilt. She rides me, grinding down against me until we're both sweating and chasing our release. Her hands come to my chest, and I grab them, restraining them behind her back while she continues to jerk against me. "Only good girls get to touch, Red. Lie to me again and watch what happens."

She whimpers, my display of dominance spurring her on, and I feel her walls contract, her release flooding her body and leaking out. I follow her, pumping myself into the condom and growling at the intensity of my orgasm.

She collapses on top of me, a sweaty, panting mess. I hold

her to me, cocooning her in my arms while we wait for our heart rates and breathing to slow down. I'd be content as fuck to just lay in bed with Red for the rest of the day, but she must have other ideas. Shifting on top of me, she pulls away from my chest and slides off my softened cock.

When she stands, a goddamn avalanche falls from between her legs, soaking her thighs and my floor. "What the fuck—?" she says, staring at the fluid between her thighs. Without even looking down at my cock, I fucking know what happened.

"Fuck, Red, the condom fell off."

1

CeCe

Four weeks later

After spending twelve years waking up at the ass-crack of dawn for school, I carefully curated my class schedule to allow me to sleep each morning until at least ten. On Tuesdays and Thursdays, I have the treat of sleeping until one in the afternoon. I don't care that my classes end at nine at night if it means that I have an easy wake-up.

This morning, my jolt from sleep is anything but peaceful. Nausea bubbles in my throat and forces me to get out of bed and to the bathroom as quickly as humanly possible. Grabbing my dorm key and phone on the dresser, I run out the door. I barely make it into the stall before I'm vomiting the entire contents of my stomach out, heaving into the toilet as I continue gagging on my own bile.

I've been like this for two days, and I'm convinced the dining hall gave me food poisoning; on Monday, they had a taco bar, and like everyone else on this damn campus, I can't say no to tacos. The meat was undeniably questionable, but when loaded with cheese, sour cream, and hot sauce, it was a good imitation of Taco Bell. Serena was disgusted by the watered-down American version of Mexican food and claimed her *abuela* would kill her if she saw her eating that shit.

Lucky for us, I'm like a human garbage disposal. I should probably be more discerning about the quality of food I eat though because, fuck, this is not good.

I flush the toilet, close my eyes, and lean back against the stall, willing the nausea to dissipate or at least lessen in its intensity. I crack an eye open and look at my phone, noting that it's not even six in the morning, and here I am, worshipping a porcelain bowl. I groan, hitting my head against the door. My parents are coming this afternoon to take me to lunch since my first class isn't until two, and they have the day off. How my father, the chief medical examiner of Haversham County, got a Thursday afternoon off is anyone's guess, especially since they are literally always working.

After waiting ten minutes for the sickness to wash away, I stand and unlock the stall, thanking every god in the universe that no one is up this early to get ready for class. If Ava had slept in our room last night, she'd probably be in here doing her hair and makeup before her morning classes. She is such a fucking freak with routines. We can finally sleep in and start our days at a more reasonable time, like noon, but she refuses to give up her early morning wake-up calls.

Turning on the faucet, I let the water run while I lather my hands in soap. Catching sight of my reflection, I double-take at the shit show staring back at me. My fair skin and dark red hair are my most striking features, but after the vomiting session this morning, the spiderweb of popped blood vessels is overpowering.

"Fuck," I sigh, surveying the damage in the mirror. I nor-

2

mally don't wear more than tinted moisturizer and mascara during the day, but I can't let my parents see me like this. With my mother as a cardiothoracic surgeon and my father as a medical examiner, they'll freak the fuck out if I show up with popped blood vessels all over the left side of my face from projectile vomiting.

Tucking my chin into my chest, I rush out of the bathroom and hurry to the safety of my dorm room, praying that I don't pass anyone in the hallway on my short walk back. I breathe a sigh of relief once I reach my door and make my way inside. Even though it's an ungodly hour, there's no way I'm going to be able to go back to sleep, so I may as well get ready. I'm never eating another fucking taco.

—

It took me two fucking hours to cover the shit on my face, and by the time I was done, I looked more ready to go out to a club than meet my parents for lunch. I'd rather them question the heaviness of my makeup than the state of my natural face, though. With more than four hours to spare before I meet my parents, I grab my backpack and head to the student center to catch up on my writing. Being born with freakishly smart and scientifically minded parents introduced me to STEM at a young age and gave me the advantage of advanced math and science classes. Lucky for me, I passed my AP tests and earned credit for college-level math and science because I hated both subjects. Earning those credits allowed me to add two English-centric electives to my schedule.

Most people opt for the quiet solitude of the library to study, but not me. There is something enchanting and riveting about the student center; I love watching the interactions of others and creating stories for them in my head. One of my electives, creative writing, challenges me to create pieces at least twice a month, be it poetry, prose, or short essays, and I use the inspiration derived from the student center to do so. Setting my bag down at one of the tables just outside the grill area, I grab my laptop and start watching the world around me.

To my left, a lone girl is standing in front of the drink display, and I imagine that she's mulling over a date she has for the night, that she's contemplating what to wear and if the guy will be the love of her life. To my right, there are two guys engaged in a heated discussion, and I picture them entwined together, secretly in love but too nervous about what people would say if they went public.

This is what I live for—creating scenarios and a reality that can live within the pages of a book. I focus my attention on the two guys and conjure up the story that I would love to see play out.

—

My phone goes off, breaking my writing spell. Glancing down, I see my mother's contact information on my screen. My mother never calls me unless the world is falling apart or she's about to arrive at our predetermined meeting place. I swipe the screen to answer.

"Hi, Mom," I greet.

"Hi, Chicken," my mother responds, and I roll my eyes. When I was a young girl, I was obsessed with Chicken Little, and she's called me Chicken ever since. "We're almost at the campus. Should we meet you at the diner, or do you want us to pick you up?"

I pull my phone away from my ear and look at the time; shit, I've been writing for almost four hours without a break. "I'm at the student center working on my writing assignment; I'm

4

a five-minute walk to the diner, so I'll meet you there."

"I know how you get with your writing, save that document and close your laptop before you get sucked into another writing vortex." I wince because she's not wrong. I'm fortunate that, even though my parents don't understand how I could ever *not* want to go into the medical field, they support my creative mind.

Kind of. When my dad does text, it normally includes a statement like, "Are you switching your major to biology yet?" or "What are you going to do with a liberal arts degree?"

"Yes, yes, Mother, I'm packing up now. See you soon," I promise and hang up. I throw everything into my bag and walk toward the heavy glass doors. Before I can push the door open, hands grab my shoulders and pull me back. I don't need to turn around to know who just manhandled me; the warm scent of wood and citrus envelopes me, and I sigh, turning around to face my tattooed weakness.

"Dante, if you keep grabbing me in public, I am going to flip you over my shoulder and laugh when I break your fucking back," I complain, shrugging his hands off.

"Damn, Red, is that any way to greet your man?" he replies, tugging my body back toward him. "I texted you last night, but you didn't answer. Do you want to grab dinner?" Since that afternoon at the barbecue, I have done everything in my power to avoid Dante. It doesn't help that we shared a bed after Ava was verbally attacked at the soccer party—okay, and that we made out in said bed until I shoved him out like Edward Cullen in the *Twilight* movie. If it were up to him, he'd put a brand on my forehead that said, "Property of Dante," but I'm more comfortable not doing this, whatever "this" is. Even Ava, whom I tell everything, doesn't know that Dante and I hooked

5

up, though I'm sure she suspects it after our interaction a couple of weeks ago in Grey and Dante's kitchen.

"You are not my man," I grumble, taking a step back. "I need to go meet my parents for lunch. Stop stalking me, you creep." I practically run out of the student center, using my parents as the excuse for my haste. I regret sleeping with Dante, not because he isn't amazing in bed or because he's actually a creep, but because he makes me feel too much. When I first got to college, I had no intention of entering a relationship and had every desire to be single, meet cute boys, and maybe go on a few dates. I wanted casual, not intense.

Dante doesn't seem to give two shits about what I want, though. He's gorgeous, kind, generous, and the biggest pain in my freaking ass.

My phone goes off, and I expect my mom's name to flash across my screen; I scowl when I see it's Dante. Opening the message, I sigh at our thread.

Dante: Red, you look like a goddess today. When can I take you out?

I hate it when he does this shit: continually compliment me and try to take me on a date. He is incapable of keeping things platonic, and it's infuriating. I thought college guys were supposed to be terrified of commitment, but it seems Ava has introduced us to a group of men who are all equally possessive and intense. I type out my typical response to Dante and hit send.

CeCe: Fuck off

Dante: I love it when you talk dirty, baby.

I stuff my phone in my pocket, not bothering to reply to him, it's pointless anyway. Approaching the diner, I can see my parents at a booth through the window and jog up the steps toward the entrance. As soon as I walk through the door, I'm assaulted by the smell of bacon grease, artificial sweetness, and eggs. I gag, trying to hold the wave of nausea back. It's not as bad as it was this morning, and I take that as a sign that the food poisoning is working its way out of my system.

I practice my breathing and will the need to vomit away, eventually succeeding. After a few minutes, when I no longer feel like dying, I step through the second set of doors and walk to the back of the diner where my parents sit. Buried in their menus, they don't notice me until I throw myself into the booth. Startled, they look up and smile at my presence.

"Hi, little Chicken," my mom says with a smile before narrowing her eyes at my face. "Why are you wearing so much makeup?"

My dad cuts in before I can respond, "You are wearing a lot of makeup. You know, the new mortician at Jones' funeral parlor does the same thing with the cheekbones on the older corpses," he says, gesturing to the contour on my face. "Makes them look fifteen years younger, I swear."

Great, now I'm being compared to dead people.

I shake my head and shrug my parents' comments and questions off. "I wanted to try a new look," I lie. "I guess I went too heavy on the foundation. Anyway"—I gesture toward their menus—"what are you getting?" I don't have to ask to know the answer to my question—my parents are creatures of habit and will probably split a soup and sandwich—but I need to change the topic.

"We're splitting the club sandwich and soup," my mother answers, confirming my suspicions.

"How exciting," I tease. I don't bother looking at the menu because I know anything other than water will set me off again.

7

"My stomach is off, so I'm just going to get a croissant," I tell them.

My mom's brow raises in question, but I shake my head. "The dining hall food is terrible," I offer with a grimace. My mother doesn't have a chance to respond because the waitress approaches, ready to take our order. I don't even have a chance to put in my order when I feel the bile rise in my throat, another wave of nausea consuming me. Both my parents and the waitress look at me expectantly, but I shake my head, covering my mouth with my hand and making a run for the bathroom. Like this morning, I make it to the stall just in time.

When I finish, my mother is waiting for me by the sinks, concern written on her face.

"Celeste, are you okay?"

"I don't know, Mom, I feel so sick one minute and fine the next. I haven't eaten since Monday night, and I'm just praying for this to pass."

My mom looks at me, surveying me in a way only a mother can. "Celeste, I need to ask you a question," she says tentatively, almost like I'm a skittish horse, and she's afraid to spook me.

I look at her, confused. "Sure."

"Is it possible..." she pauses and clears her throat. "Is it possible that you're pregnant?"

"What?" I scream. "No. Absolutely not."

"Honey, are you sure?" I look at her, horrified that she's even asking this question.

"Mother, yes. I-I..." I take a breath, the timeline of my period running through my head and giving me pause. "I'm not. I can't be," I whisper.

"Okay, Celeste. But you'll tell me if you're in trouble, right?"

my mom pleads, letting me know that while the subject is dropped for now, it won't be dropped forever.

"Let's just go back to the table. I have a class this afternoon that I can't be late for."

We leave the bathroom and make our way back to the table. Throughout the rest of lunch, my mom's question is on repeat in my head, like a broken record that plays the same line over and over and over again.

I'm not pregnant. I can't be.

2

CeCe

I'm not sure if it's phantom nausea or actual nausea that follows me throughout the rest of my day, but by the time I make it back to my dorm room, I'm ready to dive into my bed and forget the world for a bit. My mother's question is an albatross that hangs around my neck; my quick denial of a potential pregnancy sits in my stomach like a lead bomb, and something just feels off.

During my world history class, I couldn't focus and instead did mental calculations of my last period and ovulation window, as though those two factors were exact science. When I lost my virginity four weeks ago, the condom fell off, but I've been on hormonal birth control since I was sixteen, so I didn't bother taking a preventative pill afterward. Honestly, I was more concerned about a potential STD since Dante seems like the kind of guy who would stick his dick in a glory hole just for the hell of it.

The fuckhead swore that he wasn't carrying a venereal disease, but still, I worried about that more than anything else. Two days later, he sent me test results from a local clinic confirming that he wasn't a super spreader. But what if he is, but instead of flesh-eating bacteria, he has super sperm that fought its way out of a condom, through my birth control, and fertilized my fucking eggs? I sit up in my bed, where I am lying watching a movie after class, and my breathing turns heavy.

I'm well into the start of an impressive panic attack when my phone starts vibrating in my bag. Getting up from my bed, I walk to my desk, where I discarded my backpack. Reaching into the side pocket, I see a missed call from Dante, which is weird since he's never called before. My phone goes off again, this time with a text.

Dante: Celeste, pick up your phone. Emergency with Ava.

My blood runs cold, and I immediately click on his contact information to call him back. He answers on the first ring, like he was waiting for my call.

"Thank fuck," Dante's voice booms through the line. "Where have you been? Are you safe?"

"Safe? What are you talking about? I just got done with class, and I'm in my dorm. What's going on?" I ask, frantic energy builds within me, and I know, instinctually, that something is very wrong.

"Baby, I need you to stay calm," he starts. He pauses before continuing, "Ava was attacked by Felicity, and she's on her way to the hospital with Grey."

My heart plummets. "W-what do you mean attacked?" I feel the tears build, and I start pacing, feeling useless within these cinderblock walls. "Is she okay? Which hospital is she in? I'm calling a car now. Oh my God," I ramble, unable to comprehend anything bad happening to my best friend.

"Red, calm down. Working yourself up isn't going to help anyone," Dante says in a consoling voice. "I'm almost at your dorm to bring you to the hospital. Stay inside until I text you. Lincoln is picking up Serena, and we'll meet them there."

"Th-th-th," I start but can't push out my words. Sobs wrack my body, and I start shaking from the impact of my fear and emotion for my best friend. I don't even know what happened, but I can only guess that if she's in the emergency room and we're going there to hold vigil, it's not good.

"Fuck," he says under his breath. "Baby, stay with me. I'm almost at your dorm. I'm going to come up and get you, okay? Just stay where you are," he commands softly.

"I—" my voice breaks on a hiccup. "I have t-to let you in. You w-won't be able to get upstairs," I tell him.

"Let me worry about that, Red. Just stay on the phone. I'm getting out of my car now." I hear his engine shut off and the opening of a door. Moments pass before he says, "Baby, I'm coming up the stairs. Which room are you in?"

"Th-third floor," I stutter and then give him my room number. The words barely leave my mouth before there's a soft knock on my door. "Is that you?" I whisper into the phone.

"Yes, baby, it's me. Now, open up." I open the door, and I am immediately enveloped in his embrace. I collapse into him; I didn't realize how much I needed a hug until he gave me one, almost like he knows what I need better than I do.

Bringing both hands up to cup my face, Dante leans back and takes stock of my appearance. The intensity with which he surveys me is unnerving, and I feel entirely too exposed under his scrutiny. I drop my eyes and realize that my makeup rubbed off on his black T-shirt, and I wince; the splotches and popped veins from this morning are probably on full display.

Right now, that's the least of my worries. "Can you take me

to her? Please?" I ask, still not looking at his face.

He's quiet, not responding until he lifts my chin to meet his eyes. "Yes, baby. But don't think you're getting off easy. I know something is wrong." I open my mouth to refute his claim, but he shakes his head, cutting off my rebuttal. "No, don't lie to me, Red. We don't have time for this now, but later, we're talking about this."

Dante steps back and grabs my hand, pulling me toward the door. I'm barely coherent as he ushers me down the hall and into the stairwell. He must sense the rising hysteria because one minute I'm standing, and the next, I'm in his arms bridal-style and being carried down the stairs, out the door, and toward his car that's parked illegally in front of my building. With one hand, Dante opens the door and deposits me gingerly in the passenger seat before buckling my seatbelt and pausing to stare at me. The gentleness in his features contradicts everything I know about him, and I'm left speechless by his display of care and compassion.

Leaning in, he presses his lips to my forehead and mumbles, "I swear to you, Red, everything will be okay."

—

I think Dante broke every speed limit in West Helm getting us to the hospital. I'm not complaining since he got us here safely and in record time, but still, I don't think he obeyed most traffic laws. When we arrived at the hospital, he once again picked me up and raced through the lobby until we found the family waiting area. He was hesitant to let me down, but I forced him to so that I could embrace Ava's parents and siblings. The low growl that came from him when I hugged Rafe would have been annoying in any other situation, but I was too worried about Ava to care.

13

We've been waiting in this room for over two hours with Ava's family, Grey, Serena, and Lincoln. Grey's dad, Greg Jansen, just got here and pulled Grey and Mr. Gregori aside to talk. The silence in the room is deafening, not literal silence, since Mrs. Gregori and I can't seem to hold back our sobs, but the silence of information. We haven't received any update about Ava's condition or how the surgery is going. The unknown is horrifying.

I can't imagine never seeing my best friend again, never having the opportunity to graduate college with her or be in each other's weddings. I let out a soft sob and burrow my head into my hands, trying to hide from the reality of where we are and why we're here. I feel a strong, warm hand coast up my arm, settling at my shoulder.

"Red," Dante whispers. "Lean on me, baby. Let me hold you." My bravado from earlier and my prior need for distance between us are nonexistent; I release my head and turn into his body, letting his chest absorb the cries that I can't seem to hold back. His hands rub my back, pulling me closer to his embrace. "Shh," he soothes. "She's going to be okay, baby."

Dante continues holding me as families cycle in and out of the waiting room; some leave in tears, their losses weighing heavy in the room, while others shout in happiness, offering brief reprieves from the somber atmosphere. What feels like hours pass before a petite woman in scrubs enters the waiting area, asking for Ava's family.

Grey catapults himself toward the doctor, demanding answers and a status update on Ava. Despite his gruff attitude, I'm grateful that he's demanding the information that has been withheld from us. In a crisp, calm voice, the doctor introduces herself and explains, "Ava is out of surgery. We

14

were able to stop the bleeding and repair the damage done to her bladder. She will have a few complications, but this will not affect her quality of life or mobility. We will wait to go over these complications once she wakes up and we're in the clear. The next forty-eight hours are critical after surgery, and we will keep her in the trauma unit. They're weening her off the anesthesia now, and she should be coherent in a few hours. Once she's lucid, we'll bring you back to see her." Continuing, she says, "Why don't you all go grab something to eat, run home, and take a shower? When she wakes up, the last thing she needs to see is blood." She looks pointedly at Grey's blood-soaked clothing and skin.

I let out a breath I didn't realize I was holding and sag into Dante's arms in relief.

"She's okay, Red," Dante says into my ear, holding me closer. "Come on, baby, let's get you something to eat, and then we'll go see Ava when she wakes up."

—

Not to be dramatic, but waiting for Ava to wake up from anesthesia has been one of the longest waits in my life. Dante keeps trying to pry my mouth open and force stale hospital vending machine snacks down my throat, but between omnipresent nausea and the stress brought by Ava's attack, the last thing I want to do is eat.

Dante holds up a powdered donut from a package that looks suspiciously vintage and presses it to my lips. I smack his hand away and grumble, "So help me God, if you try to put another donut in my mouth, I will kick you in the fucking gonads." He somehow crammed one in, and it tasted like dirt and dead dreams.

"You haven't eaten since lunch with your parents. You're

going to pass out, and then I'll need to get a gurney for you. Do you think Ava needs to be worrying about your stubborn ass when she wakes up, fresh from a knife fight?" Guilt courses through me at his words, and I scowl, grabbing the stupid donut from his stupid hand and shoving it in my mouth.

I choke on the stale treat, reaching for water to wash it down. As I chew and swallow, Dante looks on in rapt attention, like he's making sure I don't spit it out. I roll my eyes, open my mouth, and hold out my tongue, showing him that no food remains.

"Are you happy now, you overbearing ogre?" I mumble. The asshole just smiles and holds out the package of donuts, encouraging me to take more. "Dante, they're stale, stop trying to force me to eat."

"Red," Dante begins but stops when Grey comes into the room, freshly showered and dressed in dark blue scrubs. He walks toward us, nodding his head at the others scattered about the room to join.

"She's waking up," he pauses, running a finger through his long blonde hair in frustration. "We don't know how she'll react to the anesthesia, but we think it'll be good for you guys to wait in the hall. If she's okay, you can come into the room. If she's not, I'm going to need you to get the fuck out of there so that we can take care of my girl. Understood?" He levels us with a look that is equal parts menacing and pleading, as if he's saying he'll beat the shit out of us if we overstep, but he needs Ava to know we're all here.

Normally, I'd reply with a snide remark or snap at him for ordering us around, but the look on his face makes me refrain. He knows that Ava is in this situation because of his inability to keep his dick in his pants, and I don't need to make it worse by being a bitch. I nod my head, letting him know that I'll listen, that the mental and physical well-being of my best friend takes precedence over everything else, even the ripples of nausea from the shit donuts Dante force-fed me.

Grey surveys me, narrowing his eyes and seemingly discerning my ability to follow his directive. I raise my hand and itch my nose, offering him a "fuck you" middle finger for good measure. That seems to pacify him, and with a scoff, he turns around, silently commanding that we follow him toward Ava's room.

Grey walks into the room without pause, sitting down next to Ava and grabbing her hand. From my spot in the hall, I can see her eyelids twitch, as though her mind is working, but her body is catching up. Seeing her there, bundled in threadbare sheets with unusually pale skin, has me seeing red.

When we were in elementary school, Ava and I watched the movie *Gremlins* in her parents' basement; after watching those little fur balls go from adorable to psychotic, Ava would tease me that I was the human embodiment of those little assholes. I can't deny that Ava's current state has me devolving into that state. I've always been quick to trigger, which is why my parents signed me up for martial arts at a young age. The discipline and teachings of my first sensei are in the furthest recesses of my mind, and all I want to do is kick Felicity's ass and hogtie her like a baby cow.

"Mmmph," sounds from across the room, and my eyes fly to Ava's face, the first flicker of life coming out of her.

"Vixen," Grey chokes out, his voice filled with unsuppressed emotion. Next to me, Ava's mom lets out a squeal of relief and rushes inside the room, nearly launching herself at Ava. I hang back, clinging to Dante's shirt and letting Ava's family have

17

this moment of relief. Ava's eyes are locked on Grey's; the look of reverence and adoration on her face has me choking back even more tears. I may hate what Grey did to get her in this mess, but their love is tangible, and I can't fault him for how he cares for my best friend.

Dante's arm wraps around my body, pulling me into him. Leaning down, he whispers, "I told you, Red, she's going to be okay."

—

We left shortly after Ava woke up, the doctor not so subtly kicking us out. When I attempted to order an Uber home, Dante plucked my phone from my hands and ordered my "tight ass" into his car. I tried to get my phone back, but he's over six feet and built like a damn tree. Short of climbing his body like an obstacle course, there was no winning in this scenario.

I'm also too drained to argue with him.

"How are you holding up?" Dante asks. His voice is still uncharacteristically soft and soothing; I fucking hate how that makes me feel.

"You can stop being all nice and sweet and acting like you care about me. I'm okay. Aves is going to be okay."

He laughs from his side of the car and shakes his head, acting like I just told the funniest joke he's ever heard. "Red, when are you going to understand that we're happening? You can ignore me, leave me on read, and act all tough, but baby? I know how you feel when you come. I know the spots that make you see fucking stars, and I fucking know how goddamn sweet it is after you come on my cock and melt into me, showing me just how much you need me." He reaches over the console and squeezes my thigh. "You can try to fight this all you want, but we both know that this, you and me? We're happening. Just

18

like Grey knew he and Ava were it, I know it's us. I'll fight for us, don't worry."

I'm stunned for a moment before annoyance takes over. "You realize you sound like a lunatic, right? You're veering into obsessive behavior."

He chuckles again. "Listen, you want to go out there and explore other options? Fine. But remember, you're going to come back to me, and I'm going to prove every step of the fucking way that no one can give you what I can." He releases my leg and grips the steering wheel. "Do you want a burger or tacos? You need to eat something, and don't give me any sass. You look like you're about to pass the fuck out."

His speech leaves me off-kilter. I feel like I just got whiplash from the sudden change in topic while my stomach lurches at the mention of tacos. I swallow down the bile and grip the door handle.

"Fries," I answer. Even the word "taco" makes me want to die.

He looks over at me, his eyes narrowing. Maybe it's my tone, maybe it's my easy acceptance of food? Who the fuck knows, but I recognize that I do need to eat something, even if I don't want to. Not offering any comment, he turns into a drive-thru and proceeds to order enough food to feed a family of six. I raise an eyebrow, confused by the burgers, chicken nuggets, fries, and chicken sandwiches he just ordered.

Dante offers a shrug. "I'm Italian; my mother never taught me moderation when it comes to ordering food."

I roll my eyes. "You sound like Ava and her family. I swear, every time that girl cooks or I eat at her parents' house, I gain five pounds from the amount of food they make."

"My sister is the same; she owns a few restaurants with her

19

wife. I have to be rolled out of there every time we go," he comments absently as he drives up to the window to get the absurd amount of food he ordered.

Handing me the bags, he instructs, "Grab whatever you want. Whatever we don't eat, I'll bring back for Linc." I select a container of French fries, inhale the salty, fried aroma, and feel a level of peace descend. Unlike some of my friends' parents, my mother can't cook for shit, and we lived on takeout until I was in high school. Ava's mother nearly had a heart attack when she found out my parents were either too busy working or just incapable of making a homemade meal. When I was fifteen, Mrs. Gregori included me in her cooking lessons with her daughters, and I figured out my way around a kitchen.

I'm not talented like Ava, nor do I have a deep love for cooking, but I enjoy it and can make a few things well. Once I started cooking regularly, fast food became a treat to be had during late nights and after high school football games. The nostalgia of these deep-fried potatoes gives me comfort.

"You going to eat those fries, or are you just going to smell them?" Dante's voice breaks through the memories fogging my brain. I look up and realize that Dante has parked us in front of a lake. Truthfully, I have no idea where we are in proximity to the hospital or campus.

Looking over at him, I grab a handful of fries and shove them into my mouth, chewing loudly and hoping to annoy the shit out of him. Smacking my lips as I chew, I grab more fries and reach my hand out, thrusting the fries into Dante's mouth. He laughs through the mouthful, chewing the fries and swallowing before reaching into the bag and grabbing a burger.

I watch his long, thick fingers unwrap the cheeseburger,

gripping it with such force that ketchup drips down the side, falling on his hand. Bringing his hand to his mouth, Dante's tongue darts out and licks the sauce off. The move shouldn't be sexual; there should be no tingling between my thighs or heat licking up my spine. With his large, lean body, tattooed limbs, and sinfully good-looking face, the act of eating is pornographic. I shift, clenching my thighs together at the wetness and need pooling between them.

"That was cute, Red," he says around a bite of burger. "Next time you put that hand over my mouth, I'll bite you before I taste that mouth."

I stare at him, wide-eyed and mortified that I'm so turned on by the thought of Dante biting me.

3

Dante

Fucking fuck. If Red doesn't want me to know that she's turned on by my threat of kissing her sassy as fuck mouth, she should stop shifting in my goddamn seats. With every squirm she makes, her tight ass rubs against the leather and squeaks, calling attention to how needy my girl is.

She's convinced we're not right for each other, that I can't be more than a walking cock, and has done everything she can to avoid me. After I fucked her tight cunt, she raced home and refused to answer my text messages. I'd be embarrassed if I thought she wasn't interested in me, but she left my sheets soaking wet.

Unless she has a hate kink, which would be interesting as fuck, but I could work with that.

"What's wrong, Red? Are you thinking about how good my mouth would feel on your skin?" I tease, watching her skin flush.

"I'm thinking about how good it would be to punch that mouth," she throws back. Based on the color of her cheeks under all that makeup, she's a lying little shit.

"Tsk, tsk." I reach over, prying the half-eaten container of fries from her hands. "You know, every time you lie, your cheeks flush, and you turn the prettiest shade of pink. Now, if you don't want me to think you're a little liar, tell me what you were thinking about and where you want my mouth." Setting the fries back in the take-out bag, I grab her by the waist and lift her over the center console. Depositing her on my lap, I lean back while she straddles me, putting her hot cunt right over where I want it most.

She shifts again, rubbing over my cock and making both of us groan. "I wasn't thinking about your mouth anywhere, you Neanderthal," she whispers. "I couldn't want you less." Her pelvis rocks, back and forth, back and forth, proving her words false.

"If you don't want me, get off my lap, and I'll take you home." I grab her hips and push her back, disconnecting her center from my hard-on.

She meets my eyes and lets out a dramatic huff. Spearing her hands into my hair, she yanks my head back and complains, "You're so fucking annoying," before covering my lips with hers. I let her take control of the kiss, following her lead as she traces my upper lip with her tongue and her nails dig into my scalp. After seeing her break apart today, I'll do everything I fucking can to get my hellion back.

Red's hips thrust forward. Fuck, she feels good grinding against my cock, even with layers of clothing between us. Her tongue licks the seam of my lips, demanding entrance. I pull her closer, meeting her tongue in a fucking frenzy.

There's nothing practiced about this kiss; it's wild and frantic and fucking delicious. The sweetness of her lips is coated in salt, and I lap it up, diving my tongue into her mouth over and over again until they're fucking raw.

Reaching up, I grab her hands from my hair and pull them behind her, taking control of her movements. Still writhing against my dick, she struggles and tries to pry her arms from my hold. I tighten my grip, not allowing her dominance.

"I let you take control, and now it's my turn." I nip her bottom lip, drawing it into my mouth and sucking on it. My little hellion growls at me, fighting against the restraint.

"Let go of my hands," she whines. Ignoring her request, I trail my mouth to her jawline, licking my way down until my lips meet her pulse. I taste her skin, lapping at the delicate pulse until it's beating like a fucking hummingbird's wings.

"Let me take care of you, baby." I bite down, and she groans, her body growing slack with submission. Transferring both her wrists to one hand, I use my free hand to trace a path from her knee to her slim thighs, up to her luscious ass. Despite how tiny Red is, both in height and shape, her curves are defined, perfect lines that tease a man and test resolve. I'm fucking addicted to the soft gasps she makes when I graze the back of her thigh. I'm harder than I've ever been when she lets out a soft moan as I grip her tight ass.

As my mother would say, she's got an ass like two moz-zarellas, except in her New York accent, it would come out as "muhtz-a-dells."

"No," she breathes out, and I still. Her voice is a whisper, barely audible, but it echoes in the space like a scream. "No. We cannot do this. Dante, let go of me." I lift my hands from her ass and her wrist, holding them out to the side of my head to show that I won't touch her again.

As soon as my hands are off her, it's like a dam breaks; a strangled gasp releases from her mouth, followed by body-wracking sobs. She convulses on top of me, similar to her grinding minutes ago, yet this is not in pleasure but pain. I close my eyes and breathe in her hurt, fucking willing God to transfer her internal pain to me.

"Shh, Celeste, it's okay," I murmur into the car. I slowly lower my hands until they're resting by my thighs. "Baby, let me hold you," I plead. If she says no, I'll continue to sit here, anchoring her as she cries into her hands on my lap. I catch her subtle nod.

I raise my arms and wrap them around her lightly, letting her feel the weight against her body before pulling her flush against me. My cock is still hard—she's fucking straddling my dick right now, and the warmth from her pussy is a flame against my crotch—but I shift her body so that she doesn't feel the full force of my erection.

"Tell me what I can do, Red. How can I help?"

"I-I-I," she starts, stuttering with a sob. "I don't k-know. It hurts. A-Ava could have died, and we're here. I should be at the hospital." She settles into my hold, and I pull her closer, absorbing her words.

"You know Grey wouldn't allow us to stay there." He's a possessive motherfucker—I don't blame him because I would do the same if she were lying in that hospital bed. The thought chills my blood, and I squeeze her tighter, reassuring myself that she's safe. Realistically, the hospital wouldn't allow Red to stay in the room with Ava and would instead force her to occupy a waiting room until visiting hours were open in the morning. How Grey managed to convince Ava's parents and the hospital to allow him to stay in her fucking room all night is anyone's guess.

"Baby, listen," I pause, lifting one of my arms from around

25

her waist and bringing my hand up to cradle her face. I lift her face from my chest until she's looking up at me. Her bright green eyes are glowing from her tears, making them look even greener, like fucking moss in England. "I need you to listen to me. There is nothing, and I mean absolutely nothing, we could have done to prevent this from happening, short of Grey and Ava never getting together in the first place. Felicity is sick, she needs fucking help, and her eyes were set on Ava the minute that Grey showed interest in her. Ava is okay, she is going to make it through this, and Grey will make damn sure that nothing will ever harm her again." She's no longer sobbing, but tears continue streaming down her cheeks, dripping over my fingers as I hold her face in my hand.

She shakes her head, as though she's disagreeing with my words.

"Yes, Red," I say before she can voice her disagreement. "There is nothing we could have done to prevent this. I promise you that. The fault is Felicity's and the illness that fucking consumed her."

"But I threatened her. I told her that I would come after her if she came after the people that are important to me. I-I provoked her," she says between cries.

Ah, so that's the issue. She thinks she's the catalyst for Felicity's fucked up game of possession. Fuck that.

"You're wrong, baby. Felicity didn't give a shit about you. She always had her sight on Ava because of Grey." While we were at the hospital, Grey told me the shit he found in her dorm room—the goddamn surveillance pictures, the computer, the framed photograph. It's creepy as shit.

Her eyes are downcast, but I can tell that she's processing my words.

26

"You can't make yourself the villain in this story, Celeste."

4

CeCe

Dante holds me as I break apart on his lap. After saying his piece about Ava's attack, he falls quiet and doesn't say anything to shatter the silence. With his hand in my hair—petting me rather than pulling me—and his breath in my ear, he offers me comfort in the most basic way: hugging.

After finding out about Ava, stress and anxiety about my situation were replaced with fear and trepidation for her; now, however, I'm left to ruminate.

"I feel you building walls, Red," Dante murmurs into my hair.

I shake my head and deny his accusation. It's a lie, of course, but does it count if I don't verbalize my response?

He chuckles against me, pulling me in closer. "Liar," he whispers. "As much as I'd love to keep you against me all night, we need to get you home, baby." In a swift move, he hoists me off his lap and gently deposits me in the passenger seat.

Dante wastes no time shifting into drive and pulling out of the lot. Based on Dante's relaxed body language, I can't imagine what he's thinking; it's been a shitstorm of a night, and other than Ava making it through alive, there's not much to be happy about.

We pull into my dorm's parking lot, and Dante pulls into a spot, surprising me when he unbuckles and gets out of the car. Crossing the hood and opening my door, he holds his hand out, daring me to question him.

"What are you doing?" I ask, though I already know.

"We're going to your dorm, and we're going to crash in that tiny ass bed."

"No." I shake my head. "You're going home, and I'm going to crash in my 'tiny ass bed.'"

He sighs, exasperation clear in his expression. "Come on, it's been a long day. I just want to go to sleep with my girl."

I roll my eyes and exit the car, ignoring his extended hand. "I'm not your girl," I mumble.

"You have my spit in your mouth right now, and my shirt is soaked with your tears," he responds loudly. There aren't many people out right now, but there are still a few out here who definitely heard him.

"You fuckhead," I seethe. "Lower your damn voice." I turn to him and glare, hoping to impart that I will disembowel him if he does that again.

"Red, you're a little tease. I know you like it when I get possessive—" I stop Dante with a hand, clamping it over his big, stupid mouth. His eyes show how much he's enjoying my annoyance.

"If you come upstairs, you will be quiet for the rest of the goddamn night, or I will put laxatives in your well." His house has well water, and I'm not above poisoning all the guys at this point. He responds with a nod, grinning at me when I remove

29

my hand from his mouth. "Let's go, you dick."

I swear I hear a whispered, "Your dick," come from behind me. I don't bother turning around.

The walk into my building and up to my room is quick. I breathe a sigh of relief as soon as I shut the door behind us. Dante must be taking my order seriously because he doesn't say anything, doesn't offer any smartass or sexual words, and I'm grateful that he respected my condition.

Granted, I threatened to ruin his water supply.

We undress in the silence; I don't even bother taking off my makeup or brushing my teeth, staples in my nighttime routine. Instead, I rid myself of my clothes, throw on an oversized T-shirt and boxers, and start to climb into bed. Dante's hand reaches out, stilling my movements and forcing me to turn toward him.

I look at him, waiting for his words. When he doesn't speak, I realize that he's waiting for me to tell him that he's allowed to.

"Yes, Dante?" I sigh.

"Whose fucking clothes are those?" he growls. His voice is hard, a tone that I've never heard from him before. I look down at my sleepwear and look at him in confusion.

"They're mine. Why?"

"You're wearing fucking boxers. Who the fuck do they belong to?" The menacing tone of his voice absolutely should not turn me on.

I roll my eyes. "They're mine. I bought them for myself because women's pajamas and underwear are fucking stupid and designed to be sexy. I don't want to be sexy when I sleep; I want to be comfortable and not have dental floss ride up my ass," I scoff. "Now, can we go to sleep, or do you need me to find itemized receipts?"

He stares at me before shaking his head. "Get your ass in bed," he grumbles. Sliding into the twin bed, I press my body against the cinderblock wall, giving him as much space as I can. Instead of taking the space I allotted him, he rolls into me, pulling my back against his chest and curling his form over my body. Just like earlier tonight, when he held me in his arms while I cried, I melt into him, letting his strength wash over me.

It's intoxicating, letting him take care of me. It reminds me of my parents and their give-and-take relationship; though my parents are overworked and have never spent much time at home, they have always supported each other's lives. When my dad was up for his promotion to chief medical examiner, I remember how anxious he was to take on such a prominent role. My mom was his voice of reason, sounding board, and emotional support through the initial months of the job. I've seen them offer physical and emotional comfort to each other my entire life, and it's something I demand in a partner.

It pisses me off that Dante, the biggest pain in my ass, has so many of the qualities, or has displayed so many of the actions, that I will want in a partner. He thinks I'm just resisting or being difficult, but there's more to it than that. I'm petrified of the future; there's this nagging voice in the back of my head telling me that I need to experience life and not tie myself down. However, there's a tug in my heart—and vagina—every time I see or speak to Dante.

With Dante's body curled around me, protecting me from the world outside this tiny dorm room, his possessive words from earlier flow through me. The gentle breath escaping his mouth and the firm hand pressed against my stomach feel secure.

Sleep pulls on my eyes, and I fall under, warmth at my back and a wall at my front.

5

CeCe

The first thing I realize when I wake up is that there is an inferno surrounding me. Heat and pressure run along my back and stomach, and I shift, trying to find some relief from the oppressive temperature in my bed. Keeping my eyes closed, I try to pull my blanket down, but it's not a blanket suffocating me, it's a large, tattooed arm. Confused, I look over my shoulder and see his face, perfectly peaceful in sleep.

Fuck, Dante.

I bolt upright, the prior evening rushing to the forefront of my mind and replaying like a bad movie. Ava's attack, the car ride home, the hour spent at the lake, and the ever-present nausea are all there on a loop. I rub the sleep from my eyes and groan when I look at my hands, the mascara and concealer from yesterday are smeared all over. With my red hair and raccoon eyes, I probably look like the Hamburglar right now.

My stomach rolls, and all thoughts of my appearance fall away as nausea takes over. Last night, I slept against the wall to give Dante enough space; I'm regretting that decision right now. I try to climb over his large form without touching him, but he's everywhere. Now that he's no longer pinning me to his body, he's sprawled out like an oversized starfish, taking up all the available space in the bed.

Fuck this. Not giving a shit if I wake him up, I climb over the mountain of a man and scramble toward my slippers and toiletry bag. It doesn't matter how sick I feel, I will not be walking into a communal bathroom without shoes on. Throwing my door open, I sprint down the hall and run into a stall.

Releasing a demon-like sound, the entire contents of my stomach are expunged, not unlike the scene from the original *Exorcist*, where Linda Blair's character projectile vomits all over the priest. It's disgusting but also immediately makes me feel better. I flush, stand up, and exit the stall, making my way to the sinks and vanity mirrors along the wall. My mother's question, my constant nausea for the last few days, and the nagging voice in the back of my head eat at me. I close my eyes, willing the hysteria down, and force myself to look in the mirror.

I stare at my reflection, noting the still-present popped veins and the sallow look of my skin. Despite the makeup caked on from yesterday, there's no mistaking that my skin is a mess and that I need cosmetic help.

I was smart enough to bring my bag with me and take out the makeup remover, toothbrush, and toothpaste that will hopefully improve my current state of being. Pouring the micellar water over a reusable makeup remover wipe, I cleanse my skin, hoping that it'll restore me. I look in the mirror after taking the makeup off.

God, I look like shit.

I brush my teeth and reapply a coat of makeup—foundation,

34

bronzer, blush, and mascara—before running a lip balm over my chapped lips. Surveying my reflection, I sigh. The makeup doesn't help, I still look horrible, and if anything, the shit on my face just highlights the dark bags under my eyes and the gauntness of my cheeks. I'm petite to begin with; losing weight does not do me any favors.

I grab my things and make my way back to my dorm room, preparing myself for which version of Dante I'll get this morning: possessive ass or horny frat boy.

I pause at my door, bracing myself before I open it and walk in. If Jesus loves me, Dante will still be passed out and incoherent on the twin bed.

When I step through the threshold, Dante is sitting up in my bed, back against my headboard.

"You know, Red, I've never had a girl get physically sick at the sight of me. First, you ignore me, then you throw up when you realize you're lying next to me. You're going to make me develop a complex," he says in a soft, teasing voice.

"Bad tacos," I mumble.

"That's what she said." He smirks. I grimace, though a small part of me appreciates his reference to *The Office*.

"You're repulsive." He just shrugs, as though he was expecting my reaction. I take a deep breath, square my shoulders, and walk over to my desk. Perching on the edge of the furniture, I look down at my nails, noting that my cuticles are as fucked as the rest of my life right now.

Glancing up, I meet his eyes. "Listen," I begin, "last night, I was emotional and tired and not myself." I pause, gauging his reaction. His face is devoid of emotion and unnaturally calm. "You shouldn't even be here right now. You being here is a mistake."

35

He raises one perfectly shaped eyebrow. His barber probably threads his eyebrows each time he gets a shape-up. "Why?" he questions.

Startled, I move my gaze from his eyebrows and meet his eyes. "What do you mean why?"

"Why?" he repeats. "Why are we a mistake? Why are you so fucking determined to not give this a shot?"

I explode. "Because you're too much! My God, you take up all the damn oxygen in the room and leave me breathless and annoyed and fucking feral." My breaths come out heavy. "You will eclipse me and everything that I am working toward. I came here, left home and my family, to gain an iota of independence and figure out who the fuck I am, who I want to be, and what I want to do. So far, you have designated me as yours, not caring that a relationship is the last thing I want. You fucking push, and when I pull, you take a fucking life preserver, buckle me in, and pull me through your wake. I can't do that. I can't just be yours and not figure out who I am."

He shakes his head, disagreeing with me. That fucking sets my blood on fire. "Don't you shake your head at me, you asshole."

"You're wrong," he starts, still shaking that goddamn head.

"Excuse—" I start, but he cuts me off.

"You're scared, and you're lying to both of us. You know who you are: Celeste fucking Downing. You know what you want to be: a goddamn novelist. You may not know exactly how you're going to get there, but you will get there. For shit's sake, I'm not trying to take your independence away, don't you get that?" He draws in a breath before continuing, "Since we've met, I've wanted you and only fucking you. There has

36

been no one else, and there won't be. Okay, you're scared and worried that I'll 'eclipse' you, but that's fucking bullshit.

"You should know by now that you are the fucking sun, and my life will revolve around you, not in front of you or behind you. Let me be your support system, let me help you figure out how you're going to achieve those fucking dreams, let me cheer you on. Fucking Christ, woman, you drive me fucking insane." He jams a hand in his short hair, pulling on the strands. "Red, I don't want to be your friend; I want to be your fucking family, the guy that needs to get out of the way before you throw up on him but will hold your hair back while you do it; the guy that makes you realize being in a relationship doesn't mean you're sacrificing your goddamn independence."

He stands from my bed, boxers hung low and chest heaving from the exertion brought by his words. My tongue feels thick in my mouth, dry beyond belief, and heavy, as though it's so caught up in what he said no phonemes or morphemes can be uttered.

Grabbing his clothes and yanking his pants on, he looks at me, shirt in hand, and pleads, "Don't be stubborn and don't say no yet. Just give us a fair fucking chance. Let me take you out, get to know me, and realize that the chemistry we have while fucking is there when we're lying in bed or just talking."

I stare at him, boring a hole into his forehead. He looks at me, studies my face, and nods.

"The day after we met, I bet Lincoln that you would be mine, and I know that it's true. The only thing stopping us is you. I wasn't lying when I told you that you can explore your options and see what else is out there, but you'll always come back to me. So, little Red, take all the time you need because I'll

37

fucking be here. I'm not going anywhere." He walks toward me, stopping inches from my body. "You are everything, and I will fucking worship you if you let me."

My blood turns cold and my eyes narrow at his mention of a bet. "You fucking bet on me?"

Dante shakes his head, exasperation stamped on his features. "That's what you latched onto? Yes, okay? I accepted a fucking bet because I knew you were it for me, no questions asked. The moment you handed me my ass playing *Mario Kart*, I was fucking done for, Red. I didn't plan to tell Linc that you and I fucked—and I haven't opened my fucking mouth about taking your virginity. As far as that fucker knows, he's getting a job at my sister's restaurant as a fucking dishwasher because I refused to say shit about you."

"You cocky son of a bitch," I murmur. "I'm not property or something to be won. I'm a fucking person; you and Lincoln are childish idiots if you think betting on my fucking affections is funny."

He growls, running a hand through his hair before grasping my shoulders. "You're missing the goddamn point. The bet's not going anywhere. I'm not fucking winning it, even though it'll be obvious once Linc sees you in our house, spending the night in my bed. I'm sorry you're pissed about it, but I made it because I knew that this was going to fucking happen: you and me are it. End game. There's no one else for me or you. Lie to yourself all you fucking want, but you can't lie to me.

His lips cover mine in a soft kiss, a whisper of his passion. "Call me when you're ready." With unbuttoned pants and his shirt in his hand, he leaves me, closing the door quietly behind him.

—

It's been two hours since Dante left my room, and I have residual shock from his outburst. In the time we've known each other, our interactions have been intense but infrequent. Based on his speech, you'd think we were constantly in each other's orbits. I felt the conviction of his words and don't doubt his sincerity, even though knowing I was regarded as an object to be had pisses me off.

And... that terrifies me.

I can't spend all day thinking about Dante's words, and if they are reaffirmed by his actions, I have more important shit to figure out. Forcing myself to get out of my pajama shirt and boxers, I drag on leggings and an oversized sweatshirt, pull a baseball cap over my head, and slide into my sneakers. Grabbing my keys and messenger bag, I head out of my dorm room and walk toward the student center.

Keeping my phone in my hand, I send a text to Ava, checking in on her and seeing if she needs me or Serena to bring anything while she's in the hospital. I don't expect her to answer, but she must have her phone glued to her hand because her response is immediate.

Ava: Get me the hell out of here. Grey keeps growling at the doctors and nurses. I am mortified.

I roll my eyes and release a laugh. Grey must be in extreme protector mode at the hospital right now.

CeCe: Should I sneak a horse tranquilizer in? I can jab him and have him sedated for a couple of hours.

Ava: Your knowledge of death, poison, and sedatives never ceases to amaze me.

She sends me a double text, not giving me a chance to answer.

39

Ava: No. He had a mini heart attack with everything that happened, so I'll let him be an alpha asshole for a bit. Can you bring me my pajamas, though? The hospital gown makes me feel like my dead grandmother in a house dress.

CeCe: I'll bring your muumuus.

Ava: Fuck off, bring me oversized T-shirts, sweatpants, and underwear. I'm very breezy right now.

CeCe: There is such thing as too much information, you freak. But yes, I'll pack your bag and come over with Serena. When do they think you'll get out?

Ava: Get out? I'm not in a prison. I'll be home by next weekend, hopefully.

We exchange a few more texts before Grey takes her phone, sending me a nasty message that I'm overexerting her brain with our conversation. When I see him again, I'm going to kick him in the dick.

I pocket my phone and continue the last few minutes of my walk across campus. It takes very little time to reach the student center. Marymount is designed as a small community where everything is within a ten-minute walk.

Including pregnancy tests.

Walking into the building, I follow the hallway to the campus market and pray that there aren't many people there. I've been in the store a few times to buy random things—things like notecards, bags of chips, and iced tea. The layout of the store mimics a small bodega, and I beeline for the health and wellness aisle.

I'm immediately struck by the variety of tests: pink boxes, blue boxes, generic, and name brand. How the hell am I, an eighteen-year-old, supposed to know which box to pick? Panicking, I grab one of each box, five in total, and cradle them in my arms toward the cash register. I stop on the way and grab a large bottle of water.

Dropping the bottle and tests on the counter, I feel the judgment in the check-out clerk's eyes, an older woman that has probably seen some shit at this campus.

"That will be $86.72," she says in a monotone voice.

"What? For five tests?" I ask, shocked by the price.

"If you don't like the price, you probably shouldn't have been such a hussy."

I look up, appalled and slightly amused by what I think I just heard. "Excuse me?"

"Cash or card?"

I hand over my card wordlessly, wondering if I heard her correctly or if I imagined it. She swipes my card and hands it back, pushing the boxes and bottle toward me. "Have a nice day," she mutters before turning away, showing me her back.

I toss everything into my messenger bag and hustle to the unisex single-occupancy bathroom. I'd rather cut off my left tit than take these tests in the communal bathroom in my dorm. I could call Serena and ask if I could come over, but I have the overwhelming need to be alone.

It doesn't take long for me to rip open all the boxes and grab a test from each one. Depositing the tests on the small vanity, I open the water bottle and chug it. It takes a few minutes to work through my body, but eventually, the urge to pee consumes me.

I take a deep breath, calming my nerves and pepping myself up. "It's okay. They're going to be negative. You've been on birth control since you were sixteen. There's no way he has super sperm." I grab the tests, stacking them on top of each other. One by one, I place them under me for a few seconds before bringing them back up. Capping each one, I place them back on the counter and set a timer for five minutes.

Anxiety courses through me, accompanied by heavy doses of fear, apprehension, and nausea. The nausea is always there.

I told Dante that we wouldn't work because I needed independence and to figure out what I wanted out of life, but he's right: I'm scared. I'm petrified of giving him my heart and it breaking into a million irreparable pieces. I'm terrified that I'll make him my whole world, and if it ends badly, I'll be left a shell of myself. Most importantly, I'm horrified by what these five tests are about to tell me.

My timer goes off, and I close my eyes, stealing myself for the two possible outcomes. I open my eyes and look down at the five pieces of plastic.

"Oh fuck," I whisper.

6

Dante

Dante: Good morning, Red. You look fucking beautiful today

Like all my previous texts, she leaves me on read and doesn't bother answering. It's fucking annoying, but I promised I'd be there when she was ready, and I wasn't lying; I'd wait for fucking years if that's what it took.

I didn't say anything about leaving her alone while I waited for her to get her stubborn head out of her perky little ass, though.

I drop my phone back down to my desk and start paying attention to my professor, Dr. O'Donnell, and her lesson on workers' compensation claims and reporting. As a business major, human resources management is a required course, even though it's tedious as shit. I want to make people money, not fucking deal with people. I recognize that this shit is important, especially if Grey and I are going to own a firm one day, but goddamn, there's a lot of shit you have to worry about. Health insurance, fit-for-duty policies, disciplinary action, progression programs, and a host of other things that can

43

either lead to a "Great Place to Work" certification or fucking mutiny.

My phone buzzes on my desk, and I get excited, wondering if it's Red finally fucking answering me. I pick up my phone and see a short code number on my screen. Swiping it open, it's a coupon for an online sex store.

What the fuck?

Another text comes through from my sister, Francesca, or Franki. I open her message and roll my eyes.

Franki: I sent a coupon code to your phone number. Can you send it to me?

Dante: Why the fuck is it for an online sex store?

Franki: I need a new double-sided vibrator. This is weird to tell my brother. Just send the fucking code.

I gag; my sister shared entirely too much personal information with that text. I must have been louder than I thought; the girl next to me leans over her desk, nearly falling out of her seat.

"Are you ok, D?" she asks, the use of my nickname throwing me off. She widens her eyes and puckers her lips; the face she makes reminds me of a fish.

"Uh, do I know you?"

She laughs, sounding completely unhinged. The sound reminds me a little too much of Felicity, and I lean away, putting more distance between us.

"You're so funny. I'm Giana, we've sat next to each other all semester. I lent you a pencil the first day, remember? Maybe we can grab a coffee after this?" she asks, the hopeful tone of her voice unmistakable.

"Sorry, I have a girlfriend," I reply. If it were up to me, that wouldn't be a fucking lie. I just need Red to get on the same page and stop being a little brat about everything. Giana's face drops, and she straightens, no longer on the verge of falling over.

"Oh, well, let me know if anything changes."

"It won't," I grunt, not bothering to leave the disdain out of my voice.

I look back down at my phone and type out the code to my sister.

Dante: Here, you freak. I don't need to know about the shit you and Katie do in the bedroom.

My sister and her wife, Kate, have been together since they were in high school. I've always thought of Kate as another sister, and she's always been less annoying than my actual sister. While Franki loves to give me shit about every fucking thing, Kate is a calming presence and balances my sister's crazy.

I still don't need to know about their sex life, though.

Franki: Who said anything about a bedroom?

God fucking dammit. I gag again, wanting to strangle her through the phone.

I don't bother answering her and swipe out of our conversation. Opening my social media folder, I check Red's accounts to see if she has posted anything new. Her account looks the same as when I checked yesterday; there have been no posts, no stories, and no activity on her accounts since Ava's assault three weeks ago. I scroll through her posts until I find my favorite picture of her; in the shot, she's smiling at something off-camera, and her red hair is illuminated by the setting sun. Her body is wrapped in a dark green dress that shows off every narrow curve and dip and highlights her perky tits. She looks fucking radiant and happy.

I take a screenshot of the picture and crop it, setting it as the background of my phone.

I look up and see everyone start packing their shit up, getting ready to leave. Fuck, I missed the entire class and didn't even realize it. I grab my laptop, notebook, and pen and toss them into my backpack. Standing up, my legs eat up the space between my desk in the back of the classroom and the door.

It takes me less than five minutes to get to my car, a 2018 Estoril Blue BMW i8 Coupe. It's a fucking beauty and one of the best things I've ever owned. My uncle and cousins gave me shit that I didn't opt for a Porsche or Lamborghini, but BMWs remind me of my dad. Growing up, he always had at least one BMW in our garage. After he died, my mom donated all his cars because looking at them hurt too much. Driving this car makes me feel connected to him.

I throw my bag in the back seat before getting behind the wheel and peeling out of the parking lot. Unsurprisingly, heads whip around; whether it's at the car or the driver is anyone's guess. Ten minutes later, I'm pulling into our driveway, parking right behind Grey's lifted Jeep. With all the money Grey and his family have, the asshole looks like he's about to hunt caribou in the Alaskan wilderness with his ride.

I like his Jeep well enough, but with the lift kit and modifications, the matte black truck looks like it's more suited to a fucking zombie apocalypse than the coastal suburbs of New Jersey. How Ava, who's just as vertically challenged as Celeste, gets in that monster is anyone's guess.

Walking through the front door, I'm greeted by the sound of Ava yelling at someone, a sound that I've become fairly used to in the weeks that she's been staying with us. With my family's background, the yelling doesn't faze me and instead makes me feel right at home. Rounding the corner of the foyer, I walk into the kitchen and see Grey and Linc sitting at one of the islands while Ava stirs something in a large pot on the stove. I inhale deeply, smelling the perfume of my homeland: garlic and onion.

"Shit, that smells good," I say as I walk over to the stove.

"Damn right it does," Ava mutters under her breath.

"It's fucking canned!" Linc yells, confusing the shit out of me.

I look at Grey, who's sitting there shaking his head, and ask, "Do I even want to know?"

He raises his eyes, looking at the ceiling before answering, "Linc is being a pampered little shit."

"I am fucking not. She is using canned peas instead of fresh ones. She's going to be a fucking chef, and she's serving canned peas. They lose all their fucking flavor in that aluminum, and she thinks I'll 'enjoy it,'" Linc whines.

"Then don't eat it, you pretentious, pompous asshole. I can tell you've grown up with a gold freaking spoon in your mouth," Ava replies. "This is Sera's favorite dish, and if you don't learn to make it correctly, trust me, she's not going to give you the time of day."

"I'll make it fucking better."

"It's good because it's a classic. Not everything has to be made into a Michelin-star meal."

"What are you making?" I ask as I walk over to the pot. My mouth immediately waters at the broth of peas, garlic, and onion I see. "Oh shit, are you making Pasta e Piselli?"

She points at me. "Thank God there's another Italian in this house. Yes, I'm making pasta and peas."

"My sister serves that at her restaurant. She uses bacon

47

grease instead of oil. Fuck, it's so good." My mouth waters.

"Et tu, Brute?" Lincoln says.

"Dude, if you want to impress Sera, listen to Ava." Lincoln has been fixated on Ava's younger sister, Seraphina, since she visited for Ava's birthday. Since then, he's made Ava give him a crash course in all of Sera's favorites, from movies to food.

What the fuck do they put in the water in Monroeville that every girl I've met there has someone obsessed with them?

I'd spend some time thinking that through, but I have questions that need fucking answers.

"Aves." Grey growls at my use of her nickname, and I shoot him the finger, silently telling him to fuck off. "How's Red doing?"

She shrugs, lowering the burner at the stove. "She's okay, I guess. She was here earlier but left because she wasn't feeling well."

I'm on alert by that comment. "She was here? What's wrong? Does she need me to take her to a doctor?"

"Calm down, D," Ava says, and Grey growls again. Looking at him, she throws her hands on her hips and asks, "Why do you keep growling?"

"When the fuck did you two start using nicknames?"

Ava scoffs at his questions. "You can't be serious. I've been living here for weeks, plural, because you're too paranoid to let me go home. I'm friends with Dante and tolerate Lincoln because he's a decent cook."

"I'm a fucking phenomenal cook," Lincoln calls out.

"Not the point, snob. Get over your little alpha display, Grey. Now"—she turns back to me—"CeCe just felt nauseous. She said something about tacos. I'm not sure."

Tacos? Again? I scowl, knowing there's more to the story

48

than she's letting on. Maybe I'd be able to get the truth out of her if she'd fucking answer my texts. I pull out my phone and click on the message of the one person I know will be able to help me in this situation.

Dante: Can you meet me at Mom's house in an hour? I need your advice.

Franki responds instantly.

Franki: Oh shit, Danny Boy has girl problems. I'll be there.

—

My mom's house is more of a compound than a house. Pulling up to the gate, I click the opener on my visor and head down the wide drive that leads to the living quarters. Tucked into the suburbs of New Jersey, the estate is fucking massive and comprised of a main house, three guest cottages, a pool, an accompanying pool house, a tennis court, a basketball court, and a fucking bocce ball court. It isn't gaudy or decorated in glitter and sparkles, but it's an ostentatious display of wealth. My mother didn't choose this compound, my dad did for our safety, and I think that prevents her from ever moving. Unlike my dad's car collection, the house holds memories of our family.

Since the early nineties, my mom has been on-air: talk shows, news broadcasts, and case commentary; her resume is fucking endless, as are the people that love her and hate her. She's vocal about her views and doesn't shy away from asking her guests or interviewees difficult questions. My mom's brother is a senator in New Jersey, and our family has achieved a small level of recognition that makes a lot of people uncomfortable. We're not exactly the Kennedys, but we're the less publicized Italian equivalent.

While my mom's family comes from a political background,

49

my dad's side is a clusterfuck of criminal activity, tapped wires, and payoffs. How my mother, the most law-abiding citizen, ended up with the exiled son of a mafia don is a story my sister and I have never been told. They tried to separate us as much from his former life as possible that, though I have my dad's blood pumping through my veins, my parents gave me and Franki our mother's last name. When he was killed four years ago in a hit and run, my mother never doubted that it was a hit from his family. Apparently, crime syndicates don't like when someone severs all ties to lead a nine-to-five life in anonymity.

I clench my fist, remembering the day the police knocked on our door. I was a junior in high school and had just gotten home from football practice. Ma was in the kitchen, cooking dinner, and Franki was in college with Kate. When the security announced police were at the gate, I remember seeing the knife my mother was using clatter to the ground and her normally olive complexion going pale. I answered the door, a knot in my stomach as the officer hung his head and muttered, "I'm sorry."

It was fucked.

I park in front of the stairs and get out of my car. Pocketing my keys, I jog up the stairs and don't even pretend to be surprised that it opens as soon as my foot hits the top step. I smile wide, throwing my arms around our housekeeper and pseudo-grandmother, Sofia.

"Sofie," I yell, pulling her to me in a tight hug.

"Don't mess up my hair, young man. I just had it set, and Paul is taking me out tonight," she says against my chest. "I was wondering why your mother was cooking today. It makes sense now that you're here."

"Frank is coming, too."

"Francesca is already with your mother, telling her that her knife cuts are uneven and being a little dictator in the kitchen." She pauses, and I can hear my sister's voice travel from the kitchen through the foyer. "You should probably head in there before your mother turns the knife on her."

I laugh but listen to her. Sofie and her husband, Paul, have been part of this family since before Franki was born. While Paul mainly sticks to the groundskeeping and to himself, Sofie has always had a level of authority in this house that no one, except my mother, could compete with. Even my uncle is scared shitless of her.

I walk into the kitchen and am immediately hit with the familiar smells of onions and tomatoes. Just as Sofie mentioned, Franki is yelling at my mother about the cut of the potatoes on the cutting board in front of her.

"Hey," I call out, cutting off Frank's tirade. Both my mother and sister turn to look at me, their near-identical features making them look like the creepy ass twins in *The Shining.*

"*Viso bello,*" my mom calls out, rushing over to me and grabbing my face in her hands. Despite our heritage, my mother doesn't know how to speak Italian, so her translation of "beautiful face" is probably fucked up. She could be calling me a pretty goat, for fuck's sake.

"Hi, Ma." I kiss her cheek and draw her into a hug.

"Francesca said you have girl problems. Sit down. I'm making a snack, and then we'll talk." She releases me and heads back to the stove, grabbing the cutting board of potatoes on the way.

"Ma, you're making pasta and potatoes, this is not a snack. It's going to stick to our ribs," Franki grumbles at the island.

I look at her in time to see her roll her dark eyes. Like my mother, Franki's features are classic Italian: dark eyes, dark hair, and a rich olive complexion. She has a couple of inches on my mom in the height department, but she's still under five-seven. Her short stature and pretty face hide the fucking beast contained within her.

If you ever want to see an adult cry in a fridge walk-in, go to her restaurant during the dinner rush. I had to throw away all the fucking radishes because one of the line cooks used the leaves as goddamn tissues. How Kate, her sweet, docile wife, deals with her level of intensity is a mystery.

Ignoring my sister, I sit on the opposite end of the island and watch my mom cook. At fifty, my mom looks more like a thirty-year-old housewife than the boss she is. Magazines have lauded her for her youthful good looks, but she scoffs each time, refusing interviews on superficial attributes. It's no wonder Franki is a fucking tyrant.

"The food will be ready in thirty minutes. Now, while we wait, tell me what's going on. Tell me about the girl," my mother orders.

"I never said there was a girl," I say, raising an eyebrow. There is a fucking girl, but still, I never fucking said it.

"You wouldn't have asked for a family meeting unless there was a girl or you had flesh-eating bacteria," Franki calls out. I hold out my middle finger.

"Hey," my mom snaps, hitting her wooden spoon against the counter. "Enough of that. No more distractions, tell us what's going on."

I hang my head, grab it in my hands, and pull at my hair. "There's a girl," I start.

"Fucking knew it," Franki coughs out. My mother gives her

a side eye before turning her attention back to me. I dive into the story of Celeste, leaving out the mind-blowing sex because why the fuck would I tell my mother about that shit?

When I'm done explaining how she's avoided me for the last three weeks and has a deep-seated fear of a relationship with me, my mom and Franki stare at me, jaws unlocked and mouths hanging open. My mother recovers first; snapping her jaw shut, she reaches for the bag of pasta and dumps it into the boiling, salted water, giving it a stir before turning back around.

"Dante, if you're committed to this young woman and feel like she's the one for you, don't give up. Show her that you're serious and can support her. Remember, persistence wears down resistance," my mom says.

"Did you just tell him to stalk her?" Franki asks. Thank God she said it because I had the same question.

"No, don't stalk. What are you, an idiot?" My mother shakes her head. "If you care for this girl, show her. Don't ignore her, don't wait around for her in silence. Pursue her and show her that you want to be there for her and will be a help, not a hindrance."

I look at Franki and raise my eyebrows. "Ma, I'm sorry, but it really sounds like you're telling me to stalk her."

7

CeCe

I never envisioned my life would play out like the scene from
Juno, where she's chugging a Slurpee in a convenience store
and shaking the pregnancy test like an etch-a-sketch, hoping
the result will change. The last time I saw Dante, I gave him
every bullshit excuse about why we can't be together: my need
for independence and my fear of committing to him, but this?
This changes everything.

My hand coasts down to my stomach, clenching over it...
protectively? In derision? I don't know how I feel or how I
should feel. Sometimes, I feel excited flutters, knowing that
I am growing a tiny human inside me. Those flutters quickly
transform into dread, and my body seizes in fear; how am I
even remotely capable of being a mother right now?

My stomach gurgles, and I quickly pop in a ginger candy,
sucking on the spiced sugar like it will cure me of the situation
I've found myself in. Since I found out three weeks ago in
a unisex bathroom, alone and untethered, I have avoided
interacting with nearly everyone I care about. I've seen Ava
five times since she's been home from the hospital; between

my need to vomit every ten minutes and the anxiety I am blanketed in, I'm worried that I'll break down and tell her everything. The last thing Ava needs after being shanked with a goddamn machete in her ovary is my confession:

I'm eighteen, pregnant, and fucking terrified.

I close my eyes and breathe, taking in as much oxygen as my lungs can handle. I continue my breathing, hoping that the intake of air will calm my nerves; right now is definitely not the time to freak the fuck out. Sitting in the back of my creative writing class, I must look like I'm losing my shit with the heavy breathing and sweat breaking out along my brow. My professor and the other students have given me a wide berth after my last freak-out in this class, probably because they thought I was high on drugs.

A few days after I found out about my pregnancy, I zoned out during the professor's lecture on tone and narrator's voice, and when she called on me to provide an example of an author using an unreliable narrator, I said, "*Spice World*." As in the movie... from 1997. That I have never watched.

In my defense, I watched a documentary on Victoria Beckham a few weeks ago, and I am now obsessed with all things Posh Spice.

My gaze dips down to the hand at my stomach, and not for the first time, I wonder how I can both loathe and love something at the same time. It feels so incredibly selfish to view this as the end of my freedom, a swan song for a brief college experience that didn't include stretch marks or diapers. Simultaneously, I feel so much love and affection for the little bundle of cells inside me that I know I will obliterate anyone that tries to harm her.

I'm not sure why, but each time I think of the life inside of me, I think of it as a "her." I picture her with soft red hair, a trait that seems to afflict every woman in my family, and Dante's dark eyes. I wonder if she'll have my pale skin and freckles, or Dante's olive complexion and healthy glow. My nerves rachet up; God, Dante is going to freak out. I feel my heart racing in my chest, and I'm not sure if I'm having a panic attack or a heart attack at this point.

Thoughts of Dante, *parenting* with Dante, immediately bring images up of my parents as freaking grandparents. I haven't seen my parents since they met me for lunch three weeks ago, and, unsurprisingly, their schedules have been so all over the place that they haven't even bothered calling. Sure, they've sent regular text messages to check in, but our conversations have been brief and surface-level. I'm simultaneously irritated and relieved that they've been so absent. I could be dead in a fucking ditch somewhere with my murderer responding as me, and they'd have no freaking clue.

I give myself a figurative slap in the face and pull out my phone, sending a text to my group chat with Ava and Serena.

CeCe: Question:

CeCe: Do you think it's possible to unlock someone's phone with their face when they're dead and covered in mud and blood?

My thoughts are still on me being dead in a ditch with my murderer impersonating me like Buffalo Bill.

Serena: I really, really don't want to be complicit in murdering someone today, Celeste.

Ava: Yes.

There are two types of friends in this world: there are the friends that will tell you you're wrong, scold you, and try to make you a better person. That's Serena. In the short time I've known her, I've come to accept her cautious, anxious ways and appreciate having her as a foil to my "kill first, think later" mentality.

But then, there's the other kind of friend. The kind that gives you the bottle of lighter fluid and matches and cheers when you ignite. It's the same friend that will be the getaway car but give you shit for the rest of your life when the cops eventually catch you for arson. That's Ava.

Their responses to my text exemplify their roles in my life: the angel and the accomplice.

CeCe: It's a hypothetical question.

CeCe: But also, how long does it take a body to decompose in mud? Do you think that mud would slow the process a lot or a little?

Ava: I am so confused. Your dad is an M.E., shouldn't you know the answer to this question?

Serena: I'm removing myself from this chat if you don't stop talking about criminal activity.

CeCe: Fine, you little saint.

Serena: Anyway, I miss you both. I feel like we haven't hung out all together in weeks.

Since Ava's attack, I've seen Ava and Serena separately for a few hours at a time. Before the attack, even with Grey monopolizing Ava's time, we were together constantly.

Ava: Well, I was attacked with a fucking machete and carved like a jack-o-lantern. I've been a little busy.

CeCe: No one likes a complainer, Ava. Grey is keeping you hostage with his metal dick.

When Ava first came home from the hospital, I went to Grey's house nearly every day, careful to avoid Dante, but also not willing to abandon my best friend when a psychopath tried to hack her with a fucking machete. During one of my visits, Ava was high on painkillers and told me all about the piercings lining Grey's dick.

She wanted to draw a picture to submit to evidence, but I hid the paper and pens. I didn't need to see an anatomic drawing of Grey's dick and the layout of his piercings. Some things should remain a mystery.

That's one of them.

Ava: I'm going to show him that text, and he's going to give Dante shit for your comment about his penis.

CeCe: Do it and die.

Serena: Metal dick? Did I miss something?

CeCe: Ask Ava to explain Grey's piercings. Better yet, ask her to draw, in detail, the metal balls leading up from his balls.

Ava: Fuck off, fire crotch.

—

The day speeds by, both uneventful and chaotic. My thoughts from earlier never dissipated; instead, they multiplied like a virus and infected every part of me.

By the time I make it back to my dorm, I'm exhausted and grateful for the chance to be alone. When Ava and Grey first went public with their relationship, I was a tiny bit resentful over how much he monopolized my best friend's time. If he wasn't in our room, she was staying at his house. I grew close to Serena because of their obsession, often spending my nights with her to grab dinner at the dining hall or eat at her apartment. Serena texted me and asked if I wanted to get food with her after my evening class. I could sense her disappointment through the phone when I declined and let her know I was going to eat in my room before going to sleep early.

I feel like a horrible friend for that, but I crave the solitude, even though I miss my friends.

Taking the lid off my soup, I inhale the steam wafting up from the container. The scent of parsley, onion, and bay leaves envelops me, and I relax against my desk chair, letting the comforting aroma soothe me. For some reason, the only foods I can get down are chicken noodle soup and wontons, not the ones in soup, but deep fried and covered in sweet and sour sauce. My body is sixty percent noodles and dough at this point.

I lift my spoon to take my first bite when my phone vibrates on my desk, signaling a text. Putting the spoon down, I grab my phone and swipe to unlock it.

Dante: Hi, Red.

My stomach plummets. Dante has texted me at least three times a day since he spent the night. I haven't responded, not even with a "fuck you" or "leave me alone." Guilt consumes me; he has a right to know what's going on. It's just as much his responsibility as it is mine, but I'm terrified that as soon as he knows, our relationship will change. Logically, I know that it has to. Even if he becomes disgusted by me, our lives are inexplicably linked now.

Though he's ignorant of the repercussions of our night together, he does know something is going on. Ava told me he asks if I'm okay every time they cross paths in Grey's house. My appetite now gone, I bite down on my lip, contemplating my choices. My phone goes off again, and I check the message thread.

Dante: Open your door.

"What the fuck?" My eyes widen, and I look to the door just

as a gentle knock sounds against the metal.

"Open up, Red. I know you're in there." Dante's voice washes over me, and I curse, annoyed by how much it consoles me.

"No one's home," I mumble. He releases a laugh, and it flows over me, the deep rumble making me shiver. I sigh, get up from my chair, and walk toward the mirror against the wall. "Just... give me a minute," I let out on a sigh.

I glance in the mirror and scrunch my nose. I haven't thrown up nearly as much recently, but I look sallow and too thin. I grab an oversized hoodie from my dresser and throw it on over the long-sleeved T-shirt and shorts that I changed into when I got back, hiding my body as effectively as I can. I take a deep breath and turn toward the door, opening it quickly before I talk myself out of it.

Dante's smile greets me, but it drops from his face in seconds. His jaw clenches, and his eyes narrow. I find myself dropping my head, ducking my face away from his assessing gaze.

"Baby, what's wrong? Are you sick?" He steps forward and grabs my chin with one hand, tilting my head up to meet his eyes.

I pull my chin from his grip and step back, allowing him space to enter the room. "Not in the hall," I murmur. His mouth flattens, and his brow furrows, giving his features an intimidating look. He steps inside, and I close the door, hiding us from the outside world.

I turn around and walk to my bed. I climb on and sit cross-legged before I look up. I startle at how close he is. It's no surprise that he takes up most of the space in the room, not literally, but everything seems to center around him. The dust in the air circulates, a tornado with Dante as the eye.

Leaning over me, he lowers his head until his mouth con-nects with my neck. His kiss is disarming. I gasp and try to hold back a moan, but it's useless. I feel like one of those wind-up toys that came in kids' meals in the early 2000s; I went from still to restless as soon as he touched me. I close my eyes and savor the lingering feel of his mouth, the lashes of his tongue against my pulse, and the scrape of his teeth on my skin.

"Fuck, you taste good, Red," Dante growls against my throat. "Three weeks is too fucking long."

"Dante," I murmur, pulling back. He follows my retreat, caging me in until my back is against the cinderblock wall. I stare at him, wide-eyed and flustered. His face is inscrutable, and I can't read him. Honestly, the lack of emotion on his face, coupled with the human prison he's erected around me, is worrying me.

It's also turning me on and drenching my panties, but that's beside the point.

"This is how this is going to go," he breaks the silence with a tone that should piss me off but just makes me squirm. "You're going to tell me what the fuck is going on in that beautiful head of yours, why you look like you've lost ten pounds, and why the fuck you're avoiding me." He punctuates each demand with a fist banging into the wall right above my head.

"And if you think for a single second..." He pauses and swoops down to lick a line from my jaw to my cheekbone. I shiver at the contact and arch my back. With my legs still crossed, I'm trapped beneath him and can't get close enough. He continues, "That you are going to bullshit my questions and lie to me, I'm going to handcuff those little wrists to your bed and spank the insolence out of you."

"'Insolence,' nice SAT word, superstar," I mumble. His hand lifts from the wall and lightly grips my throat. He applies pressure, not enough to restrict my airflow, but enough to show me that he's in control of this conversation.

"Does my girl need her pussy spanked?" he growls.

"Wh-what?" I stutter against the pressure at my throat. I close my eyes and, like a movie reel, picture Dante stripping me down, tying me to the bed, and spanking the most intimate part of me until I come all over his hands.

"Mmmhm," he mumbles, nipping my jaw before sucking the skin into his mouth.

"You're going to leave a mark!" I yell against him, fighting to turn my head against his hold on me. It's not that it doesn't feel good—it feels amazing—but I don't need bruises decorating my already pale, lifeless skin.

I can't shake him off, and he keeps sucking until, finally, he releases me with a pop. "I didn't leave one, but I'm fucking tempted to. I need everyone to know that you're mine and you're fucking taken." He pauses, looking at my neck like it holds the answers. "I saw my mom today," he continues. "She told me, 'Persistence wears down resistance,' but I'm fucking done with you resisting." He leans forward and latches onto my neck again, nipping the skin.

"Dante," I growl. This time, his bite is hard and punishing.

He releases my skin with a growl. "No. I'm fucking done. I'm done with the distance and the space that is manufactured because you're a fucking coward. If you didn't want this, you wouldn't be spreading those pretty legs, inviting me to sink into your pussy." I look down, horrified, to realize that my legs are spread wide, just like he said.

62

His words wash over me. Instead of heating my skin like they should, they douse the flames and my blood chills. Here is this man, ready to stake claim to me, and I've withheld critical information—information that he's entitled to—for three fucking weeks.

I have never felt more like a terrible person than I do at this moment.

I pull back as far as I can and draw my hands and legs up, pushing him back. He may be possessive and slightly barbaric, but he's not a creep, and he allows me to put distance between our bodies. "I don't care about your stupid bet. There are more important things to worry about." At my confession, Dante's brow furrows, clearly not anticipating those words.

He furrows his brow, confusion and frustration stamped across his face.

"We need to talk," I say. My voice sounds tired, and Dante's eyes narrow at my tone. "Can you sit over there?" I wave my hand toward Ava's side of the room. "It'll be easier for me to talk to you if we have some distance between us."

"Are you in trouble?" he questions as he backs up and leans against Ava's bed. With his arms crossed over his chest and his veiny forearms on display, he looks angry and ready to pounce at me.

I shake my head and take a deep breath. "I-I," I stutter. I swallow, pausing until I'm sure I can get the words out. I've never had an issue with words before; normally, they're comfort and solace and beauty. But right now, they're like a death sentence.

"Dante, I-I thought we were covered. I've been on birth control for years, and I never thought it would be possible for anything to happen. But..." I stop, letting out a breath before

63

continuing, "I've been feeling sick for weeks. I thought it was those stupid freaking tacos from the dining hall, but it wouldn't go away and, and..." I break off and look at him. His eyes are wide, and his jaw hangs open. He knows where I'm going with this.

"And I'm pregnant," I whisper into the room. I watch the emotions that transform his features: shock, fear, resolve. I expected disbelief or anger, but neither seem to be present. He remains silent for long minutes, and I can't help but fidget. Dante, who is normally the loudest, most opinionated person in the room, is struck mute.

If I weren't already watching him intently, I would have missed the minute nod of his head. He unfolds his arms and hangs them at his side. His eyes trace my face, and it's only now that I realize I have tears trailing down my cheeks and dripping onto my sweatshirt. I wipe them away with my sleeve before I bring my knees to my chest and tuck my arms beneath my thighs.

"Red," he whispers, breaking the silence. I look up at him, waiting for his next words. He closes his mouth and stares at me, his eyes cataloging every detail. In the two months that I've known Dante, I've seen him annoyed, aroused, and animated; I have never seen the earnest look he currently wears. He swallows, his Adam's apple bobbing in his throat before he asks, "Can I hold you?"

I nod my head, release my hold on my legs, and shift to the edge of the bed. He rushes forward and envelops me in his arms, pulling me tightly against his body.

"It's going to be okay, baby," he murmurs against my hair.

8

Dante

I should feel nervous, scared, resentful, or some other bullshit emotion right now, but all I feel is the relief that this girl—this woman—is finally fucking mine. The baby growing inside her is mine, and there's no fucking way that she's getting rid of me now.

At twenty-one years old, it probably makes me the biggest sap in the goddamn world, but I can't find a single worry. Three days after I met Celeste, I told my two best friends that one day, she would be my wife and carry my child. Did I think that God would use that as a fucking premonition? No. But am I mad about it? Fuck no. Red's mine, and she's finally going to get on board with me being a permanent fixture in her life.

About fucking time.

She's sobbing and shaking in my arms, and I know that now is not the time for me to stake my claim. Rubbing her back, I hold her against my chest and let her sobs soak through my shirt.

"Shhh," I whisper. "We're going to be okay, baby." My placations do jack shit, and she continues to cry. I pull back and bring my hands to her face, cradling her jaw gently and tilting her head to meet my eyes. "Red, tell me what you want to do. Tell me what you need," I tell her in the softest voice I can, a stark contrast to the tone I used when I first got to her dorm room. After speaking with my mom and sister, I wanted to come to Celeste, balls fucking blazing, and let her know that I was done with the distance she forced between us.

The last ten minutes have drastically changed my fucking thought process. I still don't want her to deny that there's something between us, but I'm not a douche, and I'm not going to steamroll her.

She closes her eyes and licks her lips; mascara runs down her cheeks, and her skin is flushed from the outpouring of emotion. She's never looked more fucking beautiful. She opens her eyes but diverts her gaze. Fuck that. I need to look in her eyes for this conversation.

"Eyes on me," I murmur. Her gaze snaps to mine, and I see pain in her pretty green eyes.

"I thought about it," she releases a laugh under her breath. "It's *all* I've thought about. I've read a lot about our options, and it's overwhelming." I don't miss that she referred to it as *our* options, not just hers. That makes me happy as shit.

"I know that you should have a say in this, but I'm keeping her." She pauses and looks down at her stomach. Hidden in the oversized sweatshirt, I have no idea if there's evidence of her pregnancy already or when she's supposed to start showing. "Every time I think of the baby, it's always a girl."

This girl. This fucking girl.

"Red, I want our baby. I don't give a fuck what their sex is as long as you and I raise the baby together. I don't want to make decisions *for* you; I want to make decisions *with* you. I told you." I lean in to brush a kiss against her soft lips. I pull back slightly and speak against her lips, "You are the fucking sun."

Capturing her mouth again, I tease it open and brush my tongue lightly against hers. It's a lazy, uncomplicated kiss, one meant to savor rather than claim. I'll fuck her mouth and her tight little pussy later, once I know that she won't break.

Fucking weeks of silence and a secret this big deserves punishment, and my girl's pussy is going to fucking weep.

She pulls back first, licking her lips like she's lapping up my taste. "Dante, we can't just bypass talking and make out."

"Who fucking says?" I growl.

"Be serious," she punctuates her words with an eye roll and drags her body back. My hands drop to my sides, and I clench my jaw, annoyed by the distance she keeps putting between us. "Get that look off your face," she orders.

"What look?"

"The one that looks like you're about to throw me over your shoulder and lock me in your room, then rub lotion on me and fatten me up until you can skin me alive and wear my skin as a suit."

I raise an eyebrow. "I'm not Buffalo Bill, drama queen."

"Close enough," she murmurs.

"You wanted to talk, so start talking." She gives me a look that would shrivel the balls of a lesser man.

"God, once I'm feeling better, I'm going to knee-drop your ass." The mention of her violent tendencies has my dick getting hard instantly, and I reach down to adjust myself.

"Red, you know I fucking love it when you show that ruthless side. If you don't want me to worship that body—that body filled with my fucking cum—then start talking."

67

"It's not filled with—" she stops and shakes her head. "Okay, you know what? It doesn't matter; I'm not giving you a ninth-grade health lesson right now. Why are you so calm about this? I told you that I'm pregnant, cried on your chest for thirty minutes, and you're acting weirdly composed."

I shrug, not feeling the least bit embarrassed. "After we met, I told Grey and Linc that I was going to marry you one day and put a baby in you."

"What the fuck?" she explodes. "What kind of stalker shit is that?" She reels back as though slapped. "Oh my God, did you break the condom intentionally to trap me?"

My irritation instantly fucking rises. "No, I wouldn't do that to you, and you should know better than to ask that. I meant in five fucking years from now, but if you think I'm disappointed that your tight little pussy milked my cock so good, I busted through a condom and fucking birth control, you're wrong." I take a steadying breath, willing myself to calm the fuck down.

"Listen, baby, the reason why I'm not freaking out is because I'm fucking happy. I get it, it's scary, and we're about to add a lot of fucking responsibilities to our lives, but I'm not worried. We'll have help, my mom, my sister, Sofie, and your family; it'll be hard, and we'll annoy the shit out of each other, but we'll get through this together. As a family." I grab her legs and pull her toward me until her legs bracket my thighs. "Red," I continue, pulling her head back by her mane of hair. "We're going to be okay. I promise."

She studies my face before asking, "Who the hell is Sofie?"

"My housekeeper, nanny, second mother, second grand-mother; she's everything, all at once," I laugh.

"You still have a nanny?" she asks, disbelief lacing her tone.

"Did you not hear all the other titles I gave her?" I shake

68

my head and tsk, running my hands up her thighs until they settle at her waist. "Sofie has been with us since my older sister was born. She's more like a member of the family than an employee. After my dad died, my mom relied on Sofie to help stay sane." Her eyes soften at the mention of my dad.

"I see," is all she says. I'm grateful that she doesn't give me pity over the loss of my dad, but I'm surprised she doesn't ask questions. In the two months I've known her, Celeste has been like a bull in a fucking antique shop, especially when it comes to information.

"You're not going to ask about him?" I question, pulling back so that I can look at her face.

"No, because if you wanted to talk about it, you would tell me."

"He died in a hit-and-run four years ago. I was a junior in high school," I say, suddenly needing her to know.

She doesn't say anything, just hums and shifts her body weight. Drawing her arms up, she circles my neck and pulls me in for a hug. I stand frozen for a moment before I relax into her embrace. This is the first time that she has initiated contact, and it doesn't escape me that it was to offer me comfort.

I clutch her body, eliminating all of the space between us. "We're going to be okay, Red. Trust me."

—

Red sleeps like the fucking dead. She passed out in my arms shortly after I told her about my dad and his accident. I tried to succumb to sleep, but between Red clinging to me like a boa constrictor and the thoughts pounding through my mind, I'm still wide awake.

I'd compare her to some cute, furry little animal, but she's more likely to bite my head off than hug me.

69

I shift her off my chest and reach to grab my phone from the table beside her. I didn't have a chance to look at her and Ava's dorm when I first got here, nor did I have the opportunity to inspect their space when I picked her up after the attack. Even in the darkness, I can tell it looks like a catalog of girly shit threw up in here. I'm not going to complain about the absurd number of pillows on the bed, though.

I remember my dorm freshman year and the utilitarian pillow I had; it was fucking lumpy as shit. She must have seven soft pillows stacked high on her bed, and the mattress pad beneath the sheets makes the limited space of the twin more comfortable.

We'd be better in my king-sized bed with a private bathroom, but when she let me hold her earlier tonight, the last thing I was going to do was act like a dickhead and force her to go to my house.

Clicking on my phone screen, I see missed calls from my mom and texts from Franki and Grey. It's after ten, so there's no way in fuck my mother will be up, but Franki still has another few hours left at the restaurant. I swipe to open her message.

Franki (6:32 pm): What happened with the girl?

Franki (7:35 pm): Fuckface, are you going to answer?

Franki (8:27 pm): I'm telling Mom you're dead.

I say a silent curse at my sister's texts; knowing her, she probably did tell my mom that I wasn't answering my phone, and that's why I have eight missed calls from her and a voicemail.

Dante: Jesus, Frank. I fell asleep at her place. What the fuck did you say to Mom? She called eight fucking times and left a two-minute voicemail.

70

I'm not going to tell my sister that I didn't sleep for shit and spent the last three hours watching Red sleep. That sounds creepy as fuck.

My sister takes less than a minute to respond. The asshole is probably loving the chaos she's created.

Franki: Damn, that sucks. Better call Ma. You fell asleep at her place? Dante, it's after ten, I texted you four hours ago.

Dante: I can do the math. I came over after her class. We were fucking busy and then passed out.

Franki: Fucking busy or busy fucking?

I grip my phone, wishing that it would transform into my sister's neck. Before I can respond and tell her to fuck off, she sends me another text.

Franki: I know when you're hiding things, D. What's going on?

Lifting my arm, I rub a hand over my face, trying to wipe away the guilt I feel at keeping this fucking bomb from my sister. For my entire life, but especially after our dad died, Franki has been my best friend and the person I tell every fucking thing to.

Dante: Working through some things. I'll talk about it when I'm ready.

Swiping out of our message thread, I click on Grey's text and note that he sent it thirty minutes ago.

Grey: Ava's trying to get in touch with the pit bull. You're not home. I assume she's with you?

Grey's a jackass; Celeste will kick his ass for that nickname one day, and I can't wait to see him get what's coming to him. I quickly type out my response.

Dante: Don't fucking call her a pit bull.

Grey: Answer your goddamn phones. Ava doesn't need this

71

stress, you dick for brains.

I respond with the middle finger emoji before locking my screen and setting it back on the nightstand. Shifting to my side, I work my way down the bed until I'm at eye-level with her chest. Lying flat on her back with her red hair spread out on her pillow, she looks like one of the princesses in the movies my sister forced me to watch when we were younger. My parents thought Franki watched those movies because she wanted to be one of the princesses.

Turns out, she wanted to kiss them.

Before she fell asleep, Red took off her oversized hoodie. Once the fabric was peeled away, I was able to see the smooth, pale skin and the swell of her perky tits. In the two months that I've known her, she's had a toned and flat stomach, but she seems alarmingly fragile. She mentioned that she's been sick, and I grit my teeth against the anger that engulfs me. If I knew what she was going through, I would have taken care of her, given her pastina, or some shit to help. Instead, I'm showing up weeks late.

Laying my head on her chest, I bring my hand up and place it on her flat stomach. With her petite frame, my spread hand takes up the width of her body. Jesus fuck, she's tiny. Rubbing my thumb over her shirt, I whisper into her body, "Hi, baby. It's your daddy."

I flick my eyes up, making sure that she's still sleeping. I have the need to talk to my baby growing in my woman's stomach, but I also don't want Red to wake up and think I'm weird as shit for talking to the tiny bean inside of her. Confident that Red is still sleeping, I turn back to her flat stomach.

"Your mama is a stubborn woman, baby, and tried to do this

herself. I'm here, though, and fuck," I pause, swallowing back the emotion that's clogging my throat. "Shit, I don't think I can curse in front of you. But I'm not going anywhere; you, me, and your mama are a family now. I don't know you yet, but goddamn, I love you. I don't know how the fuck to be a dad, but I promise I'm going to be the best one for you." I look back up at Celeste's face, relaxed in sleep. "I promise I'm going to be the best man to your mama, too, baby."

Lifting my head from her chest, I press a light kiss on her abdomen. "Now, be good to your mother and let her hold down some food. Mama needs her strength if you're anything like your parents."

With a final kiss to her stomach, I move myself back up the bed. Grabbing Red, careful not to wake her up, I pull her into my body and sigh into the mass of red hair.

9

CeCe

It took everything in me to remain silent while Dante caressed
my stomach and spoke to our baby. His quiet whispers filled
the room, and his declaration of love had tears pooling behind
my closed eyes.

I don't know why I'm surprised by Dante's response; if
anything, I should have expected it. From the moment we met,
Dante has been intense in every way: his obsession with me
and pursuing a relationship was instant, like he was a werewolf
claiming his mate.

I almost hit him when he called me stubborn, but he wasn't
wrong. These past few weeks have been miserable and iso-
lating; I was afraid to tell anyone about the pregnancy before
telling Dante, but I also wanted to avoid the behemoth of a
man at all costs.

I fall asleep hours later, just before dawn, to Dante's heavy
hand holding my stomach and his breath whispering against
my neck.

— -

When I finally fell asleep, Dante's breath against my skin

was soothing and welcoming; now, it feels like there's a dog panting at my throat. He must have woken up before me because his breath smells minty. I don't want to think about where he got toothpaste and a toothbrush since he probably used mine, but I thank God that Dante had the foresight to brush his teeth before aiming his mouth in my direction.

"Your eyes are fluttering, Red. I know you're awake," he whispers against my pulse. "I've been watching you for thirty minutes."

I roll over and push him off me, trying to create as much space between us as I can. "You are such a creep," I mumble. "What time is it?"

"It's after nine."

I growl and grab the pillow from behind my head. "It's too early. You are the antichrist," I groan. Dante's answering chuckle just pisses me off more. "Ugh, shut up."

"I have to say, this wake-up is already better than the last time I slept over." He pauses, running a hand over my stomach before continuing, "You climbing over me to puke is a memory I'd like to replace. Why don't you climb on Daddy's lap and help me?"

"Oh my God," I huff. Grabbing the pillow from over my face, I sit up and hit him with it.

"Ow, fuck, woman. How the fuck are you so strong? That fucking hurt, Red."

"Good. Stop calling yourself 'Daddy,' it's weird." Placing the pillow back on the bed, I kick the sheets and comforter off my body, welcoming the cool air against my bare legs. From the corner of my eye, I see Dante's gaze on my skin and cringe. My legs are stubbled with fine hair, a result of not shaving for a few days. Though my stubble isn't too dark, the stark contrast between the emerging hair and my pale skin is obvious. I shift my legs, attempting to hide them from Dante's view.

It's no use; I'm half-naked, and we're sharing a bed.

"Baby, don't hide those fucking legs from me." His voice is deep, coating me in instant arousal.

"I haven't shaved; I wasn't exactly expecting company." I wave my hand down the lower part of my body. Instead of disgusting him, my admission has him narrowing his eyes and leaning closer.

He stops his movement when his lips are touching my earlobe. "Are you telling me, Red, that your sweet little cunt is covered in soft red hair?" he asks, nipping my earlobe before trailing his mouth upward, peppering kisses, bites, and licks along the outer part of my ear. I shiver and feel my stomach clench. His mouth continues to work over me, sucking and tasting until I can't help but shift my legs, trying to find relief from the onslaught of sensations.

He trails his teeth lower, latching on to the skin beneath my ear and nipping. I groan, unable to hide how much I love the pain and pleasure he gives me.

"So tell me, baby, are you wet for me? Does my tongue on your ear make your pussy fucking cry for my fat fingers?" His hand rises from the bed and settles on my torso before trailing down to cup my pussy. Even though I'm still wearing the shorts I threw on last night, I feel the heat of his hand, almost like he's touching my bare skin. I arch my back and push my hips forward, craving the weight of his touch.

"That's *my* good girl," he murmurs into my ear, emphasizing his ownership. His fingers start to move, rubbing unhurried circles over my fabric-clad clit. "This is *my* pussy. I fucking own it now. You don't get to push me away again, you don't get to ignore me, and you don't get to take my pussy away from me. Do you understand?"

Words don't come out, just unintelligible sounds as his edict and ministrations consume me. Suddenly, his movements stop, and his hand lifts. I start to protest but am silenced as his hand comes back down, delivering a sharp slap against my center.

"Ahh," I cry out, arching my hips upward. The duality of pain and pleasure is heady, and I throw my head back as Dante delivers another blow against my core.

"I said, 'Do you understand?' Answer me," he commands.

"Y-yes," I moan.

"Say that you're mine," he orders. I shake my head, refusing to give in to the ridiculous name.

"Fucking say it." He spanks me again and again. "Fucking say it, Red. Let me hear those words come out of that sassy mouth." My body convulses, and I feel the impending orgasm rising within me.

"Please, Dante," I groan, pressing further into him. His tongue sweeps inside my canal, and I nearly combust at the wet heat that envelops my ear, accompanied by the sharp stings against my pussy.

"You're not coming until you tell me that you're mine."

"Dante, goddammit!" I screech. "Please, I'm yours. Please let me come." I almost sob in relief when Dante's hand steals under my shorts and panties. His thick fingers fill me, and I can't hold back my response. I explode around him, crying out his name as my release sweeps my body. Dante pulls his fingers out of my shorts and brings them to his lips. Licking my cum like it's a rare delicacy, Dante moans at the taste.

"Fuck you taste good, Red," Dante says before trying to

capture my mouth. I immediately pull back, ducking my head against his chest. "What did I say about hiding from me?"

"I have morning breath," I respond.

His hand, the one still covered in my cum, grips my jaw and tilts it upward until I meet his eyes. "You think I care about morning breath when I just had your tight cunt squeezing my fingers?" He shakes his head, chuckling as though I told him the funniest joke. "No, Red. But we can fix that." Dante pulls on my jaw until my mouth pops open. Wasting no time, he plunges his cum-covered fingers into my mouth, stretching me wide. I swallow around him and feel my saliva drip out of my mouth.

I gag against him, and he withdraws his fingers before quickly covering my mouth. This time, I offer no resistance as his tongue licks at me, and I let him. Our tongues twine. I lose myself in the kiss, not registering that his hands have worked their way to the waistband of my shorts.

Pulling back from our kiss, he whispers, "Help me take these off." I lift my hips, giving him room to slide the fabric down my legs. He throws my shorts and panties over his shoulder before grabbing the hems of my sweatshirt and the T-shirt underneath. In a swift motion, he rips the clothing from my body and throws that, too.

I'm naked, wet, and hairy in front of him, though Dante doesn't seem to mind the light-red hair adorning my skin. Running his fingers over my pubic bone, Dante runs his hands through the short hair covering my pussy. Normally, I keep it in a trimmed, tidy strip, but right now, I feel like a 1970s adult actress. Dante trails his fingers over my slit, gathering wetness in lazy, unhurried strokes.

"Dante," I sigh, spreading my legs wider, inviting him closer

78

to my center.

"I like your pussy covered in red hair, baby." Moving his hand up, he runs his fingers through the mane of red covering me, stroking it like I'm his pet. "Fuck, your hair is so soft."

"You're petting me like I'm a domesticated cat," I tease, though I love the attention he's paying to the most intimate part of my body.

Dante's caresses stop, and he lifts his hand. Shifting his body, he stands from the bed and yanks off his boxers, showing off his hard cock and the tattoos decorating his skin. Dante's body is a work of colorful art; one arm is inked in a nautical sleeve, with a diving girl plunging into his wrist. Spanning from his bicep to his triceps, a large ship dominates the space, with the eerie tentacles of an octopus latched onto the bottom of the vessel, almost like it's dragging it through the water.

On his other arm, there's a religious shrine to Jesus and the Virgin Mary, along with Catholic symbolism and imagery: a chalice, crosses, doves, and an angel. Dante's religious tattoos extend to his chest, ending just at his collarbone. A colorful lighthouse takes over most of the right side of his chest, while the left is bare. Lower on his torso, Dante has seemingly random images decorating his skin: a female profile, an eagle, and a moth with a skull. Though it's not visible, Dante's back is covered with one of the four horsemen, skulls, and roses—a beautiful and creepy homage to death.

I must take longer than I realize to survey his body because when I shift my gaze to meet his eyes, Dante has a smirk and raised eyebrow plastered on his stupidly attractive face.

"You like what you see?" he teases. I shrug, not bothering with a response. Dante grips his cock and strokes it, putting on a private show for me.

"Should I video this and post it to Campus Hotties?" I ask, though the thought of anyone seeing Dante like this—naked and hard, for me—is enough to turn my stomach.

"That pussy is mine, and this cock is yours, Red. Don't make me murder some asshole for viewing what's not for public consumption. Now..." He pauses as he walks toward the bed. "That pussy isn't going to eat itself." Before I know what's happening, Dante lifts me from the bed, holding me up in the air like my weight is inconsequential. He lays himself on the bed, lowering me until I straddle his chest.

"Get that pussy up here," he commands. "I'm fucking starving." Rolling my eyes at his authoritative tone, I brace my hands on his chest and shift my weight until I'm able to swing a leg over his body and reverse my position. With my ass now in his face, Dante grabs my thighs and pulls me back until my center is positioned over his mouth.

"Fuck yeah, Red." He latches onto my clit, sucking it lightly into his mouth before releasing the sensitive bundle of nerves. "Goddamn, you look fucking beautiful. You're fucking soaked for me, baby." Like a whip, his tongue lashes out, and he tastes my wetness, a mixture of my earlier orgasm and a fresh wave of desire. He moans at the taste and dives back in, eating at me with an intensity that has me grinding into his face.

I lose myself to the sensation of his lips and tongue and teeth devouring me. Like a man starved, Dante feasts, alternating between slow, savoring licks and sucking, like he's trying to absorb my essence into his body. I'm jerked from my pleasure-zombie state when his large hands travel up my body, stopping just below the swell of my small breasts. Shifting his hands, Dante's fingers pluck at my nipples, drawing them into stiff peaks.

I roll my hips, increasing my speed until it's *almost* too much, *almost* too fast, and I need to reach back to grip the headboard for stability. Dante's hands spread, and he cups my breasts, squeezing hard as I continue to ride him. He doesn't stop eating at me, even when an orgasm hits me with the power of a freight train. My body convulses, and I drop forward, collapsing against the length of his torso, and my hands land against his thighs. Dante's hands run up my back, making me arch until my stomach is no longer pressed against him. He continues licking at me, though it seems to have transformed from giving pleasure to cleaning me up. Still, when his tongue licks at my clit, I shiver.

Beneath my hands, his leg hair is coarse. I run my fingers through it, petting his skin and mimicking his earlier attention paid to my body. Lifting my head up, I come face-to-face with Dante's cock. I've watched plenty of porn in my life, a byproduct of having parents with hectic schedules that kept them out of the house, coupled with my love of smutty romance novels. I've seen big dicks, small dicks, crooked cocks, and veiny ones. I've even seen a penis with a single testicle, a lonely island of sperm.

But I've never seen a penis like Dante's before. Long and thick, it's like a pretty baseball bat. If Ava ever saw it, she'd say it's the perfect cock to dick-slap someone with. That thought makes me growl; I do not like the idea of anyone seeing his penis.

"Did you just growl at my cock?" Dante says from beneath me.

"No," I reply quickly, though we both know that I did. Dante laughs at my lie, causing his erection to bob in my face. Precum leaks from his cleft tip, and I lick my lips, suddenly ravenous for him.

Leaning down, I draw the head of his cock into my mouth, savoring the salty flavor. But as soon as my mouth is on him, I'm yanked off and deposited on the bed. Dante takes my legs and wraps them around his torso, holding onto my thighs to lock me in place.

"Why did—?" I start, ready to ask why he stopped a blow job, when he cuts me off.

"I don't want you to press on your stomach," he offers, and my heart stutters.

Thoughtful, annoying man.

10

Dante

Gazing down at her, my heart fucking races. Her hair is a flame against her pillow, and her cheeks are flushed, like she just finished a marathon on my tongue.

Eight weeks ago, when I first met Celeste Lauren Downing, I fucking knew I'd have her like this one day—pliant, sated, and fucking content. She's not ready to hear about how deeply I feel for her yet; she'd probably dismiss it and threaten to kick my ass.

The thought of her very real threats has me growing harder against her cunt. Ava has told me about Celeste's black belt, and I've felt the power behind her seemingly scrawny arms, and it goddamn thrills me that my woman can take care of herself. My eyes travel from her face to her stomach, pale and flat against my tawny hands. Soon, her stomach will round and harden to protect the little being cocooned between her organs. Fucking Christ, we're young, but Red will be a grizzly bear of a mother, guarding our cub against any and all threats.

Not for the first time in the past twelve hours, it strikes me that there's life growing inside Red—a life we created together—and it turns me on knowing that I've marked her in the most primal fucking way.

I feel like I'm a kid laying ownership on the playground; I licked it, so it's mine. No takebacks.

My eyes feast on her form before moving back to her face. She's watching me with an uneasy expression, almost like she doesn't know what to make of my examination of her body. Reaching out to cup her jaw with one hand, I cradle her delicate face and move her chin up until she meets my eyes.

"Do you trust me?" I ask. She hesitates, not giving me an immediate answer. Using my thumb, I stroke gently over her chin, giving her time to consider and come up with her response.

"I don't *not* trust you," she finally says. Her eyes bore into mine, and she licks her lips. "I trust you more than any other guy I've met," she finally concedes. "But don't get cocky, you still annoy the shit out of me."

I can't contain the bark of laughter that comes out; leave it to this fucking girl to put me in my place while her legs are tangled around me, and my cock's about to impale her tight cunt.

"Only fucking you, Red," I whisper, leaning down to capture her mouth. Hooking my arms around her slender legs, I unwrap them from my waist and put her feet on the bed. Adjusting my position, I lean over her and enter her slowly, careful to leave enough space between our bodies and not press on her stomach.

Her exhale fuels the space, and I set a lazy rhythm, stroking in and out of her with unhurried, deliberate thrusts.

"Faster," she pleads beneath me. I steal another kiss, pressing lightly against her parted mouth.

"No."

She lifts her hips, trying to grind her pelvis with a wildness that, at any other time, I'd latch onto. But I can't bring myself to quicken my pace or fuck her into the mattress. Goddamn, but I'm trying to make love to her, fucking worship her, and the little spitfire won't fucking let me.

"Red, let me take care of you." I punctuate my words with another slow, deep thrust of my hips, dragging my cock all along the tight walls of her pussy. Repeating the motion, I rock into her, giving her every inch of me over and over again. She mewls beneath me, tossing her head back and forth like she can't contain the sensations, like she's my puppet and I'm her fucking master.

"Dante," she breathes out, "I'm so close." I snake my hand between our bodies and rub gentle circles over her clit, giving her the pressure and friction I know she needs to come.

"Is that good, baby?" I ask in a voice that sounds like it belongs to a fucking simp. Before Celeste, I took care of the women I fucked and made sure they came, but my release and orgasm always took precedence. Now? I could have endless blue balls if it meant that she was satiated.

She's fucking ruined me.

"Just like that," she begs, running her hands from my waist, over my chest and shoulders, until finally digging her fingers into my hair. Pulling on the short strands, she tugs my head back, exposing my neck to her teeth.

A sharp sting against my neck, coupled with her tight cunt squeezing my cock like a vice, nearly undoes me. The fucking hellcat bit me; I shouldn't like it but fuck, her aggression in bed is as hot as her violence outside of it. I start listing all fifty fucking states in my head to hold back the orgasm threatening to seize my goddamn sanity.

"Fucking hell," I pant, dropping my head until my forehead presses against hers. With my fingers pressed against her clit and the steady glide of my hips, I feel her walls start to squeeze me tighter, milking my cock.

"Oh my—" I capture her words, swallowing her screams while her pussy convulses around my dick. Her orgasm triggers mine, and I push deep, stilling my hips to make sure every drop of cum spills into her.

Still locked together, I shift until she is lying next to me, her heavy breaths a soundtrack in the overly decorated room. I look over the side of the bed, my eyes landing on the cowhide rug on the floor.

"Red?"

"Hmm?" she responds, barely coherent.

"We live in New Jersey, why the fuck do you have a cowhide?"

—

"I have an appointment on Monday before class if you want to come," Red announces after a full day spent fucking and napping. I mapped her body and drew lines with my fingers as I measured all the coordinates of Celeste fucking Downing.

"I'm sure as fuck going to be there." She grunts in response. We lay silent for long minutes before I finally give voice to the questions nagging the fuck out of me. "What would you have done if I didn't show up here last night? Does anyone else know?"

She's lying against my side; her small body is plastered to me, and I feel every move she makes. I feel her body tense and her head shake, the movement causing her nose to rub against the side of my chest.

86

"Goddamn," I scowl, shifting so that I can look down at her. "You were going to go by your fucking self?"

"Obviously." I don't need to see her eyes to know that she just rolled them.

"Don't be a little brat, Red. Why the fuck would you go by yourself? What if something happened? What if you needed a ride? Fucking hell. What if the baby needed something?" My mind is fucking spinning; the only image in my head is Celeste naked on an exam table while a horny bastard looks into her tight hole. "Jesus Christ. Would you have been alone with the doctor? What if they try some shit with their wandering fucking hands."

Placing her hands on my chest, she lifts until she's sitting upright against me. "Dante, I need you to calm the hell down; you're acting unhinged." She pauses, giving me a calculated look. "I'm barely pregnant; I doubt the baby is going to ask for something while it's in fucking utero. And you clearly have no idea how gynecologists work, but they stare at vaginas all day. Just straight Homer Simpson lips in their faces. When they're not staring at vaginas, they're feeling boobs for lumps, talking about birth control, or navigating through literal shit after pulling a child out of one of the vaginas they spent the entire day looking at."

"Okay, but what if they're attracted to your pussy?"

She shakes her head at me like I just said the dumbest shit imaginable. I probably did, but it's a serious fucking question. Red has a tight little cunt with the sweetest rosebud of an asshole. You'd need to be on a dick-only diet to think it's not beautiful.

"They're medical professionals that took a Hippocratic oath. Don't be a fucking moron."

87

"Well, I'm fucking coming. No one's getting a look at your pussy without me there." I sit up, mimicking her position on the bed.

"Nope, we're not doing that." She holds up her hands and shoves me back down so that she's looming above me. "Let's get one thing straight, big guy." My cock stirs, anticipating verbal sparring. "You don't get to make demands, issue edicts, or tell me what to fucking do. I am willing to do this *with* you as a partner. But make no mistake..." She lifts one delicate hand, stabbing me with her pointer finger. "I can do this with you or without you. Don't fucking test me, Dante."

Goddamn, I love this woman.

—

After agreeing to Red's conditions—because what the fuck else was I going to do but agree?—I grabbed her from behind and spooned the shit out of her. For all her pent-up rage and tornado-like personality, Red is a phenomenal fucking cuddler and sleeps like one of the corpses she likes to threaten everyone with. Her petite body molds to mine, the perfect fit against my larger frame.

Before she fell asleep, Red detailed what to expect at the ultrasound appointment: a hospital gown, cheap ass paper coverings, and a wand that looked like a vibrator attached to a computer.

Not going to lie, I'm intrigued about this vibrator shit. When I asked if she got turned on by the wand, she threatened to strangle me with the cord.

She kicked me out on Sunday morning, telling me that she needed space from my hovering and a break from my dick. Once we're living together, she's never going to get a fucking break from my cock.

She doesn't know it yet, but I'm going to insist that she move into my family's compound with me; there's no place safer, and we need enough space and support to raise the hellion we're about to bring into this world. My cousin has two kids—sons that will probably overthrow a totalitarian regime one day—and they come with a massive amount of shit. Diapers, toys, clothes, more fucking diapers; there's no way in fuck that's fitting in a dorm room. There's also no way in hell she's raising this child in her hometown without me.

My insides light on fire at that fucking thought.

I'm surprised Red scheduled an appointment this early on a Monday. For most people, ten in the morning isn't unreasonable, but for Celeste, it's like dawn. I'm waiting in my car in front of the entrance of her building. When I texted I was here, and that I was coming up, she gave me strict instructions to stay in my car or else she would throat punch me.

My cock is still hard from her written threat. It's probably fucked up that each time she tells me she's going to kick my ass, I get hard. There's something about my small, petite woman threatening bodily harm—or fuck, murder—that does it for me. Goddamn, the only thing that would make it fucking better is if I could watch her kick some ass. Fuck if I know where this kink came from.

I pause at the mental image of Red grappling with a pregnant belly, and the thought makes me scowl. She better fucking not practice jiu-jitsu with my baby inside her.

I'm so consumed by the idea of Celeste doing stupid shit while heavily pregnant that I don't realize Red is at my car door until she opens it and throws her body inside.

"What's with the face?" she asks, her voice husky like she just woke up. Knowing her, she probably did.

89

"Are you still fucking practicing jiu-jitsu?" I explode, and it comes out as both an accusation and a question.

She rolls her eyes at me and buckles her seatbelt. Pulling out her phone, she holds it out to me, and I see an address on the screen.

"This is where we need to go. Do you know the way, or do you need to put it into your GPS?"

She's fucking infuriating. "Celeste, answer my goddamn question."

She huffs—fucking huffs—like I'm inconveniencing her. "No, you idiot. I could barely get out of bed for three weeks and have only been able to eat soup and wontons. Do you really think I had the strength to go to the dojo? The Sifu would have taken one look at me and sent my ass home."

"Good."

"But," she continues, looking me in the eye and effectively squeezing my balls with her gaze, "once I have my strength back, I will continue practicing. I'm not a moron and know that I'll need to modify my workout, but exercise is perfectly safe for pregnant women."

I scoff. "Exercise, sure. Sparring and kicking the shit out of people? Definitely fucking not."

"Like I said, modified workout. Jiu-jitsu isn't just about physical contact with an opponent." Her face is flushed, a giveaway that her anger is rising. We're going to go around in fucking circles arguing at this rate.

I give in because what the fuck am I supposed to do with a pissed-off redhead and a doctor's appointment in thirty minutes?

"Fine. But we're talking to the doctor about this." I shift to drive and pull out from the curb. "Fucking exasperating woman," I mumble under my breath.

"I heard that, asshole."

—

Despite prepping me for the appointment, nothing prepares me for the sight of my woman, spread out and naked from the waist down, with a cord hanging out of her pussy. When the ultrasound technician handed the lube-covered wand to Red, along with the instructions to "slide it in until she was comfortable," I got excited, thinking I would get an internal exam of her tight walls.

The screen is black as shit, with blobs floating around like hot air balloons. Celeste lays on her back, her face toward the monitor and technician.

"Okay, Mom and Dad," the technician begins. "Are you ready to see your baby?" I think I'm having an out-of-body experience because, holy fuck, I was not anticipating those fucking words. She's silent, but I can feel her thinking. I reach over from my position on the cheap as fuck plastic chair and grab her hand, squeezing in silent support.

Red clears her throat. "We're ready." The technician reaches down to grasp the wand shoved into Red's pussy and moves it around, giving a clearer picture of her internal system. Pointing out the ovaries, fluid, and other shit that I should have learned about in eighth-grade health class but definitely fucking didn't, the technician measures each item she brings into focus on the screen.

"Now, based on your last menstrual cycle, it appears as though you are about ten weeks pregnant. At this point, we can see some features start developing." She waves her pointer over the white blob on the screen, showing the formation of a nose, arms, and legs. "Your baby is measuring about three point five centimeters, so right on track."

"Dante," Red whispers, drawing my attention away from the screen. I look at her, and she gestures with her free hand to our linked hands—where I'm squeezing the shit out of her hand and probably cutting off circulation.

"Fuck. Sorry." I loosen my hold but don't drop her hand.

The technician glances over to us and smiles, pulling the wand out of Celeste's cunt before discarding the plastic cover that was over it and then sterilizing the wand. Placing it back on the stand next to the monitor, she turns to us while pulling off her gloves and reaching behind her.

"Okay, here are a few pictures of Baby Downing." She hands a row of pictures to Red. I feel like a primordial caveman because I nearly corrected her that it was Baby Camaro; the only thing stopping me was that Red would probably castrate me on the spot if I opened my mouth. "I'll give you both a few minutes. The doctor will be in shortly to go over the results of the ultrasound and answer any questions you may have."

As soon as the door closes, I'm on Red, pulling her body against mine as I envelop her in a tight hug.

"We're going to be parents," I murmur against her hair. I feel tears start to form in my eyes, and I'm not ashamed to admit that I'm feeling emotional as fuck.

"I know." She lets out a sob, clutching my shirt in her hands and burying her face against my chest.

"Goddamn, baby." I release her and take her hands from my shirt, keeping my hold on them as I kneel on the stained linoleum floor.

Kneeling in front of her, I grab her around the waist and plant a kiss on her abdomen. "Hi, baby, it's Daddy," I say into her stomach, repeating my greeting from last night. "We don't know what the fuck we're doing, but we're going to be okay." I glance up at Red, her eyes are wide and filled with unshed tears.

Fucking gut-wrenching.

"I love you, baby," I say into her body, hoping to speak the words through her womb and directly into our unborn child's little heart. The words are for Red just as much as they are for our little bean, though she's not ready to hear them yet.

11

CeCe

Nine-hundred nineteen: the number of times I have pulled the ultrasound photo out of my bag and stared at the black and white photograph. There's no personality yet, no hellish traits or picky eating habits that will define this collection of organs and limbs, but I imagine who that little blob will turn out to be.

A devil, no doubt, but maybe a dancer or a basketball player. Maybe that blob will become the first female president or a world-renowned skier. I have no idea what they'll like or what they'll hate, but I know that I love them. I've never been an overly emotional or affectionate person—dramatic, yes—but the love I have for the life growing inside me is overwhelming.

Do all moms feel this uncontrollable excitement doused in fear? Do parents just navigate life with this unholy combination of elation and anxiety? It's nauseating. I only just recovered from the ever-present nausea, but I feel it creeping back in.

After my ultrasound appointment earlier this week, I made Dante drop me off at my dorm, much to his annoyance.

According to him, being pregnant means that I'm incapable of caring for myself, and he argued that I should be staying with him. I told him to fuck off before slamming the car door in his perfectly smug face.

Since that appointment, Dante has been a helicopter, constantly patrolling and asking for updates on how I feel, if I've eaten, and if I need anything. He's a gnat that refuses to go away, but I'm secretly pleased that he's taken such a vested interest in my well-being.

I haven't told anyone about the pregnancy, and we agreed to wait until after the twelve-week mark to discuss it openly. It's not that I'm ashamed, or even embarrassed, but I'm nervous about the reactions of our families and friends. At eighteen, the last thing I thought I would be preparing for is motherhood; I can't imagine that our parents will be pleased that this is the course our lives have taken.

My phone buzzes on my desk, pulling me out of my intrusive thoughts. I turn my phone over and roll my eyes at the message on the screen.

Dante: I brought you options, Red <attachment 1>

Attached to Dante's text is a photo of a green smoothie, fast food burgers and fries, a salad, a Tupperware container, and a container of Chinese food. As frustrating as he is, his consistent food deliveries are enough to stave off any complaints I have.

CeCe: What's in the Chinese takeout container?

Dante: Steamed pork dumplings

Hell yes. Somehow, earlier this week, Dante engineered a conversation to find out all my favorite foods. Cacio e Pepe, potato pancakes, beef stew, and now steamed pork dumplings have all been delivered after my evening classes. I'm no longer feeling too sick to eat, and Dante has made it his personal mission to shove food down my throat.

I warned him that if he continued to spoil me, he'd create a monster, but he just laughed and said I was already a monster.

I punched him in the ribs for that comment.

CeCe: Dibs

Dante: I may have already had one...

CeCe: You're on my shit list.

"Ms. Downing, is there something you'd like to share?" My head jerks up, and I lock eyes with Dr. Ford, my creative writing professor. She looks at me critically, letting me know that her question wasn't rhetorical and she's expecting an answer.

"No, nothing," I respond, sinking low into my seat and praying I'll blend into the background.

"No? Are you sure about that, Ms. Downing? You appeared to be engrossed in your phone."

I clear my throat, uncomfortable with being the center of attention for the absolute worst reason. "Sorry, family emergency. It won't happen again."

"See that it doesn't. Now..." Dr. Ford pauses, shifting her gaze away from me and meeting the stares of the other students. "In five weeks, your final piece is due. We're going to deviate from the normal submission process; instead, you'll all be responsible for uploading your work to the public Dropbox folder. Once I review the submissions, I'll make them public to the rest of the class. It is your responsibility to read and review your classmates' work before your workshop. You'll still be responsible for your weekly submissions, but this final submission will be in place of a final exam. For this project, workshopping will be in a communal setting rather than in pairs. Any questions?"

Hands shoot up, vying for attention. "Yes, Cassidy," Dr. Ford calls to one of the students sitting in the front row.

"What type of piece are we required to submit?"

"It can be anything: poetry, prose, essay. I want you to focus on conveying your message and your meaning in a medium that feels the most natural for you."

Dr. Ford calls on another student. My eyes narrow on the guy sitting two rows in front of me. Derek, a junior on the hockey team, and his twin, Thomas, act like the reincarnation of Ernest Hemingway and don't shut the fuck up. "Is there a theme we need to follow? Or a question we need to answer?" he asks.

"No, Derek. You can write about anything you want, as long as there is no unnecessary profanity." She levels us all with a hard stare. "I understand that you all communicate through slang, jargon, and cursing, but remember that this is a level two course, and I expect professionalism."

With that parting comment, Dr. Ford dismisses the class. Gathering my things, I stuff everything into my messenger bag and join the throng of students leaving the classroom. I'm not surprised to see Dante outside of the room, waiting for me with bags of food and a cardboard drink tray.

The more I see him and the more I interact with him, the easier it is for me to accept his hovering. When it first started a few days ago, I resisted his constant attention and food deliveries, but in the days that have followed, I see his attentiveness for what it is: worry and a need to control what he can. Dante may play at being a golden retriever with a carefree attitude, but that façade masks who he truly is: a high-strung control freak.

97

"Finally, Red. That class is long as shit," he complains. "Here, give me your bag." He shifts the drink tray to the hand holding the take-out bags and grabs my messenger bag, slinging it over his muscular shoulder like it doesn't contain ten pounds of textbooks and electronics. "Come on, let's go to the picnic tables," he suggests, tilting his head toward the double doors that lead to the quad and the concrete picnic tables dispersed throughout it.

I follow his lead because I really want those freaking dumplings.

Setting the bag down on a table near the building's entrance, I launch myself at the food. The Tupperware container, opaque and heavy, is warm, almost like the food was put into the plastic bowl right after it was cooked. Holding it up, I look at Dante.

"What's in this?"

"Bolognese with rigatoni," he responds with a shrug, as though it's no big deal.

"You made this?"

Dante drops his gaze, shifting on the hard bench seat. "Ah," he clears his throat, delaying his response. "So, my mom made it this morning," his voice lowers, and the rest of his response is lost in the noise of the quad.

I lean forward, tilting my head closer to him. "What was that?" My stomach drops, and I know that whatever he's about to say is going to ruin my appetite.

He clears his throat again like he has a goddamn frog trying to jump up his esophagus. "I said, 'She said you need to make sure you eat enough for you and the baby.'" He looks away sheepishly.

Just as I suspected, my appetite evaporates, and my stomach

plummets at his statement. "You told your mom?" I shouldn't be annoyed; I recognize that and understand it's unfair for me to be angry that he told his family.

But I'm fucking pregnant, and my hormones are all over the place.

"Yes," he answers slowly, like he's testing the word out and trying to figure out if it's a livewire explosive. "I know we said we'd wait until you were twelve weeks, but my mom is like a small general and knew something was up the minute I stepped through the goddamn door this morning."

"What do you mean?"

"She fucking said, 'Hi, honey,' as soon as I opened the door."

I let out an incredulous laugh. "Her saying hi to you makes you think she knew something was wrong?"

"Fucking right, it does. My mother normally tells me to take out the trash, peel fucking potatoes, or some shit when I get home. Her being nice to me?" He pauses, visibly shivering. "That shit doesn't fucking happen."

I continue staring at him, absorbing the paranoid explanation he just provided. "You're out of your mind," I finally mutter. Shaking my head, I grab the container of pork dumplings and open it, inhaling the scents of scallion and soy like they're my lifeline. My appetite has been revived through the power of smell.

Picking up a dumpling and bringing it to my lips, I take a deep breath before asking, "What did she say when you told her?" Biting into the pillowy dough, I look at him under my lashes, noting how still he is, almost like he's afraid to move and shatter the tentative peace we've found ourselves in.

"She was... emotional," he supplies. He reaches across the concrete table and grabs the container of pasta, popping it open and placing it back down in front of me. "Eat the pasta," he commands.

Normally, I'd tell him to shove his edicts up his ass, but the fragrant smell of tomatoes, vegetables, and beef has me dropping the dumplings real fucking quick and reaching for the pasta. Grabbing a fork out of the plastic bag, I start shoveling the food into my mouth.

"Oh my God," I moan between bites. "This is so fucking good. I think this is better than Ava's recipe." I still. Shit, did I just say that? Ava isn't competitive or territorial over many things, but admitting that I like someone else's food better is a sure way of having my food privileges revoked. "You better not repeat that, or so help me God, I will castrate you."

Dante's answering smile is smug. "Listen, my mom is a phenomenal fucking cook, look at me." He gestures down his body. "Fucking cooked to perfection."

"I think I lost my appetite for real this time." I push the containers away. "Now, tell me what your mother said." With my hunger abated, the enormity of the situation crashes down on me.

"She was pissed at first, told me that I should know better than to let my dick do the thinking, but once I explained to her the situation, she calmed down." At my stare, he continues, "She knows all about you, fuck, she's known about you since the week we met, and so does my sister, Franki."

"W-what did you tell her about me?" This woman, a world-famous journalist, is my unborn child's grandmother, and the last thing I need is for her to loathe me or think I intentionally trapped Dante with this pregnancy.

Dante stands up and walks around the bench until he's standing beside me, hovering over my body like a guard. "Red, get up," he commands.

"Why?"

He shakes his head. "Can you do anything the easy way? Please, get up." I huff but follow his order. As soon as I stand up, Dante drops into the seat I just vacated, facing outward toward the back of the quad, away from the buildings. He grabs my hand, pulling me down until I'm cradled in his lap, his groin pressing dangerously close to my hip. I shift, trying to fight for more space between our bodies.

"Is this necessary?"

"Fuck yes, it is. You were looking like I just told you that your fucking parakeet died."

"Of all the analogies, a parakeet? Really?" Dante growls into my ear, nipping it before pulling away and adjusting me so that I'm facing him and nearly straddling his lap in the full view of campus.

"Don't you fucking move, Red. My cock is about to burst out of my jeans, and the only thing hiding it is your sweet ass." He palms the curve of my hip, squeezing me so that I feel the burn of his erection through our clothes.

"Put that thing away," I say through gritted teeth.

"I fucking can't. We're talking about your cunt milking my cock and your belly growing with my child. It's fucking hot." His hand runs down my leg until he cups my knee. Leaning in, Dante drops his voice to a whisper. "How do you feel about lactation play? I watched this video; fucking hell, it was hot. The guy was squeezing her tits, and milk was leaking everywhere. The sex looked phenomenal."

My gaze cuts to the people milling around us, paranoid that someone just heard his whispered confession. Leaning in, I hiss, "What the hell is wrong with you? What the fuck kind of porn are you watching?"

"I just told you, lactation play," he responds, like it's an obvious answer to a stupid question.

"Shhh." I put my hand over his mouth. "We are not talking about this at two o'clock on a Friday in the middle of the freaking campus." I eye him, keeping my hand over his mouth until he bites my hand, leaving a stinging kiss on my flesh. "Ow, shit," I mumble.

"It's okay. We'll work up to the tit play. We have a few months until these gorgeous tits start leaking anyway," he muses.

"Okay, we're done here." I would never admit it to him—even under the penalty of death—but Dante's comments have butterflies erupting in my core and wetness pooling between my thighs. I need to get the hell away from Dante before I do something stupid, like reenact the scenes he's describing in full view of twenty percent of the Marymount student population.

Hoping off his lap, I throw the containers into the plastic bags, pausing when I realize what I'm doing. "Wait, weren't these bags banned last year? How do you have plastic bags?"

Dante rolls his eyes. "Red, your best friend is Italian, you should know the answer to that question. We fucking save everything." His hands cover mine, pulling the containers and bags from my grasp. "Can we go somewhere to talk? Somewhere private where you won't be freaking the fuck out every five seconds about being overheard?"

I gnaw on my bottom lip, considering his request. Part of me wants to jump at the chance of being alone with him, the heat at my core begging me to give in to him. The other part of me is weary; though he's been nothing but considerate and accommodating, I'm still terrified to get too close to him.

Dante is an eclipse: charismatic, sinfully good-looking, deceptively smart, and observant. He may behave like an idiot half the time, but there's no disguising how attractive every aspect of him is. He overshadows everyone, including me.

He may claim that I'm the sun, but he's a complete solar system.

Dante:

God fucking damnit. I'm three seconds away from coming in my pants like a fucking twelve-year-old, and Red has no idea, just standing there, biting that damn lip while holding a container of food.

It's like every fantasy I've ever had come to life.

"If you don't stop biting that fucking lip, I'm going to pull it from your goddamn teeth," I growl, low enough so that the fuckers staring at us don't hear me. She may not notice, but every asshole in this quad has been looking at her since we sat down. With her red hair and green eyes, she's like a siren wading through the waters of this fucking school.

Fucking hell, if we have a daughter, am I going to have to deal with this shit?

"Baby, is red hair a dominant trait?" I'm going to hire bodyguards, fucking ten of them.

"No, why?"

"Thank Christ." Her answering scowl makes me think I should probably explain but telling this hellcat that I'm fucking terrified our potential daughter will have red hair and be on the receiving end of leers and carpet-drape jokes won't go over well.

Typically, Red's ire and violence turn me on—I'm a fucking masochist—but when it concerns our child and their protection, the last thing I feel is horny.

"Come on. You're thinking too hard about this." I grab the bags of food and her messenger bag and wait for her to follow me. When she's next to me, I tell her, "We're going to my car, hellion. You good with that?"

A nod is the only answer I get.

—

It takes ten minutes to walk across the quad to the lot where my car is parked. Red has been silent for the full ten minutes. Once we reach my car, she slides in without comment.

Getting into the driver's seat and starting the car, I turn to her. "What's going on in that pretty head of yours?"

She hesitates before answering, staring down at the fingers folded in her lap. "I'm just thinking about how you told your mom and sister about what's happening, but I haven't even thought about telling my parents." She looks at me, tears welling in her eyes, before continuing, "I haven't even told my best friends yet. What kind of monster does that make me?" A tear spills out of her emerald eyes, trailing down her cheek. I catch the moisture with my thumb, tracing the path of the tear before bringing it to my mouth and sucking.

"Baby, it makes you fucking human." She shakes her head, disagreeing with me. "Yes, it does, Red. You're eighteen, and we're figuring this shit out. It's ok that you haven't announced it from the rooftops. You're allowed to be scared."

More tears spill from her eyes, and sobs wrack her body, making her convulse in the confines of my car.

"Fuck, baby," I whisper before unbuckling her seatbelt and lifting her over the center console. I deposit her on my lap and gather her close, tucking her under my chin and letting her slight curves settle against the hard contours of my body.

"It's okay."

"W-what if they hate me? What if my parents and Ava and Serena think I'm a terrible person for this?" She's irrational right now, and the hormones are talking for her; I won't say that because I don't have a fucking death wish.

"Baby, no one is going to hate you. They may be concerned or confused, but no one is going to hate you."

She nods her head, burrowing into my chest. Quiet and resting against my body, you'd never know that this flame-haired woman could easily bring the entire male population of Marymount University to their knees—with the exception of Grey and maybe Linc. She continues sniffling against me.

"Red, I fucking hate seeing you upset," I say into her hair, nuzzling against the crimson mop. My hand coasts over her hair, dipping to her face and settling on her chin. Tipping her face up, I lean down and capture her lips.

She turns away, immediately breaking contact.

I growl, slamming my head against the headrest.

"Red," I moan. I sound like I'm fucking dying. I probably am.

Her head is down, chin tucked against her chest, and she's shaking her head. Letting out a sigh, I move my hand from her jaw to her hair, gently moving it out of her face. Her hair is thick and long—a fucking curtain that gives off a wicked amount of heat. I don't know how she isn't constantly sweating from the inferno attached to her head.

"Tell me what to do." I pause, weighing my words carefully. With Celeste, if I push too hard, she'll cut my dick off and run. "I thought after last week, after the appointment on Monday, we were on the same page." I run my hand through her hair and down her back. I want to push her body into mine, but I resist.

Fucking barely.

"You and me, us." She gestures between us with her delicate fingers. "Don't you think it's going to complicate things if you can't keep your dick in your pants?"

"You weren't complaining when you rode my fucking face like a rodeo queen last weekend."

"God dammit, Dante." She reaches up and pulls on my ear, a move my eighty-five-year-old grandmother has done many times.

"Ow, fucking that hurts." I flinch away, but her fingers hold my ear in a death grip. "Red, okay, I'm fucking sorry, let go of my ear." After another quick tug, she releases my ear and lowers her hand to her side.

"If I did that to you, it'd be fucking abuse, hellion. You're lucky I don't turn your perky ass around and spank you for that move." Instead of being intimidated by my words, she rolls her eyes and leans back against the steering wheel.

"I'd feel sorry if I didn't know you get turned on." She glances down as if confirming her point. "I think your penis is about to explode. But be serious. Us being together is a complication."

"Red, everything is a fucking complication. You're pregnant, I love you, and you're stubborn as shit, you like shit music, and none of our friends know that your cunt bled on my cock two months ago. We're complicated as fuck. What's one more thing at this point?"

I'm greeted with stunned silence and replay my words, stilling when I realize what I just admitted.

Fucking shit.

"Dante, I don't love you," she whispers into the car.

My chest fucking aches, but I ignore the fissure that's torn apart my heart. "*Yet.* You don't love me yet. But you fucking will."

She shakes her head, seemingly disagreeing with me, but it lacks conviction. Her eyes shift to my lips, and that's when I know I got her.

"You're going to fucking fall in love with me, Red." I lean in and kiss her lightly on the lips, surprised that she lets me. I pull back, tilting her head up to better meet my gaze. "You're going to be so fucking obsessed with me." I dive back in, capturing her mouth before biting down on her lip.

The spark of electricity that greets me is expected but still unnerving. Her mouth parts, and her tongue sneaks out, stealing into my mouth with a ferocity and need that I didn't anticipate but fully welcome. I meet her need and coax her mouth wider until I'm breathing in her air. Her full lips are soft, pliant beneath mine, and eager to please me. I taste the sweetness of tomato on her lips, coupled with the heady tang of Celeste fucking Downing. She tries to gain dominance, biting on my lip and dragging it into her mouth before diving back in with her tongue and teeth.

I break our kiss, leaning my forehead against hers to try and catch my breath. "Fucking hell. You're going to be the death of me," I mutter.

She sighs but otherwise doesn't respond.

"Can I bring you somewhere?"

She looks up at me, her green eyes gleaming from her tears. "Where?" she whispers.

"I want to take you home." I pause, clearing my throat. "I want you to meet my mom."

12

CeCe

"Are you high?" I ask, because seriously? In the past hour, I've eaten a pound of pasta, felt his dick grow hard beneath me in public, and cried into his shirt.

It's been a sixty-minute rollercoaster, and now he wants me to go to his house, meet his mom, and make an impression that will convince her that I'm not a hormonal mess. I think fucking not.

"Red," he says with a laugh. "It's just my mom and probably Sof. She wants to meet you, and I want you to see where I'm from. I know what's running through that over-active head of yours, and you don't need to worry about impressing anyone. Just be your normal, sweet, and charming self." He fucking cackles at the last part as though it's the funniest thing he's ever heard.

"I'm going to stab you." I think I really might.

"Calm down, drama queen," he says, still giggling like a moron. He looks up at me, sobering instantly at the expression on my face. Lifting one hand, he drags it over my jaw, gripping my chin lightly and tilting my face down until I'm staring into his eyes. "What do you say, Red? Want to meet my mom?"

I jerk my chin out of his grasp and look up at the moonroof of his stupid car. "No, I don't want to meet your mom right now," I start, letting out a sigh. "But I will."

We both know that no one can make me do anything I don't want to do, and if I were *really* opposed, I would get out of this car and walk away calmly. But after everything he's done for me this week, I feel like I owe it to him to meet his mother.

Dante's mouth splits into a grin, and I roll my eyes at his eagerness. He's the only guy I know who would be excited to bring home his pregnant—two-night stand? acquaintance?—with tear stains on her face to his mother.

"She's going to fucking love you." Dante grasps my waist and lifts me back over the center console, depositing me gently on the passenger side. Leaning over me, he grabs the seatbelt and pulls it, buckling me in place. I nearly yell at him for treating me like I can't take care of myself but close my mouth when his hand slides over my waist and settles on my stomach.

"You're going to meet your grandma, bean," he whispers, though his words have the force of a yell and the impact of an avalanche. Tears prick my eyes, and I look upward, willing them not to spill over.

Fucking hormones.

—

"You've got to be fucking kidding me," I murmur as we drive up to a massive gate, in front of a massive property, with a massive gold "C" in the center.

"Yeah," Dante says, almost sounding sheepish. "I promise the gate is the only gaudy thing about the place." Reaching up, he presses a clicker attached to his visor, and the gates retract, permitting us entry.

Turning in my seat, I look out the window and gape. The long, paved driveway winds and leads us through a canopy of trees and green foliage. The greenery ends, almost like it was a mirage that suddenly lifted. In its place, a sprawling lawn leads to a house that could fit six colonials. The modern chateau-style mansion looks like it belongs in the French countryside rather than in the hills of New Jersey.

"Dante?" I say his name as a question.

"Yeah, baby?" he responds, driving up the cypress tree-lined driveway like it's not an immaculate feat of landscaping and physical labor.

"Do you remember when you asked me why I had a cowhide rug in my dorm room because, and I quote, 'we live in fucking New Jersey?'" He offers a grunt in response. "Well, why the hell does your house look like it belongs to a French king named Louis, and your driveway looks like something created using CGI and Photoshop?"

He laughs. "Uh, well, I don't really know how to answer that," he supplies.

"Dante, I am wearing leggings, an oversized hoodie, and Converses that I got in tenth grade. I look like I was hit in the face with a shovel and lived to tell the tale. How am I going to meet your mother in there"—I pause, waving my hand toward the passenger window and the absurd structure beyond it—"...looking like this?"

He drives to the end of the driveway and puts his car in park, immediately killing the engine. "Red, my mom is probably elbow-deep making a pot of chicken soup. Unless she's on-air or working, she pretty much wears the same thing you have on."

I survey him, absorbing his words and mulling them over.

Something still doesn't sit right with me. "I've always known you were wealthy, D," I say, using his nickname because I know how much he likes hearing it from my lips. "But this? This is overwhelming and intimidating. My parents make a great living, but this is not the same caliber. Your mother is going to think I'm a gold digger and trapped you." I swallow a lump in my throat, surprised by just how emotional I'm getting over the thought of his family's approval.

Dante shakes his head and, without saying a word, opens his door and gets out of his car. My eyes follow him as he rounds the hood of the car and opens my door.

"Are you going to say anything?" I ask because it's not like Dante to remain silent... ever.

Shaking his head, he bends down and reaches across me to unbuckle the seatbelt. Without a single word, he scoops me up and carries me, bridal style, toward the front door. I gasp at the contact, not expecting his move.

"The car must have fucking fumes leaking because you sound like you need a tranquilizer to calm down," he finally says.

"Hey—" I start, but he cuts me off.

"No, I'm not going to listen to whatever bullshit lie you've fabricated in your head, Red. Your overactive imagination and self-deprecating intrusive thoughts end now. Get your shit together before I paddle your tight ass in front of my mother."

I narrow my eyes at him. "You wouldn't."

"Fucking try me, Red. Now, can I put you down, or are you going to make a run for it like a goddamn convict?"

"Put me down, you ogre." But before he can put me down, the door is yanked open by a small woman who looks like the personification of motherly love. Her gray hair is swept back

111

in a loose bun, and her black cat eyeglasses frame her pretty, soft face. She's tiny, maybe an inch or two taller than me, and beautifully plump.

As soon as she sees me in Dante's arms, her face transforms from happy to pissed.

Rushing out, she starts swatting at his arm. "Dante Nicholas Camaro, you let her down right now."

Dante flinches from her attack, turning his body to make sure I'm not struck with any flying hands. "What the fuck is it with people abusing me today? First Celeste, now you, Sof? What if she was fucking injured?"

Ah, so this is Sofie. I feel a blush of embarrassment creep over my cheeks that I was jealous of this woman when Dante first mentioned her. If Ava were here, she would probably tell me that my face is turning red and that I look like a tomato.

Thoughts of Ava are like a punch in the gut. Fuck, I'm a terrible friend for ignoring her and Serena. I silently vow to call them as soon as I get back to my dorm room.

Dante's comment stops Sofie in her tracks. "Sweetheart, are you injured?" she asks, a look of concern passing over her face.

Sofie's alarm brings me back to the present. "No, I'm not. He's just being difficult."

"Traitor," Dante murmurs under his breath. "I'm going to speak shit about you in Italian to our child."

"*Stupido raggazo.* Dante, you don't speak Italian, and we raised you better than to be emotionally abusive," Sofie scoffs. "Put her down. *Now*," she orders. I know she's a nanny, housekeeper, and mistress of all things domestic, but if she ever wants a career change, she could easily become a military general.

"I could learn. How hard could it be?" Dante asks as he lets me down. Once I have both feet on the ground, I turn to him and stick my tongue out.

Admittedly, it's childish. But, considering Sofie's scolding and his asinine comment about learning a language just to spite me, it seems to fit.

"Red," he growls, his threat about paddling me hanging silently yet ominously in the air.

"Absolutely not. Dante Nicholas, get your *coolie* inside," Sofie reprimands, as though she read the silent threat in his tone.

Dante huffs, placing a hand on my ass and squeezing. "Later, hellion," he mutters. I elbow him in response and step out of his hold. Sighing in frustration, he grabs my hand and leads me through the doorway and into the house.

"What exactly is a *coolie*?" I ask under my breath, terrified that Sofie is going to hear me. I'm not joking; she's fucking terrifying.

"It's Italian-American slang for butt or ass. I don't know if other regions use it, but it's a thing in New York and New Jersey. Ava's family doesn't say it?"

I think back on my innumerable interactions with Ava and her family and shrug. "If they have, I never realized it. Why doesn't she just say 'ass?'" I motion behind me to Sofie.

Dante stops, looking over at me like I committed a sin against one of the ten commandments. "Because it's a fucking *coolie*."

Okay, then.

If the outside is an ostentatious display of wealth, the inside is a reminder of family. When we first pulled up to the house, I expected the entire interior to match the obvious wealth flaunted on the exterior; however, I could not have been more wrong. The inside is filled with pictures and warm wood; Dante and his sister and another woman are displayed proudly, as though they are the heart and soul of this home. Lining the staircase, black and white photos of their family through the years tell a story of love and evolution. I see Dante transform from a snaggle-toothed child to a teenaged heartthrob to an adult that could incinerate the panties on any warm-blooded heterosexual woman.

Dante's father is pictured in some of the photos, and I'm awed to see just how much Dante looks like his dad. While his sister, Francesca, is a near-carbon copy of their mother, Dante is a copy-and-paste version of his father. Along the wall, photos of Dante and his sister are prevalent, and I'm able to see his father at a similar age, all the way up to their early adult and teen years, where he is nothing short of a silver fox.

If these are his genetics, baby C will do just fine.

"You look so much like him," I say and immediately stiffen. I turn to Dante and wince, expecting to see sadness or heart-break on his face. Surprisingly, I just see a small smile and pride radiating through his eyes.

"My mom says Franki and I are as stubborn as him, too."

Beside me, Sofie lets out a scoff. "You may be just as stubborn as him, but your sister is even worse. I swear, that girl is going to burn herself out if she doesn't slow down." She pauses, considering her words. "Or Kate may kill her first." Sofie gestures to the other woman in the pictures with Dante and Francesca, a fair blonde with seemingly light eyes. Though the pictures are in black and white, I can tell that she is the opposite of Francesca in appearance.

Where Francesca is a dark-haired, dark-eyed beauty, Kate's

skin looks milky, and her hair looks so fair that it's nearly white in the pictures.

"Kate, Francesca's wife, tries to keep these two in line, bless her soul."

"She tries, Sof, but no one can get that woman to chill. She said she wanted to open another restaurant in the East Village."

"Absolutely not. She needs to give me grandbabies first," sounds from behind me, and I turn, coming face-to-face with one of the most stunning women I've ever seen.

Dante's mother, Sylvia Camaro, stands at average height with an athletic build and cheekbones that appear to be carved from marble. Her shoulder-length curly hair is thick and unruly, a departure from her normally polished waves on television. Her face is bereft of any makeup, and her olive complexion is smooth and wrinkle-free, like she just had a facial or Botox or sacrificed a baby for eternal youth.

"Ma, we got you covered on the grandbaby," Dante says with a smug tone.

I startle and whip my head around, shooting daggers at him with my eyes. "Dante," I say through gritted teeth.

"You're an ass," his mother says at the same time.

"What, too soon?" he asks with feigned innocence.

"Excuse my son. I promise I didn't drop him on his head as a baby. His sense of humor is from his father's side." Mrs. Camaro walks over to me and envelops me in a warm hug. Her embrace is strong, like she's trying to hold me together so I don't freak out on her son. "You are just as beautiful as he said," she whispers in my ear. With a final squeeze, she releases me and steps back.

"Mom, this is Celeste," Dante says, stepping closer to me

and placing his arm around my waist. Drawing me into his body, he leans down and places a kiss on my head. Looking up at him, I give him a puzzled look as if to say, *Why the hell are we doing public displays of affection?*

He rolls his eyes and tightens his grip.

His mother's assessing gaze tracks our movements and silent conversation. She lets out a small laugh and shakes her head. "Oh, you are so screwed, *viso bello.*" Turning her back on us, she walks toward the threshold on the left side of the foyer. "Well, are you coming? I made soup," she calls over her shoulder.

"Come on, before she drags me by my ear," Dante mock-whispers. Sofie hits him on the back of the head for his comment. "Christ, Sof, stop hitting me."

"Stop being an idiot, Dante Nicholas. Now, go get this girl some food," she says, laying a hand on my arm and squeezing in reassurance before turning and walking in the opposite direction of his mother.

"Isn't she coming with us?" I ask, tilting my head toward the doorway Sofie just disappeared through.

"She's probably going to go fuck up the gardener's day. It's like a game of foreplay they play." I raise my eyebrow in confusion. "It's her husband. I think they get off on her telling him the grass is dying. And every time Phil's on a lawnmower, she's suspiciously standing at the sunroom's windows, watching him."

I blink up at him, processing his words. "Your house is so weird." It's the best I can come up with.

"You have no fucking idea, Red." Placing a hand at my back, he leads me down the same hallway his mother just disappeared through and into a mammoth kitchen.

116

CECE

If the house looks like a feat of French architecture, the kitchen is imported from Tuscany. Distressed white cabinets line the walls, while a blue and white mosaic backsplash adds a pop of color and opulence to the room. The commercial appliances are a dull silver accented in gold hardware, and if I'm not mistaken, there are two fridges next to each other.

Dante's mom stands at the stove, stirring a large pot that's filling the air with the unmistakable scent of chicken soup. It feels warm and cozy in here, like the room holds an undeniable amount of love.

"Sit," Mrs. Camaro orders, not bothering to turn and look at us. Dante leads me over to the massive square island across from the stove and pulls out a stool. Settling into the seat, I keep my back straight and my elbows off the marble, desperate to make a good impression.

Turning around, Dante's mom has two steaming bowls in her hand but pauses before setting them down. Tilting her head, she looks at me and laughs.

"Relax, Celeste. I'm not going to interrogate you. Eat some soup and get comfortable." I immediately relax my posture, allowing my shoulders to drop and my back to arch and lean against the countertop. My stance may not be elegant, but it's significantly more comfortable.

Mrs. Camaro offers a small smile and eye roll at my reformed position and pushes the deep bowls toward us. "It's Italian chicken soup," she supplies. I inhale the smell of the soup and look down. The fragrant broth is orange from blended vegetables, while pieces of shredded chicken, miniature meatballs, and greens that I can't quite identify are generously dispersed.

"Thank you," I respond, lifting my spoon to begin eating.

"Red, woah, what are you doing?" Dante asks, almost

117

horrified. I look at his mother, who turned back to the stove, and see her shoulders shake as though she's holding back a laugh.

I look at him, confused. "Eating soup?"

He shakes his head and motions to two bowls, a container of cheese, and a peppermill that's close to him on the island. "First, do you want rice or *Acini de Pepe?*" he asks, reaching over to grab two opaque bowls.

"I have no idea what that last part means."

His mouth drops, a look of dismay on his face. "I need to have a fucking talk with Ava. She didn't even teach you the right way to eat soup." He pauses, looking upward before returning his gaze to me. "Do you want rice or pasta in your soup?"

"Pasta."

He nods his head. "Good girl." Even though the context is wrong, and the setting is absolutely inappropriate, my stomach twists, and I squeeze my thighs together at his use of "good girl." Teen pregnancy, turned on from soup, and squirming in front of his mother; if I had a checklist for all the ways I was fucking up, it would be embarrassing.

Setting both bowls down, he grabs a serving spoon and drops a large spoonful of pasta into my soup. "Next, you need to add grated cheese and pepper. Then you can eat it." He finishes assembling my dish and then leans back, staring at me.

"Well, can I eat it now, or are you going to tell me I'm holding the spoon wrong?" I ask. If his mother weren't here, I'd use significantly more colorful language. As it stands, she's five feet away and watching us with a weird gleam in her eye.

"It's okay, Red. I know you want to threaten to either cut my dick off or stab me in my aorta. It's no less than what the other women in this house do," he teases. Leveling a look at his mom, he continues, "Last week, Franki told me she'd grate my finger off with a cheese grater for saying her spicy vodka sauce was too hot. And this one"—he nods his head toward his mother—"fucking laughed like my life wasn't at stake."

"Eat your soup," his mother commands, not bothering to defend herself or refute his claim. Looking at me, she says, "Celeste, if you don't like escarole, you can take it out." She hands me a side plate. "The iron is good for the baby, though."

I feel my face flush and look down, nodding my head in acknowledgment.

"Ma, that was fucking subtle," Dante says around a mouthful of soup.

"Am I supposed to pretend as though I don't know your girlfriend is pregnant? You announced it as soon as you came into the house."

"I'm not his girlfriend," I mumble at the same time Dante says, "Fuck right, she's my girlfriend." We glare at each other, willing the other to break first.

"Well, this seems like a healthy relationship," his mother offers.

Dante turns from our stare-off to frown at his mother. "Ma, really?"

"Don't 'Ma, really' me, Dante Nicholas," his mother starts. "You are twenty-one years old, and..." She pauses, looking at me. "Honey, how old are you?"

I clear my throat. "Eighteen."

"Jesus," his mother whispers. "Celeste is eighteen. Do you have any idea how difficult it is to have a child as an adult, let alone as children yourselves? Babies don't sleep, they cry, they need you all the time, and they are dependent on their parents from the moment they're born. Do you have any conceivable idea just how much responsibility you will have? Not to mention school and your own dreams and aspirations? Those are on the back burner now. As soon as that beautiful baby enters this world, your main priority will be that child. No more partying every night, no more going out and doing whatever it is you do. Do you understand that?"

His mother levels us with a serious look.

Dante opens his mouth to reply, but I cut him off. "Mrs. Camaro, I know this isn't ideal, and trust me, we used protection and did not expect this to happen." I feel my cheeks redden and my face heat. Clearing my throat, I continue, "I don't know what we're doing, and I don't know what our relationship will look like in weeks from now, let alone months or years from now, but I know that this baby will be loved and cared for beyond compare. I-I..." I pause, swallowing down my emotion. "*We*," I emphasize, looking at Dante, "love this baby already, and though we're young and have a lot to figure out, this baby has already become our priority."

"You're wrong about one thing, Red," Dante says from beside me. "Our relationship is going to be solid as fuck. There's no guessing there."

"Dante, you can't just will something to be true," his mother reprimands. I raise my eyebrows, surprised that she's taking my side.

"Ma, you're the one that said persistence wears down resistance. You wanted me to fucking stalk her."

She points her finger at him, scowling. "That is not what I meant, and you know it, Dante."

"Okay," I interrupt before they explode. "Look, Dante, one day at a time. And Mrs. Camaro, we're figuring it out, but I promise, this baby will be the center of our world."

She nods, absorbing my words and accepting them. "I don't want to see you two struggle," she says as her eyes turn glassy. "Dante, *viso bello*, I know you're a man, but you're a *young* man." She emphasizes young, shaking her head as tears start to spill over her eyes. "And Celeste, you have your whole life ahead of you. You both need to be sure, one hundred percent sure, that this is what you want, and you're prepared to accept the responsibility that is coming. Once the baby is here, that's it.

"There's no do-overs, or takebacks, or pauses. You two will be parents and will need to figure out how to pay for things like diapers, formula, and baby clothes. Dante, you have a trust fund, but I will not allow you to be a lazy slob who lives off your interest your entire life; you need to work and provide for your family, set an example of hard work for your child."

"Ma, we've been pregnant for two fucking minutes."

"Language, Dante," Mrs. Camaro huffs.

"Listen, we're going to figure it out. We have a few months to get everything sorted before the baby comes. Like Celeste said, this baby is going to be the center of our whole fucking world."

"Christ, Dante, language!" his mother chastises again. "If my grandchild's first word is 'fuck,' I'll kill you."

"I have a couple months to get that together, too." Dante stands from the stool he's been sitting on and walks around the island to his mother. Enveloping her in a tight hug, he continues, "I had the best example of a father growing up. He walked away from everything, including his fucking family for you, me, and Franki. Everything he did for us, I'm going to do for my child. I promise, Ma, I won't fuck this up."

I breathe in a shaky breath, exhaling slowly through the emotions Dante's statement just triggered. He's told me briefly about his father's death and seemed proud when I compared their appearances, but what he just shared is more.

It's heavier, more potent.

"I wish he was here," Dante whispers, loud enough for me to catch it over his mother's sniffling.

"Me too, *viso bello.* Me too."

13

Dante

I'm not fucking sure how I ended up in this position, but my mother is crying softly against me while Red is flushed and teary-eyed at the island. If Franki, Kate, or Sofie were in the room, they'd probably be emotional wrecks, too.

I pause, considering my sister. On second thought, she'd probably be slapping me on the back and saying, "Good job," for permanently locking her down.

Possession runs in the fucking family.

Peeling my mother off me, I lower my voice and tilt my head away from Red so that she can't hear me. "Ma, I love that girl, and I love that baby. Yeah, I've fucked around, fucked girls over, but Celeste? I will never fucking hurt her. I promise. She's my fucking family now."

My mother closes her eyes and lets out a long breath. "Your language is atrocious." She leans in to embrace me one last time before letting go. Reaching one tiny hand up, she cups my jaw and squeezes. "Your father would be proud of the man you've become, Dante."

"Thanks, Ma," I say gruffly, trying to hide the emotion

coursing through my veins like wildfire.

"Alright, eat before the food gets cold." My mom pushes my face away and walks around the counter to sit beside Red. "Celeste, Dante told me you're an English major. Do you like to write?"

I smile to myself. Most people don't realize the work journalists—especially television journalists—put into their craft. The time spent writing, investigating, fact-checking, and revising can hardly be measured. Growing up, my mom was the one working insane hours and hustling to keep her stories relevant and timely. My dad, with the help of Sofie, took care of most of the domestic duties while my mom was either on assignment or working on her next piece. Those lulls between her stories were filled with family dinners, camping trips, and other family bonding shit to make up for the time she was absent.

I've never resented her for the time she spent working, which is why her speech pissed me off. She established a career, had a family, and somehow made both parts of her life work successfully. It also can't be overlooked that her brother is a fucking senator, and our family is stupid rich.

From the moment I met that redheaded hellion, I knew that her love of writing and books would endear her to my mom, while her attitude and no-bullshit approach to every-fucking-thing would be a selling point for my sister. I wasn't wrong; my mom is already fucking in love with her. I can't fucking wait for Franki to meet her.

I listen as Red describes the assignment she just received in her creative writing course and silently promise to steal her laptop once she finishes her project. A view into Celeste Lauren Downing's mind without forcing myself on her? Hell fucking yeah, I'm taking advantage of it.

"What are you planning on submitting?" my mom asks.

"I'm not sure." Celeste shrugs, looking down into her bowl before continuing, "I typically write prose, but I think working on a poem may be a smart decision for me."

"What the fuck is 'prose?'" I mumble under my breath.

"It's writing that doesn't follow a metrical pattern, like a short story, or essay, or novel," Red responds.

"So why the fuck can't you just say that?" I ask her.

"For the love of God, Dante, language!" my mother yells.

—

After an hour spent listening to my mom and Celeste, I'm antsy as shit to get my girl alone. When we first got to the family compound, Red was annoyed and nervous. Now, she looks like she's about to make herself at fucking home with my mother.

I have a feeling I'm going to regret introducing them.

"... and then he said that he was on the lacrosse team and didn't need to worry about grades." Catching the end of Red's story, my anger immediately rises at the mention of some asshole on the lacrosse team.

"Who the fuck are you talking about?" My mom's going to yell at me for language again but fuck it. Who the fuck is she hanging out with?

"Someone that we met at the STD table. He was working the event with his friend and Serena."

"The fuck are you talking about, STDs?"

Red rolls her eyes and lets out a sigh. "Sigma Tau Delta, the English Honor Society. Serena is the treasurer, and that's how we met. She had to work the interest fair with these two morons who were required to be there for their class."

"Have you seen that dickwad again?"

Celeste stares up at me with a look of disbelief on her face. "Are you serious?" At her question, I lock my jaw and stare, willing her to respond. "Jesus, no. Were you even paying attention to what I was telling your mother? They were bragging about plagiarism."

Fucking good. She hates that shit.

"Is there a reason why you're asking about him?"

"Is there a reason why you're telling my mother about a random douchebag you met?"

"Oh my God," she mutters under her breath. "Yes, you fucking moron. We were talking about clubs and activities, things I like. So, I told her about the interest fair and the fucking people I met there. If you would have listened instead of zoning out for the last hour, you would have heard our conversation."

"Well, don't talk about other fucking men," I seethe. I'm being an irrational dick, and she is probably going to threaten to poison me or fuck my shit up, but hearing her talk about other guys after denying she's my girlfriend a few hours ago pisses me the fuck off.

"Okay, that's enough," my mom interjects. "My grandchild is going to know every curse word before the alphabet. God, help me." Looking between us, my mom shakes her head. "You're both as stubborn as a mule. But it's getting late. Do you two want to stay the night?"

I look at Red and see her skin redden, a clear sign she's embarrassed. Or horny. Or wants to murder me in my fucking sleep. It's probably best we leave.

"No, thanks, Ma. I'm going to get Celeste back to the house. Can I take home some soup?" Lincoln and Ava may be fantastic cooks, but no one makes food like Sylvia Camaro. I don't give a fuck how talented or trained they are.

"Are you sure? It's after eight, and the roads aren't great." My stomach sinks, and I feel guilty for leaving, but also know Red will have a panic attack if I force her to stay in my childhood home tonight.

She'll need to get fucking used to it since I'm going to force her to move in. But baby steps and shit.

"Yeah, we'll be fine, Ma. I'll text you as soon as I'm back in the house."

"Fine, but Dante Nicholas, be careful."

With a kiss on the cheek and a promise to say bye to Sofie on our behalf, I lead Red through the house, out the front door, and back into my car. Reaching over to buckle her in, I turn on the engine and wait.

Turning her head toward me, she asks, "What are you doing?"

"Waiting on you to either yell at me, kiss me, or try to kill me." I think her meeting my mother went well, but who fucking knows with this girl and her pregnancy hormones? I thought it was fine to eat one of the dumplings today, and she threatened never to speak to me again.

"Look, it's been a long day. Let's talk about it tomorrow," she says before spinning her head to look out the window, effectively ignoring me.

Fuck that.

"No, Red. I don't fucking think so." Throwing my car in drive, I start down the paved driveway and make a left once we're past the gate. Careful not to push my car too fast, I head toward my town's lake and the seclusion it'll afford us.

"Where are we going? Isn't campus the opposite direction?"

she says from the passenger seat.

"Red, I fucking love the sound of your voice. But, for once, I need you to be fucking quiet, or else I'm going to lose my shit."

I don't look over at her, but I can practically hear her jaw snap shut.

Five minutes later, I'm pulling into a parking spot on the far side of the lake. It's October, which means no one is fucking here, and we have the area to ourselves. Leaving the car on, I unbuckle my seatbelt and slide my seat as far back as it'll go. Still silent and staring at me, she lifts one perfectly arched eyebrow as if to question what the hell I'm doing.

I chuckle under my breath, "You fucked up, hellion." Leaning over the console, I remove Red's seatbelt and lift her up, careful not to bang her body into the car's interior. Settling her on my lap, I run my hands over her stomach, trailing my fingers over her still-flat abdomen.

"This okay?" I ask, my hand still grazing her middle. She nods, a small smirk on her face.

"Words, baby. I need fucking words."

"Oh, am I allowed to speak now? Five minutes ago, you were telling me to shut up." She shrugs, acting like the little brat I fucking love. "Sorry if I missed my cue, you ogre. I'm fine."

"And the baby?"

"She's fine, too."

"Fucking good." Without warning, I grab Red's face and draw it to mine, crushing her mouth against my lips in a possessive, hard kiss. She melts for me instantly, opening her mouth and allowing me to steal my tongue inside to tangle and twist and fuck hers. With this kiss, I show her who fucking owns her, to whom she belongs. Her hands lift, digging into my short strands of hair, pulling my face closer to hers while her legging-covered pussy grinds against my jean-covered cock.

Reaching up, I grab her hands from my hair and pull them behind her, taking control of her movements. Still writhing against my dick, Red struggles and tries to pry her arms from my hold. I tighten my grip, not allowing her dominance.

"Are you going to let me take care of you? Can I make you feel good?" I ask, nearly begging her to let me go further. She nods her head, giving me nonverbal permission, but fuck that. I need to hear her say the words. "Open that sassy mouth for me, Red, and tell me that you want me to finger this wet cunt," I command.

"God, yes," she cries, trying to dive back in for a kiss. I award her a soft kiss, barely grazing her lips before my hand pulls at the waist of her pants, stealing inside so that I can touch her overheated skin.

"Lift up for me," I urge. For once in her goddamn life, she listens to me. Rising to her knees, she lets me tug her leggings down until they're pooled at her knees. This could work, but I want her fucking bare. "Hands on the steering wheel," I order. "If you move, I'll stop. Do you understand?"

She nods her head, and I chuckle. "Words, Red. I said do you understand?"

She swallows and reaches behind her, placing both hands on the steering wheel. "Yes, Dante."

I lean back in, licking her earlobe before whispering, "That's my good girl." Moving my hands to the fabric gathered at her knees, I help her out of them and stare at the perfection in front of me. Like most redheads, her skin is pale and translucent; against my olive skin, she looks like one of those porcelain figurines my Nonna used to collect to make her seem more American.

Her long hair is loose and wild, framing her perfect face and falling below her chest. I grab the bottom of her sweatshirt and yank that up, moving it over her head and down her arms until it settles at her wrists against the wheel. I was hoping she'd be bare beneath the sweatshirt, but instead, a thin black shirt covers her upper body. My girl's full tits are pebbled in her shirt, letting me know that she hasn't been wearing a bra all fucking day, while her cunt is covered in a little scrap of white fabric, hiding the strip of curls that drives me goddamn crazy.

Coasting my hand up her stomach, I graze her left breast, walking my fingers over until I circle her tight little nipple. Her breathing grows frantic, pushing her tits harder into my hand. I bite the inside of my mouth, forcing myself to slow the fuck down.

Moving my hand across her chest and to her other breast, I pinch her other nipple between my fingers, watching her face as she processes the sting. Her expression morphs from surprise to pain to arousal.

Fucking perfect.

I lean in and take her nipple between my mouth, pulling the bud until it's hard as fuck between my lips. I bite down, lightly grinding the tip between my teeth before I release and offer soothing sucks.

"Oh fuck, D," she groans, and my dick becomes granite at the use of my nickname. My tough, stubborn, argumentative woman has called me every insulting name in the goddamn book, even a few creative ones that I've never heard, but she rarely shortens my name.

"Fuck, Red," I pant, releasing her nipple. I thrust up, letting her feel how fucking hard I am right now. "You feel that baby? Give me one fucking reason why I shouldn't take that wet pussy right now. I'm about to come in my goddamn pants."

"Please, please, please," she chants. Her hands remain on the steering wheel, but her body is a livewire, grinding against me and trying to find any path to release it.

"Tell me you want my cock, Red."

"Please, D," she moans, trying to increase the friction between our bodies. Her plea was the encouragement I needed. Wrenching my hand from her tits, I grasp her stupid excuse for panties and tug, ripping the fabric away from her body.

"Dante!" she screams.

I smirk. "Hope you didn't like those." Running my thumb along the seam of her pussy, I gather her wetness and push it back in, filling her tight little hole with my thumb while rubbing her clit with my pointer finger.

"More," she pants. Just to be a dick, I slow down my pace and offer languid, lazy passes over her clit and stop thrusting my thumb, leaving it still inside her wet heat. "Dante, God dammit, don't make me beg." I laugh under my breath; even when she's naked and at my mercy, she's a temperamental little hellion.

"But I love the sound of you begging, almost as much as I love the sound of you coming around my cock," I tease, but start increasing my movements. All it takes is a few thrusts and passes over her swollen clit for her to explode around me. She starts to cry out, but I cover her mouth with mine, swallowing every sound she rasps out as I steal the oxygen from her lungs.

With one hand still locked inside her pussy, I lift my hips and use my other hand to drag my jeans and boxers down, freeing my cock. She looks down, eyeing me with hunger. I pull my thumb out of her cunt and smack her ass.

She lets out the most delicious fucking groan. I lean back, taking in the sight of her half-naked, disheveled, and flushed on my lap. Grabbing her hips, I move her body against mine, dragging her pussy over my cock so that she can feel every fucking ridge.

"I'm not going to be gentle, Red. That shit you pulled with my mom, telling her that you're not my girl? That's fucked up. *You* fucked up." I pull her back, feeling her wetness drench my dick. "This pussy is mine. I'm the only one who knows how it feels clamped around my cock. I'm the only one who knows how that cunt tastes and how rough it likes to be fucked. So stop fucking around and understand that you are mine." She lets out a whimper and bites down on her bottom lip.

This time, when I move her hips, I lift her and hold her over me. "You either stop this now, or I'm going to fill my cunt up, and I'm not going to fucking stop. Do you understand that? My baby's in your stomach, my cock is going to be in your pussy, and my cum is going to drip down your fucking legs." She doesn't say a word, just writhes suspended above me, like she's fucking the air, trying to find relief. "Good girl," I say before I drop her down, impaling her.

14

CeCe

Dante drops me down, filling me up in one hard motion. My grip on the steering wheel tightens, and I let out a scream, my body adjusting to the punishing force he took me with. He's not wrong when he said I like it rough; though it feels good each time he touches me softly, it's the harsh pulls, bites, smacks, and thrusts that ignite a frenzy within me.

I'm still adjusting to the size of him—long, thick, and slightly curved; I'm pretty sure he's hitting my cervix. Impatient beneath me, Dante thrusts up and releases my hip to smack my ass.

"Ride my cock, Red. Show me how fucking bad you want it," he growls into the car. Maybe I should give him an attitude for ordering me around, tell him to go fuck himself and climb off his dick. But I can't; when he has me like this, displayed before him like his wanton slut, the only thing I want to do is please him and hear him call me his good girl.

With lust clouding my judgment, I am the antithesis of everything I am while lucid. It's like I'm a drunk, and I can't drink enough of him or his cock.

Giving in to his commands, I work my hips back and forth, searching for a rhythm that will give me the friction I need. Dante moves one of his hands from my waist and grabs my hair, winding it around his fist and pulling back. From this angle, my breasts are on display, their bra-less state evident through the thin material of my shirt. He leans in, drawing my nipple into his mouth, biting down, and stalling my movements.

He pulls on my hair and waist simultaneously, urging me to continue. "I didn't say you could stop," he murmurs against my nipple. I release a low groan, thrusting my hips and grinding my clit against his pelvis while his cock is buried inside me.

"God," I sigh, feeling the tingles of an impending orgasm shoot up my spine.

"Not God, baby. Just your fucking man," Dante growls. "Your pussy is squeezing my cock. You better say my fucking name when you come." He emphasizes his command by pulling my hair tighter, pressing my chest further into his mouth.

Unable to hold back the wave of ecstasy coming over me, I scream into the silence of the night.

"I told you to scream my fucking name," he snarls beneath me before pinching my clit.

"Dante!" I whimper, falling into him and releasing the steering wheel.

My hips buck against him, spasming on their own accord as my orgasm crashes between us. Dante pulls me into his arms, thrusting into me from below. He fucks me hard and fast, hurtling us both toward orgasm. Latching onto my neck, he eats at my skin. I know that I'll have marks on my body tomorrow, but at this moment, the sensations he's pulling from my body are too intense for me to care about anything else.

"I'm going to fill that pussy up, fucking paint it with my cum," he says against my skin. "I want to feel that cunt flutter around my cock as I come." He grabs my ass and pulls, ruthless in how hard and deep he's taking me. Between his words and his pace, I detonate, exploding around him for the third time tonight.

"Fuck," he yells, stilling beneath me and holding me tight while warmth fills me.

I drop my head into the crook of his neck, panting as I try to catch my breath.

With a gentleness that contradicts his filthy words and the way he just fucked me, he coasts his hands from my ass to my stomach. His fingers splay out on my abdomen, and he starts fanning his hands up and down, almost like he's massaging my belly.

"Was I too rough?" he asks, looking down at where his fingers caress me. "Fuck, knowing that my baby is growing inside of you makes me fucking crazy." Though we just had sex, absolutely filthy, tiring sex, I feel his cock start to harden inside of me. I shift, holding in a moan when my clit rubs against his pelvis. Dante clenches his jaw, feeling it, too.

Clearing my throat, I shake my head. "No, I'm okay."

He looks up at me, surveying me through his thick, dark lashes while his dick turns rigid inside me. "You'll tell me if it's too much? You won't fucking act tough and pretend you can take it if you can't, right?"

I glare at him silently, annoyed that he's even asking the question. "I may be young, but I'm not stupid. I would never do anything to harm myself or my child."

135

"*Our* child," he corrects.

I let out a sigh before agreeing with him. "Yeah, our child."

Dante's chuckle fills the confines of the car. "How much did that pain you to say? Stubborn little witch." He shifts, pulling my hips toward him and creating friction against my clit. "I shouldn't be fucking hard right now, but you're a fucking she-devil." Flexing his hips, I feel just how quickly he recovered.

"I'm going to fuck you slow now, Red. Remind you how fucking good it can be, so the next time you try to cut me off for a week or tell someone that you don't belong to me, you remember how good I make you feel. I need you to fucking remember that *our* baby is going to call me Daddy and that you're both fucking mine."

He moves my hips at a slow, steady pace, and I can do nothing but follow his guidance. With each drag, my clit rubs against his skin, and the fine hair decorating his pelvis, setting off tiny waves of pleasure throughout my body. Our first round was frantic, a testament to how much we both needed release. This time feels purposeful, like our bodies are saying things our mouths can't. Or, in my case, won't.

"Fuck, I'm fucking our cum back into you," Dante whispers, his eyes trained on where our bodies are joined. "God, your cunt feels like fucking heaven." He lifts his hips, grinding into me from below.

"Do you feel that? Do you feel how fucking wet you are, dripping with our fucking cum, riding my cock?" His fingers flex, and though he doesn't pick up speed, I feel his frantic energy building, like his release is on the precipice and he's waiting for me to fall over first. "Fuck, I love you," he growls. "I love how you fucking feel, I love your cunt, I love the fucking sound of those breathy moans you make when you come on

136

my cock. Goddamn, I even love how vicious you are."

Just like earlier when he told me he loved me, I stutter, my movements jerking before stilling completely. But Dante doesn't give me a minute to pause or absorb his words.

"No, you don't get to be fucking scared of those words, Red. I'm not forcing you to say them, but I'm going to force you to fucking hear them, again and a-fucking-gain. Now ride my cock and show me who owns this pussy." He urges me forward again, this time with two fingers pressed against my clit. His words, the pressure, the moment—they all come crashing down, delivering a silent but no less intense orgasm. I feel myself clench around him as my climax travels through my body.

"Fucking finally," Dante grunts, pumping his hips one final time before stilling and filling me with his release. We stare at each other through our post-orgasm haze, chests heaving and bodies flushed and sticky.

Dante breaks the silence, gathering my body and pulling me close, though careful not to put pressure on my stomach. "Only you, Red. Only fucking you," he whispers.

His voice is a bomb, exploding the remainder of the resistance I have.

—

After catching our breaths, we quietly get dressed. I catch Dante stealing glances at me while I pull my leggings and sweatshirt back on. I feel sensitive everywhere—the scrape of the cotton against my skin feels like cheap polyester compared to Dante's callused hands.

He's ruined me. Fucking ruined me.

I'll kill him for this.

"Buckle your seatbelt," Dante breaks the silence, pulling

me from thoughts of kerosene and body bags. Following his orders, I click my belt into place and watch as his wide hands shift the car into drive.

I was surprised by how close Dante's hometown was to campus. While Ava and I live over an hour from West Helm, the stupidly large Camaro compound was less than twenty minutes from campus, close to the hospital where Ava was admitted. From what Ava told me, Dante and Greyson have been friends since childhood and met Lincoln in high school. I assume Greyson's family lives in one of the other massive estates we drove by this afternoon.

Clearing my throat, I ask, "Was this the same lake from after the hospital?"

Dante snorts. "You just realized that?"

"Don't be a dick. I wasn't sure if you had a fascination with lakes." Dante drives slowly out of the parking lot, turning left to head back toward campus. As we leave, I look behind me, taking in the enormity of the lake and how well-maintained the grounds are. Unlike in my hometown, where drug addicts use the public parks as meeting grounds, this area is manicured and pristine. While we were locked together, I couldn't appreciate how beautiful our surroundings were. Now, in the silence of the car, I can take it all in.

Like the ride to the lake, Dante and I don't speak, and the radio remains off. However, there's no tension hanging over us; we fucked that out of our systems.

Turning my head to look out the windshield, I'm startled by Dante's hand grabbing mine. Looking over at him, I find his eyes still on the road. He squeezes once before lifting our connected hands and bringing them to his mouth, kissing the back of my palm while his other hand remains on the steering wheel.

He drops our hands on the center console and leaves them there, as though it's the most natural thing in the world. Surprisingly, I'm not freaked out; maybe it's the hormones finally righting themselves or the knowledge that being pregnant is more significant that holding hands in a freaking car.

Whichever it is, I don't fight him and leave our hands joined, letting the warmth of his palm seep into my skin.

"This is nice, Red," he comments.

"Don't ruin it, asshole." He answers with a chuckle and rubs his thumb over the skin between my thumb and pointer finger.

"Fucking brat," he says, though instead of an insult, it sounds like a compliment.

"Just shut up and drive."

He listens to me for once. He's silent for the remainder of the ride, letting me enjoy the feel of our hands joined without his voice nagging me in the background.

15

Dante

I'm waiting on Red to give me shit. I'm practically fucking giddy about it. We're nearing the entrance to campus, and I'm going to drive right past it.

She's going to fucking flip. I smile to myself, craving her reaction.

Sure enough, as soon as the turn for campus approaches and I don't make any indication of turning, Celeste opens her beautiful, irritating mouth.

"You missed the turn."

"No, I didn't," I respond, barely able to keep the laughter from my voice.

"Are you suffering from amnesia? You clearly just missed the turn."

"I didn't miss it because you're not going back to your dorm."

"Excuse me? When the hell was that decided, because I didn't agree to that," she seethes next to me. "You people keep doing this shit, making decisions about what we should and shouldn't do without fucking consulting anyone except your own fucked up brains." She rips her hand out of my hold and crosses her arms, her anger written all over her face.

"'You people?'"

"You, Greyson, probably Lincoln. You're all assholes who make decisions on behalf of other people without realizing how fucking annoying and out-of-control it is."

I tighten my grip on the steering wheel, annoyed by her words but not willing to engage in an explosive argument with her. "Calm down, Red. Getting so worked up can't be good for the baby."

Silence descends over the car. Not the comfortable kind of silence from moments ago, but the kind charged with tension and fury.

I fucked up, I know, before she even says anything.

"Do you think Felicity saved her machete?"

"What?" I look over at her, confused.

"Because I'm going to fucking kill you with it," she says in a voice that's eerily calm, like she's planned the path forward and has accepted it.

"You want to end up in lock-up like her, Red? Giving birth behind bars?"

She shrugs. "I look good in orange."

"Fucking hellion," I groan. "Listen." I pause, looking over at her and taking in the firm set of her jaw. "I texted Grey; Ava is having Serena come over to the house, too. We figured you girls would want to get together. Have you seen them since Ava's attack?"

Her shoulders drop, and her face loses the angry look. She looks like a dejected kitten, sulking because the fight has been depleted from her body. "Oh."

"Why do you always assume the worst?" I question.

She sighs, throwing her head back against the headrest. "I don't know. I've never been in a relationship, and I don't know what to expect. When we first met, I thought you were an idiot with your lick-to-thrust ratio, and every time you do something, I expect to be disappointed. It's like I can't reconcile that you're a good guy when you made up such an asinine concept."

"Fuck, you know about that?" I was stoned when I wrote down my hypothesis of how many licks on a girl's pussy it would take to make her come, followed by how many thrusts were ideal for sex. It sounds stupid as fuck now, but I recited it like the gospel for a few years.

"Ava told me. I guess Grey told her." That motherfucker.

I'm going to fucking kill him when I see him tonight. I pause in my murderous thoughts, my mind tracking back to the rest of what she said. I feel a smile break out on my face. "So, you admit we're in a relationship?"

"Really? That's what you're focused on?" I shrug. She shakes her head and mutters something that sounds suspiciously like, "Fucking exasperating," under her breath. "Yes, I acknowledge that we're in a relationship, as weird and unconventional as it may be."

"Fucking right we are," I say before shutting my mouth.

We drive in silence for a few more minutes, not quite as tense as we were, but not comfortable either. Desperate to hear her voice, I clear my throat, asking a question that's been on my mind since we first met. "Red, don't get mad at me, but why are you a fucking assassin in training?"

"You are undoubtedly more dramatic than I am," she scoffs. "You already know that my dad is the Chief Medical Examiner of Haversham County, and my mom is a cardiothoracic surgeon, so I grew up with that." She waves her hand as though gesturing at her words. "And I'm the only girl out of sixteen cousins. I have fifteen male cousins who made sure I knew how to defend myself, especially since my parents work so much. When I was a kid, my parents signed me up for karate when my older cousin, Wolf, offered to go with me. He's seven years older than me but has always been like a big brother to me. When I was eleven, he suggested I transition to Brazilian jiu-jitsu since that was his passion. He's a tattoo artist and owns a shop about an hour from here, but he also does amateur MMA."

"Wait, your cousin is Wolf fucking McCleery?" The guy is built like a fucking tree and is known as much for his talent behind his machine as he is for his talent in the cage.

Motherfucker. Her vicious personality is starting to make more sense; our kid is going to be a goddamn tiny tyrant.

"Yeah, you've heard of him?"

Have I heard of him? Approaching my house, I pull my car into the driveway and park behind Linc's cherry-red monstrosity. Putting the car in park, I turn and look at her. "Heard of him? Red, he's fucking famous. I think his books have been closed for two years. I tried to get an appointment for a sternum piece, but they wanted to push me out until 2025."

She looks at me quizzically. "You don't have a sternum tattoo."

"I fucking know because I'm not getting that shit until your cousin does it in 2025. I already booked him. He better not break his hand in the fucking cage. How does he tattoo and fight?"

She shrugs. "He's a smart fighter, but he's slowed down on

143

his fight schedule; he's focusing more on his tattoo career now. I wouldn't be surprised if he stopped fighting competitively soon." Fuck, that would suck. He's a maniac in the cage.

She barely spares me a glance before opening her car door and getting out of the car.

Getting out quickly, I meet her in front of the hood of the car and match her minuscule strides. For a vertically challenged person, she walks fucking fast. "Why are you speed walking?"

"Keep up," is all she says before walking up the front steps and opening the front door. As soon as we get over the threshold, a fucking tornado of brown hair slams into Celeste, jolting her body back to mine. I steady her and the fucking calamity that is Ava. I want to tell her to be careful, but I don't want to call attention to Red's fragility.

She'd fucking kill me if she knew I thought of her as fragile.

"Oh my God, why does it feel like it's been so long since I've seen you?" Ava practically cries.

"Aves, calm the fuck down. You're suffocating me," Red replies, patting Ava on the back. "Also, I think Greyson is about to kill me, so maybe stop with the affection."

Ava releases her and turns to Grey, glaring at him. "Greyson Jansen, get the fuck over yourself. She is my best friend, and I am allowed to freaking hug her." Ava raises her hands to her hips and cocks her leg. Between the stern expression on her face and her pose, she looks like my fucking grandmother.

"Calm your tits, Aves. You know I don't do hugs. Besides, are you even allowed to be touching people with the whole hack job?"

"Pit bull, what the fuck did you just say?"

"Watch how you fucking talk to her," I growl, pissed that Grey would speak to Red with a goddamn attitude. Not only

144

is she Ava's best friend and has always had her best fucking interest, but she's my woman. No one speaks to her like that. I don't give a shit who he is.

"Okay, let's all take a deep breath and get the sticks out of our asses."

"I wouldn't mind putting a stick up your ass, vixen."

"Greyson," Ava hisses.

"This is progressing interestingly. Anyway," Red says with an eye roll, "I just meant, don't you need to be careful? I don't want to pull on your stitches or cause any damage. And you." She points to Greyson. "If you continue to call me a pit bull—which, great job perpetuating stereotypes, dickwad—I'll act like a rabid dog. So, unless you want me to permanently maim you, calm down with that."

"Fucking pit bull," Grey murmurs.

"You just don't learn, do you?" Ava says in exasperation before grabbing Celeste's hand and leading her through the house. "Thank God you're here. If I had to deal with Grey or Lincoln for another minute by myself, I was going to shoot myself with a BB gun in my fucking foot. Serena will be here in a few..." Ava's voice trails off as they round the corner and head to the media room.

I stare after them as they walk away, appreciating the subtle swing of Red's hips as she disappears.

"God, you're so fucked."

I turn to look at Grey. "Like you're one to fucking talk. You're keeping Ava as a goddamn hostage here."

He shrugs. "Her parents agree that it's easier for her to stay here since the primary is on the first floor."

I let out a sardonic laugh. "Don't bullshit me. They meant that temporarily, not permanently. But let me tell you now,"

145

I pause, leveling him with a stare, "you treat my woman, the mother of my fucking child, with some fucking respect. Call her a pit bull one more time, or treat her like the fucking dirt on the bottom of your shoe again, and I'll make sure that Ava's family knows all about you playing house with their daughter."

Grey's silent for a beat, staring at me before smirking. "Daddy Dante, huh? Didn't think I'd see that this soon." Fucking hell. Red is going to kill me.

"Shut the fuck up. Don't fucking say anything."

"You expect me not to tell my fucking woman? You just gave me shit about protecting yours."

"I expect you to be my friend and let me and Red tell people when we're goddamn ready. Do this for me, Grey." I don't let my final words hang as a question; I issue them as a statement, not giving him any option to deny me.

"Fine, but she better tell her fucking soon. I won't keep secrets, D. Not even for you."

"Fuck off, you prick."

—

CeCe:

"Okay, my little gingersnap, I have a shit ton of questions, and you owe me a hell of a lot of answers," Ava announces as soon as we're behind closed doors and away from Dante and Greyson.

"Gingersnap?"

"Like a ginger, except a cookie."

"Aves, you realize gingersnap cookies are brown, right?" Shouldn't she know this?

"It just came out, go with it. So, do I need to wait for Serena, or shall I begin the cross-examination now?" I feel my body start to heat, and I close my eyes, willing my tell-tale flush to

146

dissipate and not give me away.

"Stop talking like a lawyer, you freak. And there's not much to tell," I respond, praying that Ava doesn't question why Dante and I were together today. I'm not ready to tell her about the baby yet. I know I need to do it soon before I start showing and will no longer be able to hide it. Just not yet.

"Your pants are burning, fire crotch. Don't pretend you didn't roll up to the house with him in his bright-ass car." Roll up? When did Ava become a hip-hop mogul from 2007?

I'm about to respond to her when suddenly, she collapses like a rag doll, a heap of limbs and hair on the floor.

I stare at her in confusion until I see her ankle twisted at an odd angle. God help me, but she fell on air while stationary. How does this happen?

"For the love of God, Aves. Did you just fall over the air while not moving? How the fuck do you even do these things?"

"Ow, shit. I don't know. Jesus, I think I pulled my stitches."

"Damnit, Aves. Greyson is going to yell at me again."

"I'll shove a carrot up his ass." A disturbing visual, for sure.

"Just get up, you freak, so I can take a look at your sutures and make sure there's no obvious bleeding." A part of me expects her to impersonate the commercials that feature people calling out, "Help, I've fallen and can't get up." But thankfully, for my sanity, she gets up slowly and silently.

Lifting her shirt and lowering her leggings, Ava shows me the sutures that travel from her pubic bone up to her stomach. The stitching is almost healed, in addition to being neat and precise, but there's no doubt it will scar. Observing the incision and skin surrounding it, I don't see any obvious irritation or cause for concern, though I'm not a medical professional and was just raised by them.

147

"It looks fine, but maybe call your doctor for an appointment, though."

"And scare them with my scar and my lumps more than I already do?"

"Ava Maria, shut your beautiful, annoying mouth." I hate it when she does this; self-deprecation comes second nature to her, and it takes everything in me not to shake sense into her. Since being with Greyson, she's gotten better at not being the punchline of her own jokes or looking at herself with disgust, but it's still there like a nagging virus that won't go away.

"What? I'm just saying—"

"No, shut up," I cut her off. "If I hear you bad mouth yourself one more time, I'm telling Greyson, and he's going to spank you."

The gleam that enters her eye makes me want to throw up. Dante mentioned Greyson and Ava like spankings, but the look on my best friend's face confirms it. Add that to the list of things I did not need to know.

"Will you two ever be calm and not like verbal cage fighters?" Ava immediately drops her shirt, and I turn my head at the sound of Serena's voice.

As soon as I spot her pretty, tanned face and smell her floral perfume, my stomach lurches, and I feel bile start to climb up my throat.

Fucking hell. The morning sickness—which is a fucking misnomer because it hits you all day, at any freaking time— had improved recently. Swallowing down the acid in my throat, I frantically reach into my pocket for a ginger candy, opening the wrapper and popping it in like my life depends on it. Thank God for my emergency stash.

Ava and Serena just stare at me, confusion clear on their

faces. I suck on the spiced candy, letting the hard sugar settle my stomach slightly before I offer some bullshit explanation.

"Sorry, I'm starving and just remembered I had this ginger candy in my pocket." My stomach is still churning, the nausea climbing from a mixture of pregnancy and nerves.

"That's weird," Ava says slowly, eying me like she doesn't believe me. I wouldn't believe me either. She continues, "Serena, I'm glad you're here. I was just about to call Celeste to the witness stand to discuss her arrival with Dante."

I groan around the candy. "Ava, seriously, you are not a lawyer." I bite a portion of the candy off and chew, buying myself a little more time. "But yes, Dante and I came together. We've become... friends," I offer.

"I didn't realize friends gave each other hickeys and bite marks. Serena, did you know that?"

Serena laughs, stuttering out, "N-no."

Fucking Dante.

"Just admit you like him, C. Why are you resisting this? It's exciting, we're dating friends."

Dating, procreating. Same thing.

Ava starts to open her mouth, but Serena interrupts, "Ava, she'll tell us when she's ready. You remember what it's like to speak about things before you're comfortable, don't you?" She levels her with a stare. With her words, Serena brings the last two months crashing down around us: the texts, the threats, the turmoil. The memory of Ava lying in a hospital bed joins us in the media room like an unwelcome guest.

"God, I hate it when you're all rational and nice." Ava lets out a dramatic sigh. "But fine. I'll wait until you're ready. But don't wait too long, or I'm going to have Bianca drive up here." I shiver at the thought of Ava's youngest sister, Bianca, coming to Marymount University. Though she's the most reckless of the Gregori siblings, Bianca is a human lie detector and can smell deception like a bloodhound.

I look at Serena and offer her a grateful smile that soon turns into a grimace at Ava's words. "If we can't talk about CeCe, then we need to discuss you and Dylan."

I'm sorry, I mouth. If I were a better person, I would divert the conversation back to me. As it stands, I let Serena take center stage. I look over at Ava and see the look in her eyes; she knows something.

"It's less about Dylan and more about Devin," Serena whispers, almost like she's afraid to give voice to her situation. "We were together last weekend."

My eyebrows raise. "Devin, as in the she-devil's Devin?" Serena's former neighbor, Devin, had some sort of sex thing going on with her stepsister, Marina. "And what do you mean, 'together?'"

She clears her throat. "People don't belong to other people; this isn't *Breakfast at Tiffany's.* But we slept together."

"Famous last words, Serena. And to clarify, you mean fucked?" Ava asks.

Serena's cheeks redden, and she provides a small nod.

"Holy shit. How did that happen?" Ava's eyes are wide with shock, and my expression must resemble hers. It seems we all have secrets worth keeping.

"I went to Dad's house over the weekend; he called my mom and threatened to take her to court for our house since she needed him to cosign the mortgage when they got divorced. Anyway, he told her that if I didn't start coming over at least once a month, he would make her life hell. Well, more of a hell than it already is." She lets out a breath. "Marina was at the sorority house, so I didn't have to deal with her, thank God. But I spent pretty much the entire weekend in the guest house in the back of the property. I'm not sure why my dad even bothered since he ignored me from the moment I got there. Apparently, a client was supposed to come over for dinner, but they canceled at the last minute."

"Okay, but how does Devin factor into this?"

"He was at his family's house last weekend, as well. When he's home, he stays in the guest house in the back of his property, too. He and Marina ended their relationship a few weeks ago, and he saw me bringing my bags in on Friday afternoon. He came over on Saturday." Her blush deepens, embarrassment evident on her face.

I grab Serena's hand, squeezing it until she meets my gaze. "Serena, I need to ask. Did he take advantage of you or make you do anything you didn't want to do?"

Her eyes widen, and her face loses all color, growing pale at my question. She shakes her head. "Oh, no. it was consensual. It wasn't great, slightly awkward, but he didn't coerce or force me into anything."

"Did you come?" Ava asks, and I shoot her a *What the fuck?* look. She just shrugs as though this is a normal question.

"I don't think so. It was... nice. Pleasant."

"Serena, trust me, you would know if you had an orgasm," I say.

"And how would you know that, my chastity-belted friend?"

"Ava, drop the act. I know Dante told Greyson he spent the night in our dorm room. We weren't playing Battleship."

"Anyway," Serena says, dragging out the word. "Dylan isn't happy with me. He said I betrayed him and his trust. He brought me here today but has barely spoken to me since I

151

told him earlier this week."

"Is this prick fucking shaming you? Because I'll wipe the floor with him if he makes you feel an ounce of guilt for being an eighteen-year-old." There's nothing worse than a double standard. Fucking nothing.

The threat slips out, even though I can't act on it for the next seven or so months. I press a palm to my stomach, feeling a rush of protectiveness. If anyone tries to slut shame my child, like Dylan is doing with Serena, I'll end them.

"I don't think it's a slut-shaming thing. I think it's because Devin is his friend, too. They're competitive, and I should have known better. Plus, unless it's convenient for Devin, he won't keep a secret. I'm pretty sure the entire fraternity knows by now. Marina probably does, too."

I stare at Serena, noting that while her cheeks are still red, her voice is calm and even. "Why don't you seem more upset about this?"

"I guess because I'm not ashamed. If I learned anything from Ava's situation"—she pauses to glance at our clumsy friend—"it's that I shouldn't be embarrassed by sex and intimacy. Pissing off Marina is just an added bonus."

"Does Dylan have feelings for you?" I ask.

"Truthfully, I don't think so. We hooked up a few weeks ago—"

"What!" Ava shouts, the force of her yell nearly toppling her over. I steady her with a hand on her shoulder.

"Lower your damn voice, Ava Maria. And Serena, when did this happen?"

"Right before Felicity attacked Ava. I was going to tell you guys, but with everything going on, I just didn't think it was a good time to bring it up." She twists her hands, worry etched on her beautiful, angular face.

"Serena, you can always come to us. You don't need to feel alone, especially if you're going through a crisis—boy or otherwise. Was the hook-up bad?"

"It felt like I was kissing my brother. Devin wasn't much better. Maybe I'm defective? What if my brain is the only part of my body that can be stimulated?"

"No. I reject that," Ava says. "It just means that your first two experiences weren't satisfying. It doesn't mean you'll never be satisfied. You're eighteen; you have time to figure it out."

"Both of you figured it out on the first try," Serena comments wryly.

I blanch while Ava lets out a light laugh and says, "We did, didn't we? But Rena, they're not the guys for you. You tried it, they suck. It's not your fault Devin apparently didn't know the location of a clitoris or the need to stimulate it."

Before Ava can delve into more discussion on the female anatomy, the door to the media room opens, and Dante, Greyson, Lincoln, and Dylan walk in. With them, they carry snacks and a tray of drinks in red plastic cups. I notice that Dante is holding two cups separate from the tray.

Walking over to me, he places a kiss on my forehead and a drink in my hand. "It's just ginger ale," he whispers into the side of my head.

"Thanks," I say in a low voice.

"Ava, what the fuck kind of popcorn is this?" Lincoln bellows.

"Here we fucking go again," Dante murmurs as the doorbell rings.

And then, all hell breaks loose.

16

Dante

I'm getting ready to watch Ava and Linc fucking battle about popcorn when the doorbell rings. I look to Grey, but he has a scowl on his face as he looks toward the front of the house. I look to Lincoln, who's momentarily forgotten his stupid-ass issue with microwave popcorn, and he seems just as confused.

"Who the fuck else is coming?" I ask, not expecting an answer. Striding out of the room, I head to the front door and throw it open. On the other side, looking like a fucking douchebag is Devin Grimes. "What the fuck are you doing here?"

"Where is she?"

Despite Red's unpopular opinion, I'm not a fucking moron. I know he's here for Serena; I just don't know why. "Who?"

He narrows his eyes. "Where the fuck is that little bitch, Serena?"

"What the fuck did you just say?" I may not know her well, but Serena doesn't deserve to be spoken about this way. Hell, no fucking woman does. I approach him, walking forward until he steps off the front steps. "Get the fuck off our property, dickface."

With speed I don't anticipate, Devin rushes forward, crashing into me and sending us both to the ground. I let out a grunt as my body collides with the hardwood. Twisting my body, I throw Devin off of me and straddle his torso, landing a punch to the side of his face before he elbows me in the gut.

"You fucking asshole," I grunt, jabbing him in the nose and throwing an uppercut in quick succession. My jab connects, but he moves his head, and my uppercut punches the air.

"Get the fuck off me," Devin grinds out from below me, blood and sweat mingling on his face like a fucked-up Halloween mask. He throws a fist as he says it, but I catch it before it connects with my jaw.

"Calm the fuck down, and I will. We have women here, and you're going to fucking terrify them." My mind immediately goes to Red. She could probably take this asshole, but I'd fucking kill him if he laid a single hand on her.

"I fucking knew she was here." Devin twists out of my hold, kneeing me in the balls like a little shit. "Serena! Serena, get your fucking ass out here, you fucking cunt!"

A stampede of footsteps sounds from down the hall, and I stand up in time to catch Devin by the waist and throw him against the wall before he has a chance to make it past the foyer and down the hallway. Throwing my arm up, I pin him by his skinny-ass neck with my forearm while the entrance fills.

"What the fuck is going on?" Linc asks, taking in Devin's restrained body and the blood pouring from his nose and temple.

"What the fuck did you do, you fucking slut?" Devin spits out, nearly choking on the blood pooling around his mouth.

His murderous gaze is settled on Serena, and she shrinks, stepping back into Dylan's body. Dylan doesn't raise his hands to protect Serena or shield her; he doesn't even open his fucking mouth to tell Devin to back the fuck off. If someone were coming after Red the way Devin's coming after Serena, I'd put them in a fucking body bag and send them down the Delaware Water Gap.

My dad may not have been active in the mafia when I was born, but I know shit.

Dylan just stands there like a useless waste of fucking space, letting Serena get screamed at by a man double her size. I press on his windpipe, cutting off his annoying-as-fuck tirade.

Greyson and Linc step forward, blocking Serena from Devin's view. I glance over at Celeste, taking in the fury on her face and the scowl on her lips. Like a beautiful Valkyrie, she's ready to fly into battle. I level her with a look that says, *Get involved, and I will lock you in my room until you give birth.* She rolls her eyes.

Fucking hellion.

I return my attention back to Devin as Grey speaks from behind me. "You have one chance, Grimes, before I let Dante lay you the fuck out for coming into my house like a fucking animal. What the fuck are you doing here?"

Devin pushes at my hold.

"Dante, for fuck's sake, don't kill him. Let him talk." With a scowl, I move my forearm from his neck to his chest. He spits out some of the blood pooling in his mouth.

"That cunt told Marina that we fucked. She fucking ruined everything because she's a jealous little bitch."

"I didn't say anything," Serena says in a frantic voice. Her body is still blocked by Linc and Grey, but from my angle, I can see the rapid shake of her head.

"Then how the fuck does she know?" he roars, pushing forward and trying to break my hold on him.

"I d-don't know. I would never say anything. You know that," Serena says, her voice breaking.

"She didn't say anything, I did." We all whip our heads to Dylan, who steps out from behind the shield Serena provided. "Your girlfriend deserved to know that you fuck around behind her back. You were telling all the guys in TP anyway, so it was only a matter of fucking time."

Serena's face crumbles, betrayal stamped on her features like a mask. "Dylan?"

He turns to face her, his brown hair sticking out haphazardly from jabbing his fingers through it. "How fucking could you?"

"W-what are you talking about?"

"You fucked him after we hooked up? You're a fucking whore, just like he said you'd be once you got a taste of dick."

"That's fucking enough," Linc growls. "Both of you, get the fuck out of our house."

"Yeah, I see you guys like fucking sluts. You're probably passing them around like the little cum-whores they are." Before any of us can react, Red walks up to Dylan, calm as fuck, and uses her right hand to shove his head back by his forehead. He's got a foot on her and should easily be able to stop her, but with a speed and agility none of us anticipate, she uses her left hand to hit his throat with an open palm. Simultaneously, she hooks her right leg around his foot and moves the hand from Dylan's forehead to his knee, pushing him backward until he crumbles like a fucking house.

Lifting her leg, she aims it over his dick. "Give me one reason why I shouldn't crush your balls for speaking to Serena like

157

that." I'm going to fucking kill her. I release Devin and stride over to Red, grabbing her small body and putting her behind me.

"Fuck you, you fucking bitch," he wheezes, struggling to speak after she fucking attacked his windpipe. I'm about to stomp his face in when Ava calls out from the other side of the room.

"You suck at kissing. And you," she says, turning to Devin, who's now slumped against the wall. "You're a selfish lover."

"Vixen," Grey grinds out. "Not fucking helping."

"Aves, stop talking," I growl. "Get the fuck out of this house, both of you." I have no fucking idea if it's because Red just proved she's a fucking assassin or because Devin has blood drenching his shirt and the floor, but they glare at us as they walk out to Serena's quiet sobs.

"Shh, it's okay," I hear behind me and turn to see Red and Ava embrace Serena.

"I honestly didn't think CeCe could back up her claims of killing someone. I'm fucking terrified but also intrigued," Lincoln says in a low voice to me and Grey.

"Fuck off and stay away from my woman."

"Don't be a dick, you know I'm not interested in her. What the fuck are we going to do about Devin and Dylan?"

"Kill them," Grey offers, and I glance at his serious face. The fucker isn't joking.

"No, we're going to ask Serena what she wants." I haven't been to the TP house since the night we met Celeste and Ava, but I'd gladly go to show our "brothers" how not to be assholes and talk about women after they fucked them. Not all the guys are bad; some of them are cool as fuck. Then again, Dylan was one of our closest friends until he proved to be Benedict Arnold to Serena.

I've done some shitty things in my life, but my father would roll over in his fucking grave if I ever disrespected a woman by detailing our fuck, or how she fucked someone else.

I walk over to the girls and pull Red into my body, wrapping my arms around her. My heart was in my fucking throat when I saw her lay Dylan out, and I need the reassurance that she is okay. The moment I'm able to, I'm dragging her back to my room to make sure she never pulls a stunt like that again.

"Serena, are you okay?" I ask. She's shaking and crying, so probably fucking not.

"I just want to go home," she murmurs, dropping her head so that she doesn't meet our eyes.

"I don't think that's a safe option right now. They both know where your apartment is. Why don't you stay here? Or in my dorm with me?" Red offers, and I growl. She's not fucking leaving this house.

"What is it with all the guys in this house growling?" Ava mutters to herself.

"I-I am going to go home. To my mom's house. I can't be here. H-he was my best friend. Why would he do this?" Serena says through tears, barely getting her words out. "I-I'm going to call an Uber."

"No! Grey and I will drive you."

Before Ava finishes getting the words out, Serena is shaking her head. "No, I can't ask that of you."

"You didn't ask, but we're forcing the issue. You're in no condition to be by yourself with a stranger right now," Red says. "Ava and Grey will take you to your mom's. Do you need to pack a bag back at your apartment?" At Serena's head shake, she continues, "Okay. Ava, get Greyson. Serena? This is not your fault. Do you understand?"

Serena doesn't respond, just sniffles into her chest. "They are both fuckheads that can't tell a clit from an elbow. Did you see how quickly Dylan went down? Fucking pansy. He can't even defend himself against a five-foot woman."

"You were like *Buffy the Vampire Slayer*, Celeste. I don't think he expected it," my voice is low, huskier than it should be given the situation and how Red inserted herself into violence. "Now, say goodbye to Serena while she gets ready to leave. I need to speak with you."

She raises an eyebrow and crosses her little arms. It takes fucking everything in me not to throw her over my shoulder and restrain her in my room. The only thing keeping me from doing so is the knowledge that that position and the pressure on her stomach are not good for the baby.

"Red, you don't want to fucking question me right now. Get your perky ass in my room before I pick you up and carry you there."

With an answering scowl, she turns and walks down the hall, up the stairs, and to my room.

—

"Fucking Christ, Red," I explode as soon as I close the door behind me. She sits like a queen on my bed, looking at me with a bored expression. "What the hell were you thinking getting involved? We fucking spoke about this. I asked you"—I pause to glare at her—"fucking begged you not to do your jiu-jitsu shit while you were pregnant, and what do you do? You acted like a fucking hired killer in the foyer."

She just stares, a blank expression on her face.

"Are you going to fucking answer me? Why the fuck would you do that?"

"Are you done?" she asks. I grit my teeth and nod, letting her know my tirade is finished. "You have some nerve, Dante Nicholas Camaro. We walked into that hallway, and you were covered—*covered*—in blood and trading punches. Do you think I liked seeing that? At least I had the common sense not to get punched while I incapacitated him."

Her reasoning has me seeing fucking red. "Celeste, your rationale that at least you didn't get hit is bullshit. You intentionally put yourself in danger—our fucking child in danger—to what? Prove that you're tough and know how to fight or can back up all those murderous threats you throw out?" I shake my head, walking over to my desk chair and gripping the back to stop me from wringing her neck. "We get it, you're a fucking fighter. Now think of someone other than your fucking self and keep our child safe." My breathing is labored, and my blood pressure must be through the fucking roof.

"I *was* thinking of someone other than myself, you asshole. I was thinking about Serena and the fact that two grown-ass men were attacking her for being a normal, eighteen-year-old girl. They were crucifying her for having sex, and I was not going to stand by and let that fucking happen."

"But why can't you trust me to take care of it? Why does it need to be you? Why do you need to be the fucking hero, Celeste?"

"Because he wouldn't stop, and no one was putting an end to his bullshit, so I did."

"I was trying to put an end to it, Celeste. Do you think I woke up today wanting to get into a fucking fight in the foyer? I swear to God, I'd love nothing more than to take you over my knee and paddle your ass, but I don't want to hurt you." The

161

moment she gives birth and is cleared for sexual activities, I'm going to tie her to my fucking bedpost and edge her for twenty-four hours.

"Calm down. Nothing happened, and I'm fine. I told you, and the doctor told you, that modified workouts are fine."

"Laying a man out on his goddamn back is not a modified workout, Red."

She shrugs, still unbothered by my anger. "He didn't touch me so..." she lets her sentence trail off as though it doesn't deserve an end.

Fuck that, and fuck her attitude about this.

"Undress, now."

Her face jerks back in surprise. "Excuse me?"

"Celeste, I'm this fucking close to handcuffing you to me and not letting you out of my goddamn sight. So, do us both a fucking favor, and listen to me." Her eyes widen at my words, and she makes quick work of tugging off her leggings, sweatshirt, and T-shirt. She shifts to lay back on the pillows against my headboard, waiting for my next command.

"Thank fucking Christ, your stubborn ass listened for once." I release my hold on the chair and walk toward the bed. As I walk, I take off my clothes until I'm in nothing except for my briefs. My cock is about to punch a fucking hole in them, so they're useless as shit.

"Red, I need to remind you of who you fucking belong to and why you need to be careful. If it gets to be too much, say 'stop.' We're not fucking around with safe words, or hand signals, or some other shit. You say 'no' or 'stop' and it's over. You understand?"

She nods her head in agreement. Good enough.

"I'm going to be gentle, and I won't do anything you won't

like or anything that will put the baby at risk. But I need to show you how fucking important your body is right now and why you need to not take goddamn risks with your safety. Now, turn on your side and face the wall," I instruct, having her adjust her position so that her face is directed toward my wall. Opening the nightstand next to my bed, I pull out a container of body oil and place it on the bed. "Move your hair over your shoulder." She follows my command and gathers her wild mane of hair, draping it over her shoulder.

Uncapping the oil, I squeeze some on my hand before placing the bottle on the bedside table. Rubbing my hands together to warm the oil, the smells of lavender and rosemary fill the room.

"God, that smells so good," she practically moans. She starts to turn her head to look back at me, but I stop her with my oiled hands on her back.

"Face forward. And keep your fucking hands to yourself." I run my hands up to her shoulders, pressing my thumbs into her neck and fanning them into her skin. Dragging my hands down either side of her spine, I alternate the pressure of my thumbs, loosening the tight muscles of her back.

Once I reach the base of her spine, I change from the fanning pressure to shorter, circular strokes. Focusing on her right side first, I use the oil on my hands to lightly knead from her waist to her shoulders, alternating sides every few minutes.

Red lets out a sigh under my ministrations, and I feel her muscles relax, her posture unwinding from the rigid position it's always in.

"Lay on your back," I order. Like a blissed-out zombie, she complies. "Good girl." I grab the oil and pour more onto my hands before straddling her legs, making sure to keep myself from applying any pressure or weight on her body. Once the oil is warmed in my palms, I start at her neck and travel to her perky, full tits. Red is small—petite and compact—but has the most gorgeous pair of fucking tits. Light freckles dot her chest, and I use my fingers to massage over them.

"Is this really supposed to be a punishment? Why are you so good at this?" she moans beneath me.

"Porn." She laughs like I'm joking, but I'm not. I'm not going to tell her that my porn viewing history is filled with Nuru massages, in addition to pregnant and lactating women. I was ambivalent toward pregnant women until Celeste told me that she was carrying my child. Now? It's hot as fuck to watch a woman with a large belly or tits filled with milk ride her man's cock. My dick gets harder at the thought of Red's stomach growing.

Coasting my palms over her tits, I use my fingers to rub oil into her nipples, teasing her until they're erect against my hand. Leaning down, I blow, eliciting a shiver from her that I feel in my fucking balls.

"You have the prettiest fucking tits, baby," I say, still blowing on her. Her chest rises, causing one nipple to brush against my lips. She lets out a moan at the contact.

"You want me to suck these nipples, Red? You need some relief?" She nods her head, pushing her chest up once again. I chuckle and lean back, placing more distance between us. "Too bad. You didn't listen to what I want, and now you don't get what you want." She lets out a whimper, and it's fucking music.

I'm not sure who I'm punishing, her or me, because oiled up, with her hair draped over one side of my pillow, she looks like a fucking goddess. My mouth is watering for a taste of her tits, but I have more control than that.

Pinching her nipples one last time, I move my hands down her rib cage and to her stomach. Her abdomen is still flat, though it's lost some of the definition that it usually has. Outlining the slight curve of her waist and the flare of her hips, I bring my hands back to her stomach and gently massage oil into her skin.

"It's safe for pregnancy," I tell her. After she told me she was pregnant, I Googled "shit pregnant women need," and one of the things that kept coming up was body oil to prevent stretch marks. I ordered a box of this organic shit for her.

Reaching over, I pour more oil into my hands and move further down her legs. Tracing a path from her stomach to her hip bones, I let my thumbs trail over her inner thighs as I work my fingers up and down. She presses her pelvis up when I reach the crevice between her thighs and pubic bone.

Wanting to fuck with her, I let my hands coast to her inner thighs, and my fingertips brush over her wet cunt before pulling away.

"Dante," she whimpers as she tries to spread her legs beneath mine. She huffs in frustration when she realizes I'm not letting her take control; her pretty legs are staying pinned beneath me. "Please," she murmurs, almost incoherently.

I rub another drop of oil from her pussy to her outer thighs before reaching around and grabbing her ass, rubbing the oil into her in hard circular movements.

"Please, what, baby?" I don't bother hiding the smirk from my face.

"You know what." Even though she's pinned beneath me and at my mercy, she's still a little fucking brat.

"Red, I told you, you're not getting what you want." Swinging my leg over her body, I stand and survey her. Her skin is flushed and oily from my massage, and her chest is heaving. She looks like a fucking wood nymph from that animated *Hercules* movie my sister used to make me watch.

Wiping my hands on my boxers, I pull them down until my cock is hitting my stomach. Her eyes widen, and her mouth drops open like she's hungry for my dick. She's seen me naked before, has had my cock buried so deep in her wet cunt that she could barely walk afterward. But with her shining, reddened skin and her expression, it's like she's seeing me for the first time.

Maybe she is. Maybe she's realizing after meeting my mom and seeing how fucking feral I became after she put herself in a dangerous situation that I'm not fucking around.

Or maybe she's just fucking horny. Google said pregnant women want to fuck all the time.

"Red, you're going to suck my cock like the little slut you are—*my* little slut—and I'm going to come down your throat. Any issues with that?" She shakes her head. "Good. If you're a good girl, I'll take care of you. If not, I'll spank your pussy until you're on the verge of coming and leave you to ride the fucking pillow."

Going to the foot of the bed, I grab her ankles and drag her down until she's flat on her back and not resting against my pillows. She starts to shift, presumably to get on her knees, but I stop her with a squeeze to her ankle. "You're too special to get on your knees, baby. Just relax." I'm pissed at her but won't compromise her comfort or her worth unless it means spanking her ass until she fucking listens to me.

I get back on the bed and climb up her body until I'm straddling her chest, and my cock is dripping pre-cum on

166

her face. In my position, her arms are braced by my legs, and she can't move them.

"Suck, Red. Show me how bad you want my cum." She opens her mouth, and I lean forward and grab onto the headboard, feeding her my cock. I'm not a sadist and pierced like Grey, but I'm thick and long, and my little hellion gags as she takes my dick. "Relax your throat." I pull back, giving her air before I push forward again in a shallow thrust. I keep the pace slow, letting her adjust to the feel of my cock in her mouth and my balls slapping against her chin.

I pull back my hips and get the surprise of my fucking life when she follows me with her mouth, refusing to let go as she pulls me in deeper. "Fuck baby, you're starving for my cock, aren't you?" She hums around me and uses her tongue to rub the underside of my dick. Red's the least compliant and docile woman I know, but with my cock in her mouth, she's a fuck doll just waiting to be used.

"I'm going to fuck this mouth, Red. Blink twice if you don't want it." I stare at her face, watching as her eyes grow wide, and she moves her head to suck me in deeper. My little hellion, causing mayhem with everything she fucking does. "My good little slut. This mouth is like a fucking vacuum."

Shifting my weight, I rise on the balls of my feet and brace myself over her. Her eyes track my movements as I thrust forward and feed her my entire length. She gags around me, and her eyes water; she's never looked more fucking beautiful.

"Relax your throat and tilt your head back. Fuck, yes. Just like that. Goddamn," I mutter, flexing my hips into her face as she chokes on me. I feel my balls tighten as she opens wide, and wet noises fall from her mouth. "I'm going to come baby. Swallow every fucking drop." She moans and closes her

167

mouth, sealing her lips around my cock as I pump my cum down her throat.

"Fuck," I groan, stilling as she swallows around me. I catch my breath, watching a stray drop of cum fall from her mouth. With her arms no longer bound by my legs, she reaches up and runs a finger over my cum, capturing it and bringing it to her lips. Sucking on her finger, she looks me in the eye and raises one perfectly winged eyebrow.

"Delicious," she murmurs.

"My little fucking slut." I shift down from my position over her and settle beside her. Hauling her into my arms, I take her mouth in a hungry, wet kiss. She tastes like me, and fuck if I don't love it. I curl my tongue around hers and pull her closer, deepening the kiss until she's panting beside me.

"Dante," she says against my lips. I pull back, seeing the need in her eyes.

"You need something?" I lean back in, stealing her lips before breaking the kiss. "You want my mouth or my cock, Red?" I'm hard again, though it's no surprise; every time she's near me, I'm a fucking tent pole.

"Your mouth, then your cock."

"Greedy, Red. So fucking greedy." I push on her shoulder until she's lying flat on the bed again. Standing up from the bed, I grab her legs and drag her down until her ass is at the edge, with her legs hanging off. Grabbing a pillow, I place it on the ground before dropping to my knees and draping her legs over my shoulders. I'm at eye level with her pussy, and it's fucking drenched, weeping for me like it's begging to take my cock.

I blow on her cunt, chuckling to myself when she shivers beneath my hold. "You were a good girl. You took my cock like a fucking porn star."

"You're not the only one that watches porn," she says breathlessly as I swipe my tongue up her seam. I suck her clit and hum into her, working my teeth lightly over the nerves until her hips are pumping into my face.

Releasing her clit, I flatten my tongue against her cunt and lick into her before suctioning my mouth and fucking feasting.

"Holy shit," she moans, pressing her core further into my mouth. I pull her closer to me, widening my jaw until I'm fucking latched onto her pussy, swallowing the wetness pouring out of her like a fucking waterfall. I could use my fingers to get her there faster, but I'm a determined man, and right now, I want her to lose her mind on my goddamn tongue.

Pointing my tongue, I use it to fuck her tight cunt until she breaks and comes all over my face. I clean her up with my mouth, catching all her wetness before I stand up and grab her by the back of the neck. I capture her mouth and smear her cum all over her lips and face, loving the way our shared releases taste: like she's mine, and I'm hers.

"Move up the bed and get on your side again, Red," I command, desperate for my cock to finally slide into her pussy. We fucked three hours ago, but I'm insatiable for her.

She gets in position at the head of my bed, and I follow quickly, not taking a moment to appreciate how fucking good she looks because my cock is about to erupt. Moving behind her, I grab her left leg and drape it over me, opening her up until I'm sliding inside her.

"Fuck," I grind out, dropping my head forward and burrowing it into her neck. Panting against her skin, I work my cock in and out of her. This position has me deep, and I can feel her tremble against me. I run a hand around her body and start thrumming her clit while my other hand is around her neck and playing with her tits.

In this position, she can't move without me allowing it. I love controlling her and crave the moments like this, where she's pliant and gives in to me.

"Dante, I'm close," she moans. I slow my hips but increase the pressure on her clit, giving her what she needs to come.

"Come for me, Red," I say against her skin, sucking on her neck as I hold back my release. I pinch her clit, and she explodes, letting out breathless whimpers. I follow her, coming inside her tight pussy and holding myself there for long minutes as we catch our breaths. Pulling out, I kiss her spine and stand up. I look at her in my bed—oiled, flushed, and filled with my cum. If I were a lesser man, I'd get my phone and take a picture of Red like this, soft and satiated.

After everything that happened with Ava, I won't risk it. But I fucking wish I could, just to remind myself of what she looks like when she's peaceful and not being a pain in my ass.

I lean down and grab her in a bridal hold, bringing her into the bathroom and turning the water on hot. I'd love for her to sleep with my cum in her cunt, but Google also said peeing and cleaning up after sex is important, especially for pregnant women. We didn't take care of her after we fucked in my car, so she needs to shower, even though I don't like it.

"Pee," I command.

She looks at me with a startled expression. "What?"

"You need to pee. I read it online."

"Let me guess, you consulted either Doctor Google or WebMD?"

I clear my throat. "Perhaps," I say sheepishly.

She nods, like she's confirming her assumption. "Right.

170

Well, I do need to pee, but you need to get out of the bathroom for that to happen."

"But—" I start, only to be cut off by my little tornado.

"But nothing. I am not peeing in front of you."

"I'll pee in front of you, too, if that makes you more comfortable."

"I don't want you to pee in front of me."

"Prude," I mumble under my breath as I leave the bathroom. I wait for the sounds of the toilet flush and the faucet turning on before I open the door and head back in. She glares at me, but I shrug, grabbing her hand and moving her forward until we're at the glass shower door. Opening the door, I step in first, testing the temperature before helping her step in carefully.

I move her body under the stream of water and grab the lavender body wash from my shelf. When I was in her dorm last week, her caddy was on display, and I saw that all of her shit was the same high-end brand of products. As soon as I left, I stopped at the store and got everything I could remember.

"You have my body wash?" she asks as soon as I open the lid of the bottle. I won't mention that it's half full because I used it to jerk off.

"Yep," I supply. Grabbing a loofa, I pour some of the body wash out and massage it until suds form. Gingerly, I wash her body, careful to leave her hair out of the spray of the water.

It's a quick, utilitarian shower with no elicit touching or heated glances. It's efficient as fuck, but also nice. I feel like a couple; the domestic act of showering makes me feel more solid in our relationship.

Turning off the water, I open the glass door to grab towels and quickly dry us off. Celeste is quiet and hasn't said a word since asking about her body wash. I look at her, trying to gauge any signs of discomfort or residual anger from the pee incident, but she seems oddly calm and content; that freaks me out more than when she's fucking irate.

"Red, you good?" I ask.

She nods. "Just tired." I pick her up, cradling her towel-clad body to my naked chest, and stride out of the en suite bathroom and into my room. "I can walk," she says, sounding annoyed. I relax my shoulders at the tone of Red's voice; it's fucked up that I like her as fiery as her hair.

"You're tired."

"Yes, but still functional."

"You're also pregnant."

"Yes, but still functional," she repeats as I set her down on my bed. Turning to my dresser, I grab a T-shirt and a pair of briefs. Pulling on the briefs quickly, I approach Red, remove the towel from her body, and shove her into my T-shirt. She's fucking swimming in it.

"It's a little big," she comments with a smirk.

"Humor me," I reply, grabbing the edge of the comforter and dragging it back. I let her crawl under the covers before I follow. She starts to shift to the other side of the king bed, but I stop her and bring her back to my chest, cocooning her with my body.

"You're like a furnace," she complains, though her feet are like ice and rubbing my legs for apparent warmth.

"And you're always fucking cold, so shut your pretty little mouth and go to sleep."

She grunts, not acknowledging my statement. Minutes pass, and I think she's fallen asleep until her soft voice fills the room.

"Dante, tell me about your father."

17

CeCe

He's quiet, and if I didn't know better, I'd think he was asleep behind me, virtually dead to the world. I know he's not sleeping, though, just mulling over my question and figuring out how to answer; his hand flexed over my stomach as soon as I asked about his dad.

"It's okay, you don't have to tell me," I whisper, and I mean it. When I told him that I wouldn't pry about his father last week, I was being sincere. After meeting his mother, seeing the colossal house, and meeting Sofie, I can't help but wonder who exactly he was protecting the family from.

I know his uncle is a senator. Though he doesn't mention him much, I've seen pictures of his mother and her brother online, in magazines, and in the news multiple times; they're like state political royalty. I'm not sure how I never noticed Dante before in the pictures that have circulated. He's a commanding presence, with his large body and tattoos, and he sucks all the oxygen from the room the moment he walks in.

"It's not that I don't want to tell you, it's that I don't want to scare you off."

Confused, I turn in his hold to face him. The room is dark, but the moon peeks through the blinds, providing a sliver of light. "What do you mean?"

He stares into my eyes and works his jaw before turning on his back and dragging me with him until my head is resting against his chest. I can guess that for this conversation, he doesn't want to look at me while he explains.

"Grey's been my friend since middle school, Linc since high school, and yeah, they know some parts of the shit that went down with my dad, but they don't know everything," he starts, sighing as his hand coasts through my knotted hair. "I'll share fucking everything with you, Red, rip out my soul and hand it to you like a bouquet of flowers. But I need to know that if I tell you this, you're not going to run away and hide from me."

"Why would I hide from you?"

"Just promise me, Red."

Looking up at him, I see the worried look on his face and settle deeper into his hold. "I promise," I whisper.

"Have you ever heard of the Fumero family?"

"Aren't they an organized crime family?"

"Yeah, they're one of the largest sects of the Italian mafia in the Northeast." He pauses, twisting his lips and letting out a breath. "My dad was the youngest son of the last Consigliere, Marco Silvestro, my fucking grandfather," he scoffs. "He was trained to be a soldier and was quickly rising within the organization. My dad looked exactly like me—you saw him in the pictures. A good-looking, tall, broad Italian guy gets a lot of attention when everyone else averages five-foot-eight. They used him as muscle and were training him to be a fucking professional hitman and marry into the Boss's family. They liked him; everyone fucking liked him."

I'm silent, both shocked and captivated by the story he's weaving. "When he was twenty-three, he met my mom and knew that she was it for him, despite the union that his father and the Boss were trying to form. My mom's family hasn't always been in politics. Before my uncle started his mayoral campaign in the early 2000s, my mom's family had businesses, a fucking lot of them, and worked closely with the Fumero family, 'distribution and sales,' or some shit equally as shady, but not entirely illegal. My uncle did what he could to smother our family's relationship with the mob, but rumors still circulate.

"My parents have never told us the full story of how they met or got together, but my mom has said that she made him work for it and that they snuck around until she got pregnant with my sister. My mom was an up-and-coming journalist and refused to have any open ties to the Family, and my dad had to make a choice: his woman and child or the Family and the life he was poised to have." He looks toward his window, lost in a memory. "He chose my mom and sister, and eventually me. That was the wrong choice for his family."

I let out a shaky breath, kissing his chest in a show of comfort and compassion that I rarely have. He looks down at me and smirks at my actions. I raise my hand and pinch his nipple, just to show him that I haven't gone soft.

"Hellion," he murmurs before kissing my head. "I don't know how long they snuck around or if he became the hitman they wanted him to be, but I do know that somehow, he got out. He told me he never ratted on his family, but I think he threatened to if they didn't let him leave quietly. I don't know what shit he had on them, but from what I can assume, it was a fucking lot."

"Jesus," I whisper. I hadn't expected this.

"My dad was never in WITSEC, but he did change his last name from Silvestro to Jones and then eventually to Camaro when he married my mom. Their marriage license shows Santino Jones and Sylvia Camaro as their registered names."

"I'm assuming his death is related to his family?"

"Yeah. I mean, it would seem pretty fucking reasonable to assume. My uncle was up for reelection, and one of his platforms was cracking down on the heroin epidemic in high schools and colleges in New Jersey. He was also targeting the influx of drugs from New York, which is where shit fell apart. You know, the mob doesn't like when you fuck with their money, and drugs bring in a shit ton of cash. My dad warned my uncle; he didn't tell him not to use it as a campaign platform, but he told him that his family and ours would need more security and would need to be monitored. We had fucking round-the-clock patrols and guard dogs at the compound.

"My dad was at work—he started a construction company in North Jersey and was crossing the street after he locked up the office for the day. From the traffic cameras and witness statements, a blacked-out Dodge Challenger came out of nowhere, sped down the street, and hit my father. The motherfucker didn't stop, and they didn't have registered plates."

"Holy shit."

He looks down at me. "Yeah. I'm not sure if they thought my uncle would stop his anti-drug platform because he didn't, probably just as a 'fuck you' to the people that took my dad from us. They were close, my uncle and dad; they became best friends after my mom introduced them. I know he blames

176

himself, but I don't. My dad, I fucking love him; he was a good man, a good husband, and the best fucking father. But he left loose ends and didn't disappear like his family probably hoped he would. My mom was too famous, too well known, to relocate or give up her career, and my uncle has been in the public eye my entire life. It was probably a slap in the face every time he would show up on my mother's arm to a state dinner or event. If it didn't happen then, it was going to happen later. I think my dad knew that."

"What do you mean?" I ask, trying to fully understand his words.

"Red, the mafia doesn't just let someone walk away; there's always ties, conditions. I don't know what my dad did to get away, but I do know that his family wanted him dead the minute he turned his back on them. My uncle's campaign was the opportunity they needed to get it done."

"D, I'm so sorry." I feel the tears run down my face and settle on his chest. I'm crying for him, for the heartache his family has had to endure.

"It's okay. We made peace with it. I hate that he's not here, but he was a fucking phenomenal dad. Frank and I are lucky that he raised us and gave his life for us."

My tears fall harder, and the next thing I know, I'm sobbing against him. I burrow closer into his chest, willing them to stop. I feel a hand on my chin, and Dante tips my face up until we're staring into each other's eyes.

"Red, are you feeling something for me?" he asks in a hushed voice, teasing me through the pain evident on his face.

"No, it's th-the hormones. I'm p-pregnant, you asshole." I swallow down a sob. "I-I'm sorry I made you tell me."

He laughs but shakes his head, rejecting my apology. "You

needed to know, baby. My family has skeletons, and you deserve to know what you're getting into." He clears his throat and tightens his hold on me. "Just remember what I said. I don't want you running away from me or thinking that there's still a connection to them or risk there. I've never known that side of my family, and I never fucking will."

I push up until I'm hovering over him, staring down at his serious face. "I promise," I say simply. Any more words, and I'd overwhelm him until he's sifting through their meaning and trying to figure out if there's deceit or falsehood woven within.

His eyes meet mine, and we stare at each other, sinking into the gravity of the moment. Dante breaks the silence. "It's your turn, Red."

"What?"

"I told you about my family, now tell me about yours."

Still hovering over him, I shrug my shoulder, letting some of my hair fall. "There's not much to tell. You know my parents' professions; you know they work a lot. That's the gist of it."

"Bullshit. You haven't even told your mom that you're pregnant yet."

"It's not a conversation to have over the phone," I grind out, clenching my teeth at his accusation.

"When are you going to tell her, when the baby is about to crawl out of your pussy?" he asks, raising an eyebrow like a fucking dick. I lift my hand and quickly flick him in that eyebrow, satisfied with his flinch at the contact.

"Don't be so vulgar. No, I'll tell her—I'll tell both of them—when I see them next. Thanksgiving break, I guess." I do a mental calculation and realize that Thanksgiving is just a couple of weeks away. How has the semester flown by so quickly?

"You go months without seeing them, barely talk to them, and you're okay with that? Fuck, Red. My mother would straight up rip me a new asshole if I let it go more than two weeks without visiting her."

What Dante doesn't understand is that not every family is like his; I love my parents and know that they would sacrifice everything for me. But unless I explicitly ask them to make that sacrifice, they won't. They're also so absorbed in their own world that they wouldn't realize that a sacrifice needs to be made. I know the dynamic he's speaking about—the stereotypical nuclear family where the parents are heavily invested in all aspects of their children's lives. Ava's family embodies that; mine, however, does not. I don't need to defend the way I grew up to him, even though it feels like I do.

"I'm an only child in a family that values hard work above all else. My parents gave me everything and worked their asses off to give it to me. You don't even know them, so don't judge them for how they structured our family."

I shift to get off the bed, but Dante grabs my arm before I can move off him. "Stop, don't leave."

"I'm not leaving, idiot. You drove me here, and I'm not getting in an Uber by myself at eleven at night. I'm putting space between us before I do something I can't take back."

"Fucking hell," he groans. "You know I love when you threaten me, but if you lift a fucking hand, I'm getting the handcuffs that I warned you about."

"I fucking know, that's why I'm moving away from you." I sigh, "I'm going to bed."

"No."

I let out a groan. "Dante, please just drop it. I'm tired; it's been a long day. I want to go to sleep."

"Kiss me first," he orders.

"If I put my lips anywhere near you, they're biting you. I'm not talking about biting in a sexy way, I mean that I will rip your skin off. Now, let me go and shut up for the next eight hours so that I can sleep."

He stares at me, weighing my words, before finally releasing my arm and letting me move away from him. "Fucking hellion," he mutters.

I don't bother responding to him. He knows he's an asshole.

18

CeCe

I hate to admit when Dante's right, but the comfort and space of his king-size bed are far superior to the narrow twin in my dorm room. He must sense my defeat because all he has to do is ask if I want to sleep over, and I agree. When I was there last night, he insisted I leave some of my things in his drawer to make it easier for me when I come over.

I'm not sure when the college house became a family house, but between me sleeping over and Ava practically living there, the atmosphere has changed. Before the movie night that ended in a brawl three days ago, I had only been at the house twice before: for the barbeque and after Ava's disastrous birthday.

It's always been weirdly homey, as though the ultra-masculine college guys care about décor, houseplants, and room design. I know from Ava that Greyson's dad hired a professional to design and carefully curate the space. It makes sense because it's almost too nice. The only one I can see remotely caring about the aesthetic is Lincoln; he is by far the most artistic—and egotistical—person I have ever met. If he's not cooking the minute he gets home, he's drawing or writing recipes. I've never seen someone be good at everything and look like a model; he knows it, too, which makes him almost insufferable.

Emerging from Dante's room after another night spent in his bed rather than mine, I'm greeted by the smell of bacon as I make my way downstairs. Like all mornings, it was difficult to wake up, and I practically run to the coffee pot. As soon as I enter the kitchen, I see Lincoln bent over the oven, lifting a tray of crispy bacon.

"God, that smells good."

"Of course, it does. I made it," he replies in a matter-of-fact voice. So fucking insufferable.

"It's just bacon; you put it on a tray or in a pan and cook it. It's not a difficult feat."

"I candied the bacon and baked it on low for three hours before I flashed it under the broiler. It's not *just* bacon, Celeste." His voice transforms from the cool, detached tone it normally holds to disgust. Looking at the clock on the oven, I see that it's nine in the morning—an ungodly hour. I have a doctor's appointment this morning, and that is the only reason why I'm up.

"You woke up at six to make bacon? Do you realize how weird that is?" I lift the coffee pot and pour myself a cup before opening the fridge to grab the hazelnut creamer Dante got me. My one cup of caffeine per day needs to be loaded with sugar to replace the five cups I normally drink.

"No, I woke up at five because I needed to make quiche." I pause, the creamer bottle tilted haphazardly in my hand.

"You're a twenty-one-year-old alien."

"I'm twenty-two and fuck off. You're as bad as Ava."

Like a phantom that appears once summoned, Ava walks into the kitchen and goes directly to the bacon, inspecting it like she's a judge on a cooking show.

"Did you glaze it with bourbon or honey?" she asks, eyeing it critically.

Lincoln scoffs, picking the cooled tray up from the counter where he set it and placing it on the kitchen table. "Neither. I used Grade A maple syrup and cayenne pepper."

"The cut is too thin."

"It's perfect; I sliced them myself," he retorts. They could go on like this forever, arguing back and forth about whose method is superior. It's fucking exhausting. I clear my throat, cutting both of them off.

"Okay, enough. I'm not going to stand here and listen to you bitch about bacon all day. Ava"—I turn and address my best friend—"I spoke to Serena last night, and we're going to do a girls-only day on the Saturday after Thanksgiving. We'll go for lunch and then spend the night at her apartment." I'm excited for a day and night away from Dante and the rest of the guys; Greyson has monopolized Ava's time just as much as Dante has monopolized mine. Even though I've slept here four nights in a row, I feel as though I've barely seen my best friend.

"I'm so excited. Grey is fucking suffocating me," Ava complains. I roll my eyes because I've heard her gasps; she fucking loves his suffocation.

"What was that, vixen?" Greyson asks as he walks in, immediately reaching for Ava and pulling her into his chest.

"Nothing," she mumbles against his body. He leans down and whispers something in her ear, and she elbows him in the gut as her face blushes.

"Do I even want to know what he just said?" I raise my eyebrow.

"Nope. Definitely not."

"Freaks," I mumble, taking a sip of my coffee. I close my eyes, savoring the sweetness and praying that the single cup of caffeine jerks me awake.

"You're joking, right? I was here when Dante got that box of body oil. One of you is getting a rub down. Maybe both, I don't judge, unlike a certain fire crotch." Ava's annoying voice breaks me out of my temporary caffeine bliss. I cough, barely swallowing the sip of hot liquid before it sprays from my mouth.

"The sun is barely up; can we not talk about body oil and rub-downs right now?"

"It's after nine. It's basically lunch."

I don't respond, just lift my middle finger and take another long sip of my coffee. I spend the next few minutes listening to Ava and Lincoln debate the preparation of eggs, the pasteurization process of milk, and the benefits of imported versus locally grown food.

By the time Dante makes his way downstairs, looking like a Roman emperor in his gray sweatsuit, I'm about to eat my left tit from hunger. No one has sat to eat yet, and I'd feel like a moron if I sat and helped myself to the quiche and bacon on the table before anyone else did. Dante must sense my impending food aggression; as soon as he walks into the kitchen, he takes one look at me and makes his way to the cabinet to grab plates.

Setting both down on the table, he slices the quiche and places a large portion on one plate before grabbing two slices of bacon with his fingers. After arranging a duplicate plate, he tilts his head, motioning for me to join him at the table.

184

Thank fuck. My stomach growls as soon as I sit, and I waste no time lifting a piece of bacon to my mouth and biting down. The dichotomy of the smokey and sweet bacon is incredible, and I release a soft moan, barely restraining myself from humming in pleasure. I continue eating the bacon, savoring it until there's none left on my plate.

"Fuck, Red. If you don't stop making noises, we're going back to my room." I move my gaze from my plate to Dante, who is very obviously adjusting himself under the table.

"If you remove me from food, I will bite your dick off."

"Fucking hell," he murmurs. I look at his lap and see him pressing a closed fist on his groin, like he's trying to will his boner away.

"You guys are so cute, I could projectile vomit." Ava's comment gives me pause, and I scowl at her. Her words should disgust me and force me to lose my appetite.

It doesn't. I keep eating.

I break off a piece of the quiche and sigh as the buttery, flaky texture hits my mouth. I'm pretty sure this was a big thing in the 1970s and 1980s because, before today, I had never eaten a quiche. I feel like I could eat twelve of them.

I'm lost in the thought of how to get Lincoln to make me quiche every day for the rest of my life when I feel a hard cramp in my stomach. Dropping my fork, I clutch the table and focus on breathing through the pain.

The feeling of a phantom period cramp works its way through me, and I curse myself for eating too fast. Just like Dante did against his groin—because he's a pervert with a pseudo-degradation kink—I clutch my fist to my stomach and apply pressure. It gives me a sliver of relief, as though my palm is acting as a heating pad. I close my eyes, surprised by the intensity of the cramp. Panic grips my chest, worst-case scenarios running rampant in my head, but I force myself to remain outwardly calm.

"Red, are you okay?" Dante whispers into my ear, his hushed voice concerned and urgent.

"Just ate too fast," I grind out, releasing a breath. I swallow the saliva pooling in my mouth, and my shoulders sag when the muscles in my stomach finally relax. I turn to look at Dante, an anxious look etched on his face, but shake my head, silently letting him know that everything is fine, though I'm not sure it is. He stares at me for a few moments before finally diverting his face back to this food.

Getting up from the table, I bring my plate to the counter and dispose of the remainder of my food. Turning back around, I meet Dante's assessing gaze and roll my eyes.

"Hellion," he mouths, smirking at me. I force out a small smile.

"Thanks for breakfast, Lincoln," I say as I walk out of the kitchen and head back up toward Dante's room. As soon as I walk up the stairs, another stabbing pain hits me, like a roundhouse kick to the abdomen. I keel over, the pressure from my position helping to alleviate some of the discomfort. I focus on my breathing, picturing the oxygen filling my lungs before I let it out. In and out, in and out. Minutes stretch until I finally feel capable of standing again.

I feel wetness on my chest and lift a hand to my face, almost surprised by the tears I wipe from my eyes. "Fuck," I murmur and rush down the hall to Dante's room. As soon as I walk over the threshold, I close the door and run to the bathroom. Tearing my pants and thong down, I inspect my clothing for any signs of blood but find none. Dante has Googled the shit out of all topics pregnancy related, but I haven't. I don't need to be concerned because there's no blood, right?

I fucking hope. Guilt seizes me almost instantly. When I first found out I was pregnant, I silently prayed that all five tests were false positives. After letting our circumstances marinate, I found that I wanted this baby, as difficult as raising a child at our age will be. The anxiety that something may be wrong causes bile to rise up my throat, and I know that no amount of ginger candy will help me.

It's not morning sickness I feel, but this instinctual feeling of dread. I quickly pull my pants up and exit the bathroom, not surprised to find Dante waiting for me in his room, keys in hand. My face must belie my anxiety because he rushes over and cradles my face between his hands.

"Red, what happened? Is it the baby?"

I shake my head because I don't have an answer for him. "I don't know," I say slowly. My eyebrows draw together, and I frown. "I felt fine when I woke up, but I got these two terrible cramps. They felt almost like really bad period cramps." Maybe I should shy away from telling him this, but if he's going to be changing diapers with me, he can handle this.

He doesn't seem disgusted or perturbed, just worried. "Did you have any bleeding?" He sucks in a breath, waiting for my answer. I shake my head again, and he exhales loudly. "Okay, that's good. But we're going to the doctor now."

I look over at the digital clock on the nightstand and see that it's an hour before our appointment time. "It takes fifteen minutes to get there; we're going to be early."

"So, we'll be fucking early, and they'll see us early."

"You realize that's not the way appointments work, right?"

"I don't give a shit how they work. We're getting there early, and they're seeing us early." Instead of fighting with him, I let him lead me out of the room, down the stairs, and out the front door.

Again, I don't argue with him as he guides me to the car, opens the door, and reaches across my body to buckle me in.

Dante rounds the car and slips into the driver's seat, silent as he settles himself in and throws the car into drive. It's a short, quiet, and tense drive to the doctor's office, and I find myself running through every possible scenario.

It could easily just be food cramps, or maybe I have a stomach ulcer. It could even be something as innocuous as a stomach bug. I'm desperately trying not to overreact. I look over at Dante and see his white-knuckle grip on the steering wheel. Reaching over, I pry one of his hands off the wheel and clasp it. I don't frequently—or ever—make the first move with Dante, but I can see he's struggling with just as much worry and anxiety as I am.

Dante's thumb rubs circles on the back of my palm. "We're going to be okay, Red."

I nod, fear choking the words out of my mouth.

19

Dante

As soon as I park, I fling my door open and practically run to Red's side of the car. She's already stepping out when I get to her, so I just wait until she's on both feet. I'd like nothing more than to carry her inside this fucking building and demand a full body scan of both her and the baby, but I don't think that shit will work.

Instead, I stand here like a fucking asshole and try to come to terms with the possible outcomes of this visit. Her cramps could be innocent, but the pain on her face during the first wave leads me to believe there's bad news coming. Really bad fucking news. I grab her hand lightly and walk with her toward the entrance.

When we held hands driving home from my mom's last week, it was comfortable and just fucking nice. Now? I'm trying not to squeeze the shit out of her fingers.

"Dante, loosen your grip," she says in a low voice. Fuck.

I release her hand and throw an arm around her waist, plastering her to my side. In normal circumstances, my little hellion would either threaten to beat the shit out of me or make

189

some bratty comment about needing space. She's silent and accepts my touch, which freaks me the fuck out.

"Are you okay, baby?"

"I don't know," she answers in a small voice.

I swallow my own fear and turn to her, stopping our progress toward the door. Lacing a bullshit smile on my face, I offer, "We haven't seen the doctor yet. Let's not form assumptions or theories. We're going to be okay. I promise." I know it's a promise I have no right making, but like a fucking moron, I do it anyway.

She nods, not responding to my words, and begins walking again, opening the door and holding it for me as we make our way into the sterile waiting room.

I settle on a narrow double-seated chair and watch as Red checks in.

"Do you have an appointment?" the receptionist asks behind the glass partition. Her voice sounds annoyed, like she's being inconvenienced for doing her fucking job. It takes everything in me not to walk up to the counter and demand the doctor see us immediately.

"Yes, we're early, but my appointment is at eleven-fifteen," Red responds in a frosty tone. Fucking good.

"Yes, well, you'll need to wait. We have other patients to see before you."

I look at the empty waiting room. Fucking where?

Instead of questioning her, Celeste just nods her head and turns from the counter. When she sits down next to me, she doesn't throw out an "I told you so" or a "Fuck you." She's still relatively silent, not giving me any of her sass or bratty attitude that I've craved since the moment I met her.

I grab her hand again as we sit in tense silence.

—

No one fucking walked into the waiting room, and no one walked out of the goddamn exam rooms. I stare a hole in the receptionist's head, and as if sensing my fucking anger, she closes the partition.

When a technician finally opens the door leading to the exam rooms and calls Celeste's name, I sigh in relief.

"Have you been waiting long?" the technician questions as soon as we reach her.

Red starts to open her mouth, but I answer first. "For thirty fucking minutes."

The technician's gaze cuts to me before she turns to the receptionist. "Victoria, we spoke about this. If there are no other patients, we can see arrivals early."

The receptionist, Victoria, has the fucking decency to look embarrassed that she was called out. "Whatever."

The technician shakes her head and motions for us to follow her. "Celeste, we're in exam room two. I just need a urine sample. The bathroom is right there," she says, pointing to a clearly marked restroom. "Collection cups are in there. Once you're done, come into the room, and we'll check your vitals."

Red disappears into the bathroom, and the technician leads me to the exam room. I sit and wait for her to return.

It doesn't take long for her to walk into the room. She sets the collection cup on the counter next to the sink and moves to sit on the exam table.

"Oh, we're going to need you to change into a gown. We're going to do a transvaginal ultrasound again today." Red nods and walks to the small changing closet connected to the room. I bounce my leg as she changes, unable to sit still. Every time I think we're about to get some fucking answers, there's

191

another goddamn delay.

"Excited to see the baby, Dad?" the tech says, cutting into my thoughts.

I give her a smile that sure as fuck doesn't reach my eyes. Once I see that the bean is okay, then I'll be a little more fucking joyful.

Red emerges minutes later in an oversized gown and non-slip socks. Clutching the open back of the gown, she climbs onto the exam table and grabs a paper blanket to drape over her lap. Once it's situated, she lays back and places her feet on the stirrups.

I think I've seen porn start out this way, except it wasn't filled with this much fucking tension.

After taking Celeste's blood pressure and temperature, the technician asks, "Any changes since your last scan?"

"She had two bad cramps today," I offer. Red shoots me a look, but I shrug, not willing to apologize.

The technician looks up from her chart. "What did they feel like, and how would you rate the severity?"

"Um, they felt almost like menstrual cramps, and I would say maybe a five out of ten?"

The technician nods and then instructs, "Okay. I'm going to hand you the wand, and you're going to place it inside until you feel the thick handle at the opening of your vagina." The technician hands the wand to Red. "Okay, that's good." The technician turns on the monitor with her ungloved hand before reaching over with her covered hand and taking control of the wand.

I breathe a sigh of relief when I see the tiny blob on the screen.

"I'm going to move the wand around a bit; you'll feel some

pressure but no pain. If you feel discomfort, please let me know." The technician takes over and starts measuring, charting, and taking screenshots of Red's uterus.

"How far along are you again?" she asks. Shouldn't she fucking know this?

"Almost twelve weeks, I think," Red responds in a small voice.

"Hmm," the technician says, not offering anything else. She continues to move the wand inside Red, getting different angles and looking at the screen intently as though it's going to magically fucking show her something that isn't there.

"What's going on?" I ask, pissed by her silence. When we came for our first ultrasound, the ultrasound technician walked us through each organ, each screenshot, and let us hear the baby's heartbeat. This one has remained fucking silent the entire time.

"I'm just having a bit of difficulty. I'm going to go get the doctor." She slowly removes the wand and disposes of the plastic covering. After sanitizing the stick, she places it on the holder beside the monitor and says, "You can sit up for a bit."

With that, she walks out of the room and closes the door behind her.

Red looks at me, her large green eyes betraying every emotion. I get up from the uncomfortable as fuck chair and stand next to the table and grab her hand. Bringing it to my lips, I repeat, "We're going to be okay."

—

The doctor walks in a few minutes later, looking serious in her long white coat. "Hello, Ms. Downing, good to see you again." She nods her head at me, her only acknowledgment that I'm in the room. "Nancy told me that you experienced

193

a few cramps this morning. Let's have a look and see what's going on."

The doctor goes to the monitor and grabs the wand, preparing it for Red before she hands it to her. Once inserted, the doctor turns the monitor so that our view is cut off. Red's eyes cut to mine, and I see the panic in her gaze. My eyes must hold the same emotion because her breathing hitches, and tears start to pool in her emerald depths. "It's okay. We're going to be okay, Red," I repeat for the fourth fucking time.

Just like the technician, the doctor is silent as she analyzes everything on the screen. Taking a deep breath, the doctor says, "Okay, I'm going to pull this out."

"Can someone tell us what the fuck is going on?" I say, unable to contain myself.

"Of course, let me just get this cleaned up," the doctor says, retaining her professional tone. She must be used to outbursts because she didn't even fucking flinch.

Once she's done sterilizing the equipment, she grabs a chair and pulls it over, sitting so that she's not hovering over Red. "You can sit up and cover yourself, sweetie." She clears her throat and looks into CeCe's eyes. "When we saw you last, the baby's heartbeat was strong, and they were measuring about three-point-five centimeters and just shy of eight grams. When we looked at the baby on the screen today, unfortunately, we were unable to detect a heartbeat." The doctor looks at us with watery eyes, silently communicating that this is the worst part of her job.

Blood rushes to my ears, and my heart pounds. I look down at Red and see tears streaming down her face. "Wh-what does that mean?" she asks.

The doctor's face dawns a sad expression, and she reaches

up to adjust her glasses. "You've experienced what is called a 'missed miscarriage.' The cramping you experienced is unusual, as typically, it's a silent miscarriage, and your body doesn't alert you to the change in the embryo. In layman's terms, you've experienced a pregnancy loss in which the embryo has died, but your body has not yet expelled or passed it." The doctor stops and looks between us.

Celeste's sobs fill the room, and I grab her, not giving a shit that she's basically naked in a hospital gown and we're in the middle of a doctor's office. I squeeze her to me and feel her tears soak my shirt as I bury my head in her hair. "I'm so sorry, I'm so sorry," she cries into me, and I hold her tighter, shaking my head.

I pull back and clasp her beautiful, tear-stained face. "I love you," I tell her, and that just makes her cry harder. My heart is fucking breaking and lying on the floor. I feel my own eyes start to leak, and I don't bother brushing the tears aside. I just let myself fucking feel and continue holding onto Red. The doctor clears her throat, and our attention snaps back to her.

"I know this is difficult, but we need to discuss the next steps. With a missed miscarriage, the deceased embryo is still inside your body, which is cause for concern. In most cases, the body will naturally expel the embryo in one to two weeks. However, there are some cases where the body does not expel the tissue, and either a procedure called a Dilation and Curettage, or D and C, must be performed, or medication must be taken to aid in the passing of the tissue. Based on the measurements of the embryo, you miscarried a little over a week ago. Because of the duration of time that has already passed, I do recommend either a D and C or a prescription. If your body does not release the tissue, it can cause grave complications down the line."

"Can I take the medication at home?" Red asks, her voice small and broken.

"Yes, it's inserted vaginally and usually softens the cervix within a few hours. There is discomfort, so I will prescribe a low dose of Xanax to assist in the process. In most instances, the tissue will pass on the first try. However, there are some cases where a second dose must be inserted. You'll receive two doses."

The doctor continues to explain the process, the risks, and what to look for, but my mind is fucking reeling. I continue holding Red as she asks questions and softly cries, but I don't participate in the conversation. I keep going back to the fucking mix of fear and happiness I felt when she told me she was pregnant, the immediate love I had for our little bean, and the excitement toward building our life together. I know we're fucking young, but I wanted that baby and Red. Fuck, I still want Red.

I squeeze my eyes shut, terrified that we just lost our child and that I may lose my woman, too.

20

CeCe

Dante's hold on me is the only thing keeping me together, though, arguably, my quiet sobs are an indication of my current mental state. If he wasn't here, I don't know what I'd do or how I'd be—inconsolable. Catatonic and numb are also possibilities. At this moment, I hate my body, and I mourn for the loss of a life that we never got to witness.

I also feel guilt, so much fucking guilt. I wished the baby, the "embryo," as the doctor called it, never existed when I first found out. And now that this mess of tissue and microscopic organs are nestled in my womb like the cruelest "fuck you" imaginable, I just want to cry. For days, for hours, for fucking years.

I know that a miscarriage is not rare, and I'm not special in my grief. But fuck, it hurts. My heart feels splintered and decimated.

"Are you leaning toward the medication?" the doctor asks, breaking through my heartache.

"Yes." My voice sounds so small, so weak. I clear my throat and try again. "Yes, I'd rather do it at home than have to go through a procedure."

"Okay, let me write up a script for everything you need and get you the instructions for the administration of the drug. It's important that you remain home the day of, as there will be cramping and blood. We're going to want to see you back in the office one to two weeks after to ensure there's no remaining tissue. The receptionist will have the script and instructions for you and will help make that appointment. Any questions?" She looks between us, taking in Dante's hold on me and the tears pouring from our eyes. "I know it feels like your world is ending; this is never an easy thing to go through. I always recommend speaking with someone; regardless of the stage, miscarriage and child loss are traumatic. Please let me know if you need a referral."

With that, she offers a small, clinical smile and walks out of the room, closing the door with a gentle click behind her. That sound is a detonator that sets me off. Though I've been crying since the doctor confirmed I lost our baby, choking sobs now wrack my body. I turn in Dante's embrace and let him hold me tighter.

"I-I-I lost our baby," I stutter, feeling the full weight of my culpability.

"Red, baby, no. Twenty-five percent of women suffer from a miscarriage. You cannot blame yourself. It's fucking devastating, but it happens," Dante says into my hair.

"Did Doctor Google tell you that?"

Dante moves back, looking at me with watery eyes. "Yeah, Red. It did." Leaning down, Dante kisses me lightly on the lips and then rests his forehead against mine. "I need to hold you, baby. Let's go home?"

I nod my head and wiggle off the examination table. Not

bothering to hold the back of the gown closed, I walk into the changing area and shut the door behind me. It may seem silly to close the door since it's just me and Dante in the room, but I need a moment to myself and to process the last twenty minutes.

With my back against the door, I close my eyes and take in a shaky breath. I exhale slowly, letting my shoulders drop as the full enormity of our loss settles around me, wrapping me like a cloak. I place my hands on my flat stomach, a stomach that never had the opportunity to grow and round. "I'm sorry. I'm so fucking sorry," I whisper, a fresh wave of tears falling down my face.

I allow myself a few minutes to cry and grieve, and then I get dressed. I wipe the remnants of tears from my face, and I open the door.

Dante is waiting for me in the same spot I left him, staring at the floor with a pained expression on his face.

"I'm ready," I say in a quiet voice. He looks up, startled by my intrusion into his thoughts.

"Let's go, Red." He takes my hand and leads me to the bitch that made us wait thirty minutes to find out the being inside me is dead.

—

"She's so fucking lucky I'm not an asshole. I wanted to rip that glass off the wall and throw it through the window," Dante seethes as he pulls into his driveway.

When we went to the receptionist's desk to make my next appointment and get my prescriptions, the attitude she gave us was ridiculous. I asked if they could send everything to my pharmacy so that all we needed to do was pick it up; you would think I asked her to give me her freaking kidney.

199

It wasn't until the doctor came over and told her to give me the medication instructions that she lost the edge she was treating us with. I thought I was going to need to cover Dante's mouth with how hard he was clenching it shut, keeping the words he wanted to say inside.

"We'll likely never see her again. Let it go." I gather the large pharmacy bag and the medication instructions and stuff them into my purse. Unbuckling my seatbelt, I open the door and stand on wobbly legs. The last two hours have just been complete shit.

I need to tell my parents what's going on. They've done their usual texting, but I haven't spoken to either of them on the phone in weeks. I feel guilty and annoyed at the same time. I should have told them, just like Dante said, but they also should pick up the phone and call their only fucking daughter.

I wait for Dante by his front door and watch him unlock it. As soon as he pushes the door open, I walk inside and head straight to the stairs leading to his room. I'm supposed to go to class this afternoon, but I can't fathom sitting amongst an ocean of happy, hungover college kids feeling like I do right now—like my heart was ripped from my chest and eaten by rabid wolves.

Ava, Greyson, and Lincoln are all in class right now, leaving the house empty. I thank God for small miracles; I don't think I can face my best friend without crying right now.

Closing the door behind me, I fling myself on Dante's bed, not caring to be gentle. When I found out I was pregnant, I was considerate and careful in all my movements. My body failed me, Dante, and our baby. What does it matter now?

Grabbing my phone out of my back pocket, I open my group chat with my parents and read through the texts I received from them earlier this week:

Mom: Hi, honey. How are classes going? I'm heading into surgery for the next few hours. Love you!

Dad: Miss you, C. Make sure you study hard. Are you sure you don't want to switch your major to biology? Lol jk ttyl.

Just like I did when I received my dad's message, I roll my eyes at his use of alphabetisms. My own response was short, just a message telling them I loved them and good luck in surgery.

It's sad, especially when you compare it to how close I know Dante is with his family. I may have acted annoyed with him when he brought it up last Friday, but he wasn't wrong in his belief that my family is kind of fucked up. I'm closer to my cousins than I am to my parents.

I throw my phone on the bed, annoyed with myself and my parents. When I took out my phone, I saw texts from my cousin, Wolf, asking to meet up for training, and from Ava and Serena. I've blown Wolf off every time he's texted me for the last three weeks, and I don't have the mental strength to respond to him right now. I didn't bother checking Ava and Serena's messages. I'll get to them later. I'll get to everything later—the grief, the processing, the healing.

Right now, I want to be numb, and I want to sleep. I shut my eyes and let exhaustion claim me.

—

I jolt awake and register a warm arm banded across my midsection. In the darkness, I can't see the vivid colors in Dante's tattoos, but the intricate linework looks so heavy against my pale, bare stomach. I glance back down and realize that my shirt is gathered under my chest, leaving my stomach exposed.

It was early afternoon when we got back to Dante's house, and I sequestered myself in his bedroom. Based on the shadows that blanket the room, it must be after midnight. Has Dante been with me this whole time? Holding me together in my unconsciousness? I know he's hurting too, and maybe I'm a self-centered bitch, but I'm not sure that I can take on his pain right now, too.

I squeeze my eyes shut, sinking further into his body. God, I am a horrible, selfish person. The moment we found out, Dante grabbed me, seeking to comfort me without any question. The difference between his instinctual role of protector and mine of retreat reminds me of the college commencement speech by David Foster Wallace, where he compared people to fish and their confusion about water.

I remember listening to it in my high school English class, enraptured by the way Wallace described how people are so self-absorbed and egocentric that they often believe the world revolves around their plight and their struggle. I feel like one of the fish he described right now, drowning under the weight of grief and unable to process anyone else's emotions, including Dante's.

Tears leak out, and I realize I'm crying both for myself and for how much I hate myself right now.

"Red, baby, don't cry." I startle at Dante's voice and shift until I'm lying flat on my back and staring up at him.

"I can't stop," I whisper. I look up at him, and his eyes are glistening, too. I tilt my head toward his body, giving him the only comfort I can right now—physical touch.

"I love you, Red. I know you're hurting right now, and fuck, my heart fucking breaks for us. But I promise you, I fucking swear, we are going to be okay." Just like in the doctor's office, his words have tears falling faster. I nod, not able to respond.

His eyes shut, and his jaw tightens; I know it's because I'm unable to say those three words back, especially now when he needs to hear them, needs my support. When he opens his eyes, he looks resigned. The arm across my stomach rubs gentle circles over my skin. "I saw your phone when I came in. Did you speak with your parents?"

"No."

He hums at my response, as though he's not surprised I haven't spoken to them. "I spoke to my mom and Franki. They asked how you were doing." He looks down at me, his eyes filled with an emotion that honestly scares the shit out of me. "I told them that you're my little fighter, that you're hurting—*we're* hurting—but we'll get through the pain."

I stare up at him, trying to figure out what planet this man came from. He's beautiful, there's no challenging that, but he's also kind and empathetic. He pisses me off more frequently than anyone else ever has, and I want to knee him in the dick more often than not, but he's a good man.

I move my eyes from his gaze and look at his bare chest. "My parents kind of suck, don't they?"

He groans. "I'm sorry I said anything last week. I had no right to question your relationship with your parents or how your family works."

I shake my head, disagreeing with him. "It's fine. I love them; they've given me everything I've ever wanted, except for their time and attention. You know my mom asked me if I thought I could be pregnant when they visited when my morning sickness first started?"

"No, Red, I didn't know that." His voice is low and soothing, a balm to my nerves.

"Yeah, and then she never asked again. Never asked how I was feeling, if I was still sick, if I needed a fucking doctor. Not a single fucking thing." I scowl into his body, moving myself closer. "They don't know I'm pregnant, or w-was pregnant," my voice breaks, and I fight back another onslaught of tears. I'm so fucking sick of crying today. Clearing my throat, I continue, "They don't know that I was pregnant because they don't say anything other than, 'I love you,' or ask any questions other than, 'How are classes? Did you switch your major to science yet?'"

I sigh in frustration. "My major is a fucking joke to them. They've asked more about me switching my major than they have about how Ava is doing after her attack. I love them, but they are so tunnel-visioned that they don't really engage in my life unless I am standing right in front of them."

I blow out a long breath, and I feel my body deflate.

"Do you ever reach out to them, start the conversation?" Dante asks softly, clearly playing devil's advocate.

I think about it, remembering all the unanswered messages and delayed responses. "Not recently, but I used to. It's not like my mom can have her phone when she's in surgery, and my dad gets so intense when he's doing an autopsy, so they would either go unanswered or be replied to hours, if not days later. I got sick of the nonresponse, so I stopped my sophomore year."

"But they came to see you. And your mom moved you in, didn't she?"

"Yeah, they love me. I don't doubt that they love me. They're great parents when they're present. The problem is, they aren't present much."

Dante doesn't answer or respond; he lets me sink into my

memories of my parents and all the times they haven't been there: recitals, award shows, matches. They've missed so many important milestones in my life. The reason I'm so close to my cousins and Ava and her family is because my parents foisted me onto everyone else when I was younger. They cared enough to make sure I was never alone, never unattended to, but they refused to sacrifice a moment of their career for their only child.

When I was in eighth grade, I asked them why they had a child if they were never home and never planned to sacrifice their careers. My mother sat me down and gave me an hour-long dissertation on the importance of her work and how she helps save other parents so their kids don't grow up alone. If someone ever wants to feel like an ungrateful bitch, they just need to spend ten minutes with my mom; she'll make you feel like the biggest piece of shit for questioning her life's work.

"I know I need to call them," I say, breaking out of the memories that assault me. "Maybe tomorrow. Tomorrow, I'll try to be strong and tell them what's going on. Can you just be with me tonight? Hold me together for a little while longer?" I ask, being the most vulnerable I ever have.

"Of course, baby. I'll hold us both together." His arms tighten, and I shift, placing my back to his front. It almost feels strange to be pressed against him without either the anticipation of sex or in a post-orgasmic stupor. There's no erection digging into my back, no hands grabbing at me, seeking pleasure. It's just us, two emotionally drained kids mourning the loss of our own.

I'd say it was nice—relaxing, even—if the situation wasn't so fucked up.

We're silent and still for long moments, our breaths the only

205

music in the room. I clear my throat and, in a small voice, ask, "Are you okay, D?"

He could be sleeping, and I'm not sure he'll answer my question. I'm almost surprised when his voice rings out. "I don't know, Red. I don't fucking know. The only thing I know is that I need you here in my bed, and I love you. Let's try to get some sleep, baby."

We have a lot to figure out tomorrow: calling my parents, when to take the pills the doctor prescribed, and how to move forward without breaking apart. There's so fucking much to do, to mentally unpack. But I'll worry about it all tomorrow. Like his words are an edict, I let sleep claim me and fall into unconsciousness for a few more hours.

21

Dante

"God fucking damnit, you hellion. You are the most infuriating creature I've ever fucking met." I try to keep my voice even, but there's something about Celeste Lauren Downing that makes me see red. Both literally and figuratively.

After spending most of yesterday and last night crying and wrapped in each other's arms, the fucking demon woke up ready for violence. During her speech, Red's doctor instructed her to take the medication within the next forty-eight hours or to call immediately to schedule a procedure. I've spent the last fifty minutes trying to convince my stubborn-ass woman to take it here, where I can watch over her, rather than in her shitty little dorm room.

"How dare you call my dorm room shitty. I'll have you know, I spent hours designing it. You have a problem with my rug, which is such a stupid thing to have a fucking issue with. My bed has a good mattress pad—"

"Celeste, for the love of God, stop fucking talking." I probably shouldn't have called her dorm shitty, but her emotions are turning her into a fucking maniac. "I'm sorry for calling your dorm shitty, and yes, your rug is very nice. Very, very pretty. But why would you do this there? You'd need to run down the hall to the bathroom, have to order food, or go to the common room to heat up fucking ramen noodles and not be as comfortable as you would in my bed. There would be no bathtub, and the doctor said that would help with the pain. Even if there were a tub, it would be fucking disgusting. How well do you think they sanitize shit if everyone wears fucking flip-flops in the shower? My room has an attached full bath, and I'll cook for you or order you whatever the fuck you want. Let me take care of you, Red. Stop being a pain in the fucking ass over this." I also probably shouldn't have said that last part, but the woman is a fucking tornado.

"Fine!" she yells, surprising me with her acceptance. I thought I'd have to spend at least another fifteen minutes arguing with her before she gave in. "But I swear to God, if you put on shitty TV shows, I'm leaving." She storms into the bathroom, slamming it shut behind her.

"Okay, Red. I'll give you free rein on the remote," I call out after her, not bothering to keep the laughter out of my voice over her demand. Yesterday, she was nearly paralyzed by her pain and self-directed guilt. I don't blame her for what happened; my heart is fucking torn apart, but I know that miscarriages and pregnancy complications affect more people than is advertised. Her shock and despair will eventually fade, and she'll recognize the situation for what it is—an unpreventable tragedy. We'll need to move on, cope, and eventually heal.

I run downstairs and grab the container of chicken soup my mom dropped off this morning, ladling some into a bowl and popping it in the microwave to warm. After I told her and

Franki what happened, my mom got to work processing grief the only way she knows how—cooking. When I woke up at seven this morning, I had a text from my mom telling me that she had dropped off packages on the doorstep on her way into the studio. I wasn't surprised to see containers filled with Italian chicken soup, pastina, and meatloaf, all my favorite comfort meals.

Growing up, I never understood why people hated meatloaf so much until I realized traditional American meatloaf tastes like a fucking hockey puck. My mother's meatloaf tastes like a meatball, covered in homemade tomato sauce and stuffed with fresh mozzarella and hardboiled eggs. She lines the top of the meat with bacon and bakes it until the entire loaf is a crispy, cheesy fucking delight.

I texted her, thanking her, and she let me know Franki was dropping off more food tonight. I'm hoping it's her risotto or veal Osso Bucco. Honestly, I'd fuck with both. We're not a casserole family; save the fucking green beans and tuna for a family that can appreciate it.

Grabbing the bowl from the microwave, I take a spoon, bottles of water, and napkins and place everything on a tray to bring upstairs. I don't know why the fuck we have a serving tray, but I'm not complaining.

When I get back to my room, Red is lining what looks like dog pads over her side of the bed. We agreed that we'd take today and tomorrow off of school; I have no fucking clue how she's going to react to the medication, and I'm not letting her out of my sight until I know she's safe. The fact the doctor prescribed Xanax makes me think the next two days will be a shitshow. Ava, Grey, and Linc left the house for their classes already; if they ask why we're holed up in my bedroom, I'll tell them we have a stomach bug or some shit and that we need to quarantine for the next two days.

I set the tray down on my dresser, and she looks up, giving me a sheepish expression. "I read online that there's a lot of blood. I got these at the pharmacy yesterday."

I nod, not wanting to embarrass her. I don't give a shit about blood, but it seems like she does. "My mom brought soup this morning. Can you try to eat some before you do the insert? I doubt you're going to want to eat later, and I'll feel better if you have something in your system."

Red abandons lining the bed and walks over to my desk. I pull out the chair, motioning for her to sit down. Once she's seated and eating, I approach the bed and continue her project of lining the mattress with fucking dog pads.

"You know, we could just throw the sheets away if blood gets on them." Her spoon pauses on its way to her mouth, and she turns to glare at me. I see the emotions in her eyes—fear, discomfort, annoyance—they play like a loop in the sea of green.

"Remember when I threatened to go home? That threat still stands." I chuckle silently and don't push her. I'm relieved to see the argumentative side of Red; yesterday, she was a fucking shell of herself.

When she's done, Red stands up and picks up the tray, moving toward the door like she's going to carry shit down the stairs. I rush over to her and take it out of her hands. "I got it. Get everything you need; I'll be back up, and then we'll do this."

She nods silently and goes to the bathroom.

—

CeCe:

I didn't really want to go back to my dorm room. I'm sure Dante knew that. We're in the eye of the storm right now; it's calm in his room, but as soon as I insert the mini egg-shaped pills into my vagina, I know that the faux serenity will break, and it'll be fucking chaos. While Dante is downstairs, I pull everything out of the pharmacy bag and line the items up on the bathroom counter.

Grabbing the instruction page, I read it for the eighth time. At this point, I think I have the text memorized. Popping out the four tablets, I walk out of the bathroom, cradling them in my open palm. Dante is waiting for me on the bed, watching me with a tight expression.

"I need to insert these and lay down," I tell him, though he already knows. He read the instructions as many times as I did. Plus, he Googles fucking everything.

"Do you need help?"

Do I need help shoving things up my vagina? "No."

He nods. "Do you have the Xanax she prescribed?" I shake my head. "Why?"

"I always have bad reactions to medications. I have to take this." I hold up my hand cradling the pills. "But if I have an option not to take something, I don't take it." In high school, I had my wisdom teeth removed, and they prescribed Vicodin for the pain. After two doses, I had difficulty breathing, extreme dizziness, and couldn't pee for three days. Even Tylenol with codeine messes with my system.

Inhaling a long breath, I slowly release the air from my lungs and pull my leggings and underwear down. I bend my knees and spread my legs, getting myself into a position that will allow me to insert the pills as deeply as possible. I look over at Dante, absorbing the compassion in his eyes.

In any other situation, laying half naked in bed and shoving things up my vagina, his dick would be hard as a rock, and I'd be dripping. But I'm dry, and he's flaccid.

There's nothing sexy about this; it's fucking sad.

22

Dante

There was so much fucking blood. It was like a geyser coming out of her; I've never seen anything like it before.

Two hours after Red inserted the tablets, the cramping started, and then it was like pain radiated from every part of her body, both the physical and emotional kind. I carried her into the bathroom, blood dripping down her legs and onto my clothes, and set her on the toilet while I drew a bath for her. Her pain was so severe that she started vomiting, puking her fucking guts out as cramps wreaked havoc on her stomach.

It took three more hours of her bleeding out until the tissue finally passed. It was smaller than I thought it would be, like a wadded-up used Kleenex.

She cried in my arms when it was done, the physical pain finally abated, but another kind of pain just starting. I said a silent prayer and held her as she clung to me, a bloody Valkyrie broken on my tiled floor.

She was mortified that I had to clean up everything that came out of her body, but I don't give a shit. I saw things projectile from every orifice, and I think I love her even more than I did this morning. She fucking battled, and I'm in awe of her.

Her body is depleted and worn out; she passed out two hours ago in my arms, and I'm clutching her to my chest. I'm man enough to admit that I'm terrified she's going to wake up and walk out my front door tomorrow.

I'm not going to let that fucking happen.

—

Red slept through the afternoon and night, dead to the world and barely moving. Unsurprisingly, I wake up before her and just watch her sleep, taking in the exhaustion that's stamped over her features like a mask. It sounds creepy as fuck, but I love watching her when she's unaware. Normally, her face is relaxed in sleep. Right now, her face is the picture of turmoil.

Easing her out of my arms, I go to the bathroom to grab more pads. I thought there would be tiny droplets of blood, nothing like what it was. Walking back to the bed, I roll her to her front and grab the bloody pads beneath her. Rolling them up, I toss them on the nightstand and replace them. When I brought Red to bed last night, she didn't put panties or her spandex shit back on, so the blood flowed freely. Going back to the bathroom, I grab the diapers she bought and open them, trying to figure out what the fuck this is and what I'm supposed to do with it. It looks like a goddamn plastic canoe.

I thought it would be like children's diapers, where you just wrap them on, or those adult ones that slide up like shorts. But this? This shit looks like a shitty airplane pillow with wings. Pulling my phone from the charger on my desk, I call my sister. It's early, not even seven, but I know she and Kate will be up.

"Hey, D. How are you hanging in there? How is Celeste?" My sister's voice greets me after the first ring.

"It was like a horror movie last night. She's sleeping right now, but listen, I need help."

My sister is quiet, waiting for me to continue. "She bought these, I don't fucking know, women's diapers, but I can't figure out how to put them on. How the fuck do you use these things?"

My sister lets out a choking sound but quickly covers it with a cough. "Do you mean pads?" she asks in a voice that barely hides her humor.

"I don't fucking know, Frank. But she's bleeding a lot, like a fucking ton. I don't give a shit about my sheets or clothes, but I know she does, and I don't want her to wake up feeling self-conscious. So, can you fucking help me, or should I call Kate?" I hear muffled sounds, and then a soft voice breaks in over the line.

"Dante, honey? Are you okay? It's Kate."

I sigh in relief. I love my sister, but she laughs at the most inappropriate times, like during funerals and at the mention of arson. "Katie, how do I use these things?"

"You're going to need underwear. The pad is probably an extra-large, so it'll be best if you can find full-coverage panties, but a thong would be okay, just a little uncomfortable."

I rummage through her bag and find a pair of tiny red booty shorts, almost the same color as her hair. If Franki laughs at inappropriate times, then I get horny at the worst fucking moments. Once we're past this and Red is healed, I'm going to fuck her in these shorts. I clear my throat and adjust my cock, pressing the heel of my hand against it.

"Got it."

"Okay, what you're going to do next is place the pad over

215

the interior of the underwear. Make sure the smaller part of the pad is toward the front. Try to center it so that it's evenly distributed front to back." She pauses as I follow her instructions.

"Okay, done. What do I do with these flaps?"

"You're going to take the paper off each side and adhere it around the underwear. You want to make sure that you're sticking the wing securely to the fabric so that the pad doesn't fall out as she moves," Kate's patient voice explains.

I sigh in relief when I complete the last step. "Thanks, Katie. I owe you."

Kate makes a scoffing noise. "Don't talk like that. We love you, D. Even though your sister is a moron, we're here if you need us. Okay, honey?"

I clear my throat again, getting choked up over her display of emotion. "I love you, too. And tell my sister I love her, even though she's an asshole." I hang up the phone and toss it on my side of the bed. Bending down, I slide the underwear over Red's feet and drag them up her legs until they're secure around her hips. When I searched through her bag, I also found a pair of large black sweatpants. I drag them over her legs until her body is fully covered.

Red frequently whines that my body is an inferno, but she's a fucking icicle. If she wakes up without pants on, I know she'll complain about being cold.

Pulling the covers back up, I tuck her in and round the bed. Climbing back in, I pull her back into my body and relax.

"Thank you, D," she whispers in a drowsy voice. I press my lips to her hair and let her cool body soak into me.

23

CeCe

I'm in love with Dante. There's no denying it, not after how attentive he was while I was out of my goddamn mind with pain. I haven't told him, and I'm not sure when or if I am going to. We have more important things to talk about, like if we're moving forward with this fucked up relationship.

I'm not a moron; I guessed that Felicity was the psychopath stalker within three days, and I would never run into an attic if the murderer were downstairs. But Dante and I found ourselves thrown into a relationship because of an unexpected pregnancy. Does that relationship still stand, even if the pregnancy no longer exists?

I left his house last Wednesday afternoon, determined to get back to my regular class schedule. We had originally planned on taking both that Tuesday and Wednesday off from school, but after passing the tissue on Tuesday, I knew I needed to throw myself back into life. If I let myself drown in the grief, I'll never reach the surface. My mind is as chaotic as Ava's coordination, and I can't be in the still silence of my dorm or in the warmth of Dante's arms forever. A large part of me doesn't want to feel; I just want to be numb.

I tried to place distance between us, thinking that it would allow us to come to terms with our grief independently. But Dante's having none of it.

Though I haven't gone to his house since I left, he's met me after every class and has brought me food, coffee, or just offered to walk with me to my next class or back to my dorm. It's a little creepy that he knows my entire schedule, but I'm used to his stalker-like tendencies. It's sweet, if not excessive.

Sitting in my creative writing class—my final class of the week—I'm engrossed in the teacher's instruction on form versus content when my phone starts vibrating in my purse. After being embarrassed in front of the class a few weeks ago, I've been leaving my phone in my bag to avoid temptation. It vibrates in a steady rhythm, letting me know that I either have a slew of text messages, or I have someone calling about my car's extended warranty.

Giving in to the need to check my phone, I reach down and discreetly pull it out. I'm disgusted to see over sixty text messages when I look at my screen. Most are from my group chat with Ava and Serena, but I see a few from Dante, my mom, as well as my cousin, Wolf.

Looking up, I see the professor's back to the classroom, busy at the smartboard in the front of the room. Returning my attention to my phone, I select my parents' group chat first.

Mom (4:32 PM): Hi honey, we miss you so much. We can't wait to see you. What day are you coming home? Do you need me to take off work to come get you?

Mom (4:39 PM): Shoot, I have a surgery in the morning on Monday. If you need a ride, I can grab you on Saturday.

Mom: (4:41 PM) If you want to come home next week, can

218

you ask Ava and her boyfriend to bring you home?

I roll my eyes at my mother's ramblings. Tapping on the screen, I type out a quick reply.

CeCe: No problem. Saturday is fine, I'll be ready by noon. Classes are canceled next week for conferences and Thanksgiving, so I don't have anything keeping me here.

Nothing but my guilt and tears.

My dad replies instantly with a thumbs-up emoji. I still haven't told them about the baby, the miscarriage, or Dante. I'm not sure which secret is most unforgivable.

"Okay," the professor's voice cuts through my thoughts, and I look up to find her pacing the front of the classroom. "Your creative pieces are due on December 2nd. I need you all to make sure that you're prepared to share your work in a peer-review setting. Do you have any questions?"

Hands shoot up, asking for office hours, rubrics, and confirmation on the length of the assignment. I listen to each question, writing down the answers in my notebook. After catching me on my phone last month, the professor is not impressed with me. I need to do well on this assignment, not just for my grade but also to show that I take this course and my writing seriously. Up until now, we've had writing prompts and small exercises but nothing that truly tested our artistic abilities.

I throw my books and laptop in my bag as soon as she finishes and stand up, joining the crowd of students rushing out of the room.

My head is buried in my phone, reading the texts from my cousin, when I bang into a large body and fly backward. Hands grip my waist, stopping my fall, and I look up into the dark eyes of my Italian savior.

219

"Red, I knew you were falling for me," Dante says with a smirk.

I roll my eyes, saying nothing in response to his stupid line. He sets me on my feet but doesn't step back. Instead, he surrounds me, infiltrating every sense I have with him. His smell is in my nose, the feeling of his hands is on my body, I hear his breath in my ear, and can practically taste his mouth on my tongue.

My hormones are still wild from the potent cocktail of a missed pregnancy and a medical miscarriage. I take a step back, but he follows me until I'm pressed against the wall. I take in a sharp breath, surprised to feel his hard dick pressed against my stomach.

"Dante," I scold, looking around to see if we've drawn any attention. People speed past us, so consumed in their own thoughts that they don't pay attention to the behemoth of a man corralling a small woman against a fucking wall. I'd be pissed if I were in danger and these assholes just bypassed us like this position was normal.

"Red, I've missed that attitude. You've been sad for too long." He leans down, inhaling the scent of my shampoo. "God, you smell so fucking good." With my long, thick hair, I can't use drugstore shampoo and conditioner or that shit you buy from the social media pyramid schemes. No, I must use salon-quality products that cost sixty dollars for a bottle of shampoo and smell like Sicilian oranges and butterfly jasmine, though, admittedly, I've never smelled either in real life. The result is that my hair always smells delicious.

"It's been ten days, Dante. Do you expect me to get over it so quickly?" I've distracted myself to the point of exhaustion, but our loss still weighs heavy on my mind. Could he really compartmentalize and block it out so efficiently, so quickly?

"No, baby, I don't. I just fucking miss you. Seeing you in public isn't the same. I know what you're doing." He pauses, leveling me with a serious expression. "You're avoiding me in private so that we can't talk about what happened."

I bristle, annoyed that he's calling me out. "Can you give me more than ten fucking days to process what we just went through? What my body just went through? It's not like I lost a goddamn piece of jewelry; I lost our fucking child," I whisper the last part, barely holding back my tears. I haven't cried since last Tuesday; I haven't let myself succumb to the emotion plaguing me.

"*Our* child, baby. I feel the loss just as greatly as you do. But I'm not willing to push you away and forget about what started this in the first place—you and me, in my bed. I'm not willing to forget how much I fucking love you." His voice is so low, so fierce, that he's practically growling in the middle of the humanities building.

"I know you're hurting, too. But..." I pause, looking down in embarrassment. "I don't think I can handle your pain, too. It feels like if I stop moving, everything will come crashing down around me."

Though I'm looking everywhere except him, I can feel his eyes studying me, unnerving in their intensity. "I love you, Red. And even though you're a stubborn little wench, I know you love me, too." I open my mouth to protest, just on principle, but he stops me with a shake of his head. "No, don't act tough and deny it. I know you do; you don't need to lie to me." He lifts one hand from my waist and cradles my jaw, lifting it until I meet his eyes. "We're endgame. I know you're hurting, and fuck, I am too. We'll get through this, *together*." He emphasizes the last word, not leaving any room for argument.

"Ass," I mutter, but he just laughs.

"Are you still going out with the girls next Saturday when you get back to campus?"

I try to nod, but with his hand holding my jaw, I can't move my head. "Yes, we're going to Serena's."

"Good, you need them. I'll pick you up on Sunday morning, and we can go to the diner for breakfast."

I raise a brow at his presumption. "Oh, can we?"

He rolls his eyes, but a small smile lights up his face. "Little hellion, don't be a smart ass. Let me drive you back to your dorm."

"Okay," I respond, my voice small, and follow him out of the building.

—

It took less than ten minutes to get back to my dorm room. Despite my instructions to drop me off in front of the building, Dante pulled into a parking spot facing the woods that offers us a modicum of privacy.

I reach for the handle of the passenger door just as the locks click into place.

Whipping my head around, I furrow my brow at Dante's smug expression. "Are you holding me hostage?"

"No," he laughs lightly.

"Am I a prisoner?"

"Red, you're so fucking dramatic." He reaches over and grabs my hand. "I just want to talk to you. I'll drop you off in the front. I'm not making you walk across the parking lot, even if you could kick a grown man's ass."

"Damn right, I could," I mumble. Though, maybe not right

now. Aside from laying out Dylan, I haven't trained in nearly three months.

"It's hard to speak to you through text. How are you doing? How do you feel? Is there still a lot of blood?"

I lean back in my seat and lift my head up, inspecting the moonroof of Dante's obnoxiously blue car. How am I? What an innocent, innocuous question. It sets me on edge.

"I'm not great. Yes, there's still blood, though not nearly as much as there was on the first day." I've never had a heavy period or flow, so the volume of blood was surprising. Now, it's reduced to spotting.

"Can I come with you to your follow-up appointment?"

"No." I shake my head. "I called the office, and they're doing an IUD insertion, too. I don't want you there for that." I may be devasted that I lost the baby, but there's no fucking way I can mentally or emotionally handle doing this again, at least not right now.

"How will you get there? You don't have a car."

"I'll Uber."

He scowls at that. "I'll drive you. If you don't want me to come inside, fine. But there's no way in hell I'm letting you go to and from a vagina doctor in an Uber."

I sigh, conserving my energy and choosing not to fight with him. "Fine. I'll text you the appointment details when it gets closer."

"What are you doing for Thanksgiving?" Dante asks, changing the topic abruptly.

I shrug my shoulders. "We're going to my aunt and uncle's house. My mom is a shit cook, so we never host holidays. What about you?"

"Everyone's coming to my house. Franki and my mom cook

an Italian Thanksgiving." I nod my head, acknowledging his plans. "You could, uhm..." He clears his throat and licks his lips, sounding nervous. "You could come. You know? If you want to? My family would love to have you there. I'd love to have you there."

"Thanks, but I need to see my parents. You know." I gesture toward my stomach. "I need to speak to them about everything."

"You still haven't told them?" he asks with a raised eyebrow. I just shake my head, not willing to voice my denial. He sighs at me and stares, looking from my eyes to my mouth and then back up again. My gaze lands on his lips, full and wet from where he licked them earlier. It's only been five days since I felt his lips on mine, but it feels like it's been much longer. I'm hit by just how much I want to kiss him, how much I want to feel him want me, like he did in the humanities building an hour ago.

But then I sober, remembering how the last time we were in this position, heated and needy in his car, he laid his hand on my stomach, caressed it, and told the bean inside that he loved it. I can't stop the loop in my mind, Dante calling himself Daddy or the sonogram pictures we looked at after my first appointment. I swallow back the emotion bubbling up in my throat and force my eyes to remain dry.

"Can I kiss you, Red?"

I shake my head despite how badly I want to say yes. "I-I can't, Dante. Not right now."

He closes his eyes and drops his head to his chest. With his head hanging close to the steering wheel, he looks completely dejected, and my heart hurts. But I'm also angry, mainly at myself. Dante's disappointment and my own failures come crashing down around me, a fucking tidal wave pulling me under, and suddenly I can't breathe. I feel my chest contract and a burning in my lungs. I try to suck in air, but there's nothing; I can't pull it in.

Short, shallow inhalations puff my chest out, but I can't fight the feeling coursing through my body.

"Red, Red, I need you to calm down, baby." Through a haze—fucking tears that I didn't want to shed—I see and feel Dante, his hands on my face anchoring me, his voice trying to soothe me. "Focus on your breath, just in and out. Good girl, just breathe, baby," he coaches.

Vaguely, I hear the slamming of car doors and the blur of people walking around the car as Dante brings me down from what had the makings of an epic panic attack.

When I feel as though I can finally breathe again, I close my eyes and release a deep exhale. "Thank you," I whisper.

"Let me stay with you. I can't leave you like this."

I shake my head before all the words leave his mouth. Opening my eyes, I see the concern stamped on his face. I could trace the worry lines on his forehead.

"I just want to be alone," I say in a low, weak voice. "I'll see you next week. Have a great Thanksgiving." Grabbing my bag, I quickly open the door and exit his car. His protests follow me as I run across the parking lot, reaching the entrance to my building quicker than I thought possible. Looking behind me as I wrench open the door, I see Dante's beautiful, worried face as he stands beside his car, watching me.

I offer a small smile before disappearing into my building.

24

CeCe

I spent the night staring silently at the sonogram pictures of baby Camaro. I've never called her that before, but that would have been her last name. My phone was burning; the messages from Dante, Ava, Serena, and Wolf sat untouched like bombs ready to detonate.

I didn't want to speak to anyone or pretend that I was fine. I'm not fucking fine. I spent the last ten days distracting myself from the fact that every inch of my soul hurts. I should be leaning on Dante, comforting him as he's tried to comfort me, but I submit to the solitude of my thoughts.

Last night, I thought, *Tomorrow, I'll deal with it. Tomorrow, I'll make an appointment with a therapist to talk through my emotions. Tomorrow, I'll try to be a good fucking partner to Dante and not this depressed, self-centered shell of myself.*

Well, it's tomorrow. I called the doctor's office and received the number of a recommended therapist. I felt guilty for admitting that I needed it; there are people out there who go through so much worse than I went through. Yet, I can't deny that this messed me up. Even if I only speak to them once, maybe letting my emotions out to an unbiased third party will help me move on.

My phone goes off, another text in a sea of them. Walking to my desk, I look down and see a text from my mother. Swiping it open, I read her words.

Mom: Almost there. Do you need help with your bags? Daddy can come up and grab them for you.

CeCe: No, I just have one bag and my backpack. I'll wait in the lobby.

Grabbing the small suitcase and my backpack, I shut the lights in my dorm before walking out, checking the door behind me. Dragging my suitcase down the hallway, I let the wheels hit each step as I bang down the stairwell. I move slowly, savoring each thump on my way down.

When I finally make it to the lobby, I see my parents' electric sedan out front and both of my parents waiting on the side of the car, like a welcoming committee.

"Hey," I say, walking up to them and giving quick hugs to my mom and dad. "Sorry it took so long; the elevator was out."

A lie—I didn't try the elevator.

"No problem, Chicken. Let's get your bag in the trunk and get on the road. The traffic going southbound was starting to pick up, and I'd hate to waste a charge idling."

I offer a tight smile, one that I'm sure doesn't reach my eyes. If my parents notice, they don't say anything, too engrossed in their own conversation about traffic, the remaining mileage on their current charge, and if they need to find a charging station before getting on the parkway.

I slide into the back seat, remaining silent as my parents continue to talk to each other, excluding me from a conversation that I wouldn't participate in even if they wanted me to. My eyes grow heavy, and I close them, letting their voices fade until they resemble the murmuring of the teacher in the Charlie Brown TV show.

I wake up to a jerk as my dad shifts the car into park. Disoriented, I look around the backseat and through the windows, noting the colonial homes of our neighborhood.

"We're home, Celeste," my mom practically yells as she gets out of the car.

"No shit," I grumble, unfolding my body and stretching out until my limbs regain enough feeling to allow me to exit the car. Somewhere around mile marker one hundred, we got caught in heavy, standstill traffic. I felt my eyes grow heavy and let myself succumb to sleep in the backseat.

"Your mom and I have an event for the hospital tonight. We're leaving around six, but shouldn't be home too late," my dad says from beside me, my suitcase in hand.

"No problem," I mumble.

My dad remains quiet, but I can feel his gaze on my face, studying me. "Everything okay, Celeste?"

Is everything okay? I want to scream, to yell at him that I'm not okay and that I wish I had a better relationship with my parents so that I could tell them that my heart hurts. I want to rage, but instead, I just offer a quiet, "Yep," and walk into the large house, where I'll be forgotten about until Thursday.

—

Ava: Grey and his dad are spending Thanksgiving with us today. Do you think B is going to cross-examine Greyson during the lasagna or the pie?

CeCe: Probably the antipasto. She'll ask him what his intentions are between bites of cheese and polenta.

Ava: Shit, you're right. I need to warn him that she's relentless and to stay away from her.

I release a soft laugh at Ava's worry; he saved her from almost certain death and all but forced her to move into his house so that he could watch over her as she recovered from the attack. I highly doubt anyone, Bianca included, is going to question Greyson's intentions when his actions show how invested he is.

CeCe: Do you really think that B will be that nosy? You didn't see him in the hospital, Aves. His pain was written all over his face. I don't think anyone questions his devotion to you.

Ava: It's my sister, Celeste. She's a nosy bitch.

CeCe: Don't overthink it. I need to go; I need to get ready for my aunt and uncle's house. I'll call you tomorrow. We're still on for Saturday, right?

Ava: God, yes. I need a break from Grey. He's choking the life out of me.

Smiling to myself over Ava's dramatics, especially since I've heard how much she *doesn't* mind Grey's choking, I walk into my en suite bathroom and drop my phone on my counter. Turning the shower on to scalding, I wait for the water to warm up before stepping in.

As soon as the hot stream hits my body, I relax, finding peace in the steam. I've been alone since my parents pulled into our driveway on Saturday. Ava didn't come home from school until yesterday, Greyson in tow, and I had no desire to meet up with our high school friends. Dante has texted me every day, simple, innocent texts like, "Hi, Red." Or "How does it feel to be home?"

I've answered each text with short answers, not ignoring him but also not inviting more conversation. He hasn't stopped reaching out, though, and in the loneliness of my house, his technological presence is a welcome distraction.

The last two weeks before break, I threw myself into my classes, coursework, and errands to help me avoid thinking about anything other than what was directly in front of me. I struggled with my writing, not able to produce anything that sounded better than a seventh-grade haiku, but I worked on reading assignments and short responses. I made a huge mistake coming home so early; there are only so many times that I can clean the already spotless floors and do laundry.

I know it's irrational to blame my parents, but I can't help it. They may not know about the shit that I've been going through lately, but shouldn't they be able to discern that my mood and disposition are different than normal? I'm not asking them to be mind readers, just parents invested in their only child's life.

I lower my head and lean against the cool tile. If Dante were here, he'd tell me that I was shutting down and placing expectations on my parents that they can't meet due to their ignorance over the pregnancy and miscarriage. I wince at the realization that Dante Nicholas Camaro is the voice of my subconscious.

I shake off that unsettling thought and quickly finish my shower. Steam fills the small bathroom, and I wipe away the condensation on the mirror. I look critically at my reflection. My appearance is the same: dark red hair, large green eyes, and a top lip that is almost too thin for the bottom lip. My skin is its normal vampire-like shade of pale, and my cheeks have filled out again from the weight I lost when I was throwing up every five minutes.

But I'm irrevocably changed; my eyes don't hold the same

spark that they used to. Instead, they look sunken by the dark circles under my eyes. Though my skin is clear, it looks brittle and dehydrated, as though the tears I've tried—and failed— to hold back have taken all the moisture from my body.

I'm the same but different.

Looking away from the mirror, I grab my makeup and apply a heavy coat of foundation, concealer, and bronzer to my face. I swipe on a few coats of mascara and lip gloss and then grab a brush to detangle my thick, wet hair. I have no desire to spend an hour blow-drying and styling it, so I brush it back into a tight, secure bun at the nape of my neck.

Not sparing myself a second look, I leave the bathroom and go to my closet to put on an oversized green sweater dress and my platform sneakers. Heading downstairs, I nearly run into my mother, who's putting on perfume by the front door. Just like me, my mother has dark auburn hair, green eyes, and a petite frame. Growing up, we often got mistaken for sisters thanks to her monthly Botox injections and good genetics.

"You look beautiful."

"Thanks," I reply, moving around her so that the scent of Shalimar doesn't cling to my clothes.

"Are you feeling alright, Celeste? You seem very quiet."

Like a tether snapping, I round on my mother, anger pouring out of me. "How would you know? You and Dad have barely been home since Saturday. You haven't seen me, haven't spoken to me. Don't pretend to care."

"Celeste, watch your tone," my mother scolds, her mouth set in a firm line. "I was on call Sunday morning and had surgeries and consultations this week. I'm sorry we haven't spent much time together, but you know how hectic things tend to get around the holidays."

"Okay."

"Celeste, talk to me. What's bothering you?" my mother asks, pleading in her voice.

"Why don't you call me while I'm at school? Why don't you answer my calls? Have you noticed that I stopped trying, stopped reaching out? Why is everyone else more important than me in yours and Dad's lives?"

My mother sucks in a sharp breath. "Celeste, that is not true."

"No? Before Saturday, I hadn't heard your voice since September, Mom. Do you think that's normal? Ava talks to her mom almost every day. Dante goes home once a week to see his mother. But you and Dad send me a text once or twice a week, and that's it. I could be dead, and you'd have no idea."

My mother's mouth opens and closes, and she looks like a fish gasping at air. I sigh at her expression, completely shocked and dumbfounded. "Celeste, sweetheart," my mom begins, her voice laced with pain at my outburst.

I quickly shake my head. "No, I'm sorry. I shouldn't have brought this up now. Let's just..." I pause, swallowing down the emotion in my voice. "Just forget I said anything."

My mom clears her throat and wipes the tears that have slipped from her eyes. "We're talking about this when we get back, Celeste. You are the most important thing in the world to me and your father." My mom grabs my shoulders and pulls me into a fierce hug. I feel moisture in my eyes and look up, willing the tears to dissipate before they spill over.

"I love you, Chicken. You know that, don't you?"

"Yes, Mom." My parents aren't bad people or even bad parents, but they're perpetually busy and oblivious.

I slip out of my mom's embrace and walk out the front door.

—

Thanksgiving in the Downing family is a huge production. There are over fifty of us packed in my aunt and uncle's house.

As soon as I walked into the overcrowded house, I snuck into the entertainment room where I knew all my cousins would be. One of the best parts about holidays at my aunt's house is that she hires a catering company and waitstaff, so I don't need to help prepare or clean up.

"There you are," a voice sounds from behind me, grabbing my arm and dragging me toward the couch at the far end of the room.

"Don't manhandle me, Wolf," I say in mock outrage to my favorite cousin and best friend, aside from Ava.

"Please, I'm barely touching you. But I need to know why you've been avoiding me and why you have that sad look on your face."

I look away from him, careful to avoid his gaze. "I just have a lot going on with school and classes. I've been adjusting as best I can, but it's a lot of pressure," I lie.

"You're full of shit. But I'm not going to question you right now where all our shithead cousins can hear you."

Contrary to his appearance, my big, tattooed, and gruff cousin is one of the most thoughtful and intuitive people I know. "Thanks, Wolf."

"Now, tell me about Ava. I heard she got into a fucking knife fight."

—

Dante:
Dante: Happy Thanksgiving, Red. I'm thankful for you.

I sent that text over an hour ago; it sits unread and unanswered. I feel like a fucking asshole continuously checking

233

my phone while I'm surrounded by my family, but I haven't spoken to Red since yesterday, and it's making me fucking anxious.

She didn't say so, but I know she was nervous about going home and confiding in her parents. It's not my place to judge her or her relationship with her mom and dad, but I can't understand her reluctance to speak with them. Unlike me, who tells my mom and sister shit they probably don't need to know, Red keeps her secrets closely guarded and contained.

We're opposites in almost every way: I'm friendly, she's volatile. My build is massive, while hers is petite and compact. She's fair where I'm olive. Though she's obviously talented at math and science, her mind veers more toward the creative than business, like mine. She's my perfect pair, my direct foil, and I wish that she could see how fucking well-matched we are for each other. She shut down after our loss, and I get it, I really fucking do, but I'm going to wait until she's ready to open up to me again.

I'm jerked from my thoughts by Franki plopping down next to me on the couch.

"Kate is going to be the death of me," she says, tugging on the neck of her sweater. "She always makes us color coordinate like those families on sitcoms in the seventies. The sweaters she chose for today are itchy as shit."

I look at her and notice the wool fabric clinging to her body. "Don't talk shit about Katie, Frank. Even if her clothing choices suck, she's the best thing to happen to you."

"I'm not shit-talking my wife, you idiot. I'm shit-talking the sweaters she chose." Franki gives me a look, not bothering to hide her assessing gaze. "How are you doing, D?"

I shrug and look down at my phone again; there's still not

fucking response. "I'm dealing with it."

"That's not what I asked; I asked *how* you're doing, not *what* you're doing. How is Celeste doing?" My sister has never met Celeste, but I've told her enough about her that she probably feels like she knows her already. The thing with Franki is that once she feels connected to someone, she'll go to battle for them, like in *Braveheart*. She may not be good at dealing with emotions and shit, but I know that she hurts deeply for me and Red.

"What do you want me to say, Frank? The woman I love is pushing me away every chance she can. I thought I was going to be a dad in six months, but that was ripped away from me, and I can't figure out how to make Celeste realize that our loss is not her fault."

Franki doesn't respond for a moment, looking past me at the clock hanging above the fireplace. The hands move, not giving a shit that time needs to slow down.

"So, you're saying that everything sucks right now?"

I shake my head and throw myself back against the couch. Releasing a loud breath, I turn to her. "Yes, Frank. Everything is shit right now."

"Hmm," she hums. "Did I ever tell you what happened when I finally confessed my feelings to Kate?"

I shake my head. Truthfully, I don't remember Franki and Katie being anything other than, well, Franki and Katie.

"Before me, Kate had only dated guys, though she had always claimed to be bisexual, even in middle school. I had never made a secret of being a lesbian; when I told Mom and Dad, they were relieved that they didn't have to pretend they didn't know anymore. Anyway, I had been dating another girl casually, Maria, and she and Kate hated each other. Every time

235

we were together, I would have to break up the bickering and stupid arguments they would get into. Katie either initiated or instigated most of those fights.

"Maria was from a very conservative family, and she was worried about coming out to them. We kept our relationship a secret in school so that she could come to terms with her sexuality and her family dynamic on her own terms. Honestly? I was fine with it; it allowed me to do my own thing and come back to her when it was convenient for both of us. We weren't in love, but we had a lot of respect for each other."

My sister lets out a laugh, remembering something that must be amusing to her. "Kate had a big fucking issue with our sneaking around. She would tell me that I didn't deserve to be a dirty little secret. I would talk to Dad about it, and he helped me identify Kate's feelings of jealousy. I started to pick up on looks Katie would give me, comments she would make, and ways she would 'accidentally' brush against my body. Before Maria, I had confronted Kate about my feelings, but she claimed that she saw me as a friend, and I accepted that; I moved on. But Kate was a fucking green-eyed monster as soon as I was no longer available. I ended things with Maria as soon as I realized Kate had not-so-concealed feelings for me, pinned her to the wall, and silenced her tart mouth once and for all. She needed the realization that I wasn't going to be at her beck and call anymore, that I was important to someone else, to understand what she was losing by being scared."

I absorb her words and the story, so at odds with the calm and level-headed Katie that I know. "Frank, if you're suggesting that I walk away from Red to teach her a lesson, I won't do that." Katie had to come to terms with her feelings for my sister, not the loss of their unborn child. While I can understand Franki's comparison, I won't let Red feel more alone than she already does by changing my behavior toward her.

"No, that's not what I'm saying, D. What I'm saying is that Celeste needs to face her demons first before she's able to come back to you. Encourage her to speak to someone, to process her feelings without relying on you to do so for her. She needs to feel comfortable and confident in who she is again before she can be a partner to you. If she's so marred by her own grief, how could she possibly resume a relationship? There must be a strong foundation, and you need to be patient with her as she figures it out. Be a support, but don't be a dictator."

"I know, you're right." I hate saying those words to my sister, but she's fucking right in this aspect. "I just miss her. I miss how we were." I lift a hand, rubbing over both the ache and itch on my chest. Trying not to scratch myself, I return my attention to my phone and the unanswered message taunting me.

"I know, D. You'll never go back to how you were; the shared loss won't let you. But you will grow into something better, something stronger. Just be there for her without smothering her." I nod, letting her know I understand her words.

"Dad would be so proud of you," she continues. "You're the best part of him, the part that's not a mafia lord."

"He wasn't a mafia lord. He was a hitman."

"Whatever he was, he hated it and fought to rise above the life his family laid out for him. He'd be proud of the man you became, and the loyalty you've shown to Celeste."

I shake my head. "It's not loyalty, Frank. It's love. I fucking love her, and I'm just waiting on her to realize that she loves me too."

My phone goes off, and I quickly lift it to my face, fucking beaming when I see it's a text from Red.

CeCe: Happy Thanksgiving, D.

"Why are you smiling like that?" Franki asks, leaning over my shoulder to see my phone screen.

"She texted me back."

There are two words and a letter, but I can't stop the giddy ass feeling of seeing her name on my phone.

Dante: How has your break been?

CeCe: Lonely. I'm ready to go back to school.

I sit forward, salivating at her reply like I'm a dog and it's the juiciest fucking steak. I have texted her every damn day since she went home for break; though she's replied, her answers have been short and not filled with much information. I have no idea if she finally spoke to her parents or if they've been comforting her and rallying around her. I don't know what the fuck is going on in her life right now.

Until right now. Now, I know she's lonely and ready to come back to me. I'm assuming the latter, but it seems pretty fucking obvious that that's her meaning.

Dante: Have you seen Ava at all? How are your parents? When do you go back?

CeCe: I'm getting a ride back to campus tomorrow. I spoke to Ava today. She got back home yesterday and is with Greyson.

Fuck, I forgot that Grey and his dad were spending the holiday with Aves and her family. Red's parents must have been working their normal schedule while she's been home. And like a fucking twat, I have no idea who her friends are other than Ava's sisters and Serena.

I should have shown up at her fucking house, surprised her, and kept her company, even if she didn't want me there.

238

Dante: Can I see you tomorrow?

She reads my text, and I see the dots pop up as though she's typing a reply. The dots disappear and reappear a few times until I lose all fucking hope over this conversation.

"Hang in there, D. She'll come around," my sister whispers, clutching my bicep before she stands from the couch and walks back into the kitchen, leaving me just as lonely as Red.

25

CeCe

"Celeste Lauren Downing, we are going to talk, and we're going to talk right now," my mother's voice assaults me from behind as soon as I open the front door. Hanging my head, I walk into the living room and sit on one of the club chairs around the coffee table.

Guilt has weighed heavy on my mind since ignoring Dante's text from earlier, but now it's replaced with a cocktail of anger and anxiety.

I wait for my parents to enter the living room and nearly roll my eyes at the sight of their clasped hands. They take a seat next to each other on the couch, facing me like a firing squad. It's no surprise that I'm sitting in the club chairs by myself, and they're huddled together like a unit.

Still, it pisses me off.

"Celeste, your behavior before we left was atrocious, and how you spoke to your mother was unacceptable. We raised you better than that, and you should know to speak to your mother with respect, regardless of whatever issues you face. You owe her an apology, young lady," my dad says beside my mom.

"No," I reply simply, shaking my head to enunciate my own anger.

"Excuse me?" my dad says in a quiet tone. My dad doesn't yell or scream; you can identify his anger when his voice is a whisper, a near-silent reproach.

"No. You have no idea what I've been going through. None. You two are here, living your empty-nester life and barely checking in on me. Mom," I drag in a shaky breath. "Over two months ago, you asked me if I was pregnant, and then you never followed up. Never sent me a text or called to see if I was pregnant, or if I was sick, or if I was dead in a ditch and my murderer was responding as me." I can't get that image out of my head.

My mom's face turns pale, as though she sees where I'm going with this tirade. "And you know what, Mom? I was. I was pregnant, and I was alone. I couldn't even pick up the phone to call you because I didn't know if you or Dad would even answer, let alone call me back. How fucked up is that? You say I need to treat you with respect? Well, why don't you treat me like I exist? Like I matter? Like I can come to you when I'm scared and pregnant and alone without feeling like I'm a burden. The only person who was there for me was Dante, and I can barely look at him because I'm so ashamed, so embarrassed, so freaking guilty."

"Celeste," my mom whispers, tears running down her face. My dad's knuckles are white, as though he's holding himself back from throwing something.

"No, you don't get to 'Celeste' me. I lost the baby in Dante's bathroom and bled all over his floor, while a man I met three months ago held me together."

I don't realize that I'm crying until angry, hot tears start dripping down my chin and onto the fabric of my sweater. I roughly wipe them away and cross my arms, closing myself off to my parents.

"When? When did this happen?" my dad chokes out.

"I found out I was pregnant in September. I lost the baby almost three weeks ago." And I've been pushing Dante away ever since.

"I'm s-sorry, Celeste. My little girl. Are you okay?" my mother sobs, her body convulsing from the force of her tears.

"No, I'm not fucking okay, Mom. I'm spiraling, and I'm a mess. You left me alone in this house since you picked me up on Saturday. What was the point in me even coming home? To spend a holiday with my cousins? I love them, but other than Wolf, they're all obsessed with getting their dicks wet and bragging to one another about their latest conquests. To spend time with you? Neither of you were home. I was alone and reminded of how much I've ostracized myself in the last three weeks."

I shake my head again, watching my parents cling to each other through my watering eyes. "I'm going to bed. I can't do this right now." Standing up, I walk around the couch and approach the stairs.

"Wait, Celeste." My mom jumps off the couch and grabs my hand. Pulling me into her body, she wraps her arms around me and nearly suffocates me with the strength of her hold. "I'm so sorry. I'm so sorry you didn't come to us and didn't think you could. We need to talk about this tomorrow."

I sigh, raising my hand to pat my mom on her back. How has my tragedy—mine and Dante's—led to me giving my mother comfort? "Fine," I say. "But I'm going to bed now." I peel her off my body and walk up the stairs without sparing my mother's sobs and my father's silence one more look.

—

Gentle knocking wakes me up from my weak sleep the next morning. Judging by the soft light coming through my windows, it's early. Too early to deal with the shit that's about to enter my bedroom.

Sighing, I rub the sleep from my eyes and sit up in bed before calling out, "Come in."

My mom slowly opens the door, poking her head in to make sure I'm up—even though I just told her to come inside—before slipping into my room and closing the door behind her.

"Hi, honey," my mom whispers. Her eyes are red-rimmed, and her hair is pulled back in a tight bun. She looks older, fragile.

"Hi," I croak around my morning breath.

"I have a few things I need to say and then a few questions. Will you listen to me?" I nod, letting her know that she can go ahead. She offers a sad smile before holding out a coffee mug that I didn't realize she carried. "Here, I know it's a little early for you, so you must need this."

"Thanks," I mumble, taking a sip of the coffee.

Letting out a breath, my mom begins. "First and foremost, I'm so sorry that you felt so alone while dealing with your pregnancy, though it sounds like you had this Dante by your side. For that, I'm grateful, even though I don't know him or if he treats you well. Honey, Chicken, you can always, always come to me and your father, and if you are in trouble, we will drop everything—work, engagements, research—to be there and protect you. Please do not doubt that you are the center of our world, and we will never abandon you, especially when

243

you need us.

"I won't pretend to understand why you felt that you couldn't come to us. I know that we work long hours, but we have always been there for you and have prioritized you above all else, Celeste. It breaks my heart that you think you aren't a priority. Please, if you ever find yourself in this situation, or any situation, ever again, come to me, come to your father. You don't need to be alone."

I stare at her, grimacing at her words.

"Why are you making that face?" my mom questions, pausing in her speech.

"I know you and Dad love me, and while you've taken time off to be with me for big events, you and Dad have never been there for the little things. When I lived at home, I spent most of my time at Ava's house because I didn't want to eat alone every night. I used to call you after school, on days when you and Dad were working late, to tell you about my day, and you wouldn't answer. I know your jobs are important, and I don't blame either of you for your professions, but when all I know are missed calls and solitary nights spent in this house, how could I be sure you'd answer since I didn't put it on a calendar or e-vite?"

My mom sucks in a breath, rolling her lips under her teeth. "Is that really how you feel?"

"Yes," I respond, not lessening the impact of the word. "But I also understand why. I had Dante, and he was... everything." I choke out the last word, pain lacing my voice. My mom sinks down on the mattress and reaches over to grab my hand as I try swallowing back my cries.

"What happened, sweetheart?"

I spend the next fifteen minutes telling my mom about the

shock of the pregnancy and the pain of the miscarriage. I don't leave out how Dante was there for me physically and emotionally. By the time I'm done, my mother is crying loud, body-wracking tears.

I don't handle extreme displays of emotion well to begin with. This? This is unbearable.

"I'm so sorry, honey. I-I cannot believe you didn't feel as though you could come to me and your dad." My mom sniffles and wipes her chin with the back of her hand. "And this Dante, how is he doing?"

I weigh her question and consider how best to answer her. I decide on the truth. "He's not great, either. But he's been my rock through all of this. When we first got together, he was so persistent. He's the one that brought me to the hospital after Ava was attacked. He took care of me and brought me food every day after he found out about the baby. And when we lost it, he tried to hold our broken pieces together. I haven't been good to him, not lately." I look down, shame and self-loathing coursing through me.

"What do you mean?" my mom asks in a small voice.

"I needed space; I needed to be alone. It's how I process things, you know that. Dante..." I shake my head and sigh. "He just wanted me, and I couldn't be there for him. He says he understands, but I feel guilty for how I handled things after everything happened."

"Have you spoken to him since you left school?"

I nod. "He texts every day." I reach over to my nightstand and grab my phone, not surprised to see a text from him. "He's already texted me this morning, and it's not even eight."

My mom studies me, quiet for long moments before she finally opens her mouth. "I know you want to go back to school today, but I'd like for you to see Doctor Plattner before you go back to campus for the follow-up appointment."

I open my mouth to tell her I already have a doctor, but she holds up her hand, silencing me. "I'm sure you have a doctor, but I would feel better if you saw Ruth. You may not have felt comfortable confiding in me, but I am a medical professional, and I need my daughter to see the best provider in this area. Okay?"

I look at my phone and the good morning text from Dante. I had told Dante he could bring me on Monday to my appointment, but in this instance, my mom does know her shit. "Yeah. Okay."

She nods once and stands from my bed. "The appointment is in an hour. I won't invade your privacy and go into the examination room with you, but I would like to drive you?" My mom lets the last part of her statement end on a question.

"Thanks, Mom." She leans in for a hug before walking out of my room and shutting the door softly behind her. Throwing myself back on my bed, I lift my phone up so that it's right in front of my face. I open Dante's text thread and quickly type before I second-guess myself.

CeCe: I miss you. We need to talk when we get back to school. I'm sorry for everything. I'll see you on Sunday.

His reply is instant, as though he's been waiting for my response.

Dante: I miss the fuck out of you, Red. Whenever you want to talk, I'm here.

Not overthinking it, I press on his contact information and call him, suddenly desperate to hear his voice.

"Red?" he answers on the second ring. "Is everything okay? What's wrong?"

"Nothing," I respond quickly. "I just wanted to hear your voice."

"Fuck," he replies, drawing out the word. "You can't say sweet things to me when I can't kiss that mouth, hellion. I'm half naked in my bed, and my cock is going to tear a hole through the fucking comforter."

I hum in response, unsure of what to say. I canvas my brain for things when Dante finally puts me out of my misery.

"I'm happy as fuck that you called, but you're up early, and you have never called me willingly. What's going on down there? Did something happen?"

"I have a doctor's appointment today. I told my mom about the baby, and she's bringing me to her friend for my appointment," I say in a sheepish voice.

"This doctor, is she the best at her job?"

I nod as though he can see me. "She's well-known."

"Good. You and your body need to be treated by the best fucking doctors. What time is your appointment?"

"I leave here in about two hours."

"Are you going back to school after?"

"I think so," I answer honestly. My plan was always to leave today, but I'm not sure what time I'll go back up to school. "When are you going back?"

"Today, Red." He pauses. "Are you done with the distance between us? Are you done punishing both of us for a tragedy that we couldn't have prevented?"

"That's not what I—" I pause, considering my words. "I don't like that you're hurting," I settle on.

Dante sighs, the sound heavy with feeling. "I'm sorry, baby.

247

I just fucking miss you and don't like this space. I feel like we're in one of those third-act breakups girls post about on TikTok."

"We didn't break up." I don't add that I'm not sure we were ever together in the traditional sense. He sounds too melancholy to add cruelty to this conversation.

"Damn fucking right, we didn't. I'll order you an Uber. Come over, lay in bed with me, then we'll go to your appointment. Let me fucking hold you."

"Dante, you live an hour away. I'm not coming over right now."

"Red, I fucking need you," his voice breaks, emotion pouring out of him.

I close my eyes and picture him, half-naked and a lethal combination of aroused and upset. It's a testament to how much he cares about me and grieves for us. It shouldn't make my thighs clench, and it should definitely not cause my stomach to dip and need to course through my veins.

It shouldn't. But it does. I open my mouth and do something that I haven't done in almost three weeks.

"D, what are you wearing?"

—

Dante:

"Oh fuck," I whisper. "Are we really doing this?"

I can hear her roll her eyes through the phone. I don't know how, but I fucking can. "I just asked what you were wearing," Red says, her voice laced with emotion and fire.

"I'm in boxers," I say, answering her question. I move my hand to my waist and rip the fabric down my hips until I'm flinging them across the room. Celeste normally does that shit, throws her clothes like a fucking strip tease, just to put

248

on an oversized T-shirt and sweatpants.

My little cock-tease.

Placing my phone on the bed, I set the phone to speaker so that her voice and breaths fill my room. A cheap imitation of the real thing, but I'll take whatever the fuck I can get from her.

"Now I'm not wearing anything," I taunt.

"Hmm," she replies.

"You want me to tell you what I'm thinking about? How hard my cock is for you right now?"

Her breath travels over the phone, and I hear it. I picture that I can feel it on my skin, and my dick fucking weeps precum over the mushroom tip.

"Fuck, Red, just keep breathing like that, and I'm going to fucking come."

"Dante," she laughs softly. I love her laugh, am pleased as fuck to finally hear it again after three weeks of tears, but right now, I need those breathy moans, sharp inhales, and the sighs that drive me out of my goddamn mind.

"Are you touching your pussy, baby?" I hear rustling, like she's shifting. I picture her snaking her hand down the sweatpants I know she has on and stroking between her legs. She's not cleared for penetration, and I know she won't fuck with that.

Red's always liked stimulation on her clit, though, so I doubt it's phasing her right now.

"Yes," she squeaks, and it's a beautiful fucking sound, my confident woman squeaking like a fucking sex doll.

"Fuck yes. Rub your cunt and grind against your pussy with your hand. I need you to pretend it's my hand, my fat fingers strumming that juicy clit."

249

I instruct her while moving my hand up and down my shaft, picturing her dainty hands in place of mine. I don't need lotion, lube, or fucking spit; I'm so horny and leaking so much fucking precum that my cock is soaked.

I'd be embarrassed if anyone was here or if I felt this way for anyone other than my little hellion.

"Fuck, I'm so hard. My cock is fucking crying for you, baby," I growl.

"Ah," she says, and I picture her head thrown back, her legs spread, and her gorgeous pussy on display. I don't give a fuck that it's still bleeding, I'd fucking feast on it if I thought she wouldn't tear my head away.

"Fuck, Red. I want to taste that pussy; I want you fucking messy and needy over my face before I sink into your bloody cunt." Images of me lying on my back with Red's beautiful, strong body above me have ropes of cum spurting out of my cock like a fucking bull.

"Fucking shit, baby." I just came, but I still want her. "I've got so much fucking cum on me; you should be here to lick it off."

Her breathing becomes erratic, and I hear her soft moans through the speaker.

"Dante," she whispers, and my cock pulses at my name on her lips, pleasure drenching my name.

I lean over the side of my bed and grab a towel that I dropped on the floor last night. I wipe myself clean before I open my mouth.

"That's fucking right that it's my name on your lips when you come, Red. The next time you get too deep inside that brain of yours, I'm handcuffing you to my body and will remind you every fucking day that we belong to each other. Now get those hands off that pussy and get ready for the day with the smell of your cum on your fingers to remind you of what we just fucking did. Sunday? No more goddamn distance. It's done. I need you, too. I've given you almost two weeks to push me away, and I can't do it anymore, okay?

"When my dad died, I wanted to be alone. But with this? All I fucking need is you. You could have asked me for bouts of distance—an hour, a night. But I can't do days, weeks without you. Don't fucking wreck us when we should be coming together."

I've told her this before, I cornered her in the fucking humanities building and delivered almost the same speech. But she didn't get it, she couldn't see through her own grief.

I don't blame her, and I'm not trying to guilt her, but I need her to understand that we're in this shit together, and I won't tolerate her pushing me away anymore.

"Okay," she replies, her voice soft.

"Okay," I breathe out. "I love you, Red."

I hang up before she has a chance to respond.

26

CeCe

I didn't get back to my dorm until late in the evening. After the appointment with Doctor Plattner, my parents took me for lunch, and we spoke about the last three months and the challenges we face in our relationship, their intense dedication to their job, and the fact they often overlook things like answering their phone.

When I finally got back, I was exhausted but suddenly inspired to write. After weeks of forced prompts and an uninspired output, my fingers ache to type out the words diving around my head. I opened my laptop and spent hours working on poems that felt more personal than anything I've ever written before. I had intended to submit one of the poems I wrote during last night's writing frenzy for my writing assignment, but now, in the light of day, I'm second-guessing that decision.

Cracking my laptop open, I read a poem I worked on last night and suck in a harsh breath:

Laying spread eagle on an exam table,
Stirrups support my legs as a scalpel probes

Lips waxed in consideration.
Nude beneath the hygienic parka, my nipples
Scrape paper, accepting polite
Small talk and medical fondling

As replacement for intimacy.
Gloves dance between my thighs,
Whispering, "You may experience discomfort."
I laugh; I'm no virgin.
Metal spears my slit, delving into feminine
Cavities and uterine walls as it tests for

Dead tissue and abandoned dreams. Need drips from lips
Parted in inspection; "Sorry," I say,
"It's been a while."
Latex massages my clit in understanding,
Retreating and returning until I'm left
wanting and lonely.

"Jesus," I whisper. Can I really hand something like this in? I'm jolted from my thoughts by an incoming text. Checking my phone, I see a message from Serena letting me know that our lunch plans are changing into dinner plans. Returning my attention to my computer, I nibble on my lower lip and debate the merit of the poem.

"Fuck it," I whisper into the room. Typing in the school's course management system, I pull up the class Dropbox, select the assignment date, and upload the poem. I shiver at the thought of reading this in front of the class, but there's something that feels right about handing this in.

Shutting my laptop, I set it on the desk beside my bed and

253

flop back on my pillows. Drawing my comforter up, I allow myself a few more hours of sleep before I have to face my friends and the truth I've kept from them.

—

Standing in front of Serena's door, I knock lightly, surprised by the near-instant opening of the door. Serena stands on the other side of the door, beautiful in her jeans and mint green sweater. Compared to her, I look like the fucking Loch Ness Monster.

"Celeste, are you okay?"

As soon as Serena utters those words, I break down; I just fucking lose it.

Sobs wrack my body, and I throw myself onto Serena. I've never been an affectionate person; the thought of hugging someone just to hug them seems like such a stupid concept to me. But right now, I need the physical assurance that someone is here with me and that I'm not alone.

Serena's body is frozen for a moment before she wraps me in a tight hug. "Shh, it's going to be okay, C. Whatever it is, it's going to be okay." Everyone keeps telling me that everything is going to be okay, and it's fucking annoying. I cry harder, unable to convey the words that are lodged in my throat.

Serena maneuvers my body into her apartment and shuts the door behind me. "Come on, let's go sit on the couch," she murmurs into my hair. At five foot five, Serena is the tallest of our little group. In normal circumstances, I'd laugh that I consider her tall. But right now, all I can do is move one foot in front of the other and make my way toward the cloud couch positioned against the far wall of the apartment.

Sinking down, I clutch Serena tighter. "C, what's wrong? Is it Dante? Your parents? Are you safe?" Serena's questions come out like rapid fire, and I just shake my head. If I'm going to do this, bare my fucking soul, I'll do it once Ava gets here.

A knock on the door causes both of our heads to turn toward the front of her apartment.

"Come in," Serena calls, still holding me. Once I see Ava open the door and step through the threshold, fresh tears start falling down my face in earnest.

When Ava sees me, she rushes over. "C, what's wrong? Are you okay?" I feel Serena's head shake, confusion probably stamped across her face.

"We decided to postpone lunch after you texted me and get dinner instead. She got here a few minutes ago and started crying as soon as she walked through the door," Serena explains.

"C, honey. Look at me," Ava coaxes, her mom voice in full effect.

I look up through my watery eyes and whisper the secret that's held me hostage. "I'm pregnant."

The shock on my best friend's face makes me realize that I used it in the present tense. I shake my head quickly. "I-I was pregnant. I," I cough. "We lost the baby."

"Oh my God, Celeste," Ava whispers and drops to her knees. "C, when did you find out?"

"Over two weeks ago," I say in a low voice. "But I've known that I was pregnant since before your attack." I glance up, seeing the hurt on my best friend's face. "I'm sorry, but you were going through a lot with that fucking psychopath, and I didn't want to compound it. Also, I think Greyson would have murdered me if I did anything to upset you, especially in the first few weeks."

"Celeste, don't apologize for how you handled major life

changes," Serena soothes, ever the maternal presence within the group.

"We'll discuss at a later date why you didn't tell me the moment you realized you were a fertile Myrtle," Ava adds.

"Don't ever s-say those words again," I mutter through my tears.

"Do you want to tell us what happened?" Serena asks softly, letting me know with her tone of voice that I can refuse. But I nod my head, desperate to get it out.

I take a deep breath and let it out slowly, letting my shoulders relax. Removing myself from Serena's embrace, I sit up and shift back until my body rests against the soft cushions of her couch. "Remember the tacos?" Both Serena and Ava nod. I made no secret that I would never eat dining hall tacos again after what I believed to be food poisoning. "Well, it was morning sickness. I mean, it was probably food poisoning, too. But it was mostly morning sickness. My mom suspected it when she and my dad came to take me to lunch earlier in the semester. I couldn't stomach any food, and smells were irritating me. My mom followed me to the bathroom and asked if there was a chance that I could be pregnant."

"Your mom knows?" Ava asks.

I nod my head. "Yes, but that's a whole other shitshow of a story." I level Ava with a look, and she nods, fully aware of how career-obsessed my parents are. "I took five tests in the Student Center bathroom. I think the asshole at the register called me a hussy. That's not important. After I found out, you were attacked, and I just couldn't bring myself to say anything when you got hacked with a fucking machete.

"Dante was the first person I told; he showed up at our dorm and demanded to know why I was ignoring him. I broke down and told him. The baby is his." I look at them before dropping their gazes and mumbling, "Obviously."

"How did we get from there to here, C?" Ava questions.

"Oh my God," Serena murmurs. I cut my gaze to her and see that her face went pale. "Was it because of the altercation with Dylan? Celeste, did I cause this?" Leave it to Serena to assign blame to herself.

I shake my head, reaching out to grab her hand. "No. *No*," I say emphatically. "I didn't exert any real force with Dylan; it was controlled, and I used gravity more than strength. No, this was just something that happened." Taking a page from Dante, I Googled miscarriages and know that there are a million reasons why it happens. It doesn't make it any easier.

I proceed to tell them both about the cramps, the intuition, and the fear that assaulted me. I detail the time in the doctor's office, how Dante held me, and was the strength that I didn't know I needed. When I start to tell them about the five hours I spent bleeding and vomiting on Dante, I get choked up, reliving the worst moments of my life with one of the greatest men I've ever known.

If someone were to ask me when I fell in love with Dante, it would be when he held me in his arms as I cried out in pain, covered in so many bodily fluids that my stomach rolls just thinking about it. I became obsessed when he called his sister to ask how to put a pad on my underwear to make sure I didn't feel self-conscious when I woke up. I became weak when he brought me food while I was pregnant and continued to do it after I lost the baby.

There are good men, there are great men, and then there's Dante.

"Have you spoken to Dante since this happened?"

257

I nod. "Every day. He's shown up at my classes, texted me, and made sure I never felt alone. We spoke over the break, too. I know he's hurting, too, but I just..." I pause, considering my words. "I've had a hard time dealing with my grief and being there for him. We spoke yesterday, and we're in a better place now."

"He needs you, too, C. Grey told me not to ice him out when Felicity first started harassing me, and I'm going to give you the same advice. Don't cut Dante out of your life, especially when he's in pain."

"I know. It's just been hard. I made an appointment last week to talk to someone, to get a handle on what I'm feeling and the emotions that I have."

"Good. I'm so fucking sorry, C."

"Me too. I wish we could have been there for you, but I understand why you couldn't speak with us," Serena adds.

I lift my fingers and wipe under my eyes. I didn't bother with makeup today, so at least I don't have raccoon eyes in addition to red-rimmed eyes.

"Can we change the subject now? I need to know all the bad shit going on in your lives so that I don't feel so shitty."

"I lost my virginity to my childhood best friend, was betrayed by my current best friend, and kicked out of my father's family for betraying my stepsister," Serena offers.

"I got stabbed with a machete by a sorority girl because my boyfriend couldn't keep his dick in his pants last year. Oh, and my sister interrogated Grey over the antipasto," Ava adds.

"You." I point at Serena, finally seeing clearly now that my tears have dried. "We need to unpack that shit." We spend the next hour dissecting our lives, talking about the struggles that each of us has faced throughout the semester.

Serena just finished telling us about her verbal exchange with Marina—who should be exiled to Antarctica for her terrible personality and frigid heart—when Ava's face lights up.

"Do you know what we really need?" she bursts out, causing both Serena and I to look at her with wary expressions.

"Vodka?" I answer as a question.

"No," Ava says, a mischievous smile breaking out on her pretty face. "Tattoos."

"Are we sure that's a smart idea?" Serena asks, ever the voice of reason.

"Absolutely." "No, but fuck it." Ava and I respond simultaneously.

"Are you serious, Aves? You'd get a tattoo?" I've always wanted a tattoo, but I've held off. Ava and I made a promise to each other years ago that we would go together for our first ones as a sign of support.

"Nothing could hurt worse than a knife to the ovary, so yeah. I'm in."

"Okay. I'm going to call my cousin and see if he can get us in tonight." Serena wrings her hands in worry. "Rena, if you're uncomfortable getting a tattoo, that's fine. No one is forcing you, and we're not judging you."

"It's not that I don't want one; I just don't want to regret it."

I nod my head, understanding her dilemma. Tattoos are permanent; sure, you could get it lasered off, but why would you go into it thinking that you may not want it forever?

"Just come with us for support. We need our girl with us."

Fishing my phone out of my pocket, I pull up my cousin Wolf's contact information and press the icon to call him. I get off the couch and make my way to Serena's kitchen island for some privacy.

The phone rings a few times before he picks up.

"C, what's wrong?" he answers in a gruff voice.

"Why do you assume there's an issue, Wolfie?" I ask, though he knows me too well.

"Don't call me that, you little shit. And I'm asking because you never call me. Who the fuck do I need to kill?"

"Chill, no one. I just..." I release a sigh. "I have a lot going on right now."

He's silent for a moment, absorbing my words. I don't say anything and wait for him to speak. "Dammit, Celeste. What the fuck is going on up there? I asked you on Thanksgiving, and don't think I was fooled by your bullshit excuse of being busy adjusting to college."

"I'm not going to tell you if you're yelling at me."

"Do I need to call Aunt Trisha? Because I fucking will. What the fuck is going on?"

"Listen, do you promise not to yell at me? I spoke to my parents about it, but I don't want them to worry that I'm not handling it well. Dante and I—"

"Celeste, what the fuck are you talking about? Who the hell is Dante?" Wolf cuts me off.

"I was pregnant," I let out in a whisper. I choke back a sob. "Wolf, I-I lost the baby."

"Shit, C, are you okay?" I can hear the emotion in my cousin's voice.

"No, but I'm going to be."

"Who the fuck is Dante? Why the fuck is he not taking care of you?" Wolf growls, taking on the persona of his name.

"Calm down, you animal. He's with his friends, and I'm

with Ava and Serena. I called you because I need a favor."

"You want me to kill him and dispose of the body? I have a buddy in the special forces, so it'll have to wait until he's on leave and back in town." Threatening murder is a family trait.

"What? No. I need a tattoo, and so do two of my friends. Well, Rena might not get one, but Ava definitely is. Are you free tonight?"

He falls quiet, and I can practically hear his mind working. "C, you know tattoos are permanent, right? And your friends, they're aware, too?"

I roll my eyes. "Yes, I am aware. And yes, they know."

"And you're not going to freak the fuck out over the pain? And are they going to be little princesses that get sick at the sight of a needle?"

"You may be an MMA fighter, but don't forget that I know how to kick your ass. No," I huff. "I am not going to 'freak the fuck out,' and neither are they."

"Fine, come in around eight," he says. I pull the phone from my ear and look at the time. It's after six, so we have a little bit until we have to drive over. "And C?"

"Yeah, Wolf?"

"I'm fucking sorry. I'm here if you need me. Love you," he says in a voice so gentle my heart nearly breaks all over again.

"Thanks, Wolfie," I reply and hang up the phone.

Walking out of the kitchen, I look at Ava and Serena. "We have to leave in an hour. Wolf will take us at eight."

I walk over to the couch and sink down, pulling my legs to my chest and resting my head on my knees. I'm curled up so tightly I feel impenetrable.

"Are you okay?" Serena asks in a soft voice.

"No," I answer honestly. It's been weeks since I've felt okay.

"Do you think this will help?"

"I'm not sure, but I don't think it'll hurt, at least not emotionally."

—

"Are you fucking kidding me?" I wince at Wolf's exclamation. When Serena, Ava, and I showed up at the shop, my cousin embraced me and checked to make sure that I was okay before he laid into me. But when I told him I wanted a phoenix on my ribcage, he lost his shit.

"Celeste, you don't even know the symbolism behind the phoenix. To you, it's a pretty bird with flames. To me, it's fucking six hours of work on a virgin canvas. Absolutely fucking not."

"She's not a virgin anymore, Wolfie," Ava calls from the front of the shop, where she and Serena look through pictures of previous work and stock designs. Though I poured my heart out to both Ava and Serena earlier this evening, neither of them has treated me like I'm broken or fragile.

"For fuck's sake, Ava. I meant her fucking skin, not her hymen," Wolf bellows. "This, this is why you two are always on my shit list." He points between me and the front of his shop. "I've never met two people more prone to giving me a fucking headache. How did you get that innocent one to join your gang?"

"Gang? That's a little extreme. We met her on the first day; she was overseeing the STD table," I explain, wincing at Wolf's expression. "The English National Honor Society, not sexually transmitted diseases."

He hums, letting me leaf through a booklet while he gathers his gloves, paper towels, and a machine bag. He turns to grab black ink and ink cups, placing them down on his station. I don't miss the way his gaze flickers to the front of his shop while he's prepping. Ava is like another annoying cousin to him, so I know his attention is trained on Serena.

"She's single, you know," I say in a low voice. Wolf has a shit record with women and typically pursues girls interested in his notoriety. His last girlfriend, Kelly, wasn't terrible, but she still wasn't with Wolf for anything other than his bank account, connections, and the prospect of growing her social media following.

He scoffs as though the idea is ludicrous. "She's too fucking young."

"Excuse me, you fucking fossil, she is an eighteen-year-old woman. The same age as me."

"She's sheltered," he argues further.

"It's like you're looking for a reason to not go after her. If you're not interested in her, just say so, but you don't know a fucking thing about her. So, take your judgmental dipshit attitude, and shove it up your urethra."

"Do you want a tattoo or not?" my cousin challenges.

Dropping the book of pictures, I suck in a breath and offer a strangled smile. "Okay, confession, I don't want a phoenix."

"No fucking shit. What do you want?"

I scowl, annoyed, and continue, "I want a narcissus on my forearm." I show him where I want it—my upper left forearm—and use my fingers to indicate the size I want.

Wolf rolls his eyes. "I forgot you went through that phase of obsessing over Greek mythology. We call it a daffodil in the twenty-first century."

"Don't be contrary, it's unbecoming." When I was sixteen, I became obsessed with Greek mythology after reading *The Odyssey* in English class. Odysseus was a little shit, but there

263

was something so romantic about Penelope, waiting for her man despite the suitors lined up to whisk her away. It was a gateway to my favorite legend: the myth of Persephone and Hades.

I fell in love with the lore almost immediately; the devotion between the god of the underworld and the young goddess of spring was delicious and forbidden, like a hot dog from a gas station, except it won't leave your body in shambles. I read every retelling I could find, devouring it as quickly as I could.

The story, watered down and distilled through a millennium of retelling, is that the young goddess was spotted by Hades, and he fell in love at first sight. He lured a willing Persephone down to his world after she picked a narcissus—a daffodil, as my asshole cousin insists—and the earth split, allowing Hades to snatch Persephone and bring her to the underworld in his chariot. The seasons are attributed to them and the concession they made with Demeter, Persephone's bitch of a mother: six pomegranate seeds to remain in the underworld during fall and winter.

"I'm not choosing a daffodil for my love of mythology," I say in a low voice. "I'm choosing it because of its symbolism and meaning." Daffodils are symbolic of rebirth and new beginnings; I don't want to forget my tragedy, but I want to be reborn from it.

Wolf's eyes soften, and he starts to cover his machine in the plastic bags. "I figured, C. Black and gray good?"

I nod my head and lay my arm out. Unlike Dante, I don't have a desire to have bold colors on my body. Wolf's machine turns on, and distinct buzzing fills the room.

"So, like I said, she's single," I reiterate as Wolf dips the tip of the gun in black ink. "Shut up, Celeste." He looks up at me before continuing, "Ready?"

I nod, breathing in deeply and letting the sting of the gun mellow my guilt.

27

Dante

"Vixen, are you fucking kidding me?" Greyson yells into his phone. We're at Legends, the sports bar frequented by most of the student population of Marymount University.

Linc and I shift our gazes to Grey, and his face adopts a murderous expression. I check my phone, hoping for something from Red. At this point, I'd take a fucking carrier pigeon or Morse code. I see Linc check his phone, too, disappointment clear on his face.

"You hear from Sera?" I ask.

"She's back with Mitch the Dick," Linc says in a voice that betrays just how affected he is by this.

"What the fuck? I thought Ava said that there was no way she was getting back with that shit stain?"

Linc runs his hand over his buzz cut and lets out a low growl. "Sera told me the same fucking thing. I think he has something on her. There's no fucking way a girl that smart goes back to that fucking asshole without a reason."

"Love?"

"She referred to him as 'anal invader' after the shit Bianca pulled. She doesn't fucking love him."

"Ava Maria Gregori, are you shitting me? Why didn't you tell me?" Linc and I stop our conversation and look at Grey, whose free hand is clenched in a fist on top of the bar. "So help me, vixen, if I find out you did anything to hurt yourself further, I will take you over my goddamn knee and have your plump ass red for a fucking week." He pulls the phone away and glances down, a stunned look on his face before it morphs into annoyance. "She fucking hung up on me."

I swallow down a laugh. I pity him but also empathize; Red is a fucking hellcat, too, and I love it. My laughter dies in my throat. Ava is with Celeste, and if she's up to something bad, Red is probably at the center of it.

"What the fuck did they do?"

"Let's close the tab," Grey mutters. He looks up at me, face set in grim lines. "They got fucking tattoos."

Linc rolls his eyes. "We're covered in tattoos. Get your shit together."

"Ava was just attacked by a fucking machete," he growls.

"Yeah, and Aves proved she's not porcelain. Lighten up, you fucking idiot. You're not her daddy, even if she screams that at three in the fucking morning."

"Don't talk about her sex noises, it's weird," I complain.

"It's better than Celeste, who mewls like a fucking cat."

All humor is gone. I stand up from my stool, pushing it back from the force of my movement. "What the fuck did you just say?"

Linc just rolls his eyes, unconcerned. "Chill the fuck out, both of you; I'm happy for you. I like them, even though Ava is going to be the fucking death of me with our practicals. We just need fucking Sera to get on the same page and leave that shithead."

"She's still in high school," Grey groans. "Vixen will have my balls if you fuck with her baby sister before she graduates." Grey's eyes cut to mine. "Why is Celeste getting a tattoo?"

I pick up my bottle and swallow the rest of my beer. "We lost the baby."

"What the fuck do you mean you lost the baby? What fucking baby?" Linc demands, while Greys offers a muttered, "Shit, I'm sorry."

"Red was pregnant. We found out a couple of weeks ago that we lost the baby."

"Goddamn, D. I'm sorry, man." I nod at his condolences; it doesn't do shit to make me feel better, but at least I don't feel so fucking alone. "How is Celeste doing?"

I shake my head and twist my lips. "Not good. She blames herself, even though I've told her that she shouldn't. She's been pulling away from me, getting more and more fucking distant." I don't add that I think we finally, fucking finally, made a breakthrough after our phone call yesterday morning. My dick gets hard just thinking about the breathy moans she made while riding her hand.

"D, it's been less than three weeks. Give her time," Linc says at the same time Greyson volunteers, "Kidnap her."

"What the fuck is wrong with you?" I ask Grey.

He shrugs, pulling out his card to pay the bill and handing it to the bartender. She comes back quickly, card and receipts in hand. "Here you guys go. Let me know if I can get you anything else, maybe something not on the menu." I cringe, and Grey scowls.

"Not interested, have a good night," Linc says. "This is why I don't fucking go out."

I hit him on the shoulder. "You would have been getting her number two months ago. Just admit that you're whipped by a high school chick, you fucking creep."

"Shut the fuck up," he grumbles. "She's eighteen."

"Whatever. Grey, we going to go get the girls?" I stand up and pull out my wallet, getting cash for a tip. After working as a busser in my sister's restaurant in high school, I know how important cash tips are.

"Yeah, they're at Ink and Needle." I stop what I'm doing, frozen to the spot. I'm not sure where I thought they'd go once Grey announced that they were getting tattoos, but the most famous fucking shop in this part of New Jersey wasn't it.

Though, I'm a fucking idiot for not assuming since Wolf goddamn McCleery is her cousin, and he owns the fucking shop.

"Holy fuck. How did they get an appointment?" Linc asks.

"Wolf McCleery is Red's cousin." I rub my chest, the memory of my own recent addition pushing at the forefront of my mind. It may not be a McCleery piece, but my artist did an amazing job capturing exactly what I asked for.

"You're fucking shitting me," Grey says. With Grey's dad as a famous athlete turned sportscaster, he doesn't usually get starstruck. Wolf McCleery is something else entirely, though. At six foot six inches, McCleery is a fucking tank in the cage, graceful in a way that shouldn't be possible given his large frame, and talented as fuck at art and tattooing. He's twenty-five but has made a name for himself in every fucking community he's part of. He may be an amateur fighter, but he's well-known as fuck. If MMA were his full-time career, he'd probably be pro.

"I'm fucking coming. Do you think Celeste can talk him into

269

an appointment for me?"

"Fuck off, Linc."

—

By the time we get to Ink and Needle, Red and Ava are sitting on stools around the receptionist's desk, speaking with a young woman covered in tattoos. As soon as they see us, Ava jumps up and runs to Grey, catapulting herself at him. Opposite of Ava's affectionate display, Red eyes me wearily, taking me in while she stays rooted in place.

"Hi," I whisper when I step into her space, careful not to crowd her.

"Hi," she responds, her voice so low that I can barely hear it. "How did you know we were here?"

"Ava told Grey."

"Right, of course. I should have figured that." She stands from the stool and holds out her arm. I look down at the bandage, taking in the flush of her cheeks and the heat coming from her body. Fuck, I miss her so fucking much, and not just the sex. I miss being close to her, having the right to touch her, feeling her small frame pressed against me. I'd fucking kill to pull her close, but I don't know if she'd retreat or embrace it, and I don't want to put her into the position of deciding what to do in front of a crowd.

"What did you get, baby?"

She offers a small smile before bringing her arm up. Gingerly lifting the bandage, she shows me a delicate flower on the outer part of her forearm. "It's a daffodil."

I raise a brow, waiting for her to continue. A woman like Red doesn't do shit that doesn't mean something. She looks down before continuing, "It means rebirth. I-I," she stumbles on her words, swallowing before she continues, "I want to remember her—the baby. I don't want to forget, but I wanted to feel better." Her eyes have a sheen to them, like a dam of tears is about to spill over.

I stare at her face, letting her words surround me. I don't know what the fuck to say other than the truth. "I love it. You look good with a tattoo, Red." To my surprise, she wraps herself around me and rests her head on my chest.

I waste no fucking time grabbing her small, strong body and pulling her tighter into me.

She doesn't hesitate to burrow closer, and it feels like I'm finally fucking home in my woman's embrace. Our friends are here, her cousin, too, but I could give two shits about them when I have my girl willingly in my arms.

"Will you come back to the house tonight? With me?" I ask, low enough that no one else can hear me.

"No, we're sleeping at Serena's," Red says and pulls back to look at me. I nod; I don't want to take her away from her friends, but I fucking want her with me in my bed.

"But you'll still let me take you for breakfast?"

"Yes," she answers simply. Pulling her arms from around my body, she takes a step back and looks around me. "Serena should be done; I'm going to go check on her." She starts to move around me, but I grab her hand and turn so that I'm facing the same direction as her.

"I'm coming with you. You're not getting rid of me that easily." She just rolls her eyes and leads me toward the back of the shop, where private rooms are set up for tattoos and piercings.

I've been in the shop before to make my own appointment; it's a large single-story building with white walls and grey flooring. The simple backdrop highlights the framed paintings

271

and artwork decorating every inch of available wall space. The first and only time I was here, I sat at the reception desk and had my consultation in the front of the store. I didn't get to see any of the tattoo stations or meet anyone other than the appointment coordinator. I'm surprised to see that the uniformity of the space ends once I pass the threshold of what I assume is Wolf McCleery's station. The walls are matte black with black baseboards and crown molding, and green wingback chairs are placed in the corner of the room. A floor-to-ceiling bookshelf takes up one wall, while the rest of the wall space has framed pictures of Wolf's art. It looks like a dope as fuck gothic library.

Thank God there's no cowhide rug, though I'll never admit that to Red.

Wolf is bent over Serena's body, cleaning off the excess ink from her ribs when we walk in. As soon as Wolf fucking McCleery looks up, I'm baffled by how similar Celeste and her cousin look; they have the same dark red hair and deep emerald eyes. But, more than physical resemblance, it's how they hold themselves: poised for a fight and ready to fuck shit up. Red may have softened marginally, but she's still a fucking banshee ready to go *Kill Bill* at any moment. Her cousin seems to be the same. His chin raises, assessing and judgmental before I even open my fucking mouth.

Red rushes over to Serena and puts a hand on Wolf, leaning into him with a familiarity that belies just how close they are. Logically, I know they're related, closer than a lot of siblings, and Red has, hopefully, no interest in having a kissing cousin. But my response isn't fucking logical, and I want to kill Wolf the moment Red puts her dainty little hand on his massive shoulder. I let out a growl, not giving a shit if I sound feral.

Both Wolf and Red look over at me, amusement in his gaze and exasperation in hers. "You cannot be serious," she says, an incredulous tone in her voice.

"I don't like seeing your hands on another man," I say tersely. Red looks from me to her cousin and back again, sputtering a laugh as she leans in closer to him.

"He's my cousin, you ogre. Don't make this weird." She gives me a look that communicates, *I will rip your balls off if you keep this up*, before turning to Serena. "Rena, let me see what you got."

Shifting on the tattoo table, Serena angles her body so that her delicate tattoo is on display. In script so fine, it looks like a computer typed it on her skin, a single word rests right below her left breast: mariposa.

"It looks so beautiful. What does it mean?" Red asks, directing her question to Serena. But, before Serena has the chance to open her mouth, Wolf responds.

"Butterfly."

Red whips her head to her cousin. "Since when do you speak Spanish?"

He rolls his eyes, an action that my hellion must have taught him. "I don't speak Spanish, but I asked your little siren what it meant six times and looked it up before I let her ink it on her skin. She could have fucked up and put 'scrotum' under her tit instead of 'butterfly.'"

I swallow back a laugh, noting the tense set of Serena's jaw and the glint in her eyes. To her, that wasn't funny. "Don't call me that," she says in a strained voice.

"What?" Wolf asks, confusion lacing his voice.

"Siren. Don't call me that."

"I—" Wolf starts, but Red cuts him off.

"Okay, Wolfie, is Serena all good?" He nods. "Good, let's go up front and pay for our tattoos."

"You know I'm not accepting your fucking money, Celeste," Wolf says. "Or that of your friends," he adds, eyes trained on Serena's back.

Red and Serena don't spare him a glance, just continue walking toward the front of the shop.

"You know," I say, breaking the silence. "There's something about these girls that will have you serving your balls up on a fucking platter. I can see you noticed Serena." I nod in the direction the girls just walked.

Wolf's face remains in an unreadable mask, not giving any hint of emotion. I swallow thickly. If this is the look he gives his opponents in the cage, there's no doubt they probably shit themselves before getting knocked out.

"But be careful with her. I don't know her well, but I know that she's had a shit go of it. From what I *do* know, her dad is a fucking loser, and her stepsister is a miserable asshole. Her best friend betrayed the shit out of her, and Red— Celeste—intervened and laid the guy out." Wolf's eyes darken at the mention of his cousin getting involved. "The guy, I don't fucking know, she was seeing? Was sleeping with or maybe just slept with? Fucking embarrassed the shit out of her in front of all her friends." I shake my head, disgust rising to the surface at the memory of Dylan and Devin at the house. "What I'm saying is, if you're not going to respect her, don't start shit. She doesn't need another person to let her down, and she's important to Celeste. She'd have my balls if she found out I saw that look on your face and didn't protect her friend."

"I don't know who the fuck you think you are, frat boy, but don't presume you know me." Wolf stands from his tattoo

274

chair and takes up more of the fucking room. Admittedly, I'm a big guy, but Wolf? He's like a fucking cyborg or genetically modified specimen.

"Listen, I'm just telling you, be careful and don't hurt her. She's been alone most of her life, and she needs Celeste and Ava. Don't make her lose them because you got a hard-on for a pretty girl." I have a death wish, apparently.

He considers my words, grinding his teeth so fucking viciously, I can hear them from where I'm standing, at least ten feet away. "She's too young."

"She's a legal, consenting adult who's going to graduate college next fall."

"You got eyes on her, too?" he questions, distrust and anger clear in his gaze.

"You think I'd be with a woman like Red if I wanted to fuck around with someone else? She'd castrate me."

"I'd fucking kill you if you hurt her," he says, then adds, "again." His words have me growing still.

"Did she tell you?"

He nods. "Celeste told me. I'm sorry for your loss, but if that girl suffers anymore, I'll tear your limbs from your body and use them as shark bait. Your bones will be ground under their teeth, and no one will be able to find a single fucking hair or tooth."

"What the fuck is it with your family and violence, man? I love her exactly as she is, but Jesus fuck, she's a trained assassin from a family of murderers. And not that it's any of your goddamn business, but I fucking love that woman and would die *for* her, not because of her. So, your threats are misplaced. I will do—and have done—everything to protect her, even when she doesn't want it."

"It's not a threat; it's a promise."

"One that you don't need to give. We suffered a loss—we, not just her. You don't want me to presume to know you? Well, you know jack shit about me. I will do everything to secure that girl's happiness, even if it means waiting on the sidelines until she's ready for me."

We stare at each other, locked in a battle of who will break first. Wolf's jaw is set, and his arms are folded over his chest. He probably wants to throw me through the storefront window.

Just when I think I'll have to extend an overture to settle the tension in the room, the fucker's face breaks out into a large smile, and his posture relaxes. "You're so fucked. Celeste probably already has your balls in a vice." Walking over to me, he claps me on the back, sending me forward with the force behind his hit. "Welcome to the family. But if you fuck with her, I'll personally see to your death."

Wolf leads me out of his room and into the reception area, where everyone is congregated. Red does a double take when she sees Wolf's arm on my back.

"Did you guys just become best friends?"

"Fuck off, Celeste. You." He lifts his chin toward Serena. "I didn't get to go over the aftercare instructions with you. Come back to my station, and we'll go over how to prevent infection."

"It's fine. CeCe and Ava know what to do, they can tell me," Serena says in a voice that holds more bite than I've ever heard from her.

"That's not how I do business, princess. So, either walk back into the room and sit your pretty ass on the chair, or I'll drag you there. Your choice."

"The sexual tension is just outstanding, you know?" Ava says in a faux whisper, causing all of us to look at her. "What? Don't give me that look, Greyson. He clearly wants to bang Serena, and she's not interested. Wolfie, we've got her; you can stop glaring at her now."

Wolf shakes his head and points at Serena. "If it becomes infected, you have no one to blame but yourself. Don't blame me or my shop for that shit, and don't fucking call me complaining that you messed up your tattoo."

Serena doesn't respond, all hints of her earlier bravado gone. Looking down, she offers a small head nod. Wolf's face loses its scowl and takes on a confused expression, as though he doesn't understand the sudden shift in Serena's demeanor.

"Alright, well, this has been fun. Thank you, Wolfie," Red interrupts. "I'll text you tomorrow. Thank you for doing this for me." Red waves at her cousin before turning around and walking out the front door of the shop. Ava, Grey, Serena, and Linc trail after her, like a queen leading her subjects.

I give Wolf a nod and turn to follow my woman out the door.

28

CeCe

It's late by the time we make it back to Serena's apartment, after eleven. We stopped to pick up pizza on the way home, much to Ava's annoyance.

"I could have cooked," she grumbles as we walk through Serena's front door. "This is glorified frozen pizza. It flops like a limp dick after too much whiskey."

"Are you speaking from experience? Has that ever happened to Greyson?" I taunt.

"Bite your tongue, devil woman."

I roll my eyes and place the box of pizza down before lifting the lid and ripping off a slice. Ava's not wrong—the pizza doesn't have a firm crust, and it's basically falling apart. I take a bite, and the cheesy, soft texture makes me moan. It's pizza, so it's still delicious.

"God, I did not need to hear your orgasm voice, Celeste Lauren Downing."

I roll my eyes and take another bite, chewing in consideration. "That's not how I sound when I orgasm," I say around the food in my mouth. It's not good manners, but I'm starving.

"Okay, says you. Don't forget, I was there when you spent four nights in a row at the guys' house." I don't respond, just lift my middle finger and take another bite.

"Serena, show me your tattoo; I didn't get a chance to see it over Wolf's asshole behavior and Dante's growling." Serena lets out a light, lyrical laugh and raises her shirt, displaying the bandage right under her breast. Moving her fingers over the large bandage, she peels it off slowly.

"It says 'mariposa,'" she explains, her voice transforming when pronouncing the Spanish word. "It means butterfly."

"Is there any significance?" Ava asks slowly, as though she's worried about overstepping or upsetting Serena.

Serena looks down, taking in the red skin around the tattoo and the black lettering that has yet to scab over. "Butterflies are free. They're not confined into one space, one role; I want to be free. I don't want to be the smart girl graduating early, or Marina's stepsister, or the girl from the broken family. I just want to flit, fly from place to place, not worrying about what designations may be assigned to me."

"Rena," I sigh, my heart aching for her. "You know, we see you as Serena, our kickass, sweet, loyal friend. You don't need to be anyone other than who you are or who you want to be."

"Thanks, C," Serena responds sheepishly, as though she's embarrassed that she provided so much information. "I just want to feel like I don't need to be restrained. I've been second to Marina for so long that sometimes it's hard to remember that I matter, too. You know, I start grad school next semester? I'll be the nineteen-year-old freak in grad classes with thirty-year-olds," Serena continues. "I'm used to the looks, the confusion that my presence brings, but for once, I just want to be free."

279

Serena's gaze cuts to Ava's forearm and the bandage plastered on it. "What did you get?"

"Oh, you're going to love this, my beautiful little butterfly." Ava rips off the bandage with a gusto that she has no right to have. Her wince is satisfying. "Ow, fuck. I didn't realize that would hurt so much."

"You just got a tattoo, you fucking brussel sprout."

"How is calling me a brussel sprout an insult? Anyway," Ava says, giving me a nasty side-eye. "I got a knife," she proclaims, gesturing to the outer part of her forearm. "Because, you know, the ovary and being a chef and all," she continues, as though that makes all the sense in the fucking world.

"Ava, sweetie, did you really get a knife after being attacked by a, well, knife?"

"Yes, Serena, I did. I am reclaiming the instrument."

Serena and I look at each other and start laughing. I struggle to get control of myself. "A knife does not make music, Ava Maria."

"My knife cuts are lyrical, thank you very much. I have half a reproductive system; I can do whatever the hell I want. Besides, there's a basil leaf beneath it."

I take a closer look at her tattoo and notice how intricate the design is, like a still-life photo was copied on her arm. The handle of the knife looks like wood, the grooves so realistic, it feels like I can reach out and grab it from her skin. I have no idea how Wolf was able to accomplish that in forty-five minutes.

Upon closer inspection, there's a very distinct imperfection in the bolster of the knife, one that looks strangely familiar. "Ava, is that—" I start, but Ava cuts me off.

"My New West Knifeworks 7-Inch Teton Edge Santoku with

a scratch in the bolster from when I accidentally dropped it on a whetstone the day after I bought it? Yes." She looks down at the tattoo with fondness. "I showed Wolf a picture, and he copied it freehand. Now, show us yours," Ava demands.

After showing Dante my tattoo, I didn't bother putting the bandage back on; I let it air out. It needs to stay uncovered after the first day, anyway, so I didn't think it would be that big of a deal.

Turning my arm over, I show Ava and Serena the delicate daffodil decorating my skin.

"Persephone," Ava whispers, well acquainted with my love of mythology. I shake my head.

"No, I didn't get it for Hades and Persephone. I got the daffodil for what it stands for, rebirth and new beginnings."

Serena's eyes water, and Ava's face morphs into the most unattractive expression I've ever seen her make.

"For the baby?" Ava asks, and I nod, unable to lend a voice to the words thick in my throat.

"I love you, C," she says on a shaky exhale and then throws herself onto me, nearly knocking me and my pizza to the floor in her enthusiasm.

"Collect yourself, Aves," I say as she clings to me, nearly suffocating me with her affection.

"No, you don't get to be a cold little shit right now. I want to hug you, so suck it up, you ice queen." I feel arms wrap from behind me, Serena's warmth seeping into my back.

I feel slightly claustrophobic but extremely loved right now.

After a few minutes spent smothered under their embrace, I finally work myself free. "Can you warn me the next time you both decide to go soft on me?" There's no strength to my voice; instead, it sounds raspy and clogged with emotion.

"You don't need to be tough right now, C," Ava chastises. Her words echo Dante's and all the times he's told me that I don't need to be strong, that I could lean on him for strength.

"I know, but if I don't try, I feel like I'll break."

"Have you spoken to someone? A therapist or counselor?" Ava asks. Ava has made no secret that therapy and consistent mental health checks keep her well, both physically and emotionally.

"I made an appointment with the person my OB-GYN recommended."

"Good, you need to speak to someone."

I swallow, weighing my words carefully before I voice them. "I know, in theory. But part of me feels guilty for taking up this person's time and needing to speak with them when they could be helping someone with bigger problems than I have. I know that women have miscarriages every damn day, but does it affect everyone as deeply as it affects me? Am I selfish and delusional and self-centered in needing to speak with someone to get ahold of my grief?"

"Don't talk like that," Serena scolds. "Therapy and counseling sessions aren't about comparing your problems, your struggles, to that of others. It's about dealing with your problems head-on and speaking with someone who can help you overcome the challenges."

Serena reaches over and grabs my hand, squeezing before letting go. "Therapy isn't a contest or competition. Don't fight it, just let yourself work through your emotions to help find healing and closure. No loss is too big or too small to work through, regardless of how you may feel right now."

I nod. "I was unsure if I should even show up to the appointment," I confess.

"Don't be a moron," Ava quips, reaching for a slice of the pizza she was just degrading. I raise an eyebrow, but she just scowls in response.

"Okay, enough about me. Serena, what the hell is going on with Dylan and Devin?"

Serena groans and buries her head in her hands. "It's such a mess."

Ava and I stare at her in silence, waiting for Serena to continue. "You were there. You heard what Devin said and what Dylan did. Marina told my dad I stole her boyfriend and that he cheated on her with me, and it became a nightmare. They were surprised when I refused to apologize to Marina."

"Fucking good. Fuck that cunt," I say, taking another bite of my now-cold pizza.

"They weren't happy about it, especially my dad. He accused me of trying to sabotage Marina's love life because I was jealous no boys were interested in me. I swear to God, Marina never entered my mind. It just happened." Serena shrugs, deflating in front of us. Lowering her voice, she drops her eyes and stares at the hardwood floor. "I regret giving all my firsts to Devin. He didn't deserve it, and he humiliated me. I feel like a moron for agreeing to whatever he wanted just because I was lonely and jealous all my friends were having sex, and I wasn't."

"Rena, no. That was never our intent. We never wanted you to be jealous of us," Ava cries. "I nearly died, and Celeste is dealing with her loss. There's nothing to be jealous over."

Serena offers a smile that doesn't reach her eyes. "I know that. But in the moment, I felt like I needed to participate or prove something regarding sex. When Devin came to the guest house, it was like I was drawn to him and couldn't say no."

"He didn't force you, right?" I ask, because I can't not ask that question. I know that she denied it a few weeks ago when I brought it up, but I need her to reconfirm it.

"No, it was consensual, like I told you. But I regret it. That single night imploded my entire life. I'm not even allowed back in my dad's house."

"Fuck him," Ava declares, and I don't disagree.

Serena just shrugs as though there's no reason to dwell on it.

"Speaking of guys, I noticed the way Wolfie was staring at you." Ava raises a brow as she throws that fucking missile out.

"I-I don't know what you're talking about," Serena stammers.

"Oh, I think you do. Don't pretend that you didn't enjoy the feel of Wolfie's hands on you while he put that pretty tattoo on your body."

Serena shakes her head, adamantly denying Ava's words. "No. And even if he was looking at me, he's too old, too big, too large, too much of everything. It would never work."

"Since when are big dicks a problem?"

"Ava Maria, that's enough. We are not talking about my cousin's dick, for fuck's sake."

"Whatever. But you can't deny that Serena caught Wolf's eye."

She's not wrong, but I still don't want to talk about my cousin or his dick.

"Okay, fine. I'll stop talking about your cousin's cock. It's late, anyway." Ava looks at the display clock on the microwave. "Jesus, it's after midnight. I need to go to bed. Grey is driving us up to Connecticut tomorrow to see his dad at the studio."

"You guys can take the bed. I'll sleep on the couch," Serena offers, but I immediately shake my head.

"Do not make me sleep with Ava; she's like a spider monkey that attaches to you during the night and doesn't let go."

"Hey! I'm not that bad," Ava complains.

"The last time I slept at your house, you were practically on top of me, and I had to sleep on the floor. I am not sharing a bed with you; I'll sleep on the couch."

"You're such a cold fish. Serena, we're cuddling tonight." Serena casts me a look that communicates how undesirable she finds Ava's statement. "Jesus, you too? Why does no one like physical affection?"

I shake my head as Ava disappears into Serena's room, mumbling to herself about lack of physical touch. Serena opens a cabinet next to the television and fishes out a set of blankets and a pillow. "Here you go, C. Are you sure you don't want to take the bed? I feel bad having you sleep on the couch."

I eye her plush cloud couch and shake my head. "You have fun with Ava and her tentacle arms. I will be very happy right here." Serena leaves me with a smile and goes to her bedroom, closing the door softly behind her.

Laying out the blankets, I tuck myself into the couch, letting myself finally relax. I'm not sure if it's the weight removed from finally telling my parents and friends about the pregnancy and our loss, the tattoo that acted like a cathartic release, the appointment I made with a therapist, or finally not having a brick on my chest when meeting Dante's eyes.

I fall asleep quickly, letting my mind finally shut off.

—

Incessant buzzing wakes me up, and I swat at the sound. It takes me longer than it should to realize that the sound is my phone going off like a drum during a rave. My heart rises to my throat; it's well into the late night, early morning hour, and no good text comes after midnight.

It's either a death or a sext; I'm not sure which is worse.

Dante: Are you up?

Are you fucking kidding me?

CeCe: Now I am, you asshat. What's wrong?

Dante: I'm here. Come outside.

I look at the time on my phone and note that it's one thirty-four in the morning. Fucking Dante woke me up after only an hour of sleep.

CeCe: If I see you right now, I'll kill you.

I throw my phone on the couch and turn, facing the cushion and shutting my eyes. I'm nearly asleep when my phone goes off again. Turning to my back, I grab my phone and swipe on Dante's message.

Dante: Come on, Red. It's cold as fuck out here.

I roll my eyes and lock my phone, not bothering to respond. It's not that I'm unaware of the flutters in my stomach, of the clenching of my thighs at Dante's late-night text. I'm just ignoring them, fastidiously ignoring them.

My phone's vibration transforms from a double pulse to a wild beat, letting me know a phone call is coming through.

I pick up the phone quickly, worried that the vibrations will somehow wake up the two other people in this apartment... who are in a separate room.

"Dante Nicholas, what the fuck?" I whisper yell into the phone, trying to keep my voice down. "It is almost two in the morning; why the hell are you here, and why are you calling me?"

"I'm outside, Red. Get your ass down here so that we can talk," he responds.

"I thought we agreed to speak tomorrow."

"Today is tomorrow. So, get down here and get your beautiful, grumpy ass in my car."

"Dante," I sigh. "It's the middle of the night. You know I'm a bitch under normal circumstances; did you really think waking me up was a smart idea? Lack of sleep makes me homicidal." Truthfully, I want to reach through the phone, grab Dante's balls, and twist them until I tear them off. I'll have Ava serve them as Rocky Mountain oysters.

"This couldn't wait, hellion."

"Fine. I'm coming down, but just know, I am not happy right now."

"I didn't think you would be," he replies, then quickly hangs up. He is such a dick.

29

Dante

When we got back from the tattoo shop, I tried to relax and have a beer with the guys, but my muscles were bound too fucking tight. Seeing Red tonight, hearing her breathy little moans in my ear yesterday morning, was a fucking tease, and I knew that I wouldn't be able to relax until I had her in my arms. I laid in bed for two goddamn hours, restless and annoyed, before I finally said, "Fuck it," and tracked her ass down like a fucking stalker.

I'm antsy as I wait for Red to come out of the apartment building. Five minutes pass from the time I hung up on her, and I'm ready to barge inside and kidnap her from the fucking building. I breathe a sigh of relief as soon as I see the complex's door open and Red saunter out in oversized gray sweats. I throw open my door and round the hood, stopping Red just before she gets in.

Lifting her small body, I turn us until she's braced against the hood of my car and straddling my waist. I don't hesitate, I fucking plunder her mouth, stealing every breath, every sigh, and her lips. It feels like returning home after being away, and

I don't stop.

She hates being a spectacle, so thank Christ that no one is here to witness this because she'd probably kick my ass. The thought of her feisty side has more blood rushing to my cock, growing so hard that it's nearly puncturing a hole in my jeans to get into her warm cunt.

Red rips her lips from mine, panting against my mouth. "Jesus, we're in public," she says. Her words may be sharp, but she's gasping for air and squirming against me, trying to get as close as she can through our clothes.

"It's two in the morning. No one is out here," I retort.

"Dante—" I cut her words off with my mouth, sucking her bottom lip before biting down on the plumpness. Her moans are loud, and her hands grip my hair, pulling with the force of a woman starved for physical touch. Her reaction to me has me moving my hips against her and fucking her through our clothes on the hood of my car.

I'm ready to tear off our fucking clothes and sink deep into her in front of God, the fuckers that can see us from their apartment windows, and the security cameras that are undoubtedly out here. I want everyone to fucking see that she is mine.

It's irrational and dangerous as fuck. I peel my lips off her lush mouth and drop my head into her neck, inhaling her deeply. At Wolf's shop, I wasn't able to embrace her or breathe in her scent, and it thoroughly agitated me.

"Hi?" she says, her voice sounding unsteady and breathless.

"Let's go home, hellion." I feel her nod against me, but she doesn't loosen her hold on my hair. I laugh softly and plant a kiss on her neck. "You need to unwind those pretty legs from around my hips and let go of my hair, Red."

Like she's been shocked, Red releases me and pushes me back, putting distance between us.

"Baby, those feet came a little too close to my dick and balls."

"Then move, unless you want to be a eunuch."

I pause, confused. "A what?"

She rolls her eyes and says, "A eunuch, a man who's been castrated to serve a queen."

What the fuck? "No, no, I don't want that." Grabbing her waist, I lift her from my hood and set her on the ground. "Get in the car," I command. She gives me a sharp look but follows my directions.

—

I speed home, breaking every traffic law in our college town. Red clutched the "oh shit" handle for the entire seven minutes that it took me to drive from Serena's apartment complex to my house.

I'm finally able to breathe when we pull into my driveway. I waste no time rounding the car and opening Red's door, communicating without words that I need her to hurry her ass up and get inside.

Once we're both inside my room, she walks gingerly to my bed, sitting down like a fucking queen on her throne. I almost laugh, but I'm too wound up to find much humor in our situation. I quietly lock the door and lean against the wood, studying the beautiful woman perched on top of my comforter.

"Baby, I'm going to talk, and you're going to listen for a few minutes, okay? I'm not trying to dictate you or belittle you, but I need you to know where my head has been for almost three weeks."

She nods, surprisingly not opening her mouth to respond. "Good girl." She blushes at my words but still doesn't say anything. "Now, you know I love you; I'd fucking die for you and kill because of you. So never fucking doubt that. But I loved that baby, too. You weren't the only one hurting, but you acted like you were. That shit's not cool. I told you from the beginning that we were in this together, and that means that your suffering and mine are fucking intertwined, not two separate entities. I know you were scared; I know you didn't expect this, but, baby, neither did I. You may have needed solitude, but I didn't; I just needed you.

"Shit is going to happen in life. People are going to be lost, we're going to have setbacks, but I need to make sure that you understand that we face that shit together. We don't go through hell separately, Red. Not anymore. We're a fucking team, a fucking family. You understand?" I stop and stare at her for a moment before finally saying, "You can talk now."

"I'm sorry," she says. "I've been around death my entire life, but never like this. I-I was so scared, Dante. And so guilty. I felt like I failed us, like I failed you, like I failed the baby. I know what Google says and what the doctor said, but it doesn't make me feel better to know that an insanely high number of pregnancies are either not viable or dangerous. I crave solitude when I'm hurt, and I'm sorry that I pushed you away. I should have communicated what I needed better."

"Yeah, you should have. But I'm not looking for an apology, Red. I know you were hurting—I know you're still hurting—but we're moving forward from here. You're not going to keep saying that you're sorry or that you harbor guilt. We're going to heal together, okay, baby?"

"Okay, D."

"How did everything go with the doctor?" I ask. It should have been the first fucking thing I said to her tonight, but I was so desperate to get my mouth on her that all rational thought fled the moment she walked out of the apartment complex.

"All good," she responds vaguely. I stare at her until she continues. "The doctor checked to make sure all the tissue passed—it did—and then she did the IUD insertion.

"Did it hurt?"

I catch her wince. I don't like that reaction one fucking bit. "It didn't feel good, but I've felt worse." I know she's referring to the day she spent in my bathroom, bleeding out on the floor.

I nod once and push off the door. "Now, give your man a kiss because you made me go too fucking long without you, and that shit ends now." She lifts her chin up as I approach, ready for my mouth to take hers.

—

CeCe:

Contrary to the urgency of his words, he leans in slowly, giving me time to change my mind or pull back. I do neither of those things; I wait for him, patiently impatient for the feel of his mouth.

His breath fans out on my face, caressing my skin before our lips finally connect. It's a slow kiss, chaste and almost juvenile in its execution, almost like it's a first for both of us. It's nothing like our previous kisses, which have been frantic and all-consuming. This is a kiss like embers in a fireplace or morning fog; there's nothing rushed about it, just appreciative. I've only known Dante for three months, but this kiss feels like I'm coming home.

The kiss morphs from sweet and innocent comfort to needy and possessive. His mouth opens over mine and draws my lower lip in. He sucks on it, biting down gently before releasing it with a pop. He licks the bite marks before grabbing the back

292

of my head and fusing our mouths together.

If the early stage of this kiss felt juvenile, this is fucking obscene. He's owning my mouth, laying possession to every inch of it with his tongue and teeth, and I'm helpless to stop him. I massage his tongue with my own, reveling in the feel of him.

He pulls away first, running his hand against my jaw. "I fucking love you, Red."

"I know," I tease. At his growl, I laugh softly, reaching out a hand to run it through his dark hair. "I love you, too, Dante. I've never loved anyone before, other than my family and Ava and her family, so I don't know if I'm good at it. But I'll try to communicate and tell you what's going on. When we lost it— her—I didn't know what to do. I was scared, and I know that I should have been better with coming to you, but it just felt like a solitary grief. I won't apologize for needing the space, but I will apologize for not handling the communication better."

I lean back in, grazing my lips over his one final time before sitting back and raising my hands to his chest to push him off.

"Say it again," he says, his voice tight.

"I'm sorry?" I taunt.

He nips my lips and growls. I know what he wants to hear; he's been in love with me for months and hasn't hesitated to let me know.

"Celeste," he warns.

"I love you," I whisper into his mouth.

"Fucking finally." He dives back in and steals another kiss. His lips are fierce and possessive and feel like a brand on my mouth. His lips move from my mouth to my jaw, to my neck, trailing kisses and bites as he makes his descent to my chest. Reaching for the hem of my hoodie, he tugs it off me and throws it across the room, like it personally offended him. "Do you know how fucking long I've waited to hear you say those goddamn words?" He sucks one nipple into his mouth, pulling at it with his teeth until I'm gasping and grabbing at his head. I'm not sure if I'm pulling him closer or trying to pull him away, but it feels like heaven and hell as he alternates between sharp bites and gentle sucking.

"Dante," I moan, tugging at the strands of his hair.

He releases my nipple with a wet pop before kissing a path to my other breast. "Months, Red. Fucking months. Every time I've had this sweet cunt, I wanted to force you over my knee and spank those words out of you. But you're a little hellion, a fucking demon sent to torment me for the rest of my life."

He bites the underside of my boob, and I yell at the sting. "Ow, Dante!" My words are lost as he laps at my pain, pulling the skin hard and undoubtedly leaving a mark.

"I'm going to fucking mark you everywhere; let everyone know that you are mine. These tits are going to be black and blue, and I'm going to mark your pussy with my cum. If you have any objections, say them now because once I start, I'm not going to fucking stop."

He looks up at me, gauging my reaction to his words. "I want that. I want to be yours," I say as I arch my back and pull on his hair, dragging his mouth back to my body.

Dante stops as soon as the words leave my mouth and pushes off the bed, forcing my hands to drop from their place in his hair. "What—?" I start to question but stop when Dante grips the waistband of my sweats and tugs them down, sending them flying in the same direction as my sweatshirt. I'm left in a pair of lace boy shorts and socks, which feels ridiculous. I shift my feet and kick off my socks, letting my toes breathe.

Dante's smirk does nothing to break the intensity of the moment. Looking down at my exposed toes, he reaches out to lift one of my legs up, raising it until the bottom of my foot is in line with his face.

"You've got the prettiest feet, Red." My eyes close in pleasure as he begins massaging the arch of my foot, digging his fingers into the muscles and tendons. I lose myself to the gentle pressure he's exerting; just like during the first massage he gave me so many weeks ago, I'm amazed at how skilled his thick fingers and large hands are. His fingers work over the arch of my foot, coasting over the heel and cupping my ankle in a gentle hold.

My eyes fly open when I feel wetness at the arch of my foot. "Did you just lick my foot?" I ask.

"No, I kissed it." Dante lowers my leg to the bed and repeats his massage on the other foot, ending it with another kiss to the bottom before he drops it. "I told you that I would worship every part of you," he says quietly. Dropping to his knees, he grabs the back of my legs and pulls me forward, resting my knees on his shoulders.

He looks up my body and gives me a look with so much longing and need that I let out a gasp. "Are you bleeding, Red?"

"Huh?" I question, disoriented by the attention he paid to my feet and the look on his face.

"Is your pretty cunt still bleeding?"

"I'm spotting."

Nodding, he tugs on my panties and pulls them down until they're restraining my legs. I expect him to lift my legs from their perch on his shoulders and discard them; he doesn't. Instead, he ducks under the fabric and settles into the space

295

between my legs.

"I'm going to fuck your pussy with my tongue. Stay still," he commands.

"But I'm spotting." Considering his position and vantage point, if he spread my lips, he'd probably see small amounts of blood.

"You think I give a shit about blood after what we went through almost three weeks ago? Baby, I fucking love you, but it was like a crime scene. I don't give a shit that you have a bloody cunt; I need to taste you and remind myself that you're finally here, in my bed." He pauses and opens his mouth to take a long, slow swipe of my pussy. I moan at the feeling, and Dante releases a growl. "You're right where you fucking belong."

Satisfied that I'm not going to object, Dante drags a hand to my lips and opens them for his inspection. "You're so fucking pretty, Red. Even here. I could look at you all fucking day and never get bored." He dives in, sealing his mouth to my clit and sucking hard. He works his jaw and pulls at me, drinking me in with wet, slurping sounds. It should be disgusting, the sounds bouncing around this room; I push my hips further into his face, seeking more pressure. Releasing the collection of nerves, he spears his tongue into my opening, thrusting until I'm undulating against his face. With each roll of my hips, his nose brushes my clit and sends sparks down my spine.

He pulls away, replacing his tongue with his fat fingers, piercing me until I feel like I'll be split in two. "I fucking love when you ride my face, baby." He dives back in, the combination of his mouth on my clit and his fingers pumping into me send me over the edge, and I explode.

"Dante," I cry, louder than I intend, but the force of the

orgasm knocks me on my ass.

Dante moves his lips from my throbbing clit and kisses a path to my pubic bone. "Shh, baby. We don't want to wake any of the assholes in this house up, do we?" he murmurs against my skin.

Still impaled by his fingers, I writhe against him, feeling my body start to heat again despite the orgasm he just gave me. "Dante," I whisper in a quieter voice. "Again."

He looks up from the ministrations he plays against my skin. "You think you can order me, Red?" He punctuates his words by withdrawing his fingers from my body, leaving me completely empty and bereft. I start to complain, but he silences me with a sharp bite against my thigh.

30

CeCe

"Look at this pretty blood, Red." I look at his fingers and see small amounts of blood mixed in with my cum on his fingers. I flush, both from embarrassment and how turned on I am. Dante lowers his hand and moves his fingers against my pubic bone, scrawling secrets on my skin. My eyes don't leave his face; I'm entranced by the set of his jaw and the smirk on his lips.

"Marked you. Now you're mine." I glance down my body and see Dante's name drawn on my skin in a mixture of blood and my arousal. "Fuck, you look pretty with my name on you." While I stare down, taking in the sight, Dante unhooks my legs from around his head and stands, reaching into his nightstand for a sleeve of condoms. Throwing them on the bed, he looks at me, seemingly inspecting his artwork.

"We don't need them," I say in a low voice. But pain quickly shoots through my heart when I realize it may not be for pregnancy prevention, but safety. "Unless you've been with someone else since..." I trail off, not able to finish my sentence.

Dante rolls his eyes and lets out a snort. "When would I

have had time to be with someone else when all I do is fucking chase you?" He shakes his head, driving his point home. "I just want you to be comfortable, Red. I know you have an IUD; I read up on them, but I don't want you to feel like I'm forcing us to go bare. If you want me to throw the condom on, I will. If you don't, then I won't. Tell me what you want."

I weigh his words, considering them before answering, "I want to feel you inside me with nothing between us."

Nodding his head, Dante grabs the packets and tosses them onto the nightstand. He surveys me before reaching for the hem of his shirt and drawing it over his head. I suck in a breath at the sight of his chest.

"What's that?" My voice is breathless, barely audible over the pounding of my heart. Dante looks down at the new tattoo decorating his skin. A realistic image of feminine hands holding rosary beads adorns his chest. Above the tattoo, directly over his heart, are the words, "I live for you," while beneath the tattoo is a date that will forever haunt me: November 3, 2022.

"I got it last week," he says in a careful voice, not betraying any emotion.

"Can I touch it?" He nods and approaches the bed, bending the upper half of his body over me so that I can run my fingers over the healing skin. "It's beautiful," I mutter.

"I got something else, too," he whispers before stealing a kiss. Pushing himself up, he shoves his sweats and briefs down, revealing the tattoos decorating his hips and legs. I don't see anything past his cock, which is standing tall and dripping precum. My mouth waters, and I clench my legs together.

He laughs at my discomfort. "Did you notice anything else,

Red?"

"Besides your dick?"

"Look next to it, hellion." I let my eyes trail from his groin to his pelvic bone and squint, trying to understand what new thing I'm seeing amongst the myriad of tattoos. As soon as my eyes catch on the golden tattoo six inches from his dick, I look up into his face and raise my brows.

"Is that a crown?" He shuffles closer, quite literally putting his dick in my face. Up close, I can see the jewels of the crown, the red and green gemstones giving away the symbolism. "Oh my God, you did not get the Princess Peach crown tattooed by your dick."

He gives me a goofy grin, and I can't suppress the laughter that bubbles up from my throat. My body convulses on the bed from the force of my laughter, and before I know it, Dante is above me, pinning me down with a look of wonder on his face.

I sober slowly, my mirth fading the longer I stare at him. "What?" I ask.

"I missed that sound, Red. It's been a long time since I heard anything other than tears, apologies, and sadness out of you."

"I know."

"I love you. So fucking much that it's disgusting."

I roll my eyes. "Thanks."

Dante growls and captures my lips, giving me a short but brutal kiss. "Say it, Red."

"I love you, too."

"Good fucking girl." His lips mold to mine, prying them open until his tongue can steal inside my mouth. I revel in the feel of him, his solid weight pressed against my body, and let him take control of this kiss.

Without breaking our mouths apart, Dante reaches for my

legs and hoists them up, circling them around his waist. His hands grab under my arms, and he pulls us up and off the bed before switching our position and sitting down. Maneuvering us back, Dante settles against the headboard. I pull away from our kiss and drop my head, panting against his shoulder, my eyes trained on the new tattoo on his chest.

I study the details of the artwork, choking up all over again at the beauty of the piece and the shared way we commemorated our grief. Leaning back, I look into his eyes and raise my hand to cup his jaw. I lift my other hand to the tattoo, barely touching the healing skin.

"I love you, Dante." I initiate the kiss this time, simultaneously lifting my hips and positioning myself over his cock. Drawing away, I look at where I'm hovering over him, ready to drop myself down and join us together.

Before I can lower myself, Dante grabs my hips and pulls, impaling me without warning.

I cry out, adjusting to his size.

"Holy fuck," he groans, clenching his jaw.

"Did your dick grow?" I pant, breathing through the fullness. He laughs, jiggling his dick inside me. "Don't laugh, you asshole. I need a minute."

"No," he growls beneath me, pumping his hips from below. "I need you to ride my cock before I flip you over and fuck you until you feel me in your throat." The hands on my hips drag me forward, letting my clit grind against Dante's soft pubic hair. "Don't make me tell you again, Red. Ride my fucking cock."

—

Dante:

In my next life, I'm going to be a goddamn lieutenant

because the way that my hellion follows my commands is fucking intoxicating. As soon as I ordered her to ride my cock, she let out the sexiest moan and started to move her narrow hips, grinding against me like a rodeo queen.

It's fucking embarrassing, but I had to hold myself back from coming the moment I pulled her pussy down. She's like a fucking vice, gripping me in an unrelenting hold. I look at her body, pausing on her small tits bouncing as she rides me.

I halt her movements and pull her forward, latching onto her tit and sucking it into my mouth.

"Ah," she cries out, pushing her chest further into my mouth. Far be it from me to not fucking oblige. Opening my mouth wider, I take as much of her tit as I can while strumming her other nipple with my fingers. "Dante," she moans, shifting her hips and sucking my cock deeper into her warm cunt.

Releasing her tit, I drop my hand to her clit and rub, increasing the pressure against the nerves. "I need to feel you come, baby." My voice is hoarse and sounds like I've been chain-smoking packs of cigarettes.

Red throws her head back and stills her hips, and I can feel the fluttering of her pussy as she reaches her climax. "That's right, baby." I lift her off my lap and scramble off the bed. Pulling her back, I lean over her and whisper in her ear, "Get on all fucking fours. Show me that pretty ass."

I help her into position and line my cock up with her cunt. There are faint traces of blood on it, a reminder of all we've been through and how far we've come. I thrust into her, gripping her shoulders while I piston my hips. It's hard and fast and fucking messy, but taking my frustration from the last few weeks out on Red's body feels fucking good. The trust she's giving me to ride her hard makes my cock grow stiffer until my balls draw up, and I feel the tingles of an orgasm in my spine. Pulling out of her quickly, I jerk my dick once before spilling all over her back and asshole.

Dropping to my hands, I barricade her in from behind and whisper in her ear, "I marked it so it's mine."

31

Dante

"What time is your appointment?" I ask Red, looking over to where she's lounging in my bed, huddled under the comforter like a small burrito.

"I have to be there at one," she says, sleep dripping from each word she utters. "My appointment is at one-thirty, but I need to fill out paperwork for insurance, so I have to get there early."

"I'll drive you," I murmur, diving back into bed and wrapping my arms around her. "How many fucking blankets do you have on? I can't feel your body." All I feel are soft lumps of fabric.

"It's cold in here. I'm going to die of hypothermia if you don't shut the air conditioner off. It's the end of November, for fuck's sake."

"You're always cold, Red. It wouldn't matter if we kept it at seventy-five in here, you'd still complain."

"I'm going to talk shit about you in therapy today. Just wait. The therapist is going to tell me to drop your ass."

I roll my eyes at her and work to loosen the blankets hiding her body. When I can finally see her body, I groan at the sight of the oversized sweatpants and fucking sherpa she has on. "Seriously?"

"I told you that I was cold." I sneak my hands under the massive sweatshirt and sigh when I meet her warm skin. Nuzzling my face into her neck, I inhale her scent and feel the pressure loosen in my shoulders. It's been three days since CeCe got her tattoo and she's spent every night at my house, in my bed. It's a fucking relief to have her in my arms again, not fighting me or shutting me out.

"We need to leave soon," I mutter against her neck. "It's almost noon."

A groan leaves my little hellion's mouth and I smile. "Fine, but you're feeding me before we get there."

—

After stopping for bagels and coffee, CeCe is like a different— more awake—person. Looking at her in the passenger seat, I grip the wheel to try and distract myself from the swelling of my dick at just the sight of her. In her leggings, sweatshirt, and leather vest, she looks like a present designed specifically for me, one that I can't wait to unwrap the minute we get home.

Shifting my car into park, I unbuckle my seatbelt and lean over to catch Red's lips. The kiss is brief, just a whisper of tongue and teeth. I'm proud of her that she's seeing someone today; I know she's scared shitless of being judged for a teen pregnancy and the effects of our loss, but we deserve to feel closure. I haven't told her yet, but I scheduled my own therapy appointment for next week to talk shit through and to make sure I'm the best partner for Red.

"You ready, baby?" I ask against her lips.

"Yeah, just nervous."

305

I nip her lips again, sucking her full bottom lip into my mouth before responding. "You'll be okay. I'll be here when you're done. Do you want me to come in with you?" I know that she's going to refuse; my fiercely independent woman doesn't like leaning on anyone.

Just like I anticipated, she shakes her head. "No, I'll see you later." She opens the door to slip out, but I stop her with a hand on her arm.

"Aren't you forgetting something?"

She rolls her eyes, but leans in, placing a quick kiss on my lips, and whispers, "I love you, you ass."

Smiling, I grab the back of her head, deepening the kiss for a moment before I pull back. "I love you, too, hellion."

—

CeCe:

"So, Ms. Downing, tell me about yourself," Dr. Pierce instructs softly. When I first entered her office, I was surprised to see how open and airy it was. A mix of floor and hanging potted plants decorate one wall laden with windows, while the rest of the space is designed to emulate a library. Grey floor-to-ceiling bookshelves encompass the remaining wall space, while the mixture of white and distressed oak furniture is soothing, almost like I want to cuddle up on the oversized chair and spill all my secrets to a stranger.

As far as aesthetics go, she freaking nailed it.

Without hesitation, I divulge everything that has happened since August: the sex, the pregnancy, the miscarriage, and my parents' oblivious nature. I even tell Dr. Pierce about Dante's idiotic bet and the anger I felt at being reduced to a possession to be had.

With the skill derived from being a trained professional, she listens intently, not interrupting me to ask questions. I ramble for what feels like hours but is probably only minutes. When I finish, I look up at the therapist, meeting empathetic eyes and a small smile. Reaching out, she hands me a box of tissues and it's then that I realize I'm crying.

"Thanks," I mumble, wiping my face with the soft cotton.

"You mentioned your parents. How did they react to the news of the pregnancy and miscarriage?"

"They were shocked. My mom was almost, I don't know, offended that I felt I couldn't or didn't tell her."

She nods, humming softly to herself and writing in the notebook open on her lap. "And in the conversation you had with your mother the morning after you told her about the miscarriage, what happened?"

I clear my throat, shifting on the couch at the memory of phone sex with Dante that same morning. "Uhm, she scheduled me an appointment with her colleague to have my follow-up appointment."

She nods again, this time shutting her notebook. "It's important for you to remember that how you perceive and react to situations may not be the same as others; in your mother's case, her role as medical caregiver most likely translates to how she shows her concern through things like appointments, in-person exams, or questioning, and behavior typical of a healthcare provider. It doesn't make it right, nor does it make it wrong, but understanding how she operates may help you address it. What I want for you after this first session is to examine your own love language and how that translates to things like grief, joy, and anger. Once you've identified those things, you'll work to understand how to express what you need from a partner or family member. Does that sound good?"

I stare at her confused. "So, we're not going to speak about the miscarriage?"

She smiles again, the expression making her seem so approachable. With her tight black bun, wire-framed glasses, and turtleneck, she looks like a modern Freud, just a younger, attractive version. "We will, but it's only your first session. We'll work to address the traumas that an unplanned pregnancy followed by a pregnancy loss brings, but we're going to approach it slowly. Ripping the band-aid off, so to speak, could cause irreparable setbacks for your mental and physical wellbeing, so we'll ease into it," she advises.

I nod, absorbing her words. For the first time, I believe Dante's words.

We're going to be okay. *I'm* going to be okay.

32

Epilogue

Three weeks later

CeCe

When I submitted my final project to Dr. Ford, I didn't expect praise or recognition for my writing, but I did expect an A. When I read it in class, I received a splattering of applause followed by awkward silence. My partners for my peer review were pussies and didn't share any real feedback on my work, so the uncomfortable applause was the only thing I had to go by until Dr. Ford released our grades.

I got a B- with a note that said, "This has promise, but the writing could be tighter." I was upset for forty-five minutes until Dante made me forget my anger by eating my pussy until his face was wet with my cum.

It's a week before Christmas, and I'm finally bringing Dante home to meet my parents. When Dante picked me up, he had a burlap package wrapped in his backseat. When I asked what it was, he told me not to worry about it.

Now, less than ten minutes from my parents' house, I can't help but bring it up again. "If that's a dead person, I'll fucking kill you for making me an accomplice."

"You know, Red, you haven't threatened to murder me in a few weeks. Could it be that your ice queen heart is starting to melt?"

I give him a look. "No. I'm trying to figure out the best place to bury your big ass body."

"Hellion." He puts the car in park in front of my parents' house. "You ready?" Dante asks from the driver's seat. I shrug. The relationship with my parents has been okay; they still work stupid long hours, are inaccessible more often than not, but they are making more of an effort to check in on me. We've had weekly FaceTime calls in addition to the texts, and it's helped to improve our communication.

Dante steps out of the car, leans over his seat, and grabs the package behind me. Trailing behind him, I try to grab the bag, but he holds it above his head and out of reach as soon as he sees my hands.

"Are you really not going to tell me what that is?" I pout, probably sounding like a whiny child.

"Patience, Red. You'll find out in a few minutes."

"You know I don't like delayed gratification, D." I hope the use of his nickname gets me my way.

He sighs before bringing the bag down. "Fine, but we need to go in your backyard."

"Is this where you take chloroform and knock me out so you can bury me alive?"

"Jesus, fuck no. Just get in the backyard and stop being a murderous little freak."

Keeping an eye on him while I lead him to the back of my parent's property, I stop as soon as we reach the deck and turn to face him. "Okay, we're in the backyard. What do you have for me?"

Dante drops the bag to the ground and opens it, revealing at least fifteen small brown cones.

"Are those turnips?"

"What? No. Celeste, they're bulbs." He pauses, clearing his throat. "I went to the nursery yesterday while you were in your final and asked about planting daffodils in winter. The nurseryman said that as long as the ground wasn't frozen, the bulbs could be planted and would bloom in late spring. He said they're perennials or some shit, whatever the fuck that means."

Tears form in the corners of my eyes as Dante explains, and I can't hold myself back. I fling my body into his and wrap my arms tight around his waist. He lets out a soft "oof" at the contact but hugs me back, cradling the back of my head like it's the most precious thing in the world.

"Thank you, D," I choke out. "I love them." I pull back and rise to my toes, kissing his jawline. "I love *you*."

"Can we plant them now?" I whisper into his jacket.

"Yeah, I brought a shovel," he says, pulling a trowel out of his coat pocket.

Looking up at him, I tease through a watery voice, "I'm going to need a bigger shovel to hide your body, Dante."

33

Serena

I pull my phone out with shaky hands, pacing back and forth through my apartment like an animal about to be let out of its cage. In this scenario, I'm not a lion; I'm the gazelle prancing itself into slaughter.

I've been talking to myself and walking around my apartment for the last—I check the clock on my oven—seventy-eight minutes. If I had a high-tech watch, it would probably tell me that I walked five hundred miles and burned an absurd number of calories thanks to anxiety and indecision.

"I should just call him. He may not even answer the phone. He doesn't have my contact information, and he could be one of those people who refuses to answer an unfamiliar number," I reason to my furniture. "Or I could block my number so that he can't call me back if he turns me down. He can't call to mock me if he can't get in touch with me."

I wince, remembering that he does, in fact, have my cell number. "God, I'm being such a wimp." I stop my movements and look up, dropping my head back so that I can stare at the ceiling.

Almost two months ago, I made the horrible, inexcusable, idiotic decision to sleep with my neighbor and former love? Crush? Infatuation? I compounded that mistake by telling my best friend about the night I spent with my bad-boy neighbor, and I ended up losing my virginity, my lifeline, and half of my family in one fell swoop.

As far as slip-ups go, mine is major. Maybe I wouldn't feel so much regret if I actually enjoyed the sex. It felt like a baby carrot was poking me in the vagina; I didn't even have that romance novel-worthy hymen tear that shocks the naïve virgin before she writhes under the rakehell like a brothel owner.

No, I had an abysmal experience, and my stepsister accused me of sabotage and subterfuge.

I doubt she even knows what subterfuge means.

Breathing in deep, I press the call button and bring my phone to my ear before I back out.

He answers on the second ring. "Hello?" his gruff voice sounds over the line, causing goosebumps to erupt over my skin. I can hear the soft rock music in the background, the bass notes dripping with sensuality and carnage.

I clear my throat. "Uhm, hi. This is Serena, my last name is Castillo. My name." I laugh awkwardly. "Right, this is Serena Castillo. I called because I need some help and I was hoping that maybe we could meet at the shop? I'm sorry, I got your number out of Celeste's phone. Is that an issue? I'm not sure—"

His deep laugh cuts me off, the sound jarring and beautiful. I suddenly crave hearing it in person. "Calm down, Serena. Yeah, I remember you. What do you need, princess?"

About the Author

Lola Miles is the pen name of a thirty-something living in New Jersey with her husband, children, and dog. By day, Lola is a businesswoman, and by night, she writes smut that would make your grandmother blush profusely.

You can connect with me on:
- https://www.lolamilesbooks.com
- https://instagram.com/lolamilesbooks

Also by Lola Miles

Lilies in Autumn

I planned for keg stands, kisses, and sorority recruitment. Nowhere in my plans did I anticipate him: Greyson Jansen, Viking-looking god and campus playboy.

Before Grey, my dreams were centered around my future and opening a restaurant after graduation. But from the moment we met, Grey consumed me. My dreams, my thoughts, my body, my heart, they were all his.

Not everyone is happy about our budding romance, though. Some will stop at nothing to prevent it.

Made in United States
North Haven, CT
24 August 2024

56525232R00187